The Carpenter

Salem Village - Book One

Pegg Thomas

Spinner of Yarns
PUBLISHING, LLC

S PINNER OF YARNS PUBLISHING, LLC

    Sault Ste. Marie, Michigan

In this series are many actual historical figures. The author has used her imagination to flesh out the characters for the purposes of the series. While using the known facts of the characters, they are not intended to be historically accurate in every detail.

Join Pegg's Newsletter
writing updates – sneak peeks – fiber arts updates – personal content
https://www.subscribepage.com/PeggThomas

Salem Village
Fictional Characters

Puritans

Verity Manton
Mary Scudder
Becky Simpson
Joseph Tripp
John Biddle
Jane Biddle

Quakers

Hester Fuller
David O'Sullivan
Isobel O'Sullivan
& O'Sullivan children
Elias Barwick
Arthur Stokes
Phoebe Stokes
Stephen Draper

Salem Village
Historical Characters

Puritans

Thomas Buffington
Sarah Buffington
& Buffington children
Rev. Samuel Parris
Elizabeth Parris
Betty Parris
Abigail Williams
Dr. William Griggs
Rachel Griggs
Elizabeth Hubbard
John Indian
Tituba Indian
William Good
Sarah Good
Alexander Osborne
Sarah Osborne
Rebecca Nurse
Mary Sibley

George Corwin
Lydia Corwin
Ezekiel Cheever
Rev. Increase Mather
Rev. Cotton Mather
John Hathorne
Jonathon Corwin

Quakers

Caleb Buffum
Hannah Buffum
& Buffum children

Author's Forenotes

Two towns are referred to in this series, Salem Town and Salem Village. The beginnings of the famous witch trials started in Salem Village, a quiet farming community about three miles northwest of Salem Town. As the number of people being accused grew, the bulk of the proceedings were moved to Salem Town, which was a bustling port city even in the late 1600s. Both were primarily settled by Puritans, but there were also Quakers, whom the Puritans despised.

During this time period, the "old style" or Julian calendar would have been used. For clarity's sake, I have chosen to represent the dates using the "new style" or Gregorian calendar that we use today.

Conflicting opinions abound on just when the use of *thee* and *thou* disappeared from common use in Colonial America. For clarity's sake, I have chosen to have the Puritans in this series use the pronouns *you* and *your*, while the Quakers will retain—as they historically did—*thee* and *thy*. The Quakers rejected *thou*, considering it too fancy for their preferred plain way of speaking.

The term *goodie* was used as the short form of *goodwife* and applied to a married woman. For instance, today we'd refer to Goodie Corwin as Mrs. Corwin.

While it looks odd to our modern eyes, in this time period, both men and women were named after their parents—a very common practice—were referred to as Jr., as in Hannah Jr. and Caleb Jr. in this series. I was tempted to change their names for clarity, but they are real historical figures, so I chose to leave them as they were.

Some events have been shuffled for the continuity of the fictional characters' stories, but at most by a week or two. Some events I did not have a firm date on, and so I used other data to estimate when they would have happened.

THE CARPENTER

Bible verses quoted are taken from the 1599 Geneva Bible, the version to which these characters would have had access.

Chapter 1

January 15, 1692

H AD THEIR IDYLLIC TIME near Salem Village come to an end? Caleb
hunched over the headboard of a baby's cradle he'd been commissioned to make for a Puritan goodwife who lived south of the
village. He blew a thin curl of wood from the end of his carving chisel
and glanced out the window. Someone approached with her head
down, either his wife or his eldest daughter, bundled against the cold,
making it impossible to tell which one it was.

The main door to the barn banged shut, and then the inside door
leading into the carpentry shop opened.

Hannah Jr. entered the workshop and untied the knitted wool scarf
that had covered her head, draping it over her shoulders to expose her
dark blond hair, which was covered by a linen cap. "I hope I am not
disturbing thee, Father." Snow lingered on the tops of her boots and
clung to the hem of her wool petticoats. She approached the brazier in
the middle of the carpenter shop and held her hands out to its warmth.

"Thee are never a disturbance." Caleb set his chisel aside and dusted
off his hands. "What brings thee out in this cold?"

"I am just returned from the village." And by her tone, something
hadn't gone well.

Of all his children, Hannah Jr. was the steadiest, the least likely to be worried over the strange goings-on among the Puritans there. "What happened that brings thee out to see me?"

"'Tis more of a feeling than a happening." She picked at a loose thread on her heavy cape. "While many of those in the village are standoffish to me, today was different." Blue eyes so like her mother's met his. "They scurried along the street without greetings even for each other and kept their faces down."

"'Tis cold even for January. Perhaps 'twas the wind that hurried them along without greetings." Yet her words struck hard on the tail of his own thoughts.

"I think not just the wind." She spread her hands out, palms up. "On my deliveries, there were no happy greetings. I was handed the coins, the goodwives took their cheese and butter, and then closed the door without a parting word." She glanced out the window. "Except for the Buffingtons, of course. Sarah is always kind, as are all her children." Hannah Jr.'s cheeks grew rosy, whether from the brazier's heat or her reaction to those of the village, Caleb couldn't be sure.

Even the goodwives, her loyal clients, had responded as such? That was unusual. At least, it was unusual for Salem Village. In other places, it was common practice. If a Puritan would purchase anything from one of the Friends—those whom they called Quakers—it was grudgingly and with an air of contempt meant to put them in their place.

Caleb remembered that feeling all too well, having faced it too many times. Were they to face it again? Here in the village where they'd made their home for the past twelve years?

"I know Thomas Buffington warned thee of something happening in the village, but I did not expect to feel so..." Hannah Jr. let her words fall off in a shrug.

The brewer, Thomas, to whom their son, Robert, had been apprenticed, had arrived the week prior with both Robert and the warning. There was something brewing in the village other than his ales, small beers, and ciders. Two of the village girls had fallen into some sort of fits on several occasions, and the cause was as yet unknown. Thomas felt that it would be better for Robert to remain on the farm until whatever it was had passed.

"I was very uncomfortable, Father."

"Thee are wise to be uncomfortable when confronted in such a manner."

Hannah Jr. didn't know of their history. She'd been far too young to remember their escape when he and Hannah had run from a mob of Puritans. Perhaps it was time to tell her. He didn't relish the idea, didn't want to rehash what had happened. But he certainly didn't want Hannah to have to tell their daughter of those dark days. His wife had suffered enough because of it. Caleb pulled the two stools he kept in the shop close to the brazier. "Have a seat. I believe 'tis time to tell thee about what happened before."

"Before?" She loosened her cloak and perched on one of the stools, but Caleb paced behind the other one.

"'Twas a long time ago, and thee had just turned a year old a month before. Your mother and I lived outside of a little village not unlike Salem Village in size and population, with farms surrounding it. The Friends community there was smaller and the Puritans tolerated us even less. In fact, they were openly hostile on many occasions." He rubbed a hand down his face, seeing the past among the tidy rows of tools lining the back wall of the shop. "A sickness came about in late January of that year, and many people died. Too many. The very young and the very old were hardest hit, of course. We heard of it in our Friends community outside the village, yet none of our people succumbed to the illness."

"How terrible that must have been for the poor village people."

He startled at his daughter's voice. Brought back to the moment, he sat on the stool and took her hand in his. "The Puritans came to believe that the sickness must have been caused by sin, and who better to blame the sin on than we Friends?"

Her cool fingers wrapped around his, her expression filled with empathy.

"The farm closest to the village was that of my best friend. He and his wife had married only months before. He had a nice little flock of sheep and was excited to plant a cabbage crop in the spring. But that never happened." Caleb stopped and searched the trusting depths of his daughter's eyes, wishing he could spare her from the rest. They'd raised their children to be strong and capable, unafraid to try new things and test their ideas as long as they fell within the bounds of the scriptures. He and Hannah hadn't wanted them to grow up under a cloud of fear.

But this one, their eldest, was an adult. Of all of them, she could handle the truth. And it was best coming from him. He should prepare Hannah Jr. in case they were forced to run again. With such a large family, they would need the older children to help with the younger ones.

"What happened, Father?" Concern lined her lovely forehead. If only the world didn't have such darkness in it. If only it could be as it should have been. But *if onlys* were not the world they lived in.

"The Puritans of the village—I know not who or how many—decided that the sin and sickness started among we Friends. Their proof was that none of us had died." He shook his head. "Very few of the Friends had fallen ill at all that winter, and none with the same symptoms as were reported in the village."

"Then how came they to accuse the Friends?" she asked. "That makes no sense."

"As thee know, there has long been hatred from the Puritans toward the Friends." He raised a hand to forestall the comment forming on her lips. "There have also been Friends who have acted to antagonize the Puritans and deepen the resentment they harbor toward us and our differing views of the scriptures." Nothing in life was completely one-sided. Hannah Jr. needed to understand that as well. Even if, at the time of their escape, it had been.

"But to make such a hateful accusation..."

"In their hatred and fear, having convinced themselves that the illness was our fault, they descended on my friend's house and burned it to the ground."

Hannah Jr. pressed her hand over her mouth, her eyes glimmering with a sheen of tears.

Turning his face away from her, he drew in a steadying breath. Even after all the years, the pain remained sharp. Should he tell her the rest? Would it prepare her for what might come? Or would it frighten her unnecessarily?

Give me wisdom, Lord.

He waited until he felt that familiar nudge in his spirit. Then he met her eyes again. "My friend and his wife had been locked inside."

Her gasp knifed through his chest, driving the memory deeper.

"It was just coming on dark when we saw the flames. Several of us from neighboring farms rushed to help, only to be shot at and driven away by the Puritans. Two of the Friends fell to the bullets, I learned much later. I was able to make it back to thy mother with nothing more than a bullet hole in the tail of my coat, but we could not stay. Another house was lighting up the sky by the time I arrived home." The fear from that moment still burned deep within him. Fear for his wife and child. Fear that he wouldn't be able to save them.

"I turned the cows out and saddled our horse for 'twas safer to ride through the forest than try to escape on the roads. Thy mother packed what she could carry, some food and what was needed for thee. Thee were wrapped in a blanket and rode with thy mother while I led the horse away. We could hear the raised cry of the Puritans coming after us." The pictures in his head were so vivid that sweat broke out on his back despite the chill of the shop. "There was no snow on the ground that year, thank the Lord, and they could not track us in the dark."

"Surely the Puritans knew thee would not fight back." Hannah's voice was strained. "How could they attack thee in such a way, with fire and muskets?"

"They were crazed by the loss of their loved ones, I assume. Perhaps chased by the very devil they so fear."

Hannah clung to his hand. "But thee made it safely away."

They almost had. He couldn't tell her the rest. He'd told her all she needed to know. Enough to understand what had befallen them and what could befall them again if things in the village turned bad.

"We had lost everything but what we carried and the horse. His name was Samson, and he was black. Funny how I remember that, but it probably helped us escape into the darkness. He was a good horse. I was forced to sell him when we arrived at Salem Town for enough money to pay rent and purchase food. I found employment with a carpenter there. We saved until we could purchase this farm."

"I remember the tiny log cabin in Salem Town. The door rattled in the wind."

"Aye, and it seemed I had to patch the roof every other week to keep ahead of the leaks." He'd worked night and day and saved every penny to move them out of that cabin. Hannah had skimped on even necessities to help. Caleb Jr. and Robert had been born there, but Caleb had been able to move the family to the farm before Tamson arrived, by less than a month if he remembered correctly. During the last twelve years, they'd built a successful farm and carpentry business and been blessed with two more boys. And lately, another girl, although she'd arrived as an eight-year-old, and not a babe, an orphan in need of a family.

A Puritan orphan.

Would the decision to take her into their home turn into something their family would suffer for? Would the village Puritans misinterpret their motives—added to their fear of whatever illness was upon the village—as reasons to drive them out? Or burn them down?

"I am sorry, Rachel." William Griggs hung his coat on its peg by the door and turned to his wife of nearly fifty years. "There is nothing I can do. You are her closest kin. She has no other relations who can or would take her in." With their past birthdays, Rachel had turned seventy and William seventy-four. And yet, they were raising her seventeen-year-old great-niece, Elizabeth Hubbard.

William had more than earned his retirement after a lifetime of doctoring. His joints ached, and getting out of bed in the wee hours to attend to the ill had become burdensome. There was also the nagging pain in his chest at times, the pain he kept hidden from Rachel. He couldn't do much about that anyway. Time had taught him that some ailments were meant to be endured for the long haul, not cured.

When he'd visited quaint little Salem Village in the fall, he'd fallen in love with the beautiful countryside and easy pace of life there. So different from the constant noise and interruptions of Boston. The perfect place for a Puritan couple like themselves to retire. He looked forward to relocating, settling into village life, and enjoying his waning years.

Although he'd tried to retire the previous spring, his patients had refused to allow it. Hezekiah Pond, his apprentice for more than three years and a young man perfectly capable of treating patients, worked at the practice every day, but still the people sought William out at his home. He'd never find peace if they stayed in Boston.

"I know, dear." Rachel, as unflappable as a woman could be, folded a blanket and added it to the trunk she was packing for their move. "But she is young and unhappy about being, and I quote, 'stuffed away in some backwater village with no hope of making a suitable match.'"

William sighed. Elizabeth was perhaps a little spoiled, but he was quite fond of the girl. She'd come to William and Rachel at the tender age of nine after her parents had died. But now she was a young woman in need of a husband. The problem was, the only man she'd shown any interest in was Hezekiah, who had shown absolutely no interest in her. Pity that, for William thought them well suited. Elizabeth, having learned a good deal working beside William in recent months, would have been an asset to Hezekiah in his practice. Yet one could not force the heart to be tender toward another. And the girl had no dowry to tempt a man to overlook matters of the heart.

"Besides, you are not responsible for her happiness." Rachel moved to the next items waiting to be sorted, folded, and either set aside for the poor, or packed. They could only take so much on the ship to Salem Town, where they would rent a wagon and driver to finish the three-mile trek north to Salem Village. "'Tis up to her to adjust and learn to make the most of her situation." Rachel held up a tablecloth they'd had forever and frowned.

It was a ragged piece, but no doubt held some attachment for her. Women tended to get that way over household things. He'd packed only his medical books, but they were priceless, of course. He might not have access to other copies, being halfway to the wilds of Maine. Not that he planned to practice medicine anymore, but he could still consult with the doctor in residence there over a pint in the local tavern.

"I wish we could have traveled overland and taken more with us." She folded the cloth, setting it aside.

"We would have, if not for the rumors of Indians." Which was only partly true. There were rumors, but the attacks had come from farther north than Salem Village. They'd also need to wait until late spring or even summer to travel overland, when the roads dried enough to get a heavy wagon through. William was anxious to get moved. He'd hoped to be settled before the snow fell, but they'd been delayed awaiting the previous owner's departure from the house they were purchasing.

Traveling by ship, they would board in the morning and arrive by evening, if the wind favored their journey.

"What is the name of the ship we are taking?" Rachel asked. "Elizabeth wished to know, and I could not remember."

"The *Margaret,* under Captain Peter Henderson. Her home port is Salem Town, so we shall board at the end of her return journey from the southern islands." Hopefully that did not result in yet another delay, but it had been the only ship he could secure passage on suitable for his wife and niece during the mid-winter months.

The front door opened and closed. "Aunt Rachel?" Elizabeth breezed into the room, removing the hat and revealing her sable hair, which was tidy and secured with pins. She was a striking young woman, free of any pock marks or blemishes, a bit tall perhaps, and maybe too slender for some, but William was convinced that a slender woman was healthier than a portly one. He'd argued the same over many a pint with his fellow physicians in their favorite tavern.

Elizabeth paused when she spied William. "Oh. Am I interrupting?"

"Not at all," Rachel said. "We were discussing the ship on which we are to sail."

The young woman's face went rigid with the obvious attempt not to react to the news, and William's heart softened. To be young and vibrant as she was, she was meant to live in a fast-paced, hectic city such as Boston. Salem Village must seem like a prison sentence to her.

If only Hezekiah had reacted favorably toward William's less-than-subtle remarks concerning Elizabeth. But he hadn't, and as things were, they would move to the village as soon as the *Margaret* found her way to Boston.

Once settled into their new home and among new friends in the village, Elizabeth would adjust.

Chapter 2

C ALEB WAITED UNDER THE blankets while Hannah finished braiding her hair at the maple dressing table he'd made for her the year after they'd built the house. A peacefulness settled over them with the children all abed. The curtains were closed against the cold that seeped in, no matter that he'd chinked around the windows before winter set in. It was the bone-chilling cold of mid-January, and there was no escaping it, even with the banked fire in the bedroom's fireplace, a luxury he'd insisted on when they'd moved so far north.

Hannah rose and came to the bed, flicking open the blankets and letting in the chill.

"Are thee trying to freeze me, goodwife?"

"I am trying to get into bed, but thee have the covers wrapped around thee as if to hibernate." There was a smile in her voice. She loved the winter months when things slowed down on the farm. Not that he could blame her when so much of the work fell to her the rest of the year. Planting and tending the garden, then preserving and storing enough food to see the family through another year was exhaustive work. Even with the girls to help—including Verity now—it was a daunting amount of labor.

Caleb preferred to be out working in a field, sweating underneath a hot sun. Winter was good for his carpentry work, but why did it have to be so cold?

Hannah snuggled in next to him, her feet finding his lower legs to warm themselves against. It was a small price to pay for the woman at his side. If only he didn't need to bring up the past tonight, but after his talk with Hannah Jr., it was best.

"I had a long talk with our daughter this afternoon when she came out to the shop."

"I wondered what had detained her." Hannah fluffed her goosedown pillow, then turned to face him, the gentle glow of the fire highlighting her smooth cheek. "What did thee speak of?"

He felt for her hand and twined their fingers together. "She was uncomfortable in the village today because of her customers' behaviors."

"Did any mistreat her?" Motherly concern colored her tone as she stiffened beside him.

He squeezed her hand. "Nay, not like that. 'Twas more of a general feeling of distrust and unease. Not only toward Hannah Jr., but even among the Puritans on the street."

A shiver passed over her. "Like before? Because of the sickness Thomas told us of?"

"I fear it may be, although she was quick to add that Sarah Buffington treated her well. Still, I took the opportunity to tell her about what happened in the past."

"All of it?" Her voice was wispy, hesitant.

"Nay. Not all." There was no need to say which part he'd left out. Hannah would know.

Silence stretched between them for several minutes. Not an uncomfortable silence, but an understanding one. Even after all these years, they couldn't discuss those days without shared grief and sorrow.

"How did she react?"

"Much as you would suppose. Our daughter is grown and ready to handle the truths and challenges of the world." He believed that, he wasn't just saying it to comfort his wife, but oh, how he wished things were different between the Puritans and the Friends. Perhaps, one day, they could make peace and agree on the important points of their shared faith in the Lord of Heaven.

"I wish she could have been spared, that none of our children would have to hear of it."

"In a perfect world, perhaps. But in this fallen world, they need to be aware of what can happen when they are old enough to understand. That is why I told her."

Hannah rose up on one elbow and searched his face. "Do thee think it wise for her to continue to go into the village to sell her cheese and butter?"

He'd wrestled with that very question since their daughter had left the shop. "I know not. I have been praying about it. Perhaps 'twould be well for her to deliver only to Sarah Buffington, if she is willing, and the others could pick up their orders from her."

"'Twill be another week before she makes her rounds again. We have time to pray more about it." Hannah settled back in, shutting out the cold that had stolen under the blankets during her movements. "Perhaps thee should also tell Caleb Jr. what happened back then—most of it—and we should send him with her if she returns to the village."

How would the villagers react to that? Hannah Jr. had been delivering the dairy products on her own for a couple of years, sometimes with the assistance of Tamson, but never with her eldest brother. Would the villagers be suspicious? That was always the fear, to draw attention of any kind. History had taught that the Puritans needed little excuse to persecute the Friends.

"Let us pray about that also." Caleb tugged her closer to his side. "As thee said, we have a week. God will answer us in His time. Until then, we shall do nothing to give the Puritans a reason to view us any differently."

Tension eased from his wife's form as she snuggled closer. "Thee are right, of course. The last thing we need is for them to come poking around and possibly remove Verity from us."

Hannah was so attached to the little girl. Heaven knew Verity needed a family to care for her, and Caleb agreed that the Lord had sent her to them, but at what cost? The issue was bound to come around again with the Puritan elders, bringing more attention to their family.

In the end, would the rest of his family suffer for their decision to take the girl in?

The walk from the tavern to the house seemed longer and colder than usual. William burrowed his chin further into the wool muffler wrapped around his neck as a blast of wind off the harbor hit him. It carried the scent of brine and frost and wood smoke from the many chimneys. A woman struggled toward him carrying a large shopping basket buffeted by the wind. He reached out and steadied it for her.

"Thank you, Dr. Griggs." She paused to draw a deep breath. "'Tis enough to blow a person away."

He tried to remember the goodwife's name, but names had been getting slipperier to hold on to in recent months. "'Twill be a good evening to sit by the fire."

"Indeed. I must hurry to get supper ready. Good day to you." She scurried on down the street without glancing back.

Goodie Caldwell, that was her name. He'd treated her son for a broken arm the past spring. William walked on, bent into the wind. In Salem Village, there would be fewer names to remember. Far fewer. Another good reason to board the ship and sail.

If only the ship would arrive. The expected date of January fifteenth had come and gone. Rachel and Elizabeth were packed and ready, and the new owner of their Boston house was eager to move in. But nothing would happen until the *Margaret* docked, no doubt filled with rum and molasses. And perhaps slaves.

William disliked the thought of that. Slaves were common among those who could afford them, but he disagreed with the practice. He'd tended enough of them to know they were not always kindly treated. And as for the argument that they were not fully human due to the color of their skin, well, that was lacking in any sort of logic. Human beings were human beings.

An older boy dashed out from between two buildings and knocked into William. "Slow down, lad." He managed to keep on his feet.

"Pardon me," the scamp shouted over his shoulder, never breaking stride.

"Are you all right, Dr. Griggs?" A strong hand gripped his arm.

"Only just." He pointed after the lad, who dodged around another man and disappeared down an alley. "That lad is a menace."

"The city is getting too crowded. I envy you, moving out and finding somewhere with more breathing space." Horace Crowder glanced around them at the rest of the people milling along the street. "If not for all the rumors of Indians, I would be tempted to follow after you."

"So far, I have heard nothing more than rumors." Although those rumors held a worrisome amount of detail.

"Let us pray they shall remain nothing more, shall we?" Crowder touched the brim of his hat and moved on.

"Indeed," William murmured after the man's retreating back.

William reached his house and entered, shoving the door closed behind him.

Rachel approached and helped him unwind his muffler and shrug out of his coat. "You are half frozen." She *tsked*. "Come in by the fire. I shall fetch you a cup of tea."

He enjoyed her fussing over him for a few moments, then took his favorite winged chair near the hearth and stretched his toes toward the flames.

Rachel hummed while she made the tea, dipping water kept hot over the log fire. She poured it into a chipped teapot, her good one having been lovingly packed for the journey. When it had brewed long enough, she handed him a cup, also chipped, with a mismatched saucer.

The tea's heat brought life back into his old bones. He drained the cup's contents, even though it nearly scalded his tongue.

"As you are silent"—Rachel sat in her chair across from his—"I assume the *Margaret* has yet to show her face in port."

"Perhaps tomorrow." Although he wouldn't complain if it waited for a break in the weather. As eager as he was to move, a milder day would be welcome. At least onboard the *Margaret*, they would have a room out of the elements during the journey.

"I hope it comes soon." Rachel rested her hands in her lap and gazed out the window. "Elizabeth has taken to spending all day visiting her friends. This long goodbye is not helping her. 'Tis almost morbid how she carries on about losing everything she loves. I fear she will make herself ill if she does not find peace with her station in life."

"Perhaps she will find a husband in the village."

His wife gave him a sour look. "She has determined to be a spinster for the rest of her days."

"The girl is simply high-strung." He took another sip of the tea cooling in his cup. "She is legally an adult now. 'Tis high time she faced the realities of life." He lifted his cup toward Rachel in a silent plea for more. "Wishes and wants we all have aplenty, but God provides for our needs."

"What she needs is a husband and children to keep her busy." Rachel poured the tea.

"As you had with me and our brood." Rachel was his second wife, his first having died after the birth of their fifth child. Rachel had stepped in and raised that babe and the others as if they were her own, and given William three more. Of the eight children, only three survived, a daughter married and living in Virginia Colony, a son married and living in Connecticut Colony, and another son off sailing somewhere. Other than the very rare letters, they had moved on with their lives. As it should be.

Elizabeth would find her path in due season, even in Salem Village.

Caleb glanced up from his chair near the kitchen hearth were he'd been snoozing since he'd come in from the shop. The little boys, Benji and Jonathan, played with wooden blocks at his feet. They were all that kept him from full slumber.

A gust of cold air announced someone had opened the door of the back room off the kitchen. Caleb Jr. entered and greeted them with a chagrined expression.

Hannah moved the soup she'd been stirring a little farther away from the fire where it would keep warm without scorching. "Did thee not find any game?"

Their son crossed the room and handed the musket he'd brought in to Caleb. "I did, but the gun did not fire properly." He turned to Hannah. "Sorry I could not bring thee any fresh meat."

"'Tis fine," she said. "We are far from starving in this house."

Benji stood, holding onto the arm of Caleb's chair. "I am starving."

"Of course thee are." Hannah smiled at the lad who, at five years old, was once again outgrowing his breeches. She sent Caleb a grin before calling out, "Girls, come down and set the table."

"Coming, Mother," Tamson replied.

"I fear this is beyond what I can repair." Caleb turned the musket over in his hands. "I shall have to take it to David." A chance to sit on a cold day and visit with his best friend over a pint of cider wouldn't be unwelcome. That David O'Sullivan was the best gunsmith in the area was also beyond dispute. Even the Puritans used him for their repairs, to commission new muskets and the occasional rifle if they could afford one.

"If we had another musket, I could go out again tomorrow." Caleb Jr. cast a hopeful glance at him.

Their eldest son had been wrangling for a musket of his own for almost two years. At eighteen, he certainly was old enough and had proven himself responsible, but the cost of a musket was dear, and last year's crops had been short from the drought. Maybe next fall, if the Lord provided.

"I agree, son." Caleb stood and put the musket on its rack above the door to the back room. "But we shall have to make do with getting this one repaired."

The spark of hope drained from Caleb Jr.'s face as Tamson and Verity arrived to set the table.

"Where are Robert and Hannah Jr.?" Tamson asked.

"In the dairy." Hannah held up a hand to stay the complaint forming on their daughter's lips. "Hannah Jr. needed some of the heavy items moved to be cleaned around. His muscles are well used to lifting from his work at the brewery. Fear not, he will not replace thee as her assistant."

Another gust of cold air announced the arrival of the two in question, and within minutes, all were seated at the long table. How blessed they were to have such a family when so many others lacked. With Robert back home, one side of the table held him and Caleb Jr. and the two little boys. Verity sat between Hannah Jr. and Tamson on the other side.

Caleb bowed his head along with the others for the silent prayer and thanked the Lord again for His provisions. *And please, Lord, protect our family from anything like what happened before.*

"Will thee go into the village again on Tuesday?" Tamson asked Hannah Jr.

His eldest daughter looked to Caleb.

"'Twill depend upon the weather, of course." He put off a direct answer.

Tamson pressed on. "But with the Puritans being so unfriendly—"

"'Tis not all the Puritans, just some." Hannah Jr. kept her face lowered. She spooned up another mouthful of the soup, her cheeks flushed.

Some of the goodwives had been her loyal customers for years. She would naturally feel the need to defend them, but Caleb hoped that friendship wouldn't blind her to the seriousness of the situation. Or even worse—make her a target.

Chapter 3

"**A**RE THEE SURE ABOUT returning to the village?" Caleb asked from the doorway to the dairy as Hannah Jr. packed her basket with cheese and butter. It was Tuesday, her normal day to make deliveries. It'd been two weeks since she'd come to him with her worries about the villagers. Last week, Tamson had accompanied her, and yet since then, Hannah Jr. had seemed unsettled even around the house.

"Mother asked that I take Tamson along again." She gave him a wry smile. "'Tis a struggle for her to separate from Verity."

It was true that his younger daughter and the orphan girl were practically inseparable. "How did Tamson react?"

"Since Mother had first asked Verity to help with the little boys today, Tamson was happy enough to tag along with me."

How could two sisters be so opposite? Tall and willowy, Hannah Jr. was born to follow in her mother's footsteps. She'd make some lucky young man of the Friends a good wife. Tamson, on the other hand, was strong and sturdy and as headstrong as old Buttercup, the misnamed red cow who habitually broke things in the barn. It would take a brave young man to come courting Tamson. Although she had a few years to mellow before she reached courting age.

But he admired her spunk.

"I would go with thee myself if—" He clipped off that thought as another took its place.

"What is it, Father?"

He rubbed his chin and let the notion settle for a moment, considering possible ramifications. "I *will* take thee and Tamson into the village. I need to order a new barrel from the cooper. 'Twould be a good time to do that. None would think it odd if thee and Tamson came along."

Hannah Jr. tucked a cloth over her goods in the basket. "The walk would have kept us warm on such a cold day."

"Bring a blanket from the house to tuck around thee." Caleb moved from the door, then stopped. "Ask thy mother if she needs anything from town."

"I will." Hannah Jr. lifted her basket and went to the house while Caleb went outside to catch the team for harnessing.

Standing in the corner of the paddock near the barn, Dolly and Dandy watched him approach. The matched team of heavy horses was a brother and sister, but Dolly was the rounder one with her coming foal. Having bred her to Arthur Stokes' stocky stallion, Caleb hoped for another work horse. If he could breed the mare back again in the summer, he could have a nice young team for Caleb Jr. when the time was right and the boy found himself a wife.

What was he doing, thinking about his children marrying off? He snorted, his breath fogging the air. Making himself feel old, that was what.

He had the team hitched and was pulling up to the house as the girls came out the back door.

"Mother needs yeast from the brewer." Tamson gave him a wide grin as she slid onto the wagon's seat next to him. "Benji tipped over her yeast pot this morning. He was trying to catch a spider and knocked the pot to the floor."

After putting her basket in the back, Hannah Jr. climbed up beside her sister. "I know not what bothered her more, losing the yeast or seeing the spider." She spread the blanket across all three of their laps.

"Although she can abide most things, thy mother has never been fond of spiders."

With a flick of the reins, the team leaned into their harnesses. Snow crunched under the wagon wheels. It didn't take long for Caleb to consider another difference in his girls. Hannah Jr. remained mostly silent. Tamson filled their ears with tales of what she and Verity had been up to and their future plans, including picking spring flowers and summer berries in the fields around the house, and maybe gathering nuts in the forest come fall.

In the forest.

Somehow, Caleb needed to find that cave where Verity had hidden. He'd prayed for the past fortnight for guidance concerning the mysterious illness in the village and the chanting in the forest near the cave. In his gut, he knew the two were connected.

As if he needed any more stress—William rubbed the ache in the center of his chest—Elizabeth had gone and done the unthinkable. Unthinkable for a young Puritan woman, for certain.

"How could she?" he asked Rachel, who stirred their supper at the hearth as if her life depended on it, back rigid as a fire poker.

Elizabeth's muffled sobbing reached them from her room above the kitchen. The neighbors must have been able to hear her by now.

William pushed to his feet. "I shall speak with her."

Rachel whirled from the hearth, spoon in one hand dripping gravy unnoticed to the floor. "What will you say?"

"I know not. Pray that I will find the words on the stairs." He climbed as slowly as he could, but it didn't help. No magic words appeared. He tapped on the door. "Elizabeth?"

She ignored him, her sobbing increasing to a wail.

This had to end. William opened the door.

Elizabeth lay sprawled across her bed in a puddle of petticoats, her face awash with tears, her hair in complete disarray as if she'd been pulling on it. She turned her red, swollen eyes to him.

Pity washed over William. "My dear."

That sent her off into another round of wailing until she planted her face into her pillow.

Was she attempting to suffocate herself?

William hurried to the bed and sat beside her, gathering her into his arms as he used to do when she was a young child. And as she'd done back then, she buried her face against the side of his neck.

"I am sorry, Uncle William."

"I know." He rocked her gently back and forth. "But I wish you would have spoken to me first. I could have told you—"

Her next wail practically deafened him.

"'Twill be all over Boston by the morrow." A sloppy hiccup followed her words. "I cannot show my face in this town again."

"Nonsense." He gave her a little shake. "I can assure you that Hezekiah will speak of this to no one. He is not that sort of man."

Elizabeth's sobs subsided, at least for the moment. "Truly?"

"Indeed." And William intended to make sure of it when he went to the office first thing in the morning. Elizabeth had been imprudent in the extreme—approaching a man to suggest marriage—but she did not deserve to be publicly shamed for it, especially in light of their impending departure. What would be the point of that?

If only that dratted ship would arrive.

Caleb slowed the team when they reached the village. It was as Hannah Jr. had described it—unwelcoming. More than the wind was cold as they drove along the main street. People hurried past, faces down or turned away, goodwives holding the hands of their young ones and keeping them close. Not even a loose dog or scavenging chicken roamed the street. No horses were tied at the hitching rails in front of businesses. It was eerily quiet.

Even Tamson seemed to have run out of words.

"Where will thee stop today?" he asked.

"If thee would drop us off outside the Puritan church, we could meet thee in front of the brewer's in an hour." Hannah Jr. turned and looked at the brewery as they passed. "'Twould be best to get the yeast last so it has less chance to freeze before we get it home."

"As thee wish." That would give him more than enough time to purchase a bucket. While he was a good carpenter, Caleb had never been successful in bucket-making. The art of making buckets belonged to John Biddle, the cooper.

A Puritan, John had always treated the Friends fairly. His goodwife was one of Hannah Jr.'s best clients. Or at least, she had been. Perhaps that had changed now.

"Ho, Dolly. Ho, Dandy." Caleb brought the wagon to a stop near the meeting house. "At the brewer's in an hour."

"We shall be there." Tamson scrambled down after Hannah Jr. They strode toward a line of houses on the opposite side of the street from the church.

Caleb drove the team to the cooper's shop. A square building farther up the street, it sat in front of John Biddle's house. Inside, it smelled of oak shavings and smoke from the small forge where the cooper fashioned the hoops to hold his staves together. A young man, no older than Robert, worked a draw knife along a stave at a workbench. Another, slightly younger apprentice wielded a broom across the floor. On other workbenches, kegs, hogsheads, piggins, butter churns, and buckets were on display. Business was good for the area's only cooper.

"Caleb Buffum, welcome." John Biddle stood and wiped his hands on the apron covering his clothing. The man was tall and thin with blond hair and blue eyes behind a pair of silver-rimmed spectacles. "How can I help you today?"

"I am in need of a sturdy bucket." Caleb shrugged. "One that can outlast a cantankerous cow of mine."

"Here is something that should work for you." The cooper ushered Caleb toward one of the workbenches. "This design"—he lifted a wide bucket with thick staves and handed it to Caleb—"should do nicely."

"'Tis perfect. Just what I need." He followed John to the small counter near the door and paid for the bucket. "Things are quiet in the village today."

John glanced at the two apprentices on the other side of the shop, who seemed engrossed with their labors. Then he leaned against the counter and spoke in a low voice. "'Tis this sickness that has everyone on edge. The reverend's daughter and niece"—he shook his head—"'tis all very unsettling."

"I had heard of it."

"Some be saying 'tis not a normal sickness, but you cannot know what to believe. With the doctor up and moving away last month, there are only the old grannies and their herbal remedies, none of which seem to have been effective."

"Has it not spread beyond the reverend's family then?"

John shook his head. "Praise God, it has not."

That might have been encouraging had Caleb not known about the chanting in the forest. A normal illness was one thing, but dabbling in the dark spirits, this was something else altogether. Something foolish. Something dangerous.

"I best be on my way. Good day to thee." Caleb stepped outside and put the bucket in the back of the wagon. He had time before meeting with the girls, but Thomas wouldn't mind him waiting inside the brewery, out of the cold. He climbed aboard the wagon and turned the team around.

The brewery was warm and welcoming. Steam rose from one of the vats, a young man stirring it with a long pole. One of the Buffington twins. They were around Caleb Jr.'s age and impossible to tell apart.

The young man stopped, wiped his hands, and approached Caleb. "What can I do for you, Mr. Buffum?"

"I am to meet Hannah Jr. and Tamson here. Would it be agreeable if I waited near the hearth?"

"Please do." The young man motioned toward a pair of chairs situated there. "I shall let Father know you are here. He stepped out only a moment ago."

Caleb raised a hand. "Do not bother him. I am sure the girls will be along shortly."

"'Tis no problem. He will wish to ask after Robert, I am sure." He sprinted to the back of the shop. The Buffingtons' house was located directly behind, so he wouldn't be gone long.

Caleb peeled off his mitts and was warming his hands when Thomas entered, both of the twins at his heels.

"Caleb!" His voice boomed across the room. "Good of you to come and visit." He turned to the lads. "Fetch us each a mug of cider, Benjamin."

Thomas lowered himself into the opposite chair. "What brings you into the village this raw, cold day?"

"I finished an errand I had to run. Hannah Jr. and Tamson are delivering their dairy products to the village goodwives. They planned to meet me here when they are finished. I hope 'tis no inconvenience to thee."

"Of course not." Thomas took the mugs from Benjamin and passed one to Caleb. "Always happy for someone to stop by." He sobered. "Especially now when visitors are few."

"I noticed the empty street."

"Aye. Thank goodness my business runs on deliveries. Folks barely come out of their houses these days."

"Because of the illness thee mentioned when thee brought Robert home?"

Thomas nodded, then brightened. "How is young Robert doing?"

"Chomping at the bit to return to thee." Caleb raised his mug and took a drink. The lightly spiced cider was refreshing.

"And I am eager to have him back." He waved a hand in the direction of his sons. The first had returned to the vat, stirring its contents. The second was at the counter, flipping through some paperwork there. "We could use his hands about the place."

The subject turned again to the strange illness, but Thomas knew no more than John had. Caleb was draining the last of his mug when Hannah Jr. and Tamson blew into the brewery on a gust of wind.

Hannah Jr. struggled to hold the door until Benjamin—if Caleb guessed correctly—hurried to her aid and got it shut.

"'Tis hardly a fit day for man nor beast out there," Thomas said.

"I thank thee for the hospitality." Caleb rose. "Would thee happen to have an extra keg of this fine cider for sale?"

"As a matter of fact"—Thomas held up a finger—"I have one left and 'tis yours if you wish."

Caleb nodded.

"I shall fetch it. I know which one." The other lad, Thomas Jr., set aside his pole, grabbed a smaller keg near the back of the shop, and hoisted it onto his shoulder.

Caleb paid for the cider while the lad carried it out to the wagon, Tamson following the boy outside.

Hannah Jr. remained near the door with Benjamin, speaking softly.

"When things settle, I shall send one of the boys to fetch Robert back," Thomas said. "'Tis been too long already. Surely this will pass over us soon."

"I hope thee are right." But Caleb was distracted by the flush on Hannah Jr.'s cheeks, and the way she dropped her eyes when he glanced her way. Perhaps she was flustered over losing control of the door, but what if— Surely not. His daughter couldn't be looking at a Puritan young man.

Could she?

Chapter 4

"PERHAPS WE SHOULD CONSIDER the overland route in a wagon, after all." William hung his coat on the peg by the door and stomped the worst of the snow from his boots. He'd been out to check on old Goodie Travers, who refused to take Hezekiah's advice to drink more tea laced with honey and keep a blanket over her swollen knees against the winter's chill. Yet she would take the same advice from William. "The harbormaster said if it does not warm up soon, there may be too much ice in the harbor, and the *Margaret* may have to turn back to wait out the weather in a southern port."

"Can a wagon get through on the roads with all the snow?" Rachel looked up from darning one of his socks.

"That is the question. Although I was told on good authority—"

"At the tavern?" His wife cocked her head at him.

"From a reliable source." He straightened his waistcoat. "'Twas a man who made the trek down from Salem Town just last week. He said the snow was not as deep there as 'tis here."

"Last week."

"Indeed." William grunted as he sank into his chair by the fire. "Things may have changed."

"I do weary of living like this, all our things packed and ready, using only what we'll leave behind." She bit off the thread and surveyed her handiwork, then set the sock aside. "If you think 'tis best to try overland, then see if you can find a teamster to hire on the morrow. But now"—she stood—"I shall brew a pot of tea."

The door banged open and Elizabeth flew through it. "Uncle William, you must hear wha—"

"Close the door," Rachel said calmly, lifting a brow in the girl's direction.

With a huff and a flounce, Elizabeth whirled and secured it. In just over a week, their niece had fully recovered from her social misstep. Thank goodness Hezekiah had been a man of his word. "You must hear what is being said." She paused, whether for dramatic effect or to draw breath, William wasn't sure. "Indians have attacked up north and killed off an entire settlement." She lifted her chin. "We cannot move north now. 'Tis far too dangerous."

"I heard nothing of an attack while at the tavern today."

"Mary's father only just arrived home as I was leaving. He shared the news." She looked between them, then faced William. "He heard it firsthand from one of the King's couriers riding through town. The man had been there, Uncle. He saw what had happened with his own eyes. Surely we cannot go north now." Her voice took on a pleading tone.

"I believe you should investigate this, William." Rachel, never one to show alarm, directed her gray eyes at him, and there was concern in their depths.

"Indeed." William left the warmth and comfort of his chair. "The city will be abuzz about it by the time I arrive at the tavern, I am sure."

Rachel helped him back into his coat and muffler, then handed him his hat before whispering, "Elizabeth appears truly alarmed, my dear."

He patted her hand. "If I am late, I will eat there. Do not wait supper on my account. I shall stay until we know the extent of it."

A week after Caleb's trip to the cooper's, the children were busy with their winter chores after breakfast, but he lingered at the table, staring into the dark liquid cooling in his cup.

Hannah hung a damp towel over the back of the chair beside him and leaned closer. "What troubles thee this morning?"

He planted an elbow on the table and pinched the bridge of his nose to collect his thoughts. Thoughts that had been swirling for the past three weeks since Hannah Jr.'s report of things in the village. He'd noticed it himself, and Thomas had confirmed it. The weather had kept them home this week on their usual delivery day, a misty drizzle having blanketed the area. But they wished to go into the village this afternoon, and Caleb had a bad feeling about it.

"I cannot help but wonder," Caleb said, "if the happenings in the village are related to the girls in the forest that we encountered when we fetched Verity back weeks ago."

Hannah pulled the chair out and sat next to him. "I confess to thinking the same, but I know not why. We know so little of what is happening."

"Thomas knew enough to bring Robert home. Hannah Jr. knew enough to give warning. Tamson knew enough to confirm her sister's feelings." He raised his eyes to his wife. "And thee heard the girls with the slave chanting in the forest. Thee said at the time how it unnerved thee."

"It did." Hannah drew circles on the tabletop with her fingertip. "But when we saw the girls and the slave on their way out of the forest, all seemed normal enough."

"Indeed." But did that tell the whole story? Caleb needed to know. Hannah wasn't going to like his suggestion. He pulled in a deep breath. "I would like to go back to that place in the forest and see for myself what is there."

She clutched his arm. "What good can come of that?"

"I know not, but I feel..." How could he explain it? "I must go and see what is there. Perhaps gain some understanding of what happened."

"Even if thee learn the truth of it, what would thee do with such knowledge?" Fear crept into Hannah's voice. "Thee cannot tell the Puritans what thee might find."

Caleb put his hand over the one still clutching his arm. "I could speak to Thomas about it."

"Nay!" Hannah arched away from him. "Thee cannot. If thee are even suspected of casting aspersions onto a Puritan—especially a child of their reverend—thee know what will happen. They will come for us. Again."

Naked fear crossed his beloved's face, and it pained him deeply, but something else was urging him on. The answer to his prayers? Maybe. Or maybe his own need to take control. If only he could be sure. This thing happening around them was so...so murky. Caleb had no other word to describe it.

"I may learn nothing at all, but I must go and see."

"How will thee find that place again?" There was an edge to her voice, as if she suspected what he was going to say next.

"I will need the girls to lead me there."

"Nay." Hannah stood and went to the window, arms crossed and back to him. "If there is something to be feared out there, the children must not be allowed to return." She whirled to face him. "Thee cannot risk them in such a way."

Caleb rose and went to her. "I will not risk them. I will be with them and protect them."

"If thee must go, I will take thee. I found the cave and the place where the chanting came from was just beyond."

"Thee followed Verity's footsteps in the snow, the same as I, but that snow has been long covered by more." He put his hands on her shoulders. "If I could find it again on my own, I would, but I know I could not. And neither could thee." Her expression said he was right, and yet it hurt to see it there. "I wish 'twere otherwise, but Verity knows the way. She ran straight to the cave through the snow the last time."

"Why take Tamson along?"

"For Verity's sake. I will keep the girls together and at a distance while I investigate the area."

"I do not like this, Caleb. I do not like this at all."

"I know."

She raised her face to him, the lines around her eyes deepening, unshed tears shimmering. Something he never wanted to see on his wife—distrust aimed at him. Surely, it would haunt him for a long time.

He pulled her stiff body against his. "Fear not. Because it distresses thee so, I will not take them."

Hannah's arms came around him. "Thank thee for that," she mumbled against his shirt. She wasn't a woman to use tears to get what

she wanted. Nor one to have a cross word for him. She was frightened—and had every reason to be.

He wouldn't take the girls, but he would try to find the place himself.
Because he still needed answers.

The extent of the Indian attack had been dire indeed. William nursed
a pint of warm cider with a trio of friends at the tavern, listening to
the courier who was being plied with questions—often repeated by
new arrivals—and ample amounts of ale. The tavern was packed for a
Wednesday afternoon.

The attack had happened at York, Maine. While rumors abounded
that Maine should be its own colony, it was still part of the Massachusetts charter. William fought a twinge of guilt over his relief that it
had happened well north of Salem Village and should not disrupt their
plans to move. It did, however, erase any thought of traveling overland
by wagon. They must await the *Margaret*.

"You are still set to leave us then, Doctor?" one of his companions
asked. "And move into this unstable country of the north?"

"I am, else I shall be tending to the ill of Boston until I take to my
deathbed." He drained the last of his pint and stood, shrugging into his
coat. "Goodie Griggs and I have earned a respite."

"A short-lived respite if the Frenchies have their way of it," said
another of the men at his table.

The courier had been adamant that the French were behind the
attack, having encouraged and outfitted the local Abenaki tribe to
commit the atrocities in York. The report was fifty colonists killed
outright and at least as many taken as hostages. Livestock had been
slaughtered and the whole settlement burned to the ground. If even
half of the report were true, the situation demanded a response.

"The king will have to act after this, good man that he is." William
put his hat on and tapped it in place, ignoring the skeptical expressions
of some of his companions. "I bid you all a good afternoon."

He took the long way back to the house, the weather having turned
milder, with the wind letting up and sunshine breaking through the

clouds. The rhythmical *plop* of icicles dripping from the rooftops accompanied him. The harbor came into view, the masts of many ships reaching for the blue-gray sky. A smaller boat shuttled shoreward from a ketch anchored twenty rods or more out. Had he seen that one there before? It appeared from the distance, as if the sailors were just furling its canvas.

William turned toward the shipping office. They no doubt grew tired of him lingering around the huge board marked with the names of the vessels in the harbor, but he had to know. He arrived before the small boat did. At least the weather was nicer for the wait. He tucked his hands deeper into his pockets and watched the small boat find a spot to tie at one of the long docks that jutted into the harbor.

When its sailor finally approached, William asked, "What is the name of your vessel, sir?"

The sailor was lean and dark, hair as black as night and skin permanently tanned by exposure to the elements. "She be the *Margaret*, sir."

At last. William turned to the vessel bobbing on the swells of the harbor. It looked much as any other ketch, with a tall central mast and a shorter aft mast. He knew a little about ships, having investigated some when his son had taken to the sea. The *Margaret*, while not large for its kind, appeared to be a stout vessel and double-ended. The type that would see them safely to Salem Town.

He stepped into the harbormaster's building and waited behind a line of six men, including the sailor from the *Margaret*. When it was his turn, he asked the clerk behind the counter, "When will the *Margaret* leave for Salem Town?"

The little man peered over the top of his spectacles. "You again, eh? Luck must not be on your side. That ship will not leave until the fifteenth of February, according to the captain's note."

"A full fortnight? Why the delay?"

The clerk frowned at William. "Do I look like Captain Henderson? That man do keep his own schedule and waits for no man. Be here before the morning tide on the fifteenth."

"Right." Frustration gnawing at his middle, William stepped outside, where he glared at the vessel bobbing restfully in the harbor. More waiting. The local livery was on his route home, so he stopped and arranged for a wagon to pick them up before daybreak on the fifteenth.

In the fine weather and with at least some good news to share, he made it home in no time, pushing through the door and announcing, "The *Margaret* is at the harbor."

"But Uncle." Elizabeth shot to her feet. "The Indians. The attack. We must remain in Boston. 'Tisn't safe to travel north."

He shucked out of his coat, Rachel coming to take it and hang it on its peg. "Nonsense, dear girl. You will be relieved to learn that the attack happened in Maine, far north of Salem Village."

"Was the report dreadful?" Rachel asked.

"Quite dreadful, I fear." He crossed to his chair and relaxed into it. "Seems that the French put the local Indians up to it. People killed, others taken hostage, the village burned. Quite dreadful, indeed."

"What is to keep them from coming to Salem Village?" Elizabeth asked.

"The king's army, of course." William removed his spectacles and cleaned them on his sleeve before replacing them. "There are barracks right there in Salem Town. A perfect deterrent to any mischief the French might wish to foment."

"Will we stay in Salem Town then?" Hope filled his niece's question.

"Nay, my dear." William cast a glance at Rachel, who appeared unruffled by the discussion. "Our house is already purchased in Salem Village, which is but three miles from Salem Town."

"Three miles." Elizabeth huffed. "We would all be killed and burned before they could reach us."

"Elizabeth." The rebuke in his wife's voice was clear and sure.

The girl backed up and dropped into a chair, defeat rounding her shoulders.

Rachel went to stand beside her, a hand on her arm but faced William. "When do we depart?"

"Unfortunately, not until the fifteenth of February. The captain has set the departure for that date."

"Well"—Rachel looked from William to Elizabeth and back again—"we have a date and can plan for it. We needn't move in haste."

William relaxed—fully relaxed—for the first time in longer than he could remember. No more knocks on his door in the middle of the night. No more worries about patients he'd seen, nor regrets for those who'd not responded to his treatments. No more standing at gravesides wondering if he could have done more, or done better.

Salem Village would be his place of refuge and retirement.

Chapter 5

C ALEB'S HEART SANK WHEN Hannah whirled and glared at him from across their room.

"Thee said thee would not take the girls into the forest."

"I know." He stepped toward her, but when she backed away, he stopped. "If I could think of another way to find that cave on my own, I would."

"Thee said thee would pray about it."

"And I have." Almost constantly since their talk a fortnight ago and during his several trips into the forest, when he'd tried to find the cave on his own. Nothing in his spirit warned him against going, although nothing prodded him to go either. No other options had presented themselves for him to learn more. In over a month since Hannah Jr. had first come to his shop, he'd had nothing but questions—no answers.

"I cannot believe the Lord would have thee put the girls in such danger." There was an edge to her voice that chilled Caleb.

He'd not heard it before. Was it fear, anger, or a combination of those and more? Whatever it was, it was directed straight at him. And he didn't like it. Not one bit. He fought the urge to lash back in kind. What would that accomplish? A breach between them? In all their years of marriage, that had never happened.

But they'd not faced the danger he sensed lurking around them before either. At least, not since they'd fled their last home. And he never wanted to be caught unaware and unprepared again.

"I must learn what is out there. I must know the danger, the risk, in order to safeguard our family."

"Thee should wait upon the Lord." Her words came fast and sharp.

Caleb dragged in a long breath, weighing his next words. "Last time, there were only the three of us. God had provided us with a good horse with which to escape. A horse to sell for a new start." He waited until she lifted her eyes, then suppressed a flinch at the cold blue directed at him. "We have our six children to move with us, plus Verity. I cannot form a plan of escape until I know what we are up against."

Hannah crossed her arms, chin tilted up, a mother protecting her young. "Thee should not involve the girls."

As much as it hurt him, he was going to displease his wife. "I will protect them, but I need Verity to show me the way."

Silence stretched across the room like a living thing, wrapping itself around his throat and pulling it closed. Caleb wanted to take her into his arms and reassure her that all would be well. But would it? He could keep the girls safe in the forest today, he was sure of that. His skill as a stalker and hunter was as good as anyone's. He could keep them hidden until any danger passed.

But the larger danger? The danger of what was brewing in the village? Danger brought about by wicked practices? Could he keep his family safe from that? Or should he prepare them to flee again? That was what he most needed to know.

And he must have Verity's help.

The forest was silent except for the slushy plops of their footsteps in the melting snow. The sky over Caleb threatened rain or snow, it was hard to say which, the temperature being where either was possible. It fit the mood of the forest around them, dark and foreboding.

Hannah's disapproval—her fear—followed him like a physical be- ing. He'd waited and prayed and had come up with nothing else he could do to find answers. He could scarcely walk into the village and tell the first passing Puritan about the chanting in the forest, or ask if it might be connected with the mysterious illness. That would cast suspicion on him for sure. Yet how could he safeguard his family if he didn't know what he was safeguarding them from?

If only Hannah could understand that. She'd calmed herself before they'd gone downstairs, but she'd not spoken another word to him, only hugged each girl fiercely after breakfast before sending them out the door to finish their chores.

Now, excited to see her cave again, Verity led the way. She skipped through the sloppy footing, Tamson right behind her, the occasional giggle reaching back to him. He'd talked the girls into leaving Button, Verity's dog, at the farm with their collie, Rags. It was enough of a challenge to keep the two girls quiet. The half-grown pup would have been romping all over the place, and Rags would have joined him.

Caleb just wanted to see the place where the Puritan girls and the slave woman had been chanting. He knew very little of the darker side of the spirit world, only what he'd read in the Bible and what he'd heard from men who had sailed to the southern islands. Several times, the memory of his wife's defiant yet haunted expression almost had him turning back, but he had to do something. If only he could be sure this was the *something* he should be doing.

The Friends were pacifists, and Caleb fully believed that was the proper way to honor the Lord. He had no intention of doing anything other than investigating the scene. Perhaps the girls had left some sort of clue as to what they'd been about. Although what the clue would look like, he had no idea.

He was risking his wife's good opinion to follow— What? A hunch?

"'Tis just ahead." Verity had turned to face him, walking backward. "See that clump of birch trees?"

They looked like many other clumps of birch to him, but the girl showed no hesitation when she turned around and led again, soon pointing at a split pine for another marker.

"I know I am close when I see those." She didn't stop until they arrived at a rock wall. "'Tis right here." She turned to him with an impish grin.

"Where?" Tamson saved Caleb from having to ask.

"Watch." The little girl stepped close to the rockface, then stepped sideways—and disappeared.

Tamson squealed and rushed forward, then turned back to him with shining eyes. "'Tis a secret entrance." She moved sideways and left his sight.

Caleb approached. The entrance was there, but far too narrow and short for him to enter. There was another wall of rock that blocked his view of anything beyond. It wasn't dark inside. Shouldn't a cave be fully dark? He called in the opening, "Did thee bring a candle?"

"Nay, Father." Tamson's head appeared around the rock. "There is a hole in the ceiling."

"And from there, Verity heard the chanting?"

The little girl passed Tamson and squeezed through the fissure. "Joseph and I both heard it."

"Shhh!" Tamson hissed from inside the cave. "I hear something now."

Caleb froze, concentrated. There were voices in the distance. "Go back inside, stay very quiet, and remain until I return for thee."

"Father?" Fear filled his daughter's voice, even as Verity obeyed and disappeared into the cave.

"Stay quiet. No talking at all until I return. Understand?" He locked eyes with Tamson until she nodded. "I shan't be long."

The hole must be on top of the rockface, which was taller than him, but not by much. Since it had a hole already, he shouldn't put his weight on top of it, in case more were to break away into the cave, on top of the girls. He backtracked the way they'd come and circled wide of the rock.

The voices grew clearer. They were low-pitched, female, and conversational, not chanting. He crept closer, keeping to the brush and brambles for cover, until two women came into view. One was dressed as a Puritan woman, her head covered with a bonnet and woolen muffler. The other was dark and familiar. While he couldn't swear to it, he was fairly certain it was the same slave woman he'd seen in the woods while fetching Verity home after she'd run away. There was no sign of the young girls who'd been with the slave then, only an old red hound dog and the other woman.

Caleb wasn't close enough to make out more than a handful of words, but with no leaves to provide cover, he couldn't get closer without the risk of being seen. And by the hair standing up on his forearms and the back of his neck, he wasn't about to risk that. Something was not right.

The very air tingled with an aura of danger.

"Feed it to him now." The slave's words were clear and demanding, not at all subservient as would be expected.

The woman with her, looking uncertain, held something out to the dog. The old hound sniffed it but didn't take it. The Puritan woman said something to the animal and stroked its head, but whatever she was urging on the beast, it wasn't cooperating.

In Caleb's experience, animals understood things that sometimes mankind did not. Perhaps the red hound had good reason to refuse the woman's urgings.

The slave woman appeared to argue with the other, then she took whatever it was and tried to force the dog to accept it. She pried the animal's mouth open, but the dog jerked back, its low growl reaching Caleb, adding to the overall feeling of evil that lurked in this small opening of the forest.

He shouldn't be here. Whatever they were doing, it was wrong. He crept backward, keeping them in his line of vision. They didn't notice him, their voices rising.

"You said this would tell us who bewitched them."

Caleb froze.

Bewitched.

The word hung like a specter in the cold, damp air.

"If the dog will not eat of it, it does us no good." The slave woman's accent didn't disguise her anger. "Stupid dog."

The other woman tugged on the rope tied around the dog's neck and stomped off toward the village.

The slave woman remained standing tall, wearing an odd expression, seeming satisfied with what had happened, even though whatever she'd tried hadn't worked. She turned the thing she'd wanted to feed the dog over in her hand, and then tossed it aside before walking off with all the dignity of a royal personage.

The Puritans were already a suspicious lot, what would they make of witchcraft in their village? More importantly—

On whom would they lay blame?

Caleb waited a full five minutes before he left his hiding spot and approached where the women had been. There was no circle on the ground, something he'd heard mentioned before as a device to contact the dark spirits. Snow trampled to mush covered the spot where they'd been. He searched until he found what the women had been trying to feed the hound. He didn't touch it, but hunkered over it and poked it with a stick. It appeared a normal cake of baked cornmeal.

How would a cake of cornmeal tell them who was bewitching someone? They must mean the young girls Thomas had told them about, the pastor's daughter and niece, both of them near Tamson's age. Just children.

He had his answer, proof that evil was afoot. Evil enough that a hound dog wouldn't eat a cake of cornmeal. And somehow, those two women were involved with it. A shiver that had nothing to do with the cold shook him.

Leaping to his feet, he rushed back to the cave. "Come out, girls, 'tis time to return home."

"Who was it, Father?" Tamson came out first, uncertainty in her expression.

"No one thee would know." The less she knew of the particulars, the better.

Verity slipped through the fissure. "Were the girls there? The ones I saw before? The pastor's daughter?"

"Nay, there were no girls today. Nor any chanting." He rubbed his gloved hands together. "Now let us return home and see if thy mother will prepare a few mugs of chocolate, shall we?"

The expectation of a treat perked the girls up, and they set out, with him following. Their footprints would have shown him the way, but he wanted to keep the girls in his sight. Caleb would warn Caleb Jr. and Robert to avoid the forest in this direction when they hunted. Of course, they couldn't hunt until he got the musket repaired. With so much on his mind, he'd neglected that task.

It was time to pay a visit to David O'Sullivan, not only the best gunsmith in the area, but someone who always knew what was happening around him. If anyone would know the workings of the Puritans in the village, it would be David.

But first, Caleb had to face Hannah and explain what he'd seen and heard.

After leaving the girls at the kitchen porch, Caleb continued to his carpenter shop. He started a fire in the brazier to take the chill from the room and warm the wax mixture he used as a wood finish. The crock of wax had just reached the right temperature to apply it when he caught sight of Hannah marching toward the shop.

Cold air swirled in from the outside door as she opened it. She pushed it shut, turned to him, and crossed her arms, waiting. In her eyes flashed the displeasure of both judge and jury, along with the fury of a mother who thought her children had been ill-used.

The full force of that fury branded something in Caleb's soul.

They had been through much together over their twenty-three years of marriage, and never had she looked at him like that. If they had ever exchanged harsh words, he could not remember it. Sorrow came over him, pressed down on him, and made him feel like an old man. He set the crock of wax aside.

"The children saw nothing they should not have—"

"They were there, in that cave, and they were frightened. Thee left them alone."

Anger seeped up through the sorrow. "Thee know I would never put one of our children—or any child—in danger."

"Thee just did." There was no room for discussion in her tone, nor in the flash of her eyes.

"If thee can even think that, thee know me not at all." So much for seeping. The anger now flashed through Caleb, and he lashed back.

"Perhaps I do not." With that, she twirled and left the shop, slamming the door behind her, but it bounced back on its well-oiled hinges.

The cold that settled over him had nothing to do with the open door. He rose and shut it gently, its click sounding too final in the quiet of the room. He moved the wax crock closer to the brazier to rewarm it, then settled on a stool.

Behind him, the door leading into the barn opened, ushering in the odors of hay, cow manure, and horses.

"Pa?" Caleb Jr. asked. "Is everything all right?"

Without turning to look at his oldest son, Caleb nodded. "Everything is fine."

"I heard the door slam."

"The wind must have caught it." He didn't wish to lie to the boy, but neither would he reveal the disagreement between himself and Hannah. The shop, sectioned off from the barn proper with two-inch thick planking, would have stopped their words from carrying, if not their voices, and was no doubt why Hannah had confronted him here. A child, even a grown one, didn't need to see or hear his parents—fighting.

He hated that word.

"Then I shall continue with my chores." There was a hesitation in his voice. "If thee are sure."

Caleb faced him. "I am. 'Tis nothing to concern thyself with." He finished the sentence with a nod, hoping that would be the end of it. And it was. For Caleb Jr.

For Caleb, as he worked the warmed wax deep into the woodgrain of a shelf he was finishing, his mind spun and tilted. He was angry and felt justified in his anger. He was filled with regret, yet felt justified in his decision. But deep down, he was hurt, the kind of hurt that would fester until he talked it out with someone.

He would take the musket to David tomorrow and get it repaired. David was a feisty man, who had gotten into more than one scrape with his wife, Isobel. He blamed it on his Irish roots and her freckles and red hair, but they had a good marriage and eight children to show for it. If any man could give him advice in this area, it would be David.

Caleb should talk to Hannah, of course, but the thought of facing her again brought out a fear of making things worse. That wouldn't do either of them any good. With the threat of witchcraft in the village, they needed to pull together—not apart. Of course, Hannah didn't know about that yet. She wouldn't until he told her.

The anger pushed its way to the forefront again. How could he tell her anything when she'd accused him of endangering the children and then stormed out?

Be angry, but sin not: let not the sun go down upon your wrath, neither give place to the Devil.

How often had his father quoted that scripture? Caleb pulled in a long breath. They were wise words, not to be ignored, but he was fairly certain their bedroom would be a silent chamber come the night. It grieved him that he couldn't find the strength to overcome his anger, no matter how justified.

Chapter 6

WILLIAM RESISTED THE URGE to plant his face in his hands and shake his head. Why couldn't the *Margaret* leave port yet? The waiting was intolerable. It was affecting all of them. Rachel sat upright on her favorite chair by fire in the parlor, her knitting in her hands, outwardly calm, but William knew the tell-tale signs of her distress. The normal click of her bone knitting needles was sharper, and the wool moved between them so fast that he could barely see the stitches. His goodwife didn't need all this angst at her age.

Neither did William.

And yet, Elizabeth was Rachel's niece. Family. He'd lost his first wife and understood what it meant to be left alone. Oh, he'd had his children from his first marriage, but that had made it all the more difficult. They'd been young and in need of a mother. Rachel had stepped in and taken over his household and—eventually—his heart.

There was nothing to do but wait out Elizabeth's unhappiness and pray. It hadn't been easy to take in the youngster after their children were all grown and gone. Perhaps they'd spoiled her. At seventeen, she was surely more dramatic than their own had been at that age. Those who had lived to see that age. He pushed the old sorrows aside.

Clearing his throat, William addressed Elizabeth's stiff back in front of the parlor window. "There are bound to be many young men you will meet once we are settled."

She whirled and stomped across the room. "I will never be married in a backwater little village on the very edge of the civilized world." Elizabeth sat with a thump on the chair opposite Rachel. "Certainly not to some farmer who digs in the ground for a living. I wish to remain in Boston and marry a nice craftsman of some sort."

Rachel's needles clicked along, her face remained stoic. "You cannot know the future any more than your uncle or I do. Trust in God. If He wishes you to have a husband, He will bring the man into your life." Raising her eyes from her knitting to William, a slight twitch of her lips softened her expression.

Surely God had brought them together. Maybe they had married out of necessity and not an emotional bond, but they'd gotten there in the end. William couldn't imagine a better wife. He was asking much of her, to uproot them and move away. He'd pondered it for a long time before speaking with Rachel, and she hadn't balked in the least, confirming his decision had been sound.

Neither had anticipated Elizabeth's reaction, or perhaps a better term was overreaction.

"I shall die a spinster."

"If you are set on the life of a spinster, you had best work on your charity skills, my dear." Rachel's needles never paused, but her voice had a crisper edge to it. "Spinsters take food to the poor, knit stockings for the elderly, and help nurse the unwell back to health. You shall be very busy in Salem Village, I assure you."

William had to bite the inside of his lip to keep his amusement from showing. Rachel had known exactly what to say, since their niece despised the first two of those activities and had only shown an interest in nursing in hopes of attracting Hezekiah. But that young man was all about his medical books and not the least inclined to look for a wife, no matter how many subtle hints William had voiced—and the not so subtle suggestion of Elizabeth herself.

Once the ship set sail, their lives could move on. Elizabeth would adjust in time. William and Rachel could settle in and enjoy a slower pace to their elder years.

Darkness lingered between the buildings when the wagon rumbled away from their Boston home. William took Rachel's hand on one side and Elizabeth's on the other. There'd been no room left for them to ride along with their possessions.

"Come now, 'tis not a long walk. Our belongings will be stowed belowdecks on the *Margaret* by the time we arrive." He put as much cheer into his voice as he could. Elizabeth's teary eyes he was accustomed to, but the sheen in Rachel's worried him. Yet she squeezed his hand and marched beside him without a falter in her step.

While not overly sentimental about such things, leaving the house in which they had raised their children was an adjustment for William as well. And leaving so many friends they'd made over the years, although few of his peers remained in Boston. Those not under the sod in the churchyard had moved to where their children lived to be closer to family in their declining years. But William had no desire to live in the warm climate of Virginia with its poisonous snakes and pernicious fevers, nor in Connecticut near their son who would try to rule over them as if they were children instead of parents.

"'Tis all rather exciting." Rachel's breath frosted the air in front of them. "I have never been aboard a sailing ship." She leaned over and addressed Elizabeth. "'Tis something you will tell your grandchildren."

"As if I shall ever have any." Elizabeth turned her face away but kept her hold on William's hand.

Perhaps it was best if they didn't speak more about it. They turned the corner to the harbor, and he stopped. The sun had yet to break free of the watery horizon, but the sky appeared as if on fire. An explosion of orange and magenta edged in deep purple flowed upward to the murky gray of the dark sky. Silhouetted were the black masts of dozens of ships across the harbor.

"'Tis a beautiful sight," Rachel whispered with reverence. "Surely a sign that God will be with us on our journey."

"There." William let go of his wife's hand and pointed to the *Margaret*. "The ketch at the end of the fourth pier."

"I always favored the name Margaret should we have had another girl." Rachel turned her smile to him. "'Tis fitting, I suppose."

Buoyed by her optimism, William led the way. Their shoes made hollow *clunks* on the weathered boards as they worked their way, single file, between sailors and dockworkers crowding the pier. William had his paperwork out of his pocket and ready when the steward greeted them at the *Margaret's* gangplank.

"Everythin' be in order here." The steward handed the paperwork back. "You be in the second cabin, next to the captain." He touched the edge of his brimless cap. "Welcome aboard, Dr. Griggs, ladies."

Elizabeth crowded against him as they walked up the gangplank, its wood bending beneath their weight, putting an actual bounce in their steps. Inside, a grinning old sailor with few teeth led them down a narrow hallway that reeked of brine and age and whatever cargo might have been stowed below. He showed them to their room and left them there. The room contained a set of bunks along the wall, a small round window, a table bolted to the floor, and two chairs. The furniture left very little space for people, but it was tidy and smelled faintly of lavender.

"Is this not nice, Elizabeth?" Rachel removed the pins from her hat.

"I suppose." At least the girl didn't argue.

"I shall take a walk on the deck and watch the ship sail away from port. Would you ladies care to join me?"

"I think not." Rachel perched on one of the chairs and set her bag, which probably contained knitting, on the nearest bed. "I believe I will stay here and avoid the cold wind."

"I shall stay with my aunt." Elizabeth took the other chair.

"Wise of both of you, I am sure. I shall rejoin you when we are at sea." William closed the door behind him. The walls of the ship were dark wood. Brass fittings lined them along the way, although he couldn't name a purpose for them. He reached a staircase that was little more than a ladder. It looked sturdy enough and led him to a door that opened to the deck. As he pushed the door open, the vessel lurched beneath his feet.

They were underway.

William headed for the back of the vessel, careful to stay out of the sailors' way as the men rushed about, carrying out orders shouted from a man standing on the raised aft deck. He wore a dark blue coat buttoned high on his neck, buff breeches, and boots that reached above his knees. A large tricorn hat with a black plumed feather topped his outfit. Captain Peter Henderson, no doubt.

William made his way to the aft deck and stood near the railing. Boston Harbor slipped past on both sides. Larger and smaller vessels bobbed at anchor, sails furled, awaiting their turn at the docks or for their cargos to arrive. The deck underfoot lifted and lowered in a soothing rhythm. It would be rougher once they left the harbor. William planted both hands on the railing and watched as the buildings of Boston dwindled into indistinct shapes against a darker background.

Captain Henderson yelled a string of commands. Sails overhead snapped as the wind grabbed them, and then the *Margaret* turned, her front lifting, the ship leaning toward its left—or port, as the captain had shouted. William faced the front, a jut of land to the ship's right, he was fairly certain, marking the opening to the Atlantic Ocean. A thrill washed along his veins. No wonder his youngest son had fallen in love with the sea. It was... It was majestic.

A view and an experience William would never forget. A grand start to the new life they would find in Salem Village.

"Ho, Dolly." Caleb pulled his horse to a halt outside of David's gun-smithing shop, a small log structure that had been the O'Sullivans' original cabin when they first moved to the area. Light glowed from the windows. He dismounted and tied the horse to a hitching rail near the door, removed the musket from its scabbard, then knocked.

"Enter." The call was its usual cheery greeting.

Caleb pulled the door open and inhaled the sharp scents of oiled metals and gunpowder. David O'Sullivan sat hunched over a table with a pistol in front of him. He was a sparse man, short of height and weight, but when he lifted his face, the life and humor that glimmered in his eyes made him a larger person than his frame.

"I had started to think thee had taken to hibernation like the bears." David put down a small file and the pistol and rose. He met Caleb halfway across the room to grab his hand. "We are long overdue for a visit, my friend."

"The road runs both ways, does it not?" Their banter lifted Caleb's spirit, even if it couldn't last with the problem and the news he carried.

"Indeed, that it does." A hint of David's Irish ancestors sometimes crept into his voice. He clapped a hand dramatically to his chest. "But I have been run ragged this past fortnight with no less than four trips to Salem Town for supplies to fix the firearms of the good Puritans of the village. 'Twould seem they all feel the need of their weapons of late." All humor drained out of his last words.

"And I fear I must trouble thee with another." Caleb lifted the musket in his hand. "If 'twas only that it needed the flint packed with new leather, I could have done it myself, but 'twould seem to need thy special touch."

"Let me see." David took the piece and carried it to his workbench with a lantern lit on both ends. He examined it, humming as he worked over the parts. "'Twill require a new frizzen." He looked over the musket at Caleb. "I believe I told thee last time 'twould not last long."

"And yet, it has lasted these past two years." Caleb tried to hide the twitch from his lips, bantering with David a balm after the previous night's silence.

David snorted. "Because thee raise more meat than thee hunt." He fiddled with the musket a moment more. "I have everything I need here in the shop. Will thee wait while I see it to rights?"

"I had hoped to do that very thing." Caleb stripped out of his heavy coat and hung it on a peg near the door, the room's fireplace providing plenty of warmth. "'Tis more than just the musket I came for."

"I rather thought 'twould be the case." David cocked an eyebrow at him before returning his attention to the musket. "Thee has no doubt heard of the ruckus in the village."

"Indeed."

"And of the tragedy to the north."

Caleb moved a stool closer to the workbench and sat. "What has happened?"

David sighed and wiped his hands on a rag. "A massacre in the village of York, Maine."

As if witchcraft in Salem Village weren't enough, now the Indians were attacking again? "York, that cannot be more than—"

"Fifty miles at most, aye." David rummaged in a sectioned box full of parts until he found the piece he was looking for. "Too close, if thee ask me."

"Or me."

David tapped the part on his workbench. "But the strange happenings in the village are even closer."

"Aye, and more unsettling."

David paused and looked at him. "More unsettling than a massacre?"

"Quite likely." Caleb leaned his elbow on the workbench. "How much do thee know?"

"That the village lasses are acting strangely—even for Puritans—and the town is walking on tenterhooks over it."

"Have thee heard any rumors?" Which was a bit like asking a river if it was wet. David had an ear for rumors like a hawk had an eye for a field mouse.

"Well now, I may have." David kept working on the musket while he talked. "Nothing that makes much sense, mind thee."

"Such as?" Getting the rumors out of David often took time and patience, both of which Caleb was a little short of at the moment. He must not have kept that from his voice, because his friend speared him with a pair of sharp brown eyes.

"I hear the pastor's daughter and niece have taken to fits, the cause of which no one has found."

Nothing new there. "Are there speculations to the cause?"

"Speculations?" David set the musket down and leaned his elbow against the table, matching Caleb's pose. "Not that the good villagers will say aloud to me."

"So no rumors to the cause have reached thy ears?"

"That, I did not say."

Caleb tried not to grind his teeth. "Then what *has* reached thy ears?"

"A word that should not be uttered where anyone can hear it." David's voice had dropped to a whisper, but not for his typical dramatic effect.

Caleb kept his voice pitched just as low. "Bewitched?"

David leaned back on his stool, in danger of toppling over. "So it has reached thee on the farm as well?"

"Nay. Not there."

"Then where?"

"In the forest, where I witnessed a Puritan woman and a slave woman from the village. They were speaking. I could not hear most of it, but that word was clear."

"One should not speak that word aloud. 'Twill only bring trouble. They were foolish. "

"Indeed, and perhaps doing something even more foolish, though I understood it not." Caleb described what he'd seen and heard and examined afterwards. "The whole situation has brought about a... a disagreement between Hannah and me."

David clicked his tongue. "Of everything thee has shared, 'tis this that distresses me most."

Caleb looked away but nodded. And yet, now he knew there were rumors abroad with the same word whispered among them.

Bewitched.

"'Twould be prudent to have a plan in place," Caleb said.

"A plan of escape, thee mean."

"I do." Because the last time, he hadn't had anything ready. This time, he would not be caught unprepared. "As discreetly as thee can, spread the word among the Friends. I will do the same."

"Forewarned is"—David patted the musket on the bench before him—"forearmed."

"Not that type of armed for pacifists. But that does not mean we cannot have an escape plan. Tell them that."

David had the new frizzen in place, and he handed the musket across the workbench to Caleb. "Now, what has come between thee and Goodie Buffum? I have never known thee to disagree in all the years we have lived as neighbors and friends."

"Nor have we." Caleb told him about taking the girls into the forest against Hannah's wishes.

"Thee know what thee did." David pointed a finger at him. "Thee poked the momma bear. 'Tis a good way to get bit, or raked to the bone with her claws." He shook his head. "If there is one thing I will not breach with Isobel, 'tis the say-so on what happens with the children."

Caleb fought the urge to hang his head like a young man getting berated by his father. "What should I do?"

"Apologize, of course." David's grin returned. "'Tis what we men all must do in the end, is it not?"

"But do thee not think I should have investi—?"

David pressed his hand, palm forward, toward Caleb and shook his head. "'Twill do thee no good to think thyself justified."

Justified. Exactly what Caleb had felt—still felt.

"If thee cherishes thy goodwife more than thee cherishes being right, thee will be a happy man." David cocked his brow. "But thee already know this, so why are thee bringing it to me?"

"Because this time there is so much more at stake. Our family so much larger, so many more to move and keep fed."

"Ah." David sat back. "I had forgotten. Thee have been through something like this before."

"Not exactly, that time 'twas but an illness the Puritans blamed on us." Caleb rubbed the back of his neck where the hairs prickled. "Imagine how much worse it could be should they level the accusation of witchcraft against us."

"And thee with a Puritan orphan under thy roof."

Caleb couldn't contain the wince his friend's words brought, and surely David noticed.

"Perhaps 'tis not a good thing that my gunsmithing has been so in demand." David picked up the pistol he'd been working on when Caleb entered. "Perhaps some of these will be turned on us before 'tis all said and done." He looked up at Caleb. "Keep the musket close."

Caleb could never raise a weapon to another human being. Not a Puritan, nor an Indian. As much as he hated the thought of running again, it was the better way.

Wasn't it?

Chapter 7

T HE SUN HAD CREPT behind the tops of the distant trees when the *Margaret* docked at Salem Town. William had spent an hour or so in the afternoon in the cramped quarters with Rachel and Elizabeth. The women had their knitting and needlework to keep their fingers busy, but William had been bored. He'd come back on deck and had enjoyed the movement of the ship, the crack and snap of the sails, the raucous calls of the gulls, and the cold wind combing through what was left of his hair. It had proved pointless to try to keep his wide-brimmed hat on once they reached the open waters.

When the man in the crow's nest had called out the port of Salem Town, William had gone below and brought the women up with him so they could watch the boat sail into the closest thing to a city they'd have for shopping trips for women's fripperies and whatnot.

In the waning light, the town's buildings took on a gentle glow. There were the usual harborside buildings, a harbormaster's office, warehouses, and taverns. Not the type of tavern William frequented for the latest news and gathering with friends, but those of a seedier sort often favored by sailors. Beyond them were streets that appeared neatly spaced in rows with houses not unlike those of Boston.

William turned to Elizabeth. "I dare say you will find everything you need here in Salem Town when we visit."

The girl studied the approaching town and answered without looking at him. "I admit 'tis larger than I had assumed."

"There now, we shall both feel better knowing we have a nice harbor town close at hand." Rachel slipped her gloved fingers around William's arm. "Such a pretty setting too."

The sun's descent, the mellow winter tones, and a layer of pristine white blanketing the ground may have added to the effect. But if his wife was happy with her first impression, then so was he.

Soon the *Margaret* bumped against the dock. Sailors scurried forward and aft, following the captain's bellowed orders. Sails were furled and ropes bound, lines tossed overboard to dockworkers, who lashed them to large pillars until the vessel was at rest.

"Come." William ushered the women toward the gangplank. "We will see what accommodations we can secure for the evening before I find a man to hire to take us to the village on the morrow."

Passengers were few, just a couple dressed as typical men of business. They moved aside and allowed Rachel and Elizabeth to go first. William escorted them down the bouncy plank. They stepped onto the weathered boards of the dock, and yet it still felt as if it moved beneath William's feet.

"I believe we shall have to regain our land legs, as they say." He chuckled and took hold of Rachel's arm on one side and Elizabeth's on the other. "But we should take heart that all of us proved to be good sailors."

"I had rather feared seasickness," Rachel said. "When I was a little girl, Mother told me stories of her passage from England and how ill she became during the ordeal."

Elizabeth said nothing, but swiveled her head in every direction, scanning their new surroundings. It was good to see the girl take an interest in anything after weeks of moping.

William led them to the harbormaster's office, which looked so similar to the one in Boston that it might have been built by the same carpenter. There was a line, of course, a mixture of captains and stewards and a few people booking passages or collecting cargo. A fireplace crackled cheerfully along one wall, and William shooed the women to wait near its warmth. When he finally reached the counter, he asked the clerk for a good place to spend the night with his wife and niece, then paid for their trunks to be stored in a warehouse until they could collect them.

"Everything is set?" Rachel asked as he approached. Lines of weariness tugged at the corners of her eyes. They had put in quite a day for a couple of their advanced years.

"Indeed. The clerk highly recommended a tavern just three blocks away. He suggested we order their fish chowder, which he claims has no equal in the colony."

"That does sound enticing"—Rachel turned to her niece—"does it not, Elizabeth?"

"Oh." The girl brought her attention back to them from whatever she'd been studying across the room. Or whomever, since the businessmen had gathered there. "As you say, quite enticing."

Walking worked the wobbles out of William's legs, and by the time they entered Culver's Tavern, he was more than ready for a meal of any kind and a warm corner to enjoy it in. A matronly woman showed them to a table made of what looked like ship planks, but it was clean and the chairs comfortable. The public room was lit by lanterns along the wall, a candle on each table, and light from the huge hearth that took up most of one side. It smelled of woodsmoke, something savory bubbling in the pots by the hearth, and pipe tobacco. William should have tucked his pipe and pouch into his coat pocket.

A man approached, a long linen apron covering his clothing, and introduced himself as the proprietor. "What can I get for you folks?"

William ordered a pot of tea, the fish chowder, and two rooms for the evening, connecting rooms if those were available.

"You be new to the town?" the man asked.

"Passing through on our way to Salem Village, where we have purchased a house," William said.

The man shifted in a subtle way, but years of working with people who sometimes said more with responses than words had trained William to notice such things. He waited until the man returned behind the counter, then he patted his coat.

"I did not think to pack my pipe. If you ladies will excuse me, I shall see if 'tis possible to purchase another." He went to the counter and waited.

"Did you need something?" the proprietor asked.

"A pipe and a pouch, if you keep such on hand, and a little information." William kept his voice down and didn't glance at their table.

The proprietor brought a nondescript clay pipe and a small leather pouch from under the counter and placed them in front of William. "What sort of information?"

"I could not help but notice your reaction to my mention of Salem Village."

"Ah. That." The man picked up a glass and polished it. "'Tis just that rumors have been floating around."

"What kind of rumors?" William took his time packing the pipe.

"Not the kind anyone wishes to hear. Talk of an illness that has attacked the daughter and niece of the pastor there."

William took a taper that rested on the candlestick's base near him and lit his pipe, shaking out the taper and replacing it for the next fellow who needed it. He puffed a couple of times. "What sort of illness?"

"I know not, just that it has unnerved the citizens there."

"Well"—William took another puff—"I am a doctor. Perhaps I shall be able to assist in the matter."

The proprietor's face brightened. "There is no doctor in the village. The one they had up and moved a month ago, and our town's only doctor has his hands full here. Talk is that they are anxious for you to arrive. I believe they expected you weeks ago."

"The ship was late."

"As they so often are. But Praise God, you are here now."

William made his way back to the table, Rachel's eyes following his every move. He hadn't fooled her a bit with his ploy about the pipe. Perhaps she'd also picked up on the man's reaction.

"What is it, William?" Rachel leaned forward and kept her voice low.

"An illness in the village." He gave her a wry smile. "'Twould seem there is no doctor there anymore."

Rachel relaxed against the back of her chair. "Then you shall soon set it to rights, if anyone can."

William took a long pull from his pipe. Salem Village was a fraction of the size of Boston, but still... finding out it now lacked a doctor wasn't the best start for his life of retirement.

A Quaker? William wasn't used to dealing with Quakers. The few in the Boston area kept to themselves, including having their own doctor. The fellow loading their trunks onto his wagon was most certainly dressed as such, not a wisp of lace or a stitch of decoration anywhere on his clothing. His dark blond hair was tied at the nape with a simple black ribbon, and his shoes sported leather fastenings instead of shiny buckles.

William had taken the recommendation of the livery stable owner to hire David O'Sullivan because the man was leaving for Salem Village that very morning and had a large enough wagon at the ready. He was certainly quick and efficient as he loaded everything.

But a Quaker?

Rachel and Elizabeth came down the street from the tavern, the sun catching them in its feeble winter glow. He and his family were on the final leg of their journey. The last three miles. He and Rachel had been through so much. How he'd looked forward to the retirement awaiting them, but now? What of the mysterious illness reported in the village? Had he brought them this far only to risk their own lives with something unknown?

William gave himself a mental shake. He refused to second-guess his decision now. Illness lurked everywhere, and one wasn't any more likely to catch something in a rural village than on the streets of Boston.

"Are we ready, ladies?" He greeted them with a cheerful voice.

"I believe we are." Rachel smiled at Elizabeth, who, amazingly enough, returned the gesture. Salem Town had surprised their niece with its offerings of shops and houses and the pretty town square at its center. With luck, she'd see the village in a similar light.

William turned to the Quaker. "Whenever you are ready."

The fellow wasn't very big, but he hefted the last trunk aboard the wagon with a thump and grinned. "'Tis a good thing thee had not one more of these. My poor wagon would not have held it. Let me lash down the load, and we shall be on our way."

Rachel stepped close to William. "Thee?"

"'Twould seem a community of Quakers lives north of the village, and as this man is heading that way, he was the logical person to hire."

"Indeed." But Rachel eyed the man warily.

"Where will we ride?" Elizabeth pointed to the bench for the driver that would sit two at most, and those close together.

"Begging thy pardon," O'Sullivan said while giving a tug on the rope to secure their belongings, "I left the flat-topped trunk there by the rear of the wagon for thee ladies to rest upon."

"We are to bounce around on that?" Elizabeth pointed at the trunk but faced William.

Rachel took her arm. "Our quilts are stowed in that trunk. Let us open it and bring them out to cushion the top, shall we?"

O'Sullivan glanced at William and shrugged.

After assisting the women onto the wagon's bed, William took a deep breath and moved to the bench seat. It was far above the ground. He had to step on the hub of the large wheel to climb aboard, his old joints creaking with the stretch.

In contrast, O'Sullivan leaped up and caught the edge of the bench, swinging himself aboard in one fluid motion. He appeared to be in his forties, thirty years William's junior. Watching him in that maneuver had William feeling every one of those years.

O'Sullivan untied the reins from the wagon's brake, disengaged it, and then called to the back, "Are thee ladies ready?"

"We are," Rachel said.

The fellow shook the reins over a mismatched pair of heavy work horses, one gray and the other sorel. "Hup, Izzy. Hup, Bella." He grinned at William as the horses stepped forward. "Named after my goodwife, Isobel."

William chuckled. "That must endear you to her."

"As she will not condone me applying either nickname to her, she is content that I bestowed them on such fine beasts as these two." His grin was engaging, his manner relaxed.

Perhaps the Quakers and Puritans had found an easy way of coexisting in Salem Village. In Boston, it would be a rare occasion when the two would ever speak. William had never really puzzled about that. It was just the way things were. Sharing the high bench seat with the talkative O'Sullivan for a three-mile journey proved fertile ground for pondering such things.

They arrived with the sun directly overhead, and O'Sullivan stopped the wagon in front of the house William had purchased. It looked much more abandoned than he remembered from his trip the previous fall. A cold wind blew down the main street of the village, picking up dampness from the slushy snow blanketing the ground in shades of white, brown, and gray.

The dreary setting didn't help the house's appeal much. The porch that ran the length of its front needed the top railing repaired. The roof dripped melting snow into puddles below. The windows were dark, of course, no one having lived in it for weeks as William and his family had awaited the *Margaret's* arrival. The whole place would benefit from a fresh whitewashing come summer. At least the roofline was straight, the porch level. The front steps looked solid enough.

"This is it?" Elizabeth stood on the back of the wagon, an expression of dismay leaving her mouth agape.

"I am sure 'tis perfectly adequate inside, my dear." Rachel shot William a look that said it had better be.

William climbed down and hurried to the back of the wagon to assist the women, while O'Sullivan appeared to take a particularly long time to set the brake and secure the team.

After helping Elizabeth, William took Rachel's hands and steadied her as she climbed down and shook out her petticoats, eyeing the building where they were to live out the rest of their lives.

"Shall we enter?" Her voice was at best carefully neutral. At worst, it was a warning that more words would follow when they were alone.

Had he made such a poor choice in the house? He followed the women to the door, where he took the key he'd been mailed from his waistcoat pocket, inserted it into the lock and prayed it would work. The soft click reassured him, and he opened the door before stepping aside and letting the women enter.

In silence, they took it in.

The two women walked from room to room on the ground floor, not that there were very many, and raked their eyes over every nook and cranny.

William's heart dropped to his heels.

Nooks and crannies were all there were. Not a stick of furniture remained. He'd agreed to purchase the house with all its furnishings, but it had been stripped bare except for a worktable near the hearth that was built into the wall. And by his wife's tight expression...

William was in trouble.

O'Sullivan cleared his throat, and then lowered the trunk from his shoulder to the floor with a hollow *thud*. "Ingersoll's Tavern has a couple of rooms to let upstairs. Nothing fancy, mind thee, but it has a good reputation"—he glanced around the empty house—"and furniture."

"We shall have to live in a tavern?" Elizabeth's voice rose in a controlled shriek. At least it was controlled.

"Only temporarily." William cast O'Sullivan a frantic look of appeal. Surely the man must know whom to approach for furnishings.

"Ah. Caleb Buffum is the man thee wish to see about furniture." He was a quick-witted fellow. "There is none better with wood in the district than Caleb. He lives just beyond me. I could swing by there before I return home and arrange for him to meet thee at Ingersoll's, if that suits thee."

William released a breath of relief. "That would suit us admirably. And just think, my dears, we shall have all new furniture. No doubt, 'twill outlive us and benefit thee in years to come, Elizabeth."

His cheery words did little to improve the twin dour looks directed his way.

Chapter 8

"P A, DAVID IS DRIVING up the lane." Robert's voice reached into the carpenter shop.

Caleb put down his saw and wiped his hands free of sawdust. What would bring his friend around just two days after their talk?

Unless it was bad news.

Caleb opened the outside door to the shop and waved to David.

Robert and Caleb Jr. waited outside, ready to take the team.

David pulled them to a halt. "I cannot stay long, lads. But if thee would give them each a bucket of water and tie them for me, I would appreciate it."

After the boys had taken charge of the horses, Caleb moved back to allow his friend to enter. "Welcome." He shut the door behind them. "I hope thee are not the bearer of bad news."

"Nay. Nothing of the sort." David's usual humor lit his expression. "In fact, 'tis good news I come with. Good news for thee, but not so much for the village's new doctor." He explained the situation.

"They need a whole houseful of furniture? 'Tis a windfall for me, to be sure." He would be able to purchase that musket Caleb Jr. wanted, and Hannah needed a few new things for the house. "The poor man, to come so far and learn he had been cheated."

"Aye. If thee could have seen the look his goodwife bestowed upon him in that empty shell of a house." A low whistle escaped between David's teeth. "I envy not that man when she gets him alone tonight."

An unhappy wife was nothing to jest about. Caleb knew that all too well. He never thought he'd miss Hannah's cold feet against his legs, but he did. That and the sound of her voice when they were alone. "Thee said he will be at Ingersoll's tomorrow?"

"Where else could he be?" David shrugged. "'Tis the only lodging in the village. 'Twas either that or haul him and his women back to Salem Town."

"Women?"

"Aye. He brought a young lass with him. His wife's niece, I think he said. Looked to be about my Mary's age, old enough to have the young men sniffing around."

"I can see him in the morning before the meeting at the meeting house," Caleb said.

"What meeting?"

"I thought thee would have heard. Word of this sort carries on the wind."

"I was in Salem Town and had to stay the night. The silversmith did not have my parts ready as he had promised. 'Twas why I was happy to haul the doctor and his family back. It refilled my pocket for the room and meals the trip cost me."

"After we spread the word about the Puritan women in the forest, the elders decided we should meet. All should know what has happened and have a chance to discuss our best way forward. 'Twill be at noon, adults only."

"Aye, and for sure. 'Tisn't a topic for the wee ones." David turned back to the door but stopped with his hand on it. "I must get home, but tell me, how are things progressing?" He tipped his head toward the house.

"Not good." Caleb shrugged. "I did as you said. I apologized. What more can I do?"

"Wait. And then wait some more. Hannah is a sensible woman and will come around to forgiveness." David winked and left the shop.

As Friends, they were taught from childhood that forgiveness was essential, not for the one forgiven, but for the one holding onto the hurt. The Bible said as much. Holding onto unforgiveness turned a person bitter.

Being the one unforgiven didn't feel very good either.

A serving girl delivered a tray to their room, and William moved the two ladderback chairs closer to the small round table as Rachel set the tray on it. William sat while Rachel prepared their tea, its fragrant steam rising between them. If only they were enjoying it in their new home and not the village tavern.

They'd barely spoken a word to each other since awakening, and little enough the evening before. Seeing their empty house had been a shock to him, but even more so for Rachel and Elizabeth. Especially Elizabeth, as if that girl needed one more thing to be dissatisfied with. Rachel had wisely suggested the girl sleep late that morning.

William took the cup Rachel passed him and sipped. It was sweetened the way he liked. He waited until she'd seated herself, then cleared his throat. "I am truly sorry, my dear."

"You were not to know." She sighed and spread some sort of berry preserves from a little pot onto the toast, then cut each piece into quarters and nudged one plate closer to him. "I do not blame you for another's cheating ways."

"I might have inquired more into the man's character before taking him at his word and entering into the agreement."

"'Tis not your way." She gave him a sad sort of smile. At least it was a smile. "'Tis probably what has made you such a good doctor. You are slow to form negative opinions of others. You assume all men will be as honest and forthright as you are."

He bit into the toast and savored its tangy preserves.

Rachel sipped her tea, then cocked her head. "The idea of all new furniture is growing on me. I have always loved cherry-wood, and we had only the one piece."

"Your mother's side table." He finished his toast. "We should have made room for it."

"'Twas on its last legs." She chuckled. "Literally. Had we not had the other three repaired already?"

"True, but the sentimental value—"

She stopped his words with a wave of her hand. "'Tis not as if the children wanted it. And I had the enjoyment of it for these many years. 'Twas enough."

How he admired—loved—the strong woman across from him.

Someone knocked on the door, probably Elizabeth. "Come in," William called.

A man opened the door, dressed in a plain brown coat, a darker brown waistcoat beneath, and worn buff breeches. On his head was a slightly battered tricorn hat, which he did not remove. If William remembered correctly, that was a mannerism of the Quakers.

"Are thee the new doctor, William Griggs?" he asked.

Thee. Definitely a Quaker. William stood. "Indeed, and my good-wife." He gestured to Rachel, who inclined her head.

"I am a carpenter, Caleb Buffum. David O'Sullivan asked me to call on thee regarding furniture for thy new house."

"Mr. Buffum, do come in," Rachel said.

"Thank thee. Please call me Caleb. We Friends prefer the familiar address rather than the formal."

"Indeed, I shall strive to remember," William said.

The Quaker glanced around the small room. "Perhaps I am too early. I can return this afternoon if that better suits thee."

Rachel looked out the open door toward the room across the hall-way where Elizabeth still slept, the tavern not having any adjoining rooms. "I think that would be best. Our niece will accompany us then."

"Very well. I must attend a meeting at noon. I shall return afterward."

Without another word, the plainly dressed man left them.

"What is your first impression of him?" Rachel asked.

"If I had not misjudged the former owner of the house so badly, I would say he is a no-nonsense man who will get things done." William gave her a wry look. "But we shall wait and see, shall we not?"

Words were still sparse between Caleb and Hannah. She wasn't avoiding him, not exactly, yet even in the same room, she might as well be a mile away. The rift between them hurt, but he hadn't found a way to close the gap. Not even enough for her to agree to attend the meeting with him.

Elias Barwick, being the eldest among them, raised his hands and called the Friends to order. It was uncommon for them to gather outside of a Sunday meeting, but these were unusual circumstances. Perhaps even dire. That accounted for the good turnout.

"We all know why we are gathered here." Elias lowered his hands. "'Tis a troubling thing happening in the village. Let us first start by sharing any reliable—and I stress the word *reliable*—accounts by those who have them to share." The old man took a seat on one of the benches.

There was a short pause before Caleb stood. He cleared his throat and searched the faces around him. His friends. His neighbors. His community. Was it all to come crashing down?

Not if he could prevent it.

"Hannah heard voices in the forest to the east of our farm more than a month ago, and young Verity heard them as well. 'Twas some sort of chanting."

A murmur broke out among those gathered, as well it should. After all, this was a firsthand account from Hannah. If only she had come with him to share it.

"She is certain the words were in English, though not clear enough for her to understand. They were not the guttural speech of the Indians nor the flowing cadence of the French. She did not try to approach or see who it was. However, I met with her and Verity on the trail shortly thereafter, and on our return to the farm, we crossed paths with a slave woman and the Puritan pastor's daughter and niece, both of whom Hannah could identify."

Isobel O'Sullivan, David's wife, rose. "'Tis those two girls they say be having the fits."

"Never did trust that pastor," one of the men grumbled. "Always looking down his long nose at us."

"Chanting could mean calling to the spirit world," said a woman from the back of the building.

Caleb raised his hands to quell the flurry of comments that were tripping over each other. "I returned to the same spot in the forest three days ago." He lowered his hands when the others quieted. "There was a slave woman there, and a Puritan woman whom I know not. With them was an old red hound dog. I could make out little of what they said until they grew frustrated and raised their voices." He paused a moment, recalling what he'd witnessed.

"Frustrated at what?" A man in the back asked.

"They were trying to feed what looked like a common cake of cornmeal to the hound, but the dog would not take it."

Hester Fuller, the midwife, stood with her hands folded in front of her. "Did they say any words over the cake?"

Caleb pressed his thumb and finger on the bridge of his nose and tried to remember. Those gathered sat in silence and waited. But he couldn't recall, or maybe he hadn't been close enough to hear. "I only heard one of them saying that if the dog would not eat of it, it would do them no good. The slave woman blamed the dog. But the Puritan woman said, clearly enough for me not to be mistaken, that whatever they were doing would tell them who had bewitched someone."

A collective gasp sliced through the meeting house. Then bedlam broke out. Voices rose and words tangled until it was impossible to discern what was said.

Hester, who had remained on her feet, raised her voice. "I fear I know what these women were doing." She shot a worried glance at Caleb, and he nodded for her to continue. "There is a belief in the old country that if a cake is baked using the urine of the bewitched person and fed to a dog, that the dog will identify the witch who has possessed that person. 'Tis something I read about in a very old book passed down to me by another midwife. 'Tis not witchcraft itself, thee understand, but 'tis too close to dark magic for me to ever condone its use." She sat and smoothed her petticoats, tucking her chin to her chest.

Caleb resumed his seat as Elias rose, the old man's face more ashen than before. "This news is grave indeed. I trust we have all heard of the witch trials of Connecticut Colony in Hartford in 1662 and Boston in 1688. If this spreads, the same might befall Salem Village."

Hester stood again. "I know of only one family in the village who owns a dog such as you have described. He's a gentle beast with a graying muzzle." She looked across the room at Caleb, and he nodded that it described the dog he'd seen. "Sam and Mary Sibley, whom I have always found to be kind people and generous to the poor. If Mary did this thing, I trust it was an attempt to help—not to harm."

Murmurs erupted again, and Elias let them run their course. It was probably best to let the people have time to digest what had been said. After several minutes, the old man raised his hands again. "What say thee? What shall we do to safeguard our community from being drawn in by these troubling events?"

Hester said, "I believe we should remain at home as much as possible." Of all of the Friends, she might be the most sought out by the Puritans. Her reputation for assisting in healthy births brought her into their homes to attend to their women. Plus, she lived in a rented cottage in the village. She would suffer a loss of income until all this passed.

If it did.

Arthur Stokes stood next, another farmer and as steady a man as the Friends had. "Perhaps 'twould be best for a while to make the trip into Salem Town for our needs, and never send the women alone. They should go in a group watched over by one or more of us men."

That was sage advice. Hannah Jr. would be dismayed, but her safety—the safety of their entire community—was worth the sacrifice.

"And prayer." Isobel stood and turned to survey the room. "We need to pray daily for this...this rumor of a witch in their midst to be scrubbed from the village. God alone is able to conquer evil." She plopped back onto her bench with a nod that bounced the red curls escaping her bonnet.

More suggestions poured forth, but they all boiled down to avoiding the Puritans, letting them manage the mischief in their midst, and praying it stayed contained within the village limits.

Would the Puritans show up at Caleb's door, threaten his family, and destroy everything they'd worked so hard to establish?

How was he to avoid the Puritans when one lived under his roof? Verity was but a child, yet they might return for her at some point. That would break Hannah's heart.

For that reason, Caleb would do everything within his power to keep the child with them, even pick up his family and move.

Chapter 9

T HE MEETING OVER, AND Caleb not wholly reassured by what had been agreed upon there, he sat on his wagon outside Ingersoll's Tavern for several minutes. How was he to tell the doctor that he couldn't accept the work? What excuse could he give without making matters worse? But there was no help for it. The Friends had come to a decision. He would obey the decree.

He climbed down and entered the tavern.

Four men in Puritan clothing gathered around a table near the hearth, pints in front of them. They watched Caleb as he walked through the room and up the stairs. He rapped his knuckles on the doctor's door.

Dr. Griggs opened it, his white hair neatly combed, blue eyes peering up at Caleb from behind round spectacles. "Mr. Buffum, Caleb." He stepped back to allow Caleb to enter.

Wishing he didn't have to, but also not wanting to speak in the hallway where they might be overheard, Caleb stepped inside the room. "I am sorry to tell thee this." There was no point in drawing things out. "But I cannot take the order to make thy furniture."

"Whyever not?" Goodie Griggs rose from her chair, the matching chair occupied by a much younger woman.

"Thee have only just arrived in the village, so thee may not have heard." Caleb picked his words as carefully as he'd pick fried fish from its bones. "There is a sickness of some sort." Mentioning the word witchcraft would likely land him in trouble, if not with the doctor, then with whomever he might repeat it to. "Our meeting today was a gathering of the Friends—thee refer to us as Quakers—about the problem. 'Twas decided that we should avoid the village until it passes, for our own safety."

"Indeed, a wise decision if 'tis contagious." The wrinkles on the doctor's brow deepened. "I am sure I will be advised of it before long."

"May we contact you again when the danger has passed?" asked the goodwife.

"Indeed," Caleb said. "I would be grateful for the work. I wish..." He let the words trail off, not sure what else he could say.

The doctor returned to the door. "None can appreciate the wisdom of your church's decision any more than a doctor, rest assured." He let out a sigh and opened the door. "Unhappy timing for us, but 'tis for the best." The glance he directed at his wife was loaded with regret.

On her part, Goodie Griggs appeared resigned to the wait. The young woman, however, lowered her face into her hands.

Caleb touched the brim of his hat and left, walking past the men at their table without a word or glance. Back on his wagon, he flicked the reins over the team. "Hup, Dolly. Hup, Dandy." Stomach growling because the meeting had dragged on into the afternoon, and then several men had stopped him and asked more questions of what he'd seen, Caleb let the horses set a brisk pace for home. He had until then to settle his heart before he must explain what had been said to Hannah.

Who should have been with him.

On the porch, Caleb knocked the slush from his boots before entering the back room and closing the door gently behind him. The house smelled of rosemary, which meant Hannah had a pot of his favorite chicken and noodle soup simmering. The clatter of horn spoons against dishes said they hadn't waited the evening meal on him. Why would they, when they knew not his time of return? His stomach grumbled even as he wiped nervous sweat from his palms.

He dreaded telling Hannah what had been decided at the meeting and upsetting her further.

Caleb closed his eyes and drew in a deep breath, then let it seep back out along with the anger he harbored. Anger wasn't the answer. Anger would only deepen the rift between them. She was reacting out of fear. Fear of what the Puritans might do. Fear of having to run.

Fear of losing another child.

Her fears weren't groundless.

He pulled off his boots and entered the kitchen in his stockinged feet.

Hannah glanced up from where she was mopping a spill near Jonathan's bowl.

"Father, thee are returned." Hannah Jr. rose, filled a bowl with soup, and placed it in front of his chair while he hung up his coat and then took a seat.

"Thank thee, daughter."

Hannah Jr. cast a glance at her mother, then a worried look back at Caleb. He gave her as reassuring a smile as he could muster. He bowed his head. *Lord, thank Thee for the food Thee has provided, and help Hannah and I to heal this breach soon.* He'd been praying the same silent prayer for four days, but so far, to no avail. God was able. Caleb had to trust in His timing.

Hannah finished cleaning Jonathan's mess and took her seat at the far end of the table, which further symbolized the distance between them. "How did the meeting go?"

Caleb swallowed his first spoonful of the savory soup. "Well enough, I suppose."

"What was decided?" She cocked her head in an almost challenging manner, and all eyes focused on him, the four boys on one side of the table, the three girls on the other.

Why did she wish to discuss this in front of the children? Hannah was usually the one who insisted they not bring things up for all to hear until they'd discussed them between the two of them. Did she not even wish to speak to him alone? Or did she just not want to be alone with him?

His anger surged again, and he struggled to not let it show, either on his face or in his voice.

"'Twill be best for the time being if we all keep our distance from the village." He nodded at Robert. "As we already discussed when Robert came home."

"But only for a time, thee said." A worry line inherited from Caleb creased Robert's brow.

"Indeed. Whatever is happening amongst the Puritans will run its due course. Until then, we have plenty of chores to keep everyone busy here on the farm." Caleb took another spoonful of the soup that was cooling in his bowl.

"What of my cheese and butter sales?" Hannah Jr. asked.

"I am sorry, but 'twill have to be delayed until this situation has resolved."

His oldest nodded and returned to her soup, shoulders rounded.

"Of course, thee may continue to deliver to thy customers among the Friends," he said.

"What if we run out of salt or thread or something we must purchase in the village?" Tamson's voice rose. That one was their reactionary child.

"'Twas decided when we have a need for supplies, we shall make the journey to Salem Town." He raised a finger and made sure everyone was listening. "Not alone, but as a group, at least one of the men accompanying the women and children."

"Sounds like a plan." Caleb Jr. sopped the last of his soup from his bowl with a crust of bread and popped it into his mouth. After he swallowed, he said, "If I may be excused, I need to finish repairing the milking stanchion." He gave his mouth a hasty wipe with his napkin. "Buttercup broke the head gate this morning. Again."

That cantankerous cow with the mild moniker. "I shall be out in a few minutes to give thee a hand."

"No bother." Robert wiped his mouth and rose. "I can do it." The brothers left together.

"I help too," Jonathan said, a piece of noodle hanging from his chin. Benji crammed his mouth full and spoke around the mass, "Me too."

Hannah Jr. laughed and rose. "I will take them out, if Tamson and Verity will wash up."

Verity nodded and Tamson gave a shrug, but both girls stood and began their task.

Leaving Hannah and Caleb without anything pressing to do. Would she talk with him if he asked her into the parlor? Or would she make an excuse, again, to avoid that? It felt too much like courting, this uneasiness between them. The uncertainty of her reactions, his hesitancy to initiate.

He hated it.

Caleb pushed back his chair and stood, his soup only half eaten, his empty belly ignored. "Hannah." He held out his hand. "Join me in the parlor." He did his best not to make it either a question or a command. Just a statement between a husband and wife, as it should be—but as it hadn't been for too many days.

Her brows rose. She took his hand and followed him into the parlor. A small step, but a start to their healing.

He hoped.

William and Rachel's room at Ingersoll's tavern was more than adequate. It was clean and comfortable, with homey little touches like the lace-edged curtains on the window that overlooked the main street, a tatted doily covering the round table that rested between two brocade-cushioned chairs, and the subtle scent of lavender in the air. Elizabeth had her own room across the hallway but spent the day with them in theirs. In sleepy Salem Village, William wasn't too concerned that riffraff would come up from the public room below.

He sank into one of the chairs as Rachel and Elizabeth unpacked the necessities from the two trunks O'Sullivan had hauled up the steep stairs for them.

Someone pounded on the door.

"Merciful heavens." Rachel turned to him. "Who else could even know we arc here already?"

"Word travels fast in a small town, they say." William rose and answered the knock.

The man in the hallway wore a dark coat that reached to his knees, and tall boots that met its hem. He held a hat in his hands, turning it as if he might screw it onto his midsection.

"Can I help you?"

"You can if you are Dr. Griggs."

"I am he."

"Thank God." Relief relaxed the lines of the stranger's face. "I need you to come at once. My daughter and niece, they are in a terrible way."

Daughter? Niece? The proprietor of the tavern back in Salem Town had mentioned them. "Then you must be the pastor here."

"What? Oh. I am. Reverend Samuel Parris"—he sketched a quick bow—"at your service."

William mimicked the movement. "Dr. William Griggs at yours." He turned to Rachel. "Hand me my satchel, dear. I shall return when I can."

She handed him the worn leather carryall he'd planned to stow away on the top shelf of a wardrobe once they arrived. He slipped the strap over his shoulder, then smiled at the pastor. "Lead the way."

"Of course." The younger man bolted for the stairs, calling over his shoulder, "But do make haste."

They rushed two doors down along the main street in the opposite direction from William's new house, to the rather run-down house next to the church. A side door opened long before they reached it, a frail-looking woman somewhere in her thirties wringing her hands in the entrance. "They have calmed down, but only just," she said as they marched past her.

"This way." The pastor never broke stride, leading William into the house's main room where two dark slaves, a man and a woman, stood over two girls prone on the floor.

Both girls had dark blond hair, one older than the other, both breathing rapidly, faces toward each other, eyes wide and fearful.

"What happened?" William knelt beside the younger girl.

"They have been having fits," Reverend Parris said. "At first not too extreme, but lately, they have turned violent."

"Violent?" William leaned back and looked at the man.

Reverend Parris retreated a step. "Indeed, to the point of Abigail trying to throw herself into the fire." He motioned toward the slaves, who had backed away against one wall. "I have to post my slaves as guardians so they do not hurt themselves."

William bent over the younger girl again. "What is your name?"

"Betty." The voice was breathy, her eyes not fully focused but pupils equally dilated.

"Are you in pain, Betty?"

The girl shook her head. "Not anymore."

He patted the back of her hand. "Just rest here." He moved to the older girl. That they were related was unmistakable. Except for the age difference and eye color, they could almost have been twins. "And your name, my dear?"

"Abigail." This one's voice was stronger, her eyes sharper.

"Are you in any pain?"

She clamped a hand on her upper arm. "Here. 'Tis where something bit me during the fit."

"Bit you?" William took her arm in his hands and started to push the sleeve up. "May I examine it?"

She nodded, sitting upright on the floor.

He eased up the fabric and uncovered not what he'd expected, some sort of an insect bite, but the partial oval of a human bite. The imprint of teeth was visible in dark red, the skin not yet showing a bruise. The mark was on the back of her arm. Years of practice kept his face in its professional mask. "You say this happened while the fit was upon you?"

"Aye, and hurt it did." Her blue eyes widened, and tears shimmered on the lower lids.

"I see. Were you hurt anywhere else?"

She shook her head. "Not this time."

"Then you have been bitten before?"

"Nay, I was pinched many times, and once poked in the back as if with a fire poker."

"I was pinched and poked too." Betty had sat up and rubbed her upper arms.

"What is it, doctor?" The woman from the doorway stood just inside the room, a younger girl clinging to her petticoats.

"Pardon, doctor, this is my wife," said the reverend, "and our youngest, Susannah."

"Goodie Parris." William addressed the distraught woman. "I will need time to study this before I can render any diagnosis. When did these fits begin?"

"More than a fortnight past, but they came infrequently then." The woman wrung her hands together. "'Tis every other day now, it seems like."

"Indeed, they are becoming more frequent and more violent." Frustration rang in Reverend Parris's voice.

"Have the girls had a change in their diet? Their routines? Have you brought any new pets into the household or some other foreign object?" William worked to keep his tone level while his mind raced to places he'd rather it not go. There had to be a scientific reason behind the girls' distress.

But that bite mark.

From the direction of the teeth marks, one thing was certain. The girl could not have made that mark on herself. That fact hung over his head like the specter he didn't want to think about.

Chapter 10

C ALEB DREW HANNAH OVER to the window, keeping hold of her hand. They watched the boys walking out to the barn, Caleb Jr.'s laughter reaching them as their older son shoved his brother in that companionable way boys did.

"'Tis good to see them back together." Caleb squeezed Hannah's fingers gently, but she didn't respond. "Soon they shall be grown and gone, I suppose, so we had better enjoy them during this season."

"What was said at the meeting this morning?" Hannah ignored his comments, but she didn't withdraw her hand.

He took some measure of comfort in that. "Hester believes she knows what the ritual I witnessed in the forest meant."

Troubled blue eyes rose to his. "What had she to say?"

He turned his face back to the window as Hannah Jr. led Benji and Jonathan toward the barn, holding a hand of each. Would they still be living here come spring? Or were these his last days to secret away memories of this place with his family? He sighed, closing his eyes for a moment before facing his wife again.

"She believes they made a witch's cake."

That brought a reaction. His fingers were nearly crushed in her grip. Her eyes grew cloudy with worry.

"Hester said that the ritual is not witchcraft itself, although she does not condone its use, but 'tis an old remedy used to detect one who may be a witch."

"Do thee believe it?" She searched his face. "Do thee believe witches truly exist?"

"The Bible says they do."

"But here? In Massachusetts Colony?" Her voice rose. "In Salem Village?"

"Quietly, dear. The girls will hear thee from the kitchen."

Hannah pressed her hand to her mouth, but her eyes never left his face.

"Evil exists. This we know because the Bible tells us many examples, and we have taught our children not to court it. Did we not have that very discussion with them in our wagon several weeks ago on the way home from a meeting?"

"We did." She blinked several times, then stepped closer to Caleb.

He put his arm around her until she leaned into him. A wave of thankfulness washed over him, and an increased urge to protect her, as well as the children from what might come.

"But we cannot live in fear of evil when we have the Light of Christ on our side." He cupped the side of her face and pressed a kiss to her forehead. "'Little children, ye are of God, and have overcome them: for greater is He that is in you, than he that is in this world.'"

A soft sigh slipped from her. "One of my favorite verses from First John."

"I remember." He rested his chin on the top of her head, her hair soft against his throat. "'Tis a good reminder that the Lord is in charge of things, not us."

"He might direct our paths away from here, might He not?"

Caleb wanted to stay in this place they had built together by the sweat of their bodies and the love in their hearts. But the choice wasn't his to make, not really. "He might. But whether we stay or go, we will be together."

"All of us?" There was a tightness in her voice, like a warning, and she moved out of his embrace, eyes wary.

"We have two strong horses this time, which is a blessing. Depending on the weather and roads, we may not be able to take the wagon.

And not if we must escape into the forest. Caleb Jr. and Robert are both old enough to carry packs of essentials. I think we would—"

"Caleb." Hannah cut him off. "I asked if *all* of us would stay together." She meant Verity, of course.

He took a step toward her, but she moved farther away, faced him, and said, "We cannot leave if we do not leave all together, including Verity."

How he wanted to reassure Hannah that they would keep the girl with them forever. It was a promise he lacked the power to make, yet her eyes pleaded with him for that very assurance.

"I will do everything I can to keep her with us. 'Tis the best I can promise."

She turned her back to him, arms wrapped around her middle, fingers drumming nervously against her sides. "I cannot leave her, Caleb. I will not lose her."

That was the root of it all for his wife, the fear of losing another child.

He could not comfort her in the way she wished—the way she needed—because there were six other children involved. Their own children.

It was Caleb's job to protect them all.

Several silent moments passed, and then Hannah stalked from the room.

The fear of losing another child was pulling his wife apart, and there was little that Caleb could do about it.

Supper had already been served by the time William returned to Ingersoll's, but Rachel had put a bowl aside for him, as well as a plate with three thick slices of bread. How many times over the years had she done the same? Too many to count.

Elizabeth had retired to her room, and after seeing him settled in a chair with his bowl and plate, Rachel took the chair beside him. "How bad is it?"

He stared into the bowl of lamb stew, thick with potatoes and turnips, its rich aroma tempting him, and sighed. "'Tis bad enough. I know not what I am dealing with for sure."

"What are the symptoms?" Rachel often asked such questions, knowing it helped him think the situation through. And through the years, she'd gained nearly as much knowledge of healing as he had. He could trust her opinion.

This time, maybe more than ever before, he was going to need it. "Fits that threw the girls to the floor when they first started have now turned violent, to the point where one of the girls has to be restrained from throwing herself into the fire."

Rachel shrank back in her chair and pressed a hand to her throat. For his unflappable wife, her reaction said she understood the gravity. "And you think it may be—" She cut the sentence off abruptly.

"I know not. But the older girl had a bite mark—a human bite mark—on her arm." He pointed to the spot on the back of his arm. "'Twas in a place she could not have inflicted on herself during the fit." He'd seen that once before, a person who had bitten himself during a fit. The poor soul hadn't been right in the head. These two girls, however, had recovered to full rationality. They had spoken to him for well over an hour before the reverend had instructed them to be about their household chores.

Then he'd demanded William give him an answer.

If only it were that simple.

The word he didn't want to utter was coating his tongue like thick pine tar. He mentally pushed it aside and took a bite of the warm stew. It was delicious, and he was hungry, so he scraped the bowl clean while Rachel resumed her needlework beside him. When he had finished the last of the bread, he pushed the dishes to the center of the table and belched.

"I am sorry, my dear," he said, "that the Quaker carpenter cannot make your furniture. I will try to locate another craftsman as soon as I am able."

Rachel sighed, letting her needlework rest on her lap. The poor woman wanted her own home, not a room above a tavern. But the reverend had already claimed William's time for the next day to meet with the village elders. When he told Rachel as much, she simply nodded, but there was a tightening at the corners of her mouth as she lifted her needlework again.

"'Tis not what I had envisioned."

"'Twill all work out in the end." She kept her needle moving through the fabric in smooth strokes, creating a pattern of some kind that would grace their new home. In time.

"'Tisn't fair to you, though. My dragging you across the colony only to find that I had been swindled."

"Nay, dear." Her hands paused, and she raised her eyes to his. "'Tis but a setback. We shan't make more of it."

"I can only imagine Elizabeth's disappointment."

"She is young." Rachel shrugged. "'Tis things like this that will shape her character. If one knows no adversity, how will one learn to rely on the Lord to overcome it?"

"You are a wise woman, my dear. What would I do without you?"

"I expect you would muddle along." But the smile that skirted her lips said otherwise.

William settled deeper in the chair and let his head rest against its high back. "What I saw this afternoon, it makes things like furniture seem...seem unimportant."

Rachel paused her needle again. "Do you wish to talk about?"

"Not yet. Let me mull it over. I have a medical book in the trunk I want to consult." Would that help? Would it bring him closer to the answer? He'd read each of his medical books at least three times through. Nothing he'd seen that day resembled anything he'd read.

At least, not in a medical book.

Reverend Cotton Mather's book, however, had touched on such things. And if what the good reverend had written was true, there was nothing William could do to help those girls.

Nothing at all.

The jingle of harnesses pulled Caleb from his thoughts as he bent over the piece of wood he was measuring in his shop. After his talk with Hannah, he'd decided to make Verity a dressing table. The girl deserved something of her own, not just hand-me-downs from Tamson. It would also please his wife.

"Whoa, there." The voice outside was a familiar one, and the muscles in Caleb's shoulders eased. David had a way of bringing joy wherever he went. Always upbeat and outgoing, some people mistook that for a lack of depth, but Caleb knew his friend better than that. More voices rose in greetings. David had brought some of his brood along to visit with Caleb's offspring of similar ages, no doubt.

He grabbed a rag and brushed off the sawdust and wood curls that clung to the front of his coat. Even with the brazier lit, it was cool in the shop. Crossing to the window, he watched four of David's children hop off the wagon and mingle with his own. The oldest boy took control of the team while David strode to the shop.

"Have thee a moment to spare this fine afternoon?" David came through the door already speaking and unwinding a muffler from around his neck.

"Always a moment to spare for thee." Caleb grinned in return.

David sobered and lifted his brown eyes to Caleb. "Even after yesterday's meeting?"

"At which thee were unusually silent." Grabbing the other stool, Caleb sat across the brazier from his friend.

"Aye, and what could I say? There are dark days coming, I fear."

"I see not how it can be otherwise." The word *witch* had the power to change the very landscape. It had done so before, in other towns and villages, even across the ocean in Europe. The thought of people being hanged, or in England burned or drowned, based on such a claim was more than sobering. It was frightening. Families torn apart, lands forfeited, children left orphaned... It was too much to think about.

David rubbed his chin. "With thy animals and stores, I trust thee are well-provisioned."

"Indeed. We shall be fine without Hannah Jr.'s sales to the Puritans." Caleb stiffened when a thought struck. "But what of thee?"

Most of David's business came from the Puritans. The Friends kept muskets for hunting and keeping their livestock safe from predators, but generally only one or maybe two pieces per family. The Puritans, however, had pistols and muskets, and some, if they had enough money to afford them, even had rifles. Puritans were forever commissioning guns to be made and others repaired. If David lost their trade, it would be difficult for him, his goodwife, and their eight children—although the eldest two boys often hired out as laborers and brought income to the house.

"'Twill not be easy." David stood and paced the length of the shop, then he whirled and faced Caleb. "Why decide on so drastic a decision? We had few enough facts."

"Thee were there and heard all that was said. Why did thee not stand and speak?"

"'Twould have done me little good, and maybe some harm." David returned to the stool and plopped onto it. "Thee know I am seen as one who gads about, maybe even something of a rebel."

True enough, a personification his friend generally embraced. But not now.

Then he speared Caleb with a shrewd glance few others ever saw. "Do thee believe the Puritans will come after us? Try to blame us for whatever they have gotten themselves into?"

Years ago, Caleb had shared the story of their past with David. "I know not, but neither can I trust them."

"Nay. Thee cannot." David shook his head. "We cannot. But to lose my income, 'tis a hard blow."

Most of the Friends were farmers, at least in part, and could weather the isolation. Isobel, David's wife, kept a backyard full of chickens, a flock of ducks near their small pond, and two milk cows. David brought one round every year to breed to Caleb's bull. Other than a large garden and hayfield, they grew no crops.

"If thee need anything—"

David raised his hand and cut off Caleb's words. "I know. We shall be fine." But there was a gleam in his eye that said he wasn't settled on the matter of not interacting with the Puritans or the village.

"Perhaps 'twould be a good time to extend thy reach to Salem Town and find more clients there." He went between the town and the village more than anyone else among the Friends. "Oh." Caleb snapped his fingers. "We should spread the word that thee would be available to take the women to Salem Town when they need a shopping trip. Thee know it best, after all, and thy wagon is one of the largest. If one or two of thy sons went along, the women would be more than adequately chaperoned."

"Not a bad idea," David murmured, but his thoughts seemed elsewhere.

The Friends would pay for the service, of course. Most with a gift of something off their farms. Hannah Jr. would give some of her cheese, for sure. It wouldn't be enough to keep David's family going, but it would help.

If his friend decided to follow the decree of the meeting. Caleb understood—as most of the men among the Friends would—that the man must take care of his family.

The same as Caleb must take care of his.

Chapter 11

S TORM CLOUDS GATHERED BENEATH the dark sky, closing like a fist and choking off the light of the moon. Caleb pulled the curtains closed across their bedroom window. "If I could have filled the doctor's order for furniture, 'twould have been a good opportunity to put some money aside for a rainy day." Whether those clouds would produce rain or snow would be answered in the morning. He stripped to his shirt, getting ready for bed, while Hannah braided her hair at her dressing table.

"But the Friends were wise to limit our interaction with the village." She glanced at him in the looking glass mounted on the wall. "Thee said as much, did thee not?"

"I did, but I had not realized all the implications of it." He pulled back the covers and slid between the fresh sheets, the scent of dried roses rising from them.

Hannah turned on her chair and looked at him, hair half-braided, pausing with the strands between her fingers. "What implications?"

He tucked his hands behind his head and stared at the beams in the ceiling. "I knew 'twould impact Hannah Jr. with her cheese and butter business, but she lives here and we can continue comfortably without her income. She will lack for nothing and neither shall we." He turned his face to her. "But others like David and Isobel will lose almost all their income."

Hannah's fingers moved again, plaiting the long blond strands. "I had not thought of that either. We Friends shall have to pitch in and see they do not suffer."

"Arthur Stokes sells many of his piglets to the Puritans for their back gardens. If this should drag on until the spring, he will be hurt by it."

"Will thee be short of commissioned work?"

Caleb shrugged. "I finished and delivered my last piece days ago. It has been a slow season in the carpenter shop."

Hannah tilted her head. "And yet, thee spent the entire afternoon out there."

"I am working on a surprise."

She rose, braid tied and swinging to her hips, and joined him in the bed. "Should I keep the children away? Or is it something for me?" Her smile was genuine, the first he'd seen since that awful trip to the forest.

It warmed his heart and thickened his voice. "'Tis not for thee, but 'twill please thee."

"Are thee not going to tell me?"

"Not yet." Mentioning Verity might send Hannah back into the fearfulness from which she seemed to have crawled out. That was the last thing Caleb wanted. He would do everything in his power to keep the family together—and at peace with each other.

"Fire!"

The word shot through the dark house, jerking Caleb from a deep sleep. He bolted out of bed while Hannah scrambled from the other side.

"Fire! Fire in the barn!" Caleb Jr.'s voice carried as footsteps pounded in the upstairs hallway.

Caleb grabbed his breeches and yanked them on, saying over his shoulder, "Tell Verity to keep the little boys in the house. Bring Hannah Jr. and Tamson with all the blankets thee can spare. Tell the girls to dress first. Frostbite will not save the barn or the animals."

He wrenched open the door.

Caleb Jr. stood on the other side, eyes wide but not in a panic, shirttails hanging to his bare knees.

"Where is Robert?"

"Getting dressed."

"Go do the same, wear coats and gloves and hats. Join me at the barn as soon as thee can."

Caleb started down the stairs.

"Caleb," Hannah called after him, "wait for help."

He turned on the stairs. The fear on Hannah's face tore at him, but as much as he'd like to calm her, he couldn't. "I must get the livestock out." He half-ran, half-tumbled down the remaining steps, stomped into his boots, pulled his coat off its peg, and rushed the door, Rags and Button racing beside him.

Rags barked when the flames came into view, and Button joined him. Good. Their noise might make it easier to get the livestock moving. Frightened animals were often difficult to move because they sought what they knew as a place of safety—the barn. They didn't understand the dangers of fire and smoke.

Caleb's ankle twisted when he came down on a rut, yesterday's slop having frozen solid overnight. He hopped a couple of steps and kept going. It wasn't serious, but he needed to be careful.

He reached the barn's main door and wrenched it open, smoke pouring through the gap. "Rags, Button, stay." Trusting they would obey, Caleb bent low, keeping under the smoke, and raced toward the horses first. Not that the cows were less important, but good horses were hard to come by this far north in the colony. Dolly being closest, he untied her first, and then the gelding, Dandy, backing them out of their stalls. Both tossed their heads at the smoke, snorting, and pulling on their lead ropes.

"Come on. Trust me now." He kept his voice as soothing as he could. By the time he'd coaxed them out the door, Robert was there. He thrust the ropes into the boy's hands. "Tie them at the house, on the side away from the fire. Do not let them go or they may try to return to their stalls."

Robert crooned to the prancing horses and led them away.

Caleb plunged back into the barn. The cows were on the far side, bellowing in distress. Fire crackled to the right of him where the farm tools were stored. All of them. But he had to save the livestock first. The smoke thickened, and he hurried to where the cows were loose in their large stall. There was no time to put a rope on each of them. He bent over and coughed out some of the smoke.

"Pa!" Caleb Jr. called.

"With the cows." Caleb undid the gate and swung it open.

Rags raced through the smoke and straight for the milling herd.

"Rags! Come out of there!" Caleb started to go in after the dog, but Caleb Jr. grabbed his arm.

"Wait, Rags has them moving."

Caleb backed up and watched as the black-and-white dog nipped at the cows' heels, getting the reluctant animals moving. Even Buttercup was more fearful of Rags' teeth than the smoke.

"Good dog. Way to go, Rags." Caleb Jr. coached the animal. "Bring them out this way. Good dog."

Caleb coughed and wiped the smoke from his eyes as the cows flowed past him and out the door. "Follow them. Make sure they do not turn and run for the barn again. I have to get the bull."

"Be careful." Caleb Jr. took off behind the last cow.

The bull was in his own enclosure at the back of the cows' pen. The animal was stomping its feet and bellowing, angry to be left behind. And dangerous. Caleb unwound the heavy rope that tied the enclosure shut and called to the bull, "Come on, fellow, I shall get thee out, but thee have to behave."

In reply, the maddened bull bellowed again.

When it moved to where Caleb could trap it behind the gate, he shoved the gate in and planted his feet to keep it tight against the huge animal. When the bull swung its head toward him, he slipped his fingers into its nose ring and threaded the rope through it.

How was he going to get the maddened animal through the barn and out the door?

"Pa!" Caleb Jr. appeared through the smoke.

"Grab the rope." Caleb shoved it toward his son. "'Twill take the both of us to get this beast outside." He kept his finger on one side of the ring while Caleb Jr. kept the rope tight on the other. Even so, the bull half-dragged them out of the barn. When they reached an oak tree on the side of the barn farthest from the fire, Caleb tied the animal fast, nose ring snubbed to the bark. "That should hold him." Caleb coughed.

"Thee and Robert start on the fire with buckets, use the blankets as soon as the women get here." He pointed to the house, where Hannah and the girls were coming down the porch steps.

"Where are thee going?" Caleb Jr. asked.

"To release the sheep."

Caleb ran into the barn, bent almost in half to keep below the thick smoke. The barn was built against a hill, and the sheep byre was on the lowest level, its walls the barn's rock foundation. Caleb lifted the trap door that opened into a chute used to drop hay to the flock. Glad he hadn't put on too much weight over the years, he lowered himself through the opening and slid down the chute into the midst of the pungent, woolly animals. Their flock was small, just eight ewes—all pregnant—and the ram, the beast glaring at him from its corner pen.

"Come on, girls." The smoke was lighter down there, and Caleb had the door open in no time. Once he shoved the lead ewe outside, the others followed willingly enough. Then he went for the ram.

It eyed him in the dim interior and backed against the far wall.

Caleb opened the gate, and the ram lowered its head and charged. At the last moment, Caleb stepped aside. Seeing the open door, the ram bolted through it.

"Caleb!" Hannah's panicked voice reached him.

He dove through the lower barn door, pulling in lungsful of clean air. "I am fine!" He shut the door to prevent the sheep from returning, and ran around to the front, where angry flames licked up the barn's side.

Caleb Jr. and Robert heaved water on the flames, while Hannah Jr. and Tamson hauled buckets from the springhouse, which was thankfully only fifteen feet from the barn.

"Where are the cows?" he asked.

Caleb Jr. pointed toward the house, where the cows milled in a circle, Rags and Button sitting to one side, eyes on them. The old collie was showing the pup what to do.

"Hannah." Caleb motioned for the girls to bring the buckets of water to their mother. "Douse the blankets and beat out any flames thee and the girls can reach. Robert, keep the fresh buckets coming. Caleb Jr. and I will throw the water." They were the two tallest, not that it would help much, the northeast corner of the barn was already in full blaze.

They were going to lose the barn.

Time seemed to stand still as they battled the flames.

He'd lost count of how many buckets he'd heaved, the muscles in his arms growing weary, when the freezing rain started. *Thank thee, Lord.* A downpour would have been better, but freezing rain would slow the fire.

Then it changed to sleet, slanting hard, driven on the wind that had picked up, lashing right into the corner of the barn that burned, sizzling and popping amid the flames. Soon all of them were soaked with the water they were throwing, the wet blankets they were wielding, and the mixture of snow and rain. But the fire was dying down.

It could have been so much worse.

Dawn pinked the sky, even through the storm clouds. The extent of the damage wasn't as bad as he'd feared from all the smoke. The roof remained, thanks to the freezing rain and sleet, even though parts of it were scorched and would need to be replaced. The barn's northeast corner was in ruins. The northeast corner—and the tools he needed to plant crops in the spring.

The carpenter shop was in the southeast corner, so the fire hadn't started from his brazier, which had been his first thought. Although he was always careful with the fire in there, it was a risk. One he might not take again after this night.

The fire was down to a smolder within another hour. Caleb, Caleb Jr. and Robert had taken buckets inside the barn, as well as Hannah with her blankets. She'd balked at the girls entering, and he didn't blame her. Dresses and long braids didn't belong around flames. He'd rather Hannah had stayed outside as well, but she was a determined woman, and he hadn't had the time or breath while flinging buckets of water to argue with her. The girls had taken over carrying water once the others had moved inside.

Now his family stood in a bedraggled group, growing cold without the constant activity.

"What do thee think caused it, Father?" Hannah Jr. asked.

He shook his head. "I would only be guessing. Once everything cools, I shall walk through and see what I can learn, but we may never know."

Or he may find evidence of arson. Had the madness already started? Had some Puritan come in the night and started the fire? It had happened before.

"At least we saved all the animals," Robert said.

"Rags and Button were a big help." Tamson pointed to where the dogs still watched over the cows, which had settled enough to paw through the frozen crust to graze on the cured grasses below.

"Does anyone know where the sheep ran to?" Caleb Jr. looked around in the pale morning light.

"If they do not return on their own, I imagine a neighbor will drive them back eventually." Hannah wiped her brow with the back of her wrist. "I hope the ewes do not lose their lambs over the stress of it all." She spoke from experience, and it hit Caleb hard.

Losing the lambs would be a blow. They relied on their wool to keep the family in socks and mittens, hats and scarves, and even a sweater or two each year. If they had to purchase that, it would be another drain on the budget.

But it was nothing compared to what Hannah had lost the last time.

He pulled his thoughts from the past with a shake of his head. The biggest drain on their budget would be the loss of his farming tools. How would he be able to replace those in time for the spring planting?

If they were still here. If the fire hadn't been set by someone from the village to chase them off. So many ifs.

Chapter 12

W ILLIAM HAD BARELY SLEPT that night. After dinner, he'd walked
to the new—empty—house and retrieved his copy of Cotton
Mather's *Memorable Providences, Relating to Witchcrafts and Posses-*
sions from the trunk containing his collection of books, thankful he'd
decided to bring them all. Reading through it hadn't encouraged sleep.
Quite the opposite. There were too many similarities between what
Mather described happening in Boston in 1688 with the Goodwin
family and what William had witnessed the day before at the Parris
household.

Far too many similarities.

But witchcraft? Everything from his scientific training warred
against what the Puritan pastors preached from their raised platforms
on Sundays. William firmly believed that people were created by the
one and only God of the universe and saved by the death of His son
on the cross. But science was also real and—in William's mind—also
created by God. One must balance the known world, that which could
be seen and heard, tasted and felt, against the unknown world, the
heavenly things.

What he'd seen at the Parris household did not display anything
heavenly—nor could he detect anything scientifically amiss.

So that left the unthinkable, which he'd pondered throughout the night.

Rachel roused from the bed, rising on her elbow to look at him, her hair covered with a nightcap, her face soft from sleep. "You are up early." She frowned at the stub of a candle next to him, then reached behind her and patted the bedcovers that lay undisturbed on his side. The frown deepened. "Or did you sit up all night?"

He lifted the book on his lap, and let it fall again. "I had much to consider."

She scooted until she sat upright against the headboard, resting against the pillow. "You need sleep, William, lest your own health suffer."

"I know, my dear." He rubbed the back of his neck, stiff from his night in the chair. Well, that and his advancing age. He'd rub the ache in his chest, but Rachel would question such a move. "But 'twas a worrisome thing I witnessed yesterday."

She folded her hands on the quilt covering her lap. "Are you ready to discuss it?"

How well she knew him. "I am. But I warn you, it involves an issue I do not like."

"I gathered as much." She pointed to the book. "I have read that volume by Reverend Mather, and I cannot say I agree with all his...his findings."

An advantage of being married to an educated woman. "Nor do I. Or at least, I did not until yesterday." He drummed his fingers against the book's thick leather cover. "But what I saw has made me question... Everything."

"Why do you not start at the beginning?"

He told her what he'd witnessed, as well as the answers to the questions he'd asked, then he lifted the book again. "Reverend Mather is convinced that evil spirits walk among us. And while I have as many years of education as the good reverend, my learning is in a different field. I work with the physical. His expertise is the spiritual."

"Then let us start with what you know." Rachel had the faraway look in her eyes that she got when deep in thought. "You found no sign of illness in the girls. Nothing of fever, skin appearing healthy other than the bite marks, and both well-nourished. To all outward appearances, they are healthy girls."

"Correct."

"What about the internal? Perhaps a parasite?"

"Their hair appeared shiny enough, and both exhibited bright and clear eyes once the fits dissipated. Each carried adequate weight."

"So unlikely 'tis a parasite."

"I could find nothing that indicated anything internal."

Rachel pointed to Mather's book. "Which is why you are searching the spiritual."

"Indeed." He thumped the book against his thigh. "You know I have reservations about Mather's conclusions."

"Aye, we have discussed that before."

"But in this case"—William shook his head—"the descriptions in his book are comparable to what I witnessed yesterday. Eerily comparable, I would say."

Rachel pulled their Bible from the nightstand where she'd left it, having unpacked it when they arrived. They routinely read from the Scriptures in the evenings. "If I remember correctly, when the devil was cast out, he took a good portion of the angels with him."

The Book of Revelation wasn't one they spent much time reading. Rachel had probably read it more often than William. He found it too confusing and conflicting and privately held the opinion that man wasn't meant to understand it until the end times came.

"Here." Rachel poked a finger on a page. "It says, 'And the great dragon that old serpent, called the devil and Satan, was cast out, which deceiveth all the world: he was even cast into the earth, and his angels were cast out with him.'" She raised her face to him. "The devil is not working on this earth alone."

"But witches?" There. William had said the word aloud.

Rachel closed the Bible and splayed her hand across its cover. "There are many mentions of witches in these pages as well."

True. He'd read them. Mather had quoted them. But it still felt—unscientific.

"I am not saying witchcraft is involved, my dear." Rachel laid the Bible aside. "But I am saying that it does exist."

Maybe that was William's problem. He didn't want to admit it. Spiritual things were beyond his skill to ease, or heal, or correct. They left him...completely powerless. And that was a most uncomfortable feeling.

Two nights had passed since the fire, and Caleb and the boys were finally walking among the cooled ashes. They had shored up the northeast side of the barn with fresh-cut timbers to make it safe. At least they'd been able to house the livestock in the basement of the barn after rigging makeshift stalls for the horses, the fire having reached their stalls. The cows and sheep were mingling together, except for the ram in his corner pen where he couldn't pick a fight with the bull that was penned in the opposite corner.

Caleb used a shovel that had been left near the cow pen, for once glad someone hadn't put it away, to move and sift through the ashes. As he'd suspected, most of his farm tools were damaged beyond repair. They could salvage the iron for the blacksmith to melt down and fashion into the new parts, but all the wooden pieces—the handles and frames—needed to be replaced.

The blacksmith bill would be more than Caleb had set aside.

A lot more.

Which left him to reconsider furnishing the new doctor's house. It would go against the wishes of the meeting, for sure. How would Hannah react to that? They had been on firmer footing since the fire, with no obvious signs of the fissure between them, although Caleb sensed it still lurked in the background, fueled by an old hurt that he couldn't fix. A hurt he shared, but could a man truly understand the loss of a child born too soon? A mother had held that babe inside, nurtured it with her own body, felt it move and grow within. Caleb had simply held his wife while their premature daughter died in her arms. The last thing Caleb wanted was to stir up those old pains.

Yet he needed the money or there would be new pains—hunger pains—in their home.

"Boys, find a crate and box up all the iron bits thee can find, even the smallest parts. Stephan Draper can melt it down for the new pieces we shall need." Thank goodness they had a blacksmith among the Friends. At least he wouldn't need to approach the village for that.

Robert lifted a twisted piece of iron off their blackened and crumbling hay wagon. "Like this?"

"Anything iron, even an old horseshoe if thee see one." Thank goodness the harnesses had been on the other side of the barn. Other than smelling of smoke, they were in good shape. And their main wagon had been on that side as well.

"Pa." Caleb Jr. frowned at a twisted piece of iron that had once been the head of a hoe. "Can thee replace all of this?"

"Eventually. This summer we may need to use wooden garden tools." Not nearly as good as iron, but they could make do. "I shall need both of thee to help in the shop to fashion what we can ourselves. All the handles, for sure."

"And the blacksmith?" Caleb Jr.'s creased brow said he'd figured what that bill would be.

"I have a plan, but I must discuss it with thy mother first." He might as well get it over with. "Get started here while I do that."

He strode toward the house. The weather had turned mild, and his boots slopped through the last of the melting snow. Winter wasn't over, but it seemed to be taking a break. He had two months or a little more before the fields would be ready to work. Two months to raise the money and have the equipment made. Enough time if he didn't wait to get started.

The kitchen was warm with the hearth fire and fragrant from the fresh loaves of bread wrapped in cloth and cooling on the sideboard. He drew in a deep breath.

Hannah washed dishes while Benji and Jonathan played near her feet. The girls would be in the dairy, the younger two keen to learn from Hannah Jr.

Hannah looked up as he entered, hope in her face.

How he hated to bring her bad news. He shrugged out of his coat and removed his boots, but that was only a delay. There was no softening what he had to tell her. "'Tis a total loss of the tools, except for one shovel. The hay wagon is gone, the plow, scythes, pitchforks, and hayforks, as well as all the garden tools. We have not a hoe nor a rake remaining."

"Oh, Caleb." She dried her hands. "What will we do?"

"The wooden parts I can make, of course, but the iron parts." He removed his hat and tossed it on the table. "Those will take money for the blacksmith."

Last year's drought had limited their crops, leaving them plenty to feed their family—even with the addition of Verity—and the livestock, but little to sell. The coins in their crock over the hearth were few.

Caleb cleared his throat. "The new doctor's furniture—"

"Thee cannot." Hannah cut him off.

Benji and Jonathan stopped their play and looked up at the sharpness of her voice, but that didn't stop her.

"The decision has been made for the good of all Friends. Thee said so thyself."

"I did, and 'tis sound advice, but without those tools, I cannot see how we will plant our crops this spring. Without the crops, how will we feed our livestock and family next winter?"

"Thee could sell the mare." Hannah nodded toward the barn. "She is in foal and would bring a good price."

"Then I would have to plow with one horse." Caleb shook his head. "Dandy is young and strong, but I would get less ground worked and planted. And we need two horses to pull the wagon. 'Tis too large and heavy for a single hitch."

"A cow then, or two, or some of the sheep." Desperation crept into her voice.

"We barely have enough sheep to keep thee in wool to clothe our family now. I had planned to retain this coming spring's ewe lambs to enlarge the flock." If only they hadn't lost so many of last spring's lambs to a bad run of scours, her suggestion might have worked. "If we sell any of the cows, 'twill cut into Hannah Jr.'s cheese and butter sales. While we could survive without that income, 'tis helpful in the fall when the children all require new shoes."

Hannah thrust her hands into the soapy water and attacked a poor bowl with enough vigor to slosh water onto the floor. "Can thee not bring in more carpentry business from our neighbors?"

"Thee know as well as I that most of my work comes from the Puritans in the village. And I suspect our neighboring Friends will be watching their wallets closely as they are also impacted by the decree."

"Aye, the decree." She slapped down the wet rag and turned to him again. "Thee cannot ignore it. What will the elders say? Our neighbors? What kind of example will it provide our children?"

Caleb glanced down at Benji and Jonathan, both watching him with mouths slightly open, then back at Hannah. "The example that sometimes a man must make hard decisions to provide for his family."

"Provide for the family?" Hannah crossed her arms, not in belligerence, but a gesture that said she wasn't secure in what she was about to say. "The Lord will provide what we need."

Caleb let those words settle over him. They were true. They had always been true. During the worst time of their lives, God had provided for them. But... "What if He already has?" Caleb let his voice drop to a gentle tone. "What if the doctor's arrival on the very day before the fire was the Lord's way of providing the income we need?"

"Or what if," Hannah shot back, "thee are using that as an excuse to take matters into thy own hands and not wait upon the Lord?"

The little boys' heads swiveled from one parent to the other. He needed to put a stop to this. They shouldn't witness the rift widening between him and their mother.

"Thee could be right. We should both pray about it throughout the day and speak of it again this evening."

But the stubborn set of her chin said she wasn't about to change her mind.

Chapter 13

K NUCKLES RAPPING AGAINST THE heavy wooden door drew William from sleep. He blinked against the daylight filtering in around the drawn curtains. Why was he sleeping during the day?

The door creaked open, and Rachel's voice reached him. "The doctor is lying down. What can I help you with?"

"'Tis my daughter again, and worse than before."

Reverend Parris.

Memory flooded back, and William rose, steadying himself for a moment until the room stopped spinning. He was too old to rise that fast anymore. He was too old to be reading through the night, much less three nights in a row. He straightened the clothing he'd fallen asleep in and joined Rachel at the door.

"'Tis all right, Rachel. I will handle this." She quirked an eyebrow at him but disappeared into Elizabeth's room across the hallway. "Come in, Reverend."

"I need you to come to the house. Now."

"And I need to put on my shoes. Come in and wait."

"Of course." The flustered man entered.

William shut the door. "What are the symptoms this morning?"

"Morning?" The reverend gave him a narrow-eyed look. "'Tis afternoon, doctor."

"My apologies. I was up late into the night reading medical books, researching your situation." William smothered a yawn and dropped into a chair to put on his shoes. "I have lost track of time catching up on my sleep."

"I see." In his agitation, Reverend Parris tapped his toe, perhaps without realizing he was doing it. "What did you discover in the books?"

"Very little that was helpful."

"Today it started with Abigail, but within a minute, Betty hit the floor as well." Reverend Parris tore off his hat and smoothed the top of his hair with one hand. "There is no one thing that seems to start it. Just now, they were doing needlework in the parlor, Lizzy and Susannah with them, and Tituba. Lizzy was reading out to them all while they worked."

William pulled on his coat. "What was she reading?"

"What does that matter?" the reverend shot back.

"Perhaps something they heard started the fit." William retrieved his satchel. He was grasping at straws, but what else did they have?

"'Twas the Bible, of course, for the girls' instruction."

If there was a demonic component to these fits, the Bible could very well be what had brought them on. It taught that evil thoughts and deeds were sin, after all. William filed that away in his memory as he opened the door and motioned the other man out. He then tapped on Elizabeth's door and let them know where he was going before following Reverend Parris home.

The scene was even more chaotic than the first time he'd seen it. Had it been only three days? It seemed like a month.

Abigail was rolling on the floor, shouting that someone was pinching her. Betty was seated on the floor, her arms wrapped around herself, rocking on her haunches, muttering sounds but no words. Or at least not words William understood. The hair on his forearms tingled in response. Before he could set down his satchel, Abigail rose and raced for the hearth and its glowing embers.

"Stop her!" Goodie Parris shouted from her chair where she clutched their youngest daughter on her lap.

Her husband leaped across the room and grabbed the girl by the upper arms. She fought him, screaming about the burning, her head contorting in a position so unnatural that William feared her neck might snap.

Hands trembling, William dug into his satchel and pulled out a bottle of laudanum. Sedation was in order this time, in all haste. "Hold her head still."

The reverend tried, but the slave woman had to help, and even with the two of them, William could barely get the girl's mouth still enough to let some of the liquid dribble in. She fought and sputtered, some of it spewing out, so William dribbled in a bit more.

"What about Betty?" Goodie Parris asked.

Betty appeared to be recovering on her own, no longer rocking, eyes still glazed, but she'd focused on her mother as she spoke.

William knelt beside her. "What do you remember, Betty? What happened to you?"

The young girl's eyes cleared as she blinked several times. "I know not."

"What is the last thing you remember?" He kept all hint of his frustration from his voice.

"I was darning one of Father's stockings." She looked around, then pointed to a tangle of yarn and a wadded stocking that appeared to have been flung against the wall. "That one."

"And then?"

"And then there was Momma's voice asking about me."

Which told him nothing useful, but William smiled and patted the back of her hand. "How do you feel now?"

She clapped a hand to the back of her shoulder. "It hurts here."

"Let your mother unfasten the back of your dress so I can see." William helped her to her feet and climbed to his own, knees creaking.

Goodie Parris made quick work of the dress fastening and peeled it away from Betty's shoulder, then gasped.

William leaned over and examined the bite mark on the girl. He raised his eyes to her mother's. "Did anyone touch her during her fit?"

Pale eyes met his as the woman's face blanched.

She pitched forward in the chair in a dead faint.

He caught her, then steadied the youngest child, still clinging to her lap, with his other hand.

"Lizzy!" Reverend Parris pushed the sedated Abigail into the slave woman's arms and rushed to his wife's side. "What happened?"

The youngest girl started to cry.

"She fainted." William handed the littlest girl to her father, then knelt beside Goodie Parris' chair and chaffed her wrists. "Goodie Parris? Can you hear me?"

Betty wailed, clinging to the back of her father's coat.

William needed another helper, or at least another set of hands.

And answers.

There was no way that child could have bitten herself. And if none other touched her—none other who could be seen—then the only answer left was the unthinkable one.

Caleb had prayed the afternoon away while working in the carpentry shop. He'd moved Verity's dressing table to a corner. The garden tool handles weren't fancy things, but necessary, and they left him time to pray and think. He wanted the right answer to their problem—the Lord's answer. *Ask, and it shall be given you: seek, and ye shall find: knock, and it shall be opened unto you.*

If only it were as easy as that.

After all the prayer, he kept coming back to the one solution already before them—build the new doctor's furniture. Surely the Lord had provided such an opportunity at the exact time he needed it. Outfitting an entire house would cover the cost of the iron parts of the equipment he couldn't build for himself and then some. It would ensure their survival the following winter.

It would also alienate his wife.

Their midday meal had been a stilted affair, during which their older children had cast glances between him and Hannah. They understood that something was wrong, but not what. Nor should they. It was a father's role to provide and protect.

His role. His decision.

He wanted Hannah's approval, of course, and her support. But in the end, it was his responsibility. All that was left was for him to tell his wife.

And slam a bigger wedge into the rift between them.

He approached their room that evening with an equal mixture of dread and conviction. Hannah hadn't entered yet. The door to the younger girls' room across the hall was slightly ajar, her voice low behind it. Caleb leaned against the wall in the hallway and listened.

"Of course we shall be fine. Thy father will make new tools for the garden." There was a rustling of blankets. "Perhaps he will make thee each a new hoe to keep the weeds away." A high-pitched groan dissolved into giggles. "Now thee both need to go to sleep. No more talking. The morning comes early with plenty to do." Murmurs of agreement followed, but Caleb doubted his wife's sage advice would be followed. For as quiet as Verity had been when she first came to them, Tamson had brought the girl out of her shell. The two were inseparable and always talking.

Hannah backed into the hallway and closed the girls' door. When she turned and saw him, she took a step back and pressed her hand to her chest.

"I did not mean to startle thee." Nor did he want to have the conversation that awaited, but sometimes a man must put the welfare of his family above his own desires. Pushing aside his feelings, he ushered Hannah into their room and closed the door.

Hannah whirled and faced him. "Thee are going to make that doctor's furniture." Each word was an accusation.

"I am."

"Thee are going to expose our family to whatever evil is lurking in the village." Did she even know she'd wrapped her arms around her middle, as if protecting an unborn child? "Thee are endangering our family."

"I am going to accept the provision the Lord has placed before me." He met her eyes squarely and put every bit of conviction he could into his tone. "And trust that God will protect us."

Hannah stalked to her dressing table and sank onto the bench, jerking the pins from her hair. "As thee will not be dissuaded, there is nothing more for me to say."

True to her word, her lips remained sealed while Caleb readied for bed and waited for her to join him. When she came to bed, she lay with her back to him, not even her feet touching him.

Sleep eluded Caleb for a long, long time.

William was grateful Reverend Parris had sent around a request to meet him at the church that morning. Even after a full night of sleep without opening a book, William was still drained from events of the previous day at the Parris house.

The church had a light covering of frost so that it sparkled in the morning sunshine, a bright and cheery sun for the middle of February. So at odds with the ominous thoughts swirling through William. He'd have to tell the reverend his findings this morning. He couldn't leave the man without some sort of an answer.

Even a horrific one.

He grasped the handrail outside the church and climbed the steps. Before he reached the large double doors, the one on the right opened.

Reverend Parris had dark circles under his eyes and weary lines creased his cheeks. His coat had been hastily buttoned, one button having been missed mid-torso and another only half secure in its opening. His neckcloth was rumpled, and judging by their wrinkled state, those breeches had been slept in. The poor man had been knocked about through all this.

William was about to deliver another blow.

"Thank you for coming, doctor." He pulled the door wider and ushered William in. "Come back to my office. We shan't be disturbed there."

There was no hearth in the church, of course, the risk of fire too great to allow that. On Sundays, the number of bodies warmed the building to a tolerable extent, but the two of them in the small office did little to mitigate the cold.

"I apologize for not having a brazier in here." Reverend Parris chafed his hands together. "I still have not received the allotment of firewood I was promised with this position." Bitterness colored his tone. As well it might in the middle of winter without a proper amount of fuel. But that wasn't the issue today.

"'Tis warm enough with the sunlight in the window." William took the chair the light shone upon after the other man moved to the one behind his narrow desk.

"I asked you here so we could speak freely without Lizzy or the girls overhearing." Reverend Parris rubbed a hand across his face. "Lizzy is not well. She hasn't been for some time, since Susannah's birth. After she swooned yesterday..." He shrugged.

"The restorative drink I recommended should help. I trust your slave made it as prescribed and has given it to her."

"She did, straight away. And to the girls as well." He raised his eyes to William. "Will it help the girls?"

"Not in the way you wish." William crossed his legs and folded his hands on top of them. Now came the difficult part. "I fear what ails your daughter and niece isn't physical."

"A disease of the mind, then?" The reverend's countenance almost begged William to say it was.

How he wished he could. Insanity would be preferable to what he had to say. "I think not. I fear 'tis something much darker. Something I wish I did not have to say aloud."

Reverend Parris hung his head, forehead cradled in his palm. "I know. 'Tis the word I have been dreading."

Nevertheless, William was duty-bound by his profession to utter it. "My research, my observances, and my examinations, both physical and through questioning, lead me to the sad conclusion that the girls are bewitched."

Bewitched. The word hung in the cold room like an eerie vapor.

"What am I to do?" the poor man asked without looking up. "How am I to handle this?"

"I wish I could tell you, but in this area, I feel you are more the expert than I."

The reverend let his hand fall and tipped his head back against the chair, face toward the rafters overhead. "If only that were true."

William pointed to the bookshelf behind the desk. "I see you have a copy of Cotton Mather's book on the events of witchcraft in Boston. I read through my copy. Perhaps you might glean more meaning from his writings than I could."

"I reread it when all this started, even as I hoped you would find something else." There was a tinge of rebuke, maybe even accusation, in the man's voice, but William couldn't fault him. Were it his child involved, he'd probably feel let down by the doctor as well.

William stood. "Then I shall leave you. I will stop in and see your goodwife again on the morrow. And, of course, you can find me at the tavern until I can get the house outfitted for my family."

Reverend Parris waved a hand in dismissal without saying a word.

William didn't blame him for that, either, and left without a parting word of his own. What could be said after he'd delivered such a devastating diagnosis?

Chapter 14

C ALEB ENTERED NATHANIEL INGERSOLL'S tavern. The savory scent of
meat roasting warmed the room, along with a roaring fire in the
deep hearth that took up most of one wall. The gathering place of
Puritans. Passing a pair of men nursing pints at one of the round tables,
Caleb approached the long bar, where Nathaniel wiped his hands on
the smudged linen apron that covered his waistcoat and breeches.

"Hello, Mr. Buffum. Are you here for the doctor again?"

"I am. Has he been down yet this morning?"

"Out and back and looking as if he carried the weight of the world
on his shoulders, poor man."

"'Twas a blow to find the house as he did, I am sure."

"Ah, that. Messy business." Nathaniel frowned. "That tight-fisted old
bugger sold him the house fully furnished, and then drove away with
every last stick. Short of tracking the man down and dragging it all
back—if he has not sold it somewhere along the way—the doctor will
be out-of-pocket for everything."

"I will keep my prices as reasonable as I can."

"So you will be making his furniture?" The tavern keeper's brows
raised.

The doctor appeared on the steps leading from the rooms upstairs.

"Doctor," Nathaniel greeted him. "Let me highly recommend Mr. Buffum for his carpentry work. 'Twas he who built the cupboards in the kitchen for my goodwife, who assures me they are the very best she has ever had."

"Have you changed your mind?" the doctor asked.

"Indeed. If thee are still in need of a carpenter."

"I am." He held up one finger. "Wait but a moment while I fetch my goodwife. She will have her say in this matter." The doctor turned and headed back up the stairs. For a man his age, he was limber enough.

"Make yourself comfortable," the tavern keeper said. "I have yet to meet a woman who could be at the ready in *but a moment*. I shall be just down the hall if you need anything."

Caleb moved closer to the hearth and enjoyed the warmth, settling on a nearby chair for the wait.

But in defiance of the tavern keeper's opinion, the doctor returned with his goodwife in short order. Where Dr. Griggs had a kind and congenial air, Goodie Griggs had a broad face and a no-nonsense jawline without a trace of his gentleness. Here was the person Caleb would need to please. Behind them came the girl on the threshold of womanhood.

He rose as they approached.

"Mr. Buffum." The doctor turned to indicate the women. "You have already met my goodwife, and this is our niece, Elizabeth Hubbard."

"Please call me Caleb. I am at thy service."

The goodwife looked him up and down as she might a goose hanging on market day. Judging by her crisp nod, he must have passed inspection. "Let us begin then, Mr. Buffum." She stressed the formal name.

The doctor shot a look between Caleb and his wife.

Caleb lifted one shoulder in a small shrug and followed them out the door. He wouldn't belabor the point. The Puritans would call him what they willed. He was used to it. What they did after he made his wishes known was their own affair.

He followed them a couple of doors down to the house the doctor had purchased. It appeared reasonably well cared for on the outside. He would suggest replacing some of the wooden steps that sagged beneath his weight. No sense in waiting for one to crack and perhaps cause a fall. At the couple's age, they couldn't afford that. The house wasn't very large, but its emptiness made it feel that way.

"What would thee like me to start with first?" He addressed the goodwife.

"The bedsteads, I should think. Even if we must eat at the tavern for a time, we could at least sleep here." She turned to the young woman. "What say you, Elizabeth?"

"We shall need a trio of chairs as well." There was a sullenness to the young woman's voice. "We cannot stand or be abed all the day."

"Quite right." The goodwife turned to Caleb. "Two bedsteads and three chairs will suffice to begin."

"I have three chairs I can loan thee, if thee wish," Caleb offered, "while I make a full set of chairs that match for thy table."

That earned him a stiff smile, but it seemed genuine. "Thank you, Mr. Buffum. That is very kind."

"I want to reassure you, Caleb," said the doctor, who'd remained in the background while the women spoke. "I will be paying you with coin upon completion of each piece." Caleb started to protest that it would be fine to wait until the whole order was done, but the older man shook his head. "On this I insist. No one knows better than a doctor the importance of collecting a fee. And in a timely manner."

How many times had the doctor not received a fee at all to make such a point? "However thee wish," Caleb said.

They continued through the house, Caleb asking questions and jotting notes on a smooth board with a piece of charcoal he'd brought for that purpose. All together, the work would bring him a tidy sum, enough to replace everything they'd lost in the fire and more.

Or, if they were forced to run again, enough cash for some sort of a new start.

While Rachel and Elizabeth discussed with the Quaker carpenter the types of bedsteads they wished made, William strode around the empty parlor, gazing out the windows and pondering whether they should find another ship and sail back to Boston. He had money enough to cover the passage and probably to purchase a modest house on the outskirts, but he would be forced back into full employment to cover the cost of furnishings and whatnot until this house in Salem Village sold—if it sold.

Who would buy a house in a place bewitched by evil spirits?

He wouldn't be surprised if word reached Boston before he could get his family back there. Bad news spread like a town fire in high winds, leaping from one house to another. They might return to Boston only to be turned away by a crowd fearful that they brought the evil with them.

"William?" Rachel's voice cut through his thoughts. "What is your preference?"

Since he hadn't heard a word, he could hardly say. "Whatever you wish, my dear."

"'Twill be your office." She raised a brow at him. "Surely you want some say in the matter of its furnishings. At least as far as your desk and bookshelves." Bless her. Rachel knew him so well and had supplied him with enough to pick up the conversation.

"I have always been partial to oak with its warm tones. And I like a desk with drawers on both sides, but not too wide."

The Quaker made notes on his board, the *scritch* of charcoal loud in the empty room. "And for a chair?" he asked without looking up.

"Something with a bit of padding on it." William chuckled. "Old age makes one appreciate small comforts."

The Quaker looked up, a twinkle in his eye that said he understood. "Some nice horsehair stuffing then." He wrote more on the board before straightening and glancing around the room. "I have enough to keep me busy. I shall bring the bedsteads and chairs as soon as I can."

"Are you able to start straight away?" Rachel asked.

"Indeed. This very afternoon."

"Excellent." Rachel nodded to Elizabeth, who seemed to have perked up somewhat with all the talk of furnishings and such. Women did like those sorts of things. "Once you bring them, we shall move in."

Which was what had to happen. For all his musings, William couldn't see moving them back to Boston. Even if he could afford it—barely—the risk of the stigma following them was too great. To bankrupt them only to be ostracized in the process wasn't an option. Not at their ages.

Startled when the door to his shop opened and David strode in, Caleb smacked a sawdust-covered hand to his chest. "Are thee trying to stop my heart?"

With an unrepentant grin, David helped himself to a stool and straddled it. "Never, my friend. Thee must have been much absorbed not to have heard me arrive."

"Indeed." Caleb set aside the bedpost he'd been shaping and dusted off the front of his leather work apron. "And welcome."

David pointed at the wood. "What are thee making?"

It was an innocent enough question, the question most people asked when they entered his shop and saw him working. But this time, Caleb resented it. And he shouldn't. It was his own doing, going against the decision of the meeting—against the wishes of his wife. There was nothing to do but own up to it.

"Furniture for the new doctor in the village."

David's jaw dropped open. "Thee took the job after all?"

"Yesterday." Caleb motioned toward the other side of the barn. The burned side. "I lost almost all my tools and equipment in the fire. I cannot replace it all, and I cannot plant in the spring without it. Well, I cannot plant enough to sustain my family and livestock, anyway."

"In the manner to which thee have grown accustomed."

Caleb drew out the other stool and sat. "True." They had lived more than just comfortably, although not lavishly, on what he and the boys were able to produce. "But we also have another mouth to feed, another body to clothe."

David wagged a finger at him. "Blame not the girl for thy decision to disregard the decree of the meeting."

"Thee are right." Caleb squashed a grimace.

"I know I am." David turned the finger to himself and stabbed it against his chest. "Because I have done the same."

"What have thee done?" Although Caleb wasn't surprised. David had always been the non-conformist in their midst. And yet, he brought such a joy to the community, and always a willing hand. He'd been the first on the scene after the fire to help in the cleanup.

David shrugged. "I am newly returned from Salem Town, where I picked up what I need to make two new fowling pieces for Thomas Buffington. But thee are not to tell." He held a finger to his lips in dramatic fashion. "They are gifts for his twin sons. I am to make them as alike as the lads themselves except for their initials carved into the stocks."

"If anyone can do that job, 'twill be thee." David was more than just a gunsmith. He was an artist in his profession.

"And while I was in Salem Town, I picked up another order for a rifle." His grin widened. As well it should. Rifles brought a fine price.

"At least that one is not in violation of the decree."

"I also bring news from the town." He leaned forward. "The new Massachusetts Charter has been signed. And here is the good part. It includes religious liberty for all—including the Friends—and leaves the Maine territory attached to the colony as well."

"Religious liberty for all?" Caleb was stunned—in the best possible way, but still stunned.

"Well, almost all. They did exclude the Papists and Jews."

Of course. If there was one thing Puritans hated more than the Friends, it was the Catholics and Jews. Caleb didn't know much about those religions, but he felt a moment of sorrow for their continued struggle.

"Perhaps this new charter will ease things between our people and the village," David suggested.

"Perhaps." Caleb didn't put much conviction in his voice.

"Thee think not?"

"I think once the word *witch* is uttered aloud"—Caleb barely whispered the word even between the two of them—"no one will be safe from suspicion. Not Friend nor Puritan."

"Thee are sure 'twill come to that?"

No matter how much he wished otherwise, Caleb nodded.

David sighed and slouched on his stool, then cocked his head at Caleb. "Did thee ever find out what started the fire?"

"The boys and I combed through the ashes and found nothing. If it had started in the shop here, I would say the brazier, but in the tool room? We keep nothing in there that would shed a spark."

David dropped his voice to a whisper. "Have thee considered arson?"

Caleb had worked hard not to. The idea that someone hated him enough to torch his barn and attempt to kill his livestock was more than unsettling. If it were true, would they come after his house next? His family? Such thoughts had chased away more than one night's sleep.

Thoughts he couldn't share with Hannah.

They had been through so much together. She'd always been as steady as a rock beside him. But these days, the separation between them was almost a physical thing. The fear of the Puritans rising against them—like the last time—had put her in a fragile state. The way she clung to little Verity, as if the girl were a replacement for the one lost so many years ago, was unsettling.

Caleb taking the doctor's furniture order had only made it worse. But he needed the money to take care of the family. And he truly believed the Lord had sent this opportunity for him to provide for the family.

If only Hannah could see it as a blessing too.

Nobody had to tell William that word had leaked out about the Parris household. As he walked to the general store for a pouch of pipe tobacco, curtains were pulled shut despite the sun shining overhead. The few people on the street scuttled along with their heads down, clutching shopping baskets or their children's hands. Not a word of greeting rang into the still air.

He was almost to the store when an old woman exited the building. She was more than old, closer to ancient, and she shook a gnarled finger at him. "They took away my children. How am I to survive without them, I ask you?" Then she wrapped a tattered shawl around herself and stalked off, muttering more he couldn't understand.

William entered the store and went to the counter.

"Sorry about that, Doctor," the young clerk said. "I gave Widow Scudder a handout yesterday, half a loaf of bread, but she comes nearly every day now. The church do give her a stipend. She ought not to confront people on the street."

"She mentioned children."

"Aye, she took in orphans, you see. But they were poorly cared for, and the elders situated them with other families for their wellbeing."

A prudent move, as the old woman seemed muddled in the head. That wasn't uncommon for one of her advanced age. "Is there no one to care for her?"

The clerk frowned. "She will have none of it, other than her stipend and a handout when she can get one. But to move in with another? Nay. She will have none of that."

Proud then, as so many elderly were. William gave a mental snort. How far behind her in age was he? "I need a pouch of pipe tobacco." He slid his empty pouch across the counter to be filled.

"Certainly." The clerk moved down the counter and brought a canister out from storage underneath. He quoted William the price—substantially higher than in Boston—and William handed over the coins. Perhaps he should give up smoking, but it was the one luxury he enjoyed in the evenings. He tucked the pouch in his coat pocket and left the store.

Halfway to the tavern, the reverend charged in his direction.

"Ah, there you are. 'Tis the girls. Again." Reverend Parris panted and pointed back toward his house. "Make haste."

"I shall need my satchel from the tavern."

"Please, make haste to the girls. I shall fetch your things." The fear in the reverend's voice raised the hairs on William's neck.

An unearthly shriek greeted William when he burst through the Parris's door, out of breath. He rushed into the parlor, where Indian John, the Parris's male slave, physically restrained Abigail, the source of the shriek. Her hair was uncovered and unbound, flailing around in her struggles against the large man. Her eyes rolled back in her head, and her body stiffened as William approached, arching until he feared her spine might snap.

Without his satchel and its laudanum, there was little he could do. He grabbed her hand and chafed her wrist. "Abigail, do you hear me?" He had to shout to be heard over her screams. He tapped the back of her hand. "Abigail?" No response, but she'd ceased her fight with Indian John. William slapped her cheek softly. "Abigail?"

"Will she die?"

He turned at Betty's voice, who was curled into a ball, sitting on her haunches against the wall. "Will we both die?"

Leaving the unresponsive girl in the big man's arms, he knelt in front of Betty. "Did you have a fit this afternoon as well?"

She shook her head.

"Can you tell me what happened with Abigail?"

"She was seized again. I know not why I was spared this time." Then her eyes grew wild. "Or if I will be seized yet before 'tis over."

"Calm down, Betty." He took the child's hands. "No need to think that."

"Doctor?" Indian John called.

William glanced toward where the slave held Abigail upright. She'd gone completely limp. "Lay her on the floor." William got to his feet. "Well away from the hearth." They didn't need a repeat of her attempts to throw herself into the fire.

"Where is Goodie Parris?" he asked.

"Tituba took her upstairs with the little 'un. The lady be not well."

There was nothing William could do for the girls without laudanum, and he couldn't attend to the goodwife until the reverend arrived. He examined Abigail on the floor. She appeared to be in a deep sleep. Her heartbeat was strong and her breathing steady, even after the seizure, the apt word Betty had supplied.

But what—or who—had seized the girl?

Cotton Mather's book had offered only theological musings, no practical suggestions for combating this evil. Would it return for Betty or anyone else in the village?

And most importantly, how could it be stopped?

Chapter 15

"**F**ATHER?"

In the parlor, Caleb glanced up from sketches he'd been working on of a side table for the doctor's house.

Hannah Jr. paused in the doorway to the parlor.

Hannah rested nearby, her hand over the chair's arm, fingers stroking the long hair around Rags' ears. It was unusual for one of their children to return downstairs so late in the evening.

Hannah Jr. was an adult, of course, but the habits of the family were set.

"What is it?" he asked.

Their daughter carried a lantern, one that burned whale oil, the kind she preferred in the dairy because it gave better light than a candle. The lantern wasn't lit, but it trembled in her hand, and her shoulders were hunched as if under a weight.

"I fear I know how the fire started."

Caleb sat straighter, as did Hannah. Even Rags perked up.

"How?" he asked.

She held out the lantern. "There is a hole here." She pointed to a small opening where a seam in the reflective metal had worn through from age and use. "The evening of the fire, I had used the large push broom to clean the dairy. The last thing I did was return it. I had the lantern lit to show the way, since it was late and getting dark."

Caleb took the lantern from her. "A spark could have escaped from that. 'Tis a large enough opening, and walking while carrying it... 'Tis possible."

"Then the fire was my fault."

"Nay." Hannah rose and wrapped her arms around their daughter. The two being nearly the same height and coloring, the same in beauty and poise, they could almost be sisters.

"Thy mother is right." Caleb stood and joined them, one hand on a shoulder of each. "'Tis not thy fault."

"But if I had inspected the lantern—"

"'If wishes were horses, beggars would ride,'" Caleb quoted. "Thee have no fault nor error. Sometimes, things happen and we know not why. But God does. And He works all according to His will in the end."

"Even a fire that ruins the equipment thee need for the farm?" Hannah Jr.'s brows drew into a line. "I cannot understand such things."

"Nor do I." He gave a soft chuckle. "If we could, we would be gods ourselves, would we not?"

"I suppose so." Hannah Jr. looked between her mother and him. "But how will thee farm in the spring?"

"Thy father has taken on a client for carpentry work." Hannah kept her face toward their daughter. "'Twill more than supply our needs to replace the lost equipment."

Hannah Jr. gave them both a tremulous smile. "Then the Lord has already provided?"

Hannah remained silent, so Caleb answered. "I believe He has."

Hannah Jr. took the lantern. "I will take this to Stephan tomorrow and see if it can be repaired." She left the room, her shoulders straighter than when she'd entered.

Hannah followed her toward the door.

"Hannah?" he said.

She stopped and faced him, her hands clasped in front of her.

"Our daughter saw the Lord's hand in this. Can thee not see it now?"

"What of the meeting's decree? Does that mean nothing?"

"Of course it does." He stepped closer to her. "Yet they are but mortal men, doing their best. Only the Lord knows what is to come."

"And thee truly believe He brought this work to thy hands at this time? In spite of the potential danger to our family? To our whole community?"

"I do. I would not have agreed otherwise." He took her hands in his. "Never would I put money or possessions ahead of my family."

A half-sigh, half-sob slipped from her, and she pulled her hands free. "I know."

"I am glad to learn the fire wasn't arson, was not set by anyone who meant us harm." He left unsaid that it also hadn't been started by anything evil that might be stalking the village. "That is a relief."

Hannah turned and left the room.

Swallowing his frustration—or trying to—Caleb returned to his chair and picked up the sketch of the side table. With an effort, he squashed the urge to throw it across the room. How long was the fissure between them going to last?

"Any better today, Goodie Parris?" William entered the Parrises' bedroom, where the poor woman had lain for the past two days. Her pallor didn't encourage him, but her voice was reasonably steady when she answered.

"I believe so." She was seated upright with pillows behind her, blankets pulled high to keep her warm.

Half a cup of beef tea steamed on the bedside table, its savory aroma testifying to its strength and the slave woman having followed his instructions. Goodie Parris needed the fortifying brew. She was little more than a skeletal form beneath the covers.

"I want you to finish that cup before I leave." He pointed to it. "'Tis an important part of your getting well again."

"I will, but"—she gestured to the door—"how are my girls? Will they recover?"

While William had agreed with the reverend to keep the truth from his wife until she was stronger, it left him in a touchy position. "They are young and otherwise healthy. We have every reason to hope for the best." That was as good as he could do, for he would not lie to her.

He patted her knee, which was covered by the thick blanket. "I shall return again tomorrow to check on you."

"You will see the girls before you go?"

"Of course." He picked up his satchel. "Good day to you."

"Thank you again, Doctor, for everything."

He left the room and eased the door shut behind him. For everything? It was precious little. Goodie Parris had been allowed to decline for years. Why had the previous doctor not insisted on better nutrition? 'Twas easy enough to see her need. Although he suspected the birth of her last child, now aged four years, had been the start of her decline. Like too many women, she may have succumbed to the melancholia that followed childbirth. They would care for the child but not themselves, and in the end, would weaken in such a way.

Halfway down the stairs, a knock sounded on the front door. Its hinges creaked and a female voice said, "I must speak with Reverend Parris."

William didn't know enough of the village's residents to guess the owner, but the higher voice that answered was one of the girls.

William met the reverend at the bottom of the steps and followed him to the door. "Thank you, Betty. You may return to your studies." Her father dismissed the girl.

"Oh, Reverend Parris, I must speak with you." The distraught woman lowered her voice, glancing around them as if looking for someone before she continued. "I have done a dreadful thing."

The reverend rocked back on his heels. "Goodie Sibley, this is unexpected. Perhaps we should go to my office in the church."

"Indeed." She bobbed her head. "I believe 'twould be best."

He turned to William. "Thank you for coming."

"The doctor should hear what I have to say," the goodwife whispered, still glancing around as if fearing others would overhear.

"Ah. Well." The reverend cleared his throat. "If you wish. Doctor, have you the time?"

Affairs of the church were hardly his concern, but there was something about the woman's mysterious attitude that intrigued William, so he followed them out the door.

The frosty weather was on Caleb's side as he loaded the last of the bedstead parts into the wagon, which he'd fitted with runners after the night's snowfall. Thanks to the drop in temperature, the wagon would slide over the snow with less drag, making the drive into town easier on Dolly and Dandy. The matching team of sorrels was already harnessed and tied at the hitching rail, ready to go.

After three long days working in the shop, Caleb was ready to deliver the first of the doctor's furnishings, including the fancy side table. He rechecked the wooden pieces, some cushioned in blankets scorched from the fire so they wouldn't rub together and mark the beeswax and bayberry finish he'd rubbed into them.

"Father?" Hannah Jr. came across the snow toward him, a basket in her hands.

"What have thee there?"

"'Tis a gift basket for the new doctor and his family, some of my best cheeses and a towel I stitched."

"I am sure they will appreciate it." He took the offering from her and set it on the wagon's seat. "I will see thee get the basket returned."

"Actually." She tucked the edge of a shawl inside her heavy cloak. "I was hoping thee would allow me to ride along."

He hated to disappoint her. "Thee know we are trying to restrict interaction with the village."

"And yet, thee are going." Her clear blue eyes held no hint of censure or mockery. She was merely stating the fact. His no-nonsense daughter was like that. Perhaps a little more like him than was good for her.

He untied Dolly and brought her to the wagon, hitching her while he worked to find the right words. He didn't want to add to her lingering guilt over the fire. He repeated the process with Dandy and then turned to her.

"I am, and 'tis not without its risks."

"Then perhaps thee should not go alone."

So that was it. She worried for him, as he would worry for her should she manage to talk her way onto the wagon. "The sickness in the village—the evil, if what we suspect is true—has touched young girls, not old men."

"Thee are not that old, Father." She tilted her head at him. "And I am not that young."

She wasn't. She should be married and settled, but Hannah kept assuring him there was plenty of time for that. "What did thy mother say?" Because she wouldn't have left without making sure Hannah could spare her.

"She said 'twas up to thee."

Of course she had. Caleb was clearing his throat to disappoint his eldest when Robert came pelting across the barnyard, something in his hands. "Good. Thee have not yet left." His face, reddened by the cold, split into a wide grin. "May I come along and deliver this to Benjamin at the brewery?" He held out the project he'd been working on in Caleb's shop over the past few days, after his work on the wooden tool handles was done.

"I thought thee were making that for thyself." Caleb took the box, which was well-made if without any frills.

"I can make myself another. Benjamin has nothing like it to keep his buckles and whatnot in." Robert shrugged. "And he will know that I miss him." A touch of sadness crept into the boy's tone.

The situation in the village was hampering too much of their lives. If Caleb hadn't seen firsthand how out of control things could become—and how fast it could happen—he'd give in to Hannah and Robert both. But he had. And he couldn't risk it again.

"Thee both need to remain here." Neither argued, but the disappointed faces were almost harder to take. "I wish 'twere otherwise, I do, but things in the village are... Well, they are to be avoided as much as we can." He put his hand on Robert's shoulder. "Which is why Thomas brought thee home. 'Tisn't only my feelings on the matter."

Why Hannah Jr. appeared just as stricken, he wasn't sure.

He climbed onto the wagon. "I am sorry it must be this way, and I pray it shan't be for long." He clicked to the horses, who leaned into their harnesses. As he passed the house, the curtain at the kitchen window dropped back into place. Was Hannah satisfied that he'd left the children behind?

Or disturbed that he went on alone?

Still pondering those questions, Caleb halted the wagon in front of the doctor's house. He engaged the brake and was about to walk to the tavern when the doctor approached. "Good day to thee, Doctor. Thee must have seen me coming."

"What?" The older man looked confused, or maybe just distracted. Caleb repeated his greeting.

"Nay." He waved a hand in dismissal. "I left the church and saw you here."

In church on a Monday? But then, the Puritans might be meeting to discuss what they should do regarding the situation, as the Friends had done the previous week. "Shall I unload and assemble thy bedsteads?"

"Indeed." The doctor hurried over and opened the door. "Can I assist you with unloading?"

"No need." Caleb hefted the first piece and swung it over his shoulder. "'Twould be easier if I did it, since I know the order in which I shall need each bundle." A man of the doctor's age didn't need to be toting heavy wooden pieces.

It didn't take long to get everything inside. The doctor's wife and niece arrived as Caleb set down the final of four chairs he'd brought for them to borrow. "I brought thee an extra, should anyone stop by."

"Very thoughtful of you," the goodwife said.

"And I had time to fashion a small table to set between them." Caleb picked up the smaller piece he'd already brought in and positioned it between two of the chairs, then topped it with the basket from Hannah Jr. "The cheese is my daughter's handiwork. She is quite skilled in the dairy. She included a towel as a gift."

The goodwife sat on one of the chairs and traced the subtle carving Caleb had worked into the front panel of the table. Leaves and vines intertwined in a pattern that looked more complicated than it was. "'Tis beautiful. Thank you, Mr. Buffum."

"I am happy it pleases thee."

"'Tis good we finished sewing and stuffing the mattresses last night." The doctor's wife stood. "Elizabeth and I will return to the tavern and pack our things."

"If thee wishes, we can bring them here on my wagon when I have finished assembling the bedsteads."

"Very good. Come along, Elizabeth." The two women whisked out of the house with an air of purpose.

"What can I do to assist?" the doctor asked.

Caleb wanted to know the goings on in the village, but dare he ask? "Thee could hand me the tools as I need them. That would help. My son, Robert, would have come, but..." He let that thought run out. He shouldn't even have started it.

"Happy to help. 'Twill take my mind off of...of other things."

Caleb set to work assembling the first bed in the larger room upstairs. The room was light and airy with two windows, one overlooking the street. It was also cold. He stopped a couple of times to blow warm breath on his fingers.

"I am sorry to say I have no firewood yet."

Caleb grinned. "Perhaps thee should see to that before thy goodwife moves thee out of the tavern."

The older man chuckled. "'Twould be prudent."

"I have heard the brewer's son will help with firewood. As I must stop by the brewery on my way home, I would be happy to inquire for thee."

"That would be kind." The doctor leaned back against the wall and gazed out a window. "'Twill be good to solve at least one problem today."

The comment was an invitation to ask, so Caleb did. "Thee are speaking of the Parris children, are thee not?"

"Indeed. As is everyone in the village." The old man spread his arms and then let them drop to his sides. "'Tisn't anything I can help with."

A chill climbed Caleb's back. "An illness thee have not dealt with before?"

"Illness? Nay. You might as well know the full of it." The old man ran a hand across his unshaven face. "'Tis a bewitchment. The girls are bedeviled, for sure."

The confirmation of what he'd already known wasn't comforting in the least. He sat on the floor and looked up at the doctor. "Thee are sure?"

"Unfortunately so." He let loose a weary sigh. "I have never felt so helpless. And then just now"—he pointed down the street toward the church—"one of the goodwives came and admitted to a part in it."

The chill broke into a cold sweat. "What did she do?"

"She and the reverend's slave cooked up some idea of a witch cake and tried to feed it to a poor dog. The beast wanted no part of that and"—the doctor leaned over and peered at Caleb"—are you all right, Mr. Buffum? You have gone white as the snow."

"I saw them." The words came out before Caleb could think. He might as well finish it. "In the forest, the slave woman and another with an old hound."

"'Tis true then." The doctor shook his head and looked away. "I had almost convinced myself she was telling a story, as sometimes people do, to get attention." Then he snapped back to Caleb. "Your community, the Quakers, they live outside of the village, do they not?"

"We live on farms and homesteads nearby."

The old man squatted down to Caleb's eye level. "Has there been anything unusual happening among your people? The young girls especially? Any sort of a fit or seizure. Anything you cannot explain?"

Caleb leaned back, fear drying his throat. "Nay. Nothing of that sort." Had Hannah been right? Was he bringing suspicion on their community just by delivering and assembling furniture? His heart rapped against his ribs like a woodpecker on a dead tree. "We are fine."

"'Tis glad I am to hear it." The doctor pushed back to his feet. "One family stricken is one too many."

"What will thee do?" Caleb rose and dusted off the seat of his breeches.

"Reverend Parris has sent word to two other ministers to come and pray with him over the girls. As 'tis a spiritual battle, that is the best course of action."

"Indeed, 'twould seem so."

"If thee will excuse me. I must speak with the good reverend and tell him that you have confirmed the woman's testimony."

"Nay." Caleb took hold of the man's arm, but let go immediately, flustered. "Pardon. I ask that thee do not mention my name to the reverend, or anyone else."

The doctor removed his spectacles, wiped them off, and replaced them. "What do you fear, man?"

What did he fear? Torched houses and barns, flames high against the night sky, and men armed with muskets, mounted on horses and hunting the Friends. The images were burned into Caleb's memory. "I fear for my family and the entire community of Friends—those thee call Quakers—should a finger of suspicion be pointed our way."

Chapter 16

T HE CHURCH STOOD FIRM against the cold blasts of winter air that buffeted William as he approached, one hand on his hat to keep it from flying off, the other clutching his medical satchel. He'd received a summons, via John Indian, to appear at the church. He chafed at the situation.

Rachel was cooking their first breakfast in the new house. He should be lounging at the table, watching her, enjoying the aromas in anticipation of her offering. The way a retired man would do.

He should not feel obligated to be at Reverend Parris's beck and call. After all, he'd moved here to retire, and even though the situation with the bewitched girls was dire, there was nothing he could do about it. It was a spiritual issue—not medical—therefore it was the purview of people like the reverend.

With those disgruntled thoughts, he pulled the door open against another blast of frigid air and entered. The door slammed shut behind him.

"Doctor, I am glad you are able to join us." Reverend Parris ushered William through the church building to his office in back. "Let me introduce you to Reverend John Hale of Beverley and to Reverend Nicholas Noyes of Salem Town. Gentlemen, this is our newly arrived doctor, William Griggs."

The men rose, and they exchanged the usual greetings. Reverend Hale lived up to his name, a hale and hearty appearance not wanting for a meal. Reverend Noyes was his exact opposite, somewhat frail with a sallow complexion that said he lacked the health and well-being of his robust counterpart.

"The reverends have come at my request"—Reverend Parris motioned them all to be seated—"to pray over the girls in an attempt to exorcise the evil that has overcome them time and again."

"What use am I in this?" William took a seat next to Reverend Noyes in the cramped office.

"We asked to speak with you regarding your diagnosis." Reverend Hale's voice filled the room, as large and impressive as his physical appearance.

William bristled at the tone that indicated he may have been in error. It was one thing to question himself, quite another to be questioned by one unlearned in the physical sciences.

"Not to question it." Reverend Noyes raised a thin hand, his voice much quieter. "But to understand how you came to the conclusion, or perhaps better put, what possible physical things you eliminated to arrive at your decision. So that, should this spread or emerge elsewhere, we have a basis of understanding to work with."

William forced himself to relax. The request was reasonable when stated that way. But spread? Surely not. Bewitchment or bedevilment, however one worded it, was not a contagion as they understood such things.

He walked them through the process of his determination, including his research sources. Both men seemed impressed with his knowledge of Cotton Mather's opinions, nodding along when he spoke about that. When he finished, he laced his fingers in front of his belly and waited for them to digest all he'd said.

"In light of all this," Reverend Noyes said, "I believe the doctor's diagnosis is correct."

Reverend Hale nodded, his chin quivering beneath his fleshy jawline. "A perfectly reasonable assumption, and perfectly frightening. You were quite right to call us in on this, Samuel. Quite right, indeed. 'Tis a matter for the church to address."

"A matter of prayer, first," Reverend Noyes said. "Will you bring the girls in here, or should we attend to them in your house?"

Reverend Parris stood. "Let us go to the house. The girls will be more at ease there."

"Of course." The other two reverends rose.

William also stood. "If you will excuse me, gentlemen—"

"Please, doctor." Reverend Parris turned to him. "Join us. Should the girls become distraught, they may require your medications."

Though William wanted to return home to his breakfast, the reverend made a valid point. "Very well." He followed the rest out into the wind and across the churchyard to the house beyond.

Betty and Abigail were already in the parlor. The older girl held four-year-old Susannah on her lap. Betty worked her letters in a piece of linen cloth. Tommy, the Parris's only son, read aloud from a book. It was good that the reverend saw to the education of his children. William approved of both girls and boys learning to read and write. Ignorance was a situation easily remedied in their tender years.

Tituba entered with a tray containing a large teapot, cups, and some variety of tarts. She must have been expecting them.

Reverend Parris introduced the other pastors to his children.

"Where is Goodie Parris?" asked Reverend Hale.

"She is unwell this morning." Reverend Parris looked at William, a weary acceptance etched on his face.

"I will see to her when we are done here." Even though there was little William could do other than encourage the woman to eat and drink, especially the fortifying beef tea that he'd already prescribed.

William half listened as the girls told their stories and half brooded about Goodie Parris and what else he might do for her. He focused on the conversation again when the reverends started asking pointed questions.

"Have you seen anything—or anyone—actually pinch, poke, or bite you?" boomed Reverend Hale.

"I have." Abigail rose, set Susannah on her feet, and pointed at Tituba who stood with her back to the wall near the doorway that led to the kitchen. "It was Tituba."

Betty rose as well. "She told me stories of evil things." Tears welled in the girl's blue eyes. "And she forbade me to tell anyone, or something bad would happen to me."

Tituba remained standing, her face the expressionless mask a servant wore, giving no indication that she'd even heard the girls.

"What is this, Tituba?" Reverend Parris faced his slave woman. "Is it true?"

"I have told the girls stories to entertain them. Stories from my childhood."

"Stories of witches and evil spirits," Abigail said.

Bedlam broke out, filling the house with voices. William couldn't follow all the questions that flowed.

Goodie Parris, still wearing her nightcap and wrapped in a blanket, entered the room.

John Indian also entered. There was barely room to turn around in the small parlor.

Then Goodie Parris collapsed into a chair.

"Take her back to her room." William picked up his satchel and squeezed around bodies to reach the door, following Reverend Parris, whose wife was in his arms, up the staircase. Once her husband laid her on the bed, William bent over her. She was breathing well, her heartbeat a little erratic beneath his fingertips on her neck. Then her eyelids fluttered.

"What happened?" She tried to rise.

"Rest easy." William put gentle pressure on her shoulder. "You swooned, and you need to recover."

"My girls. What is happening to my girls?"

"That is what we are trying to find out, my dear." Reverend Parris moved closer, and William backed out of the way. "But you must rest, as the doctor said."

"Will you send the children to me?"

"I will send Tommy and Susannah straight away. Betty and Abigail, we need to question first, I think. Then I will send them up as well."

She clung to her husband's hand. "Will they be all right?"

"If the Lord wills it. Now I must return below." Reverend Parris left the room.

"You need to take care of yourself." William moved back to the bedside. "Have you been drinking the beef tea three times a day?"

"Maybe, I am not sure."

By the weakness of her voice, he doubted it. "Goodie Parris, I can do nothing for you if you will not follow my instructions."

She nodded but didn't look at him. Frustration clawed his insides. There was nothing he could do here, either upstairs or down.

He remained with the poor woman until the younger children arrived, then he picked up his satchel and fled the house, the booming voice of Reverend Hale's prayer over the girls following him out into the cold. *Please, Lord, heal them of this evil. Spare the town an outbreak as happened in Boston in 1688.* He was too old and too tired to go through anything like that here in Salem Village.

The wind had calmed enough throughout the day that Caleb heard the jingle of harness. He went to the shop's window in time to see David hop off his wagon and speak to Robert, who had met him outside. The boy took hold of the horses and led them to the hitching rail. Caleb returned to the table he was working on, rubbing in the beeswax and bayberry finish, which brought the rich woodgrain to life.

Entering the shop with a basket in his hands, David pulled in an exaggerated breath. "I love the smell of bayberry."

"Good afternoon to thee as well." Caleb grabbed a rag and wiped his hands.

"Did I not greet thee first?" David's grin was infectious. "'Tis entirely thy own fault for making such a good-smelling wax." He put a fingertip on the tabletop and whistled between his teeth. "'Tis like touching a pane of glass."

Caleb snorted. "Hardly, but thank thee all the same."

"'Tis for the doctor, I assume."

"His goodwife is very particular in what she wants, but she has good taste, I will say."

"Aye. 'Tis a beauty to behold. I told them rightly when I said thee made the best furniture in the colony."

Caleb tossed aside the rag and moved the stools closer to the brazier. "So why am I getting compliments from thee today?"

David dropped onto the opposite stool. "Thee get compliments because thee earn them, but I speak lightly while I can, for I have heavier news to deliver." He handed over the basket. "But first, I am to return Hannah Jr.'s basket from the brewery. She left it behind on her last delivery there."

"Thee finished the matching fowling pieces for Thomas's sons then?"

"Nay. I needed to ask a question on the particulars. Then he gave me the heavy news."

Caleb waited, since David's storytelling had only one speed.

"'Twould seem the good reverend called up two other pastors from neighboring towns this morning. The doctor has determined the Parris girls' affliction is of the spirit and not the body."

"I heard the same from the doctor himself just yesterday when I delivered the bedsteads."

David's brows rose. "And thee kept that to thyself?"

"We had already come to the same conclusion, had we not?" Caleb rubbed the back of his neck. Even talking about witchcraft without using the word caused the hairs there to tingle.

"We did, but the doctor has confirmed it now. That makes it more"—he shrugged—"more real."

"I fear 'tis very real indeed."

Caleb didn't wish to discuss the village issues anymore, and it seemed David was of the same mind. They changed the topic of conversation to the weather, the likelihood of a late planting of crops due to the recent heavy snows, and a new musket David had taken an order for that would require some intricate detailing the purchaser desired carved into the stock.

After his friend left, Caleb put Hannah Jr.'s basket on the workbench. He tossed in a handful of rags that needed washing, and something crinkled. Caleb removed the rags and lifted the checkered cloth with which his daughter had lined the basket. A folded sheet of paper, sealed with a blob of wax, sat on the bottom. He picked it up and turned it over. *Hannah Jr.* was written in bold strokes across the other side.

Caleb tapped the paper against the palm of his hand and gazed toward the house. What had Hannah been trying to tell him a couple of weeks ago about their eldest daughter? They hadn't quite gotten to her point when they'd been interrupted, but Hannah had been leading up to the interest of a young man, Caleb was fairly certain.

Could it be one of David's boys? His eldest was a couple of years younger than Hannah Jr. and the next eldest born just a year after him. Both old enough to start looking for a wife.

That didn't make sense. David had said he'd come straight from town. Unless, of course, he was in on it and had stowed the note there for one of his sons, which would be like him. Caleb wouldn't be against a marriage between their families. But he'd never noticed Hannah Jr. paying special attention to either of those young men, despite their sister, Mary, being one of her best friends.

Who else could it be?

He slipped the note back in its hiding place and set the rags on top. It was past time for his daughter to settle on a young man and start her own family. Caleb Jr. was just four years behind her at age eighteen. If she didn't hurry up, he'd find a wife before she was settled. Not that he was in a hurry for any of their children to move on, but he wouldn't mind being a grandfather someday.

After another hour of rubbing finish into the table, he cleaned his shop and took the brazier outside to burn itself out in a snowbank. While it hadn't been the cause of the fire, he wasn't taking any chances. The old saying "once bitten, twice shy" had taken on a whole new level of meaning after the fire.

At the house, he stomped the snow from his boots and entered the back room off the kitchen, greeted by Rags and Button. He had to push their noses out of the way to bend over and get his boots off. Coat hung on its peg, he entered the kitchen that smelled of cinnamon—his favorite.

"Who has been baking for me?" He made a show of sucking in the spicy fragrance.

"Verity," Tamson piped up. "She made us cinnamon scones with currants, and they are delightful."

Caleb crossed his arms and cocked his head. "I think I should be the judge of that."

Verity giggled, then sliced a piece and handed it to him, gray eyes wide and expectant.

He held the delicate pastry high, examined it, sniffed it, and then took a pinch between his finger and thumb and popped it in his mouth. He hummed while he chewed, eyes half closed, while Verity clasped her hands beneath her chin and Tamson bounced on her toes. Even the young boys were paying close attention.

"I do believe that is one of the best cinnamon scones I have ever tasted. Well done, Verity."

The girls hugged and chattered while Hannah crossed the kitchen and squeezed his arm. "Thank thee for that," she whispered. "She was hoping to please thee."

"Was she the only one? Did thee not coach her on my favorite?"

"Tamson did." Hannah held out her hand. "Let me take the basket."

He suppressed a sigh of disappointment that she hadn't been involved in making the treat for him. "Nay, 'tis fine. I shall give it over to Hannah Jr." He glanced around the room. "Where is our eldest?"

"She went upstairs to change after Jonathan spilled a cup of milk on her lap."

Ignoring his wife's puzzled expression, he headed up the stairs, meeting Hannah Jr. in the second-floor hallway. "I have something for thee. David brought it back from the village." He held out the basket. "And a few rags that could use a good washing when thee have time."

"Of course. I shall wash them with the rest on Thursday." She showed no particular interest in the basket, nothing to show she was expecting the note.

That deepened the mystery, but he wasn't going to pry. She was an adult, after all, and she'd never been in any way indiscreet. He had no fear that she'd start now.

Later, he would ask Hannah what she knew about it, for surely his goodwife was more perceptive to matters of the heart than he was. He'd clearly demonstrated that when he'd gone against Hannah's wishes and stoked her fears. How much longer would he have to pay the price for that?

Chapter 17

A GENERAL MEETING AT the church had been called by the elders for that Wednesday evening. William blew on his fingers to warm them as they took a seat in their box to wait for everyone to arrive. Rachel had thought to bring a blanket, which she unfolded and spread across their laps. Elizabeth sat on the opposite side of the box and unfolded her own blanket. The church should consider putting in a fireplace or two, hazard or no. The older he got, the more the cold settled in his bones.

Once families were seated in their boxes and the single people on the benches that outlined the room, two of the elders and Reverend Parris walked the steps up to the pulpit. When the reverend raised his arms, the gathering quieted.

"Thank you for coming on such a cold evening." His words frosted the air, making his appearance almost ghostly. Hardly the image anyone needed considering the gravity of the situation. "'Tis our intent to share the details of what has happened in our midst." Pain cut through the man's voice, as well it should. How difficult it must be for him, their spiritual leader, to have to admit to what was happening in his own household. It was sure to bring on condemnation or at least finger-pointing from some among the congregation.

"As many of you already know, two pastors from the area came to our village yesterday and consulted with me on what has happened to my daughter and niece." He inclined his head toward the box where the girls sat with their brother and the slave woman.

Why had the reverend allowed that woman to come into the church? And to sit with his children? Perhaps, with Goodie Parris confined to her bed, he'd had no other option. But after Tituba's confession of telling the girls stories of witches and evil spirits the day before, her presence made William uneasy.

"'Tis been determined that the girls have been tormented by an evil spirit, perhaps even the specter of someone here in the village."

A gasp went up from those assembled, and people turned to look at their neighbors in the other boxes.

A specter? When had that been discussed? Clearly not until after William had left. But why had the reverend said it? Did he not understand it could induce a hysteria? The people of the village were uneasy enough without putting additional fears upon them.

The reverend went on to describe what had happened, when it started, and what had been tried to date, ending with the lengthy prayers of the visiting pastors before they left the day before. He asked for more prayers from the church body. They collectively bowed their heads, and then—

Abigail rose, clutched her hands to her throat with a loud moan, and then dropped to the floor of her box, writhing.

Tituba knelt at her side.

Gathering their children in their arms, the surrounding women backed away. Voices rose until it was hard to distinguish who said what.

Reverend Parris slapped the pulpit and called for quiet—but was ignored.

Then Elizabeth rose and clutched the front of her cape, swaying as if unsteady.

The poor girl must be traumatized after everything that had happened. Being rejected by Hezekiah, the move from Boston, the disaster with the house, waiting to move in with only the minimum of luxuries, and all the talk of witches, it was too much for her to bear.

She looked at William and opened her mouth, took a small step back, and then sank to the floor.

"Elizabeth!" Rachel knelt beside the girl before William could un-tangle himself from the blanket and join her.

Back arching, eyes rolling toward the top of her skull, a low moan escaped Elizabeth's lips.

"Do something, William." Rachel's eyes pleaded with him.

Never had he felt so helpless.

"Ann Jr. is down too!" someone shouted.

Two boxes over, another was a flurry of activity, an older woman knelt on the floor with a girl.

What was happening?

William pressed his hand to his chest against the dull pain that nagged him there. "I did not bring my satchel," he said in a low tone to Rachel. "The girls would benefit from a dose of laudanum. 'Tis the only thing that calmed the others."

Someone touched William's shoulder through the slats that separat-ed them from the next box. "I could run and fetch it." It was a Buffington boy, one of the twins who had brought them firewood. "Tell me where to find it in your house."

"Hanging on a peg near the door. 'Tis the only one."

"I shall run." The young man sprinted from the building.

Even with young legs, it took him several minutes to return. In that time, Betty had also fallen into a fit. Once the medication arrived, William went from girl to girl and dosed them.

When some semblance of order was restored, Reverend Parris, ashen-faced at the pulpit, raised his hands again. "As you can see, something is tormenting these girls, and now I fear 'tis spreading. If we can but discern the source of—"

Elizabeth rose from the floor of their box and pointed a finger at Tituba. "'Tis her!"

"And more than her." the one called Ann Jr. also climbed unsteadily to her feet. "I saw Sarah Good amongst us. She did torment me."

A gasp rippled through the building.

And then the room went eerily silent.

Who was this Sarah Good? William hadn't met her. He glanced around the room, but no one stood to defend herself.

"Beside Sarah Good was Sarah Osborne and Widow Scudder." Ann Jr. held the sides of her head and moaned.

Rachel grabbed Elizabeth's hand, urging her to be seated as William returned to their box. Rachel wore as stark an expression as he'd ever seen. "What is happening?" she whispered in a ragged voice. "Who are those women?"

"I know not." Although, he'd heard the name Scudder before. Ah, yes. The old woman who had bemoaned the loss of her orphan children.

"Someone should bring those women here. Now," shouted one of the elders behind Reverend Parris.

That brought a whole new level of chaos to the room until the reverend once again raised his arms and slapped the pulpit, shouting for order. "The girls have been given a draught to calm them. Let us return them to homes and beds. We can meet here again tomorrow afternoon."

"Reverend." Ingersoll stood. "'Tis much warmer in my tavern's public room, what with the fireplace and all. Let us meet there and speak in some degree of comfort with those who are afflicted and their immediate families."

"And the accused women." Mr. Putnam rose and shook his fist. "These girls should face their tormentors. We should be allowed to question them."

"'Tis decided then. Tomorrow an hour past noon at Ingersoll's." With that, the reverend and elders descended from the pulpit.

William took Elizabeth by the arm while Rachel went to her other side. "Come, my dear. Let us get you home and abed."

If only a good sleep would make all of this go away—the accusations, the fear in his wife's eyes, and the pressure that was building in his chest.

With the helping hands of both Caleb Jr. and Robert, Caleb had more furniture ready to deliver to the doctor sooner than he could have managed on his own. He clicked his tongue to get Dolly and Dandy moving. Twin plumes of white lifted above their heads, breath frosting in the crispness of the morning, hooves squeaking in the new inches of powdery snow. The frozen surface was helpful to deliver these two heavy pieces of furniture to the doctor. If it were muddy, the pull would be harder on the horses, and with Dolly drawing near her time to foal, he wished to be careful with her.

Should their family need to flee their home too soon after the foal's birth, Caleb would hate the decision he'd have to make. He wouldn't risk the well being of his wife and children. A newborn foal couldn't keep up, and the mare wouldn't leave a living foal behind. He sighed, sending more frosty breath into the air.

So many things could go wrong. So many repercussions could reach them.

Since their conversation three days prior when he'd delivered the bedsteads, Caleb believed he'd built some degree of understanding with the doctor. The man didn't look down on Caleb and seemed genuinely interested in the health and wellbeing of the Friends. Then there was Thomas. He might also speak for the Friends' community should it come down to that. But two Puritans against the rest? The odds weren't in their favor.

The village street was empty when he arrived, which was strange for that time in the afternoon. Or would have been, before the girls had started having fits. Caleb passed windows with curtains still drawn and businesses that should be open—but weren't. He stopped the team in front of the doctor's house and set the brake before climbing down and knocking on the door.

It opened, and the doctor looked out, blinking behind his spectacles. His hair was mussed, dark circles shadowed his eyes, and his waistcoat was as rumpled as if he'd slept in it. "Oh. Mr. Buffum. Caleb." The older man pushed his spectacles up and pinched the bridge of his nose. "I was not expecting you this morning."

"If 'tis a poor time, I could return another day."

Shaking his head, the man peered beyond Caleb. "Nonsense, you have the wagon loaded and here. Do you need my help unloading?"

The doctor's condition made the answer easy. "I believe I will ask the brewer to loan me one of his strapping sons for a hand. The sideboard is especially heavy." He took a step back. "I shall return shortly."

The doctor waved a hand in acknowledgement and closed the door.

The brewery wasn't far down the street, so Caleb left the wagon and walked. Unlike several other businesses he passed, the brewery was open, its rich aromas of roasting barley, steeping hops, and tangy apple cider swirling around him when he opened the door. "Hello?" There was no one in sight until Thomas emerged from a back room.

"Caleb Buffum!" His booming voice filled the space. "Have you brought any more of those delicious cheeses your daughter makes, by chance?"

"I am sorry to say I have not." He should have though to inquire before he left, but his mind had been on weightier matters.

"Well, then, what can I do for you today?"

"I should like to hire one of thy sons to assist me in unloading furniture for the new doctor's family. The poor man hardly looks fit for the exertion this morning."

Thomas's normally jovial countenance fell away. "I can imagine that is so, after yesterday."

A chill crept up Caleb's neck. "Yesterday?"

"Aye. 'Twas bad." Thomas held up a finger. "Let me get us both a mug of cider, and I will tell you what happened. Have a seat." He pointed to a pair of benches that faced each other near the fireplace.

Although part of him just wanted to be on his way and finish the job, the other part wanted to hear Thomas out, so Caleb took a seat. Thomas joined him, passing over a brown mug, that steamed with the aromas of apples, cinnamon, and cloves. Caleb took a sip. The mixture was sweet and tart and tangy all at once, its warmth chasing the chill away.

"Last evening, we met at the church to discuss the"—Thomas leaned forward and lowered his voice—"the charge of witchcraft in our midst. You may not have heard of that yet."

"I have."

"Ah. Bad news travels the fastest, as they say. It came to a head last night, and two more girls cried aloud that they were being tormented. And then"—Thomas sat back, glanced out the window—"they named their tormentors, that slave woman of the Parris household, Sarah Good, Sarah Osborne, and Widow Scudder."

Caleb's mouth dried despite the cider. Names. All Puritans, but still, they were naming people as—as witches. The chill came back, wreaking havoc with the hairs on his neck and spreading to his chest.

And Widow Scudder? The woman who had cared for Verity before she came to them. Would that tie their family to what was happening in the village? It took all he had to remain seated and not bolt for the wagon and send it racing back to the farm.

"I can see I have shocked you." Thomas raised his mug as if in a toast, and then drained it. "I can assure you, we were all shocked. *Are* all shocked. The whole village."

"I can imagine." Caleb's mind reeled with all the ways this might impact his family—especially Verity—and the Friends. Thoughts raced too fast for him to even separate them.

"And one of those young women afflicted last evening was the doctor's own niece, Elizabeth Hubbard." Thomas set his mug aside and slapped his hands to his knees. "So you will understand that I will not allow my sons to enter that house. However, I shall assist you myself. The good doctor's family will need their furnishings. 'Twas a crime how the last resident cheated them. If we in the village had but known the details of their arrangement, we could have stopped him. But alas, we did not."

"I would appreciate thy assistance, if thee are sure."

Some of the good humor returned to the brewer's face. "At my age, I doubt any witch would bother about me. 'Twould seem only the young are at risk." Then he sobered again. "'Tis glad I am to have returned young Robert to your care." He glanced at the door to the back room. "I fear for the orphan boy, Joseph. Fingers are pointing toward the village's outcasts, I fear. And with him having been in Widow Scudder's care, he might be singled out."

What prompted him, Caleb couldn't be sure, but he said, "Would thee like me to take the boy until this passes?"

"Would you? Your goodwife would not mind?"

Another mouth to feed, but they were in no danger of starving. And Hannah would take in any child in need. Even another Puritan. Would the village see that as a noble gesture? Or was this another way to trip them up in the eyes of their neighbors? Either way, it was too late to call back his offer.

"'Twould be no problem at all. We can squeeze him into the older boys' room."

"Joseph!" Thomas bellowed toward the back room.

The boy popped his head around the corner of the doorway, straw-colored hair poking out from under his cloth cap. "Aye?"

"Come here, boy." Thomas pointed to Caleb. "You remember Caleb Buffum, I assume."

"Aye, sir. How is Verity?" His blue eyes were sincere, so the attachment between the orphans remained.

"She does well and speaks of thee often."

He grinned, exposing a gap between his front teeth.

"Joseph, I think it best if you were to go with Mr. Buffum for a while, until things calm down here in the village."

"Because of the witches?"

Thomas made a shushing motion with his hands. "Best not to toss that word around, my boy. Discretion is in order."

Joseph nodded, but his brow wrinkled in either question or confusion.

"I am to assist Mr. Buffum for a bit," Thomas said. "You go and pack what you need, planning to stay for some time. When we return, you will join him and see your little friend Verity again."

The grin returned, but it was hesitant. "Will I ever return here?"

"Indeed." Thomas stood and clasped the boy's shoulder in a meaty hand. "You are going to make a fine brewer. We cannot lose a boy of your talents to a farm, now can we"—he turned to Caleb and winked—"Caleb Buffum?"

Caleb rose. "I should say not."

Relief filled the boy's expression before he scampered off to pack his things.

"A fine boy. He will be no trouble to you."

Caleb followed as Thomas strode out the door and down the street. *No trouble to you.* If only the rest of the Puritans would follow suit and bring no trouble their way.

Chapter 18

U NLOADING THE TABLE AND sideboard took no time at all with Thomas's help. The doctor had murmured his appreciation, but his goodwife and niece had not come downstairs. Which was probably for the best. Not that Caleb feared the evil spirits taking him over. *For greater is He that is in you, than He that is in this world.* In the earthly world, Caleb would fear the evil of his fellow humans, but in the spiritual world, he was covered by the Light of Christ.

By the time Caleb stopped the team in front of the brewery and Thomas had climbed down, Joseph had popped out the door with a sack across his shoulder.

"Mind your manners and do as they say," Thomas told the boy, who grinned wide before climbing onto the wagon and joining Caleb on the high seat.

"Next time I come to the village," Caleb said—although it may be a long time with more girls having fits—"I will not forget the cheese."

"I shall look forward to that." Thomas raised a hand in farewell before disappearing inside.

"Well, then, young man." Caleb slapped the reins on the broad rumps of Dolly and Dandy. "We should be back in time for supper."

"With cheese?"

Caleb chuckled at the eagerness in his voice. "Thee might get tired of cheese before thee are done with us. 'Twould seem to be what we have the most of."

"I could never get tired of cheese, especially Hannah Jr.'s. 'Tis the best I have ever eaten."

They finished the rest of the trip in a companionable silence broken only when a trio of deer, a doe with last spring's fawns, crossed the road in front of them. Caleb drove to the barn, and Robert came out to help with the horses.

"Joseph." Robert stopped, open-mouthed.

"Tend to the horses for me"—Caleb climbed down from the wagon—"while I explain to thy mother why she must make up a pallet in your room."

"He is staying?" Robert's brows rose to touch the knit cap covering his hair.

"For a while." Caleb sighed. "For the same reason as thee."

"'Tis bad in the village then?"

Caleb looked between the two boys. Joseph was the younger but wise beyond his years. "I am sure Joseph will fill thee in on the details." He headed for the house.

Hannah was in the parlor with Jonathan and Benji, who were cuddled together, napping on a quilt on the floor. She touched her finger to her lips when he reached the doorway, then set her knitting aside and came to him. With a gentle touch, she led him back to the kitchen, which was quiet for once.

"Where are the girls?"

"In the dairy." She turned to face him. "What has happened?"

Was it written on his face? Or had twenty-three years of marriage made him transparent to her? He related what he'd learned in the village, and she didn't interrupt.

"Caleb, this frightens me." Her voice was low. "Will we need to flee again?"

"I know not. I do not wish to leave Salem Village. 'Twould be complicated now, with so many of us. Oh." He tipped his head in the direction of the barn. "And one more. Thomas sent young Joseph home with me. 'Twould seem that those being accused as witches are the outcasts of the village."

"And he being an orphan boy..."

Caleb nodded. "I knew thee would not mind."

"Mind?" She crossed her arms. "Does not the Lord say in the Bible that we are to look after the widow and the orphan?"

"Indeed, He does. But thee should know, Widow Scudder is one of those accused of witchcraft."

Hannah touched his arm, her blue eyes growing troubled. "Accusing the widow might point a finger at our family, now that we have two of her orphans with us. Some might think the children tainted by her."

"Since we have Verity, we were already in that situation."

"Where is Joseph now?"

"With Robert, putting the team away. And since they are already friends, who knows what mischief they shall get up to next."

"Perhaps we should put them all to work these next days." She tapped her bottom lip with one finger.

"He can help me in the shop with the other boys." Caleb shrugged. "There is only so much one can do in February."

"We can prepare this time. Pack the things we would most need and have them ready to grab at a moment's notice. The girls and I can bake hardtack, boil down portable soup, and sew small sacks to store and transport our dried provisions. The boys can hunt for meat to dry at the hearth."

His ever-practical wife was, as usual, a step or two ahead of him.

She looked into his eyes. "To where would we run?"

That was a question he'd pondered since the first whiff of danger. The hostile Indian risk was north and west of them. East was the ocean. That left the south, but could they leave their troubles behind if they went in that direction? After all, Puritan Boston had been the site of the last witch trials and was no advocate for the Friends. To go farther, to Connecticut Colony or even Virginia Colony, would take weeks, if not months of travel. Spring would be upon them soon, and the roads often impassible with rain and mud.

The short answer to her question, he didn't know. But north or west toward the Indians would mean they'd be less likely to be followed and dragged back to stand trial—and possibly hang. Some Indians were starting to recognize the Friends as people who respected them and would deal fairly with them. But many didn't. In that direction, his family faced the possibility of a violent attack. Was that any better than hanging? What a horrible choice to have to make.

William arrived at Ingersoll's Tavern with Rachel and Elizabeth shortly after noon. Making his way through the wall of people, he led them to the benches nearest the roaring hearth, where Betty and Abigail were already seated next to Reverend Parris. The man was pale, elbows on his knees, his hands jittering where they dangled. He was the picture of a man who wished authority rested on anyone else at that moment.

The elders were seated off to one side.

The Putnams arrived with Ann Jr. and took their places on the benches. As crowded as the tavern was, space opened up around the afflicted girls and their families. Nobody wanted to be too close.

A woman's voice rose outside, angry and shouting. When the door opened, William rose to see who it was. Two of the church elders held between them a woman of middle age, disheveled, and dressed in clothing that had seen better days. She continued to spew words at them, cursing them both, until they wrestled her through the crowd and stopped in the open space before the benches.

"Sarah Good, you have been accused of using witchcraft to torment these girls," one of the elders said. "What say you?"

William sank to the bench again, the pressure in his chest stealing his breath.

"I do not know these girls." The woman sneered at them. "Why do you drag me out of my bed to accuse me of this?" She tilted her head to her right.

Abigail and then Betty tilted their heads to the right as well. Then Elizabeth and Ann Jr. followed.

William leaned over and looked into Elizabeth's face. "What is happening?"

"Something is pushing against my head," she said.

One of the other girls cried out in agreement.

Sarah Good tilted her head to the left, and all four girls did the same.

A gasp filled the room, then a riotous collection of voices, too many and too fast to be understood.

"We should take her home." William leaned close enough for Rachel alone to hear. She nodded, so he stood again and took Elizabeth by the arm.

"Where are you going?" asked the reverend.

"Whatever is happening here, 'tis not healthy. I am taking our niece home where I can tend to her."

Reverend Parris objected, but William ignored him and the rest of the voices around them. The crowd parted as if no one wished to come in contact.

That was fine. William simply wanted out. The stifling atmosphere, the heat from hearth and all those bodies crammed together—it was too much. He opened the door and stepped out into the cold, dragging in a cleansing breath.

Without a word, he took his family home. The others could figure out what was happening back there. It wasn't medical, that much he knew, and whatever else it was, it could happen without him. And his wife and his niece. He wanted nothing more to do with any of it.

If only they had stayed in Boston.

A knock on the door interrupted William's evening meal. As a physician, one came to expect such interruptions, but after the meeting at Ingersoll's, the sound brought a lump of dread to his throat. He rose from the beautiful table they had only taken possession of that morning. It was a shame to spoil their first family meal shared on it.

"Excuse me."

Rachel gave him an understanding nod, but Elizabeth didn't look up. She pushed the meat around on her plate, which she'd been doing since they'd finished the prayer. Thank goodness the strange sensations had left her as soon as they'd stepped from the tavern.

William opened the door to a young man in his early thirties who wore an anxious expression. "Dr. Griggs?"

"Please, step in out of the cold." William moved aside to make way, and then shut the door.

"Thank you, doctor." The young man took off his hat. "We have not met yet. I am John Biddle, the village cooper." The man was tall and thin with blond hair tied back with a black ribbon and blue eyes behind a pair of spectacles.

"A pleasure to meet you, Mr. Biddle. What can I do for you?"

"'Tis our youngest, Patsy. The missus is worried about her, what with her not breathing right."

William slipped his coat from its peg in the hall and called back to Rachel, "I shall return when I can." Then he took up his satchel that he kept by the door. "I have no horse or buggy yet."

"Our house is just down the street. This way." The energetic young man took off at a half-run.

"Whoa there," William called after him. "I cannot move so fast as that."

"My apologies." Mr. Biddle rushed back. "'Tis only that our children have been so healthy until now."

"I understand." He asked questions as they walked to keep the man's attention focused. There were four children in the house, including an older orphan girl they'd taken in to help with the three young ones and another babe due come spring. The girl with the breathing problem was only a year old, which worried William. Problems in the lungs at that age were difficult to overcome. Despite all William could do for them, so many children died before they reached their second birthday.

They entered a house similar to the one William had purchased, except it was far more crowded. Goodie Biddle took his coat and then showed him to an upper bedchamber where an older girl with blond hair sat next to his patient in a wooden cradle. The child was covered with a colorful quilt.

The girl stood and offered him the only chair in the room. William sat and peeled the quilt away to reveal a little girl with a ruddy face and clear eyes. There was a definite hitch in her breathing. He picked her up and set her on his knee. He pressed one hand to her chest and the other to her back. Each of her breaths moved her chest as it ought, and he heard nothing alarming, but something was not right.

"What is it, doctor?" The goodwife wrung her hands in the apron covering her extended waist.

The little girl began to cry and reach for her mother. As William started to hand her over, a glimpse of something caught William's eye. He pulled the child back and let her howl, looking into her mouth. "Goodie Biddle, when did you last prepare fish for your family?"

"'Twas last evening."

William kept the screaming child still with one hand and fished a pair of tweezers from his satchel with the other. "Hold her still, please," he said to the woman. "But keep her crying, I need her mouth open wide."

He watched closely. There it was again, the shine of a bone. William timed it between the child's breaths, pinched the sharp bone with his tweezers, and removed it in one quick motion. He held it up for the goodwife to see. "'Tis naught but a fishbone. When she drew in a breath, this pressed against her throat and caused her a small pain. She will be fine."

"Oh, doctor, I cannot thank you enough." Relief gushed with her words, the sobbing child's arms now wrapped around her neck.

William almost thanked her in return. Ever since they'd arrived in Salem Village, he'd been faced with situations beyond his control. But this—this felt good.

"How much do I owe you, doctor?" Mr. Biddle asked as William shrugged into his coat at the door.

"No charge. I was not here long enough even for my dinner to grow cold."

"That is very generous of you." Mr. Biddle put on his own coat. "I shall walk you back." He chuckled. "Slower this time, I promise."

With a flurry of activity, Goodie Biddle wrapped something in a cloth and handed it to William. "At least take some of this cake. I baked it just this morning."

He could hardly ignore the pleading in her eyes, so he took the offering with a smile.

Once the house was behind them, the man said, "You left the tavern early, so you will not know what happened."

Nor did he wish to, but William listened to the tale of more accusations and the final conclusion that the local authorities needed to be brought in from Salem Town. "'Twas decided that all shall meet again once the sheriff arrives. Not tomorrow," he was quick to add. "'Twas thought it might be bad luck to meet on the twenty-ninth of February, so the next day."

On that disturbing bit of news, William bid him a good night and returned to finish his supper. And worry over what this turn of events would bring to his family.

Chapter 19

C ALEB PUSHED HIS EMPTY plate away and surveyed the crowd around his table. Hannah, their six children, and the two orphans were finishing their breakfast of sausage, eggs, cheese, and biscuits. The youngest two wore white smears of milk on their upper lips and biscuit crumbs on their chins. Their chatter was free-flowing and easy with more than a little teasing thrown in, some of it directed at Joseph, who sat next to Verity on the girls' side of the table. The boy took it all in good fun.

How fortunate Caleb was. They all were. They prospered, even under the shadow of dark things happening close by. But for how long? Others were starting to feel the struggle of keeping away from the village, away from commerce with the Puritans. He ignored the niggle of guilt over his flaunting of that decision, even though none had faulted him for it. Most were farmers who understood his family's need after the fire.

There was something he could do to help one family.

"Hannah." He waited while his wife finished wiping Jonathan's face and turned her attention to him, along with the curious looks of the children. "What say thee about inviting the O'Sullivans to dinner this evening? 'Twould not have to be anything elaborate, just a family dinner with friends."

"Oh! Please say we can, Mother." Tamson bounced on her chair. Two of the O'Sullivan girls were close to her in age, and they were fast friends.

Hannah tipped her head at Tamson and Verity. "Would thee both work extra hard this afternoon to prepare enough for everyone?"

Tamson shouted, "Aye!" while Verity, much more reserved that his boisterous daughter, nodded.

"And thee, boys"—she turned to the other side of the table—"will thee clear a space in the parlor and set up a trestle table and benches for all the young men?" They would need the extra seating with David and Isobel and their eight children.

"We will." Caleb Jr. spoke first. The two oldest O'Sullivan sons were near his age, and the third was the same age as Robert. The families had grown up together, often visiting and eating together in the warmer months when they could sprawl outside.

Hannah faced Caleb. "'Twould seem we are all in favor of thy idea. Will thee send Caleb Jr. with the invitation?"

"Indeed."

"Then make haste," she said to their son. "Ride over before Isobel starts preparations of her own. Tell her she is not to bring a thing. We have all we need."

Caleb chuckled. "Thee know she will bring something anyway, as would thee were the invitation reversed."

His wife waved off his remark and set the rest of the family in motion, clearing the breakfast table and starting on dishes. Robert and Joseph she sent to the barn to make sure there were clean stalls for the O'Sullivan team to rest in while they were there. She even gave young Benji the task of collecting spoons and carrying them to the wash basin. While only five years old, he could do that small chore. None of them balked or sulked or dragged their feet. His simple suggestion had breathed a measure of excitement into the room.

"Shall I ride Dandy?" Caleb Jr. asked him. "Dolly is getting too round."

"Dandy has not been ridden as often, remember. Be careful with him."

"I will." Caleb Jr. grabbed one last biscuit off the plate Hannah Jr. was clearing from the table, then dashed for the back door.

When Hannah came to his side, he said, "Thank thee for being willing to prepare a feast on such short notice."

"'Tis a lovely thought." She glanced at their children, busy about their tasks. "A bit of normal for us all is very welcome, I think."

Normal. That one word crashed into him and brought all the rest back. The doubt, the unknown, the waiting, and the stress.

"I shall get out of thy way and return to the shop."

"How goes the doctor's furniture?" Her voice held the note of wariness to which he was getting far too accustomed. When would things between them get back to normal?

"Lord willing, I will finish the kitchen cupboard this afternoon. Then I will start on the two bedside tables, the writing desk, and the goodwife's dressing table."

"We shall miss the chairs thee loaned out today"—the wariness turned to censure—"but the boys will do fine on makeshift benches."

He took her arm and led her away from the bustle of the kitchen and into the parlor, where they could speak in private. As soon as they entered, she moved away from his touch on her arm and looked out the window.

"I am doing what I must to provide for our family." Caleb paused, but she didn't turn to face him. "I am utilizing an opportunity I believe God provided. Can thee not believe in that—in me?"

Hannah spun to face him then. "Thee *believe*, but thee do not *know*."

"Neither do thee." The words came out sharper than he'd intended, but he wasn't going to apologize. Not when she glared at him from across the room. Even in the heat of her glare however, her fear stood out.

"None of us knows what will happen next." He did his best to gentle his voice. "We may have to flee, or we may have to barricade ourselves here at the farm."

"I had planned to start sewing the travel sacks this afternoon, but 'twill wait until the morrow." She raised her eyes to his. "There will be one for each of us."

What followed was a pause in which he knew he should say something, but as he didn't know what she wished to hear, he waited.

With a sigh, Hannah half-opened her arms and then let them fall back to her sides. "Verity goes with us." She lifted her chin, the fear now naked in her expression.

Caleb crossed the room and took both of her hands. "She cannot replace the one we lost."

Hannah snapped her head back to look up at him. "Nay. I never thought that. As dear as she is to me, she is her own person, and not a shadow of the other." She let her head drop down. "I still think of her sometimes."

Something eased around Caleb's heart as he squeezed his wife's hands. It was an odd time and place to have this discussion, and yet, it felt right. "As do I."

"Verity is part of our family now. I know Joseph is here only for a season, but Verity I hold as one of our own."

"She is ours now. If we must run, Verity goes with us. Have no fear of that." He'd hold the fear inside for the both of them. Fear that the Puritans would never let them go if the child was with them. Fear that they would chase his family to the ends of the earth. And the larger fear—that it would forever damage the bond between him and his wife.

A thin curl of wood came up under Caleb's nose, fragrant and fragile, as he bent over the planer and smoothed the last dovetailed joint. He stood and slid the drawer into place, the dovetailed joins fitting snuggly. He was giving it a pat of satisfaction when laughter reached him. He grabbed a rag to wipe his hands and walked to the shop's window.

David's wagon, fitted with runners, entered the farmyard with snow flying from the hooves of the team. The family, minus Mark, who had returned riding double with Caleb Jr. to help get everything ready, filled the wagon. Hannah Jr., Tamson, and Verity came out onto the porch, their voices adding to the uproar as they called to their friends.

Caleb untied his work apron and hung it up, then carried the brazier outside before greeting their guests. Isobel and the girls were already at the house, and the crowd of boys were caring for the horses.

He reached David. "'Tis glad I am that thee could come."

"We would not have missed it. 'Twas only a day or so ago that Isobel lamented our solitary state ever since the goings-on in the village started. 'Tis as if we Friends are afraid to mingle amongst ourselves." He shook his head. "Thy invitation was a reminder that all is not lost in this world as of yet." His friend's grin was contagious, until it faded.

"What is it?" Caleb asked.

"I hesitate to ruin an evening with bad tidings."

Caleb glanced at the house. The women wouldn't miss them for a while, and there were more than enough hands to do the farm chores. "Robert," he called to his closest son, "see that the cows get milked. Thee have plenty of willing hands to help thee."

"We will."

"A good boy," David said. "Does he miss the brewery?"

"Aye. He looks forward to returning." Caleb motioned toward the small barn door that opened into the shop. "Come, we can speak privately in here."

Settled on one of the stools in the small room that lacked the warmth of the brazier, Caleb stuck his hands under his armpits. "What ill tidings do thee bring?"

"I was in Salem Town this forenoon and heard disturbing news. Arrest warrants have been issued for the pastor's slave woman as well as Sarah Good, Sarah Osborne, and"—David paused a moment—"Widow Scudder. The slave woman I can understand, based on what thee witnessed in the forest, but the other three? What do thee suppose they have done to be accused of witchcraft?"

"What does anyone need to have done?" Caleb shrugged. "Thee remembers the stories from Boston, fingers pointed at unsuspecting women, accusations that lacked any credible evidence, and yet, they were hanged for the crime of witchcraft."

"I know little of the two Sarahs. The one is a disagreeable person by all accounts. She is rough in appearance as well as language and known to smoke a pipe. A social outcast, they call her."

"Thomas Buffington said as much to me when I saw him in town yesterday. 'Tis why he sent young Joseph home with me."

"The orphan boy who brought Verity to thee?"

"The same. Thomas worried for his safety. The other Sarah, Goodie Osborne, is also a social outcast. Her crime was marrying her indentured servant."

David shifted on his stool. "The Puritans think that a crime?"

"Apparently."

"Fools."

Caleb didn't disagree. The Friends believed that all men and women were equal in the sight of God, none higher, none lower. The Puritans, however, clung to the British tradition of hierarchy.

"And the widow?" David raised a brow.

"That one worries me the most." He tipped his head toward the house. "But as we already have Verity, I do not think Joseph brings us any more danger than we were already in. Did thee hear if the women were to be taken to Salem Town?" That would move the danger farther away from the community of Friends.

"Nay." David rubbed his jaw. "What I heard was that they would be tried here in the village at the church. Starting on the morrow."

"So soon?" Caleb's plans to deliver the rest of the furniture crumbled to dust. There was no way he'd enter the town with a trial going on. No way he'd tempt fingers to point at him or anyone in his family.

"There is a more disturbing part to this." David's brow furrowed, and he looked away for a moment. "The arrest warrants were signed based on the accusations of Thomas Putnam, Ann Jr.'s father." He glanced back at Caleb. "Are thee aware of the conflict between Sarah Osborne's deceased husband and Thomas Putnam?"

"Nay. I cannot say that I ever spoke to either of them."

"'Tis over a parcel of land both men claimed, but Osborne ended up with." David shook his head. "Whatever happened with those first two girls might very well be evil from an unknown source, but I fear more evil is being stirred up with this turn of events. The evil of one man against another."

"I like not the sound of that."

"Nor do I, but if 'tis the Puritans turning on each other, perhaps we Friends can breathe more freely."

If only that could be true, but it wasn't what had happened the last time. Caleb shook his head. "Once they run out of each other to blame things on, they will look for another scapegoat. Trust me, my friend. I have seen it before."

David and Isobel had moved to the Friends community outside of Salem Village a couple of years after Caleb and Hannah had arrived and started their farm. The two families had been close ever since. But even with David, Caleb hadn't shared everything.

"I know thee and Hannah had difficulties in the past..." David let the words hang between them, an invitation to continue or let the matter drop, whichever Caleb wished.

As this was to be a day of merriment, Caleb chose the latter. "Let us put aside worries of the future—and sorrow over the past—for this evening." He stood. "Come and see how Dolly is coming along. I expect her to foal by the end of March, but thee can give me thy opinion on that." He ushered his friend out of the shop and into the main area of the barn to check on the mare and keep an eye on the boys milking the cows. All homey tasks. Normal tasks. The kind done by people who were not worried about witchcraft and warrants and possibly fleeing for their lives.

At least for this one evening.

William rested with his hands behind his head, elbows out on the pillow, as Rachel combed and braided her hair for bed. How many times had he watched her do the same? Fifty years, it must be. He should ask her, she would remember, but then she'd chide him for not remembering... so maybe not.

"What are you pondering?" she asked without turning around. She'd always been able to read him, even without looking. Early in their marriage, it had been unnerving. But he'd grown used to it.

"About tomorrow." Which wasn't an untruth, because that was where his thoughts had been when he'd first gotten in bed.

"I worry about what might happen." Rachel tied the end of her braid with a ribbon and turned on the borrowed chair to face him. "I wish they would not question Elizabeth about it."

"They will need to know what she felt, what happened to her."

"Therein lies the problem." She rose and joined him in the bed, pulled the thick covering over her and settled against her pillow. "What she said in the beginning, and what she is saying now, they do not seem to match."

"What is this?" He moved onto his side to face her.

"'Tis as if her mind has shifted. Her recounting of details has changed."

"What has changed in her recounting?"

"Remember at first she claimed someone was touching her, that she was bent over and forced to the floor?"

He wasn't likely to forget the horror that had seized him at seeing their niece collapse and writhe in the church. "Surely she is not refuting that it happened to her?"

"Nay, but she is now saying that a specter was visible to her."

"If that were true, why did she not say so at the time?" William couldn't imagine hiding such a thing in the midst of the trauma.

"That is what worries me. She spent the afternoon with Ann Jr., I saw no reason to disallow it. I thought 'twould be healing for her to speak with another who was likewise afflicted, even though Ann Jr. is quite a bit younger. Now I wonder if I should have kept them apart."

With a tingle of alarm racing through him, William asked, "Why?"

"Because now she claims to know these three women, Sarah Good, Sarah Osborne, and Widow Scudder, but she has never met any of them. She would not have been able to pick them out of a crowd at the time of her collapse."

"You think..." William chose his words carefully, not wanting to upset Rachel further by disparaging her niece. "You think perhaps this other girl, Ann Jr., planted ideas in Elizabeth's head?"

"I wish 'twere only that."

"Then what is it you fear?"

"That Elizabeth is... is enjoying the attention she has received since her supposed affliction."

William eased onto his back. He'd seen the Parris girl and her cousin contorted into positions unthinkable for even a nimble youngster, had touched the bite marks, had listened to their ragged breathing and witnessed their cloudy eyes. The girls had been touched by something... evil. He was sure of it.

But Elizabeth? He tried to remember her condition when she'd cried out and collapsed. He'd been so shaken, taken so unawares. Had he even examined her before dosing her with the laudanum? Not that he could recall.

What if Rachel was correct? What if Elizabeth was not truly afflicted at all, but working out her unhappiness by getting attention in a very unhealthy way?

If that were true, others might also be tempted to behave that way. In the middle of winter in a northern village with little to excite, little to entertain, such behavior could spread.

Even worse, the truth of what William had witnessed could be overshadowed by false accusations.

Chapter 20

As CALEB PULLED ON his heavy coat, Hannah returned to the kitchen. "How is she?" he asked. Verity had left the room before breakfast, complaining of a cough and sore throat. Hannah had sent her to bed.

"She has a slight fever and the cough." Worry lines marred her brow. "A cold, I think, nothing worse."

"I shall keep her in prayer throughout the day." He glanced around the messy kitchen, where Hannah Jr. scrubbed at a spill near the hearth. "Are thee sure I should not stay and help thee put all back to rights?"

Hannah waved a hand at their two daughters. "We will have it tidied up in no time. 'Twas all worth it to see our friends again, to laugh and enjoy each other's company."

It had been a night of merriment and good for all of them. Caleb had provided the lion's share of the laughter—at his own expense. He'd failed miserably at the parlor games after the meal, to the delight of his children.

"Will thee go into the village today?" Hannah asked the question, but Hannah Jr.'s brows raised in response.

"Nay. Not today." Why did his daughter look disappointed and turn away? He cocked an eyebrow at Hannah, who shook her head.

Whether that meant she didn't know what was up, or that he wasn't to ask, he had no idea. They could speak about it in private later. "I will start on Goodie Griggs' dressing table today. But first, I will pop up and see Verity."

He took the stairs in his stockinged feet and approached the door cautiously lest she be sleeping. But when he put his head in, she gave him a wan smile as she stroked Button's head where he curled beside her.

"Hannah says thee have a cold."

She nodded, then coughed.

"Can I bring thee anything? Would thee like someone to sit with thee?"

She nodded again. "Joseph." Her voice was raspy, and she coughed again, tugging at Caleb's heart.

Even as close as she and Tamson were, it was Joseph she asked for. The bond between the two orphans would probably last their lifetimes.

"I will send him to thee shortly."

"Thank thee." Her use of the Friends' *thee* warmed him, a reminder of her acceptance in spite of being raised Puritan before she came to them.

"Rest now. Sleep if thee can."

He returned downstairs. "She is asking for Joseph. I will send him in to sit with her."

Tamson's head snapped up. "Joseph?"

"Fret not. 'Tis he she knows best of all. When in discomfort, one wishes to have those who are familiar around them. It does not mean she loves thee any less." He smiled at his youngest daughter, then pulled on his boots and headed to the barn.

Dolly and Dandy trotted around the paddock, kicking up snow and shaking their manes. The milking had been done before breakfast, as usual, the chore going faster with Robert and Joseph both helping. The cows were out on the snowy pasture, nosing through the white, looking for a wisp of last year's browned grass to nibble.

Laughter came from the horse stalls. Robert and Joseph were mucking them out when Caleb arrived.

"Verity is asking for thee, Joseph. Would thee sit with her for a while?"

His grin evaporated. "Is she bad sick?"

"Hannah thinks 'tis only a cold."

"Go on," Robert said. "I can finish here.

Joseph left at a run, as attached to the girl as she was to him.

"Verity will be all right, will she not?" Robert asked.

"The Lord willing, but thy mother thinks so."

"Pa." Robert stuck the thick tines of the wooden pitchfork in the straw and leaned against it. "What will thee do if the Puritans come for Joseph and her?"

"Joseph will return to the Buffingtons eventually. 'Tis his choice, of course."

"Aye. He is keen to be back there. As am I." He gave Caleb an apologetic look. "Not that I dislike it here."

"I know, son. Farming is not thy calling. The Friends have not a brewer here among us, and learning the trade will be a benefit to all should things sour between us and the Puritans."

"Do thee think they will? Sour, I mean?"

Caleb had dodged the first question. He couldn't ignore this one, but how much should he say to his sixteen-year-old son? "'Twill be as the Lord wills it." The simple truth was always the best.

"I know, but what do *thee* think?"

"I think..." He released a long breath. "I think we should strive always to get along with our neighbors. The Bible tells us, 'If it be possible, as much as in you is, have peace with all men.' We should do this. But the Puritans have different notions about things."

"Not all of them." Robert was quick to defend his friends. "Mr. Buffington and Benjamin and Thomas Jr. treat me as a friend as well as a worker. Mrs. Buffington is nearly as nice as Ma."

"I know. 'Tis why I agreed to apprentice thee there. Thomas and his goodwife have always dealt fairly with the Friends. As have a few others." But too few. Too few to stand up for them should fingers begin pointing their way.

He left Robert to finish his chores and entered the carpentry shop. The pile of boards to make Goodie Griggs' dressing table was stacked neatly along the back wall, but what drew his eye was the half-finished dressing table for Verity. It'd been pushed to the side after the fire and the need to raise money for the tools to do the spring planting. Now that he could not deliver more furniture to the doctor, he might as well finish it. Maybe it would bring a smile to the sick child.

With that thought, much more uplifting than worrying about their Puritan neighbors, he moved the girl's dressing table to his bench and set to work.

The tavern was, if possible, even more crowded than the last time. William took a seat on a bench near the fire with Elizabeth and Rachel. He'd been introduced to John Hathorne and Jonathan Corwin when they'd arrived, the magistrates of Salem Town who would be overseeing the questioning.

Questioning. That word brought a ripple of something unpleasant through William. Not fear exactly, but more of a dread, the kind of dread when one knows something will come to a bad ending but has no power to prevent it.

Rachel sat stony-faced on the other side of their niece.

Elizabeth, however, sat straight and tall, the merest hint of a smile making her appear regal, and with an air of expectant calm, hands folded on her lap.

He'd attempted to converse with her that morning at the breakfast table, but to no avail. Not that she was silent, just that she didn't say anything useful about what had happened to her. Was that because nothing had? Had she simply mimicked the other girls for attention?

Elizabeth had been so unhappy about moving to the village. But even further back, she'd been unhappy in Boston. For reasons he was not privy to, the young men had passed her by while several of her friends had married the previous year. The girl was just seventeen and hardly in danger of becoming an old maid, but girls put great stock in finding a husband and settling down.

People grew restless around them, many muttering amongst themselves.

One snippet of conversation caught William's attention. "We had no trouble here before all those Quakers moved in."

"Go on with you. Some been here more than twenty years."

"I still say, they be suspect, being heretics and all."

William craned his neck to try and locate the women speaking, but John Hathorne stepped to the long table that had been added to the room facing the families of the afflicted girls and banged a gavel for everyone's attention. "Let us begin the questioning." He banged the gavel again. "Who is to be brought first?"

Corwin approached the table holding the arm of the Parris slave woman. "Tituba will be the first."

The dark-skinned woman was serene in her simple gown with her hair braided above her brow and a white cloth wrapped around the rest of her hair. The magistrates had not clamped her in irons. She stood before them unrestrained.

Someone else joined Hathorne behind the table. William had met him before, a local man named Ezekiel Cheever. He had a stack of papers he put down along with three quills and an inkwell. Obviously, he would be the scribe for the proceedings, which made the whole thing feel even more ominous.

Tituba answered their questions, at first denying any witchcraft, but after no more than half an hour, her story changed. Those inside the tavern had to be quieted several times, the last upon threat of removal if they did not remain silent, as the slave woman confessed to being a witch and then named both Sarah Good and Sarah Osborne as fellow witches. Notably, she did not mention the widow, who apparently couldn't be found that morning. Tituba added many details of possession, spectral travel, and personally meeting with the devil. On that last detail, two women in the tavern swooned and had to be removed from the building before the magistrates could continue.

William wished more than ever that he'd never brought his family to Salem Village. Regret rode his shoulders and added to the ache in his chest. Rachel retained her stony appearance, but he knew her too well to be fooled. The slight tightening of the corners of her mouth, the whiteness of her knuckles on her clasped hands.

In complete contrast, Elizabeth appeared to be enjoying the proceedings. Nodding and even smiling at several of the slave woman's comments, she leaned forward as if to ensure she missed not a word.

The rest of the morning was a painful blur of people coming and going. Goodie Ingersoll was pressed into service to look over the

women for any type of devil's mark upon their bodies. Hathorne had
at first asked William to do the examinations, but he'd refused.

For one thing, he didn't believe in a devil's mark. Plenty of people
were born with marks upon their skin. As a physician, he'd seen
hundreds. It was normal—not a sign of anything evil. Others developed
marks as they aged, moles and dark spots and old scars. All perfectly
normal. He refused to be part of any such examination which all but
required that the examiner condemn these women.

Sarah Good's husband was called forth. A slovenly man, he reeked of
drink, whether because his clothes were stained with it or he'd taken to
the bottle at an early hour, William couldn't know. But the man told the
magistrates of a mole upon his wife's back, and the woman was taken
for Goodie Ingersoll's examination in the back room of the tavern.

Sarah Osborne professed her innocence before the crowd and the
magistrates, and William believed her. Obviously in poor health, the
woman was frail and should have been home abed. She was in no
condition to pinch or bite or haunt anyone. Anger that these men had
forced her from a sickbed to the tavern further stirred the ache in his
chest.

Sarah Good was brought back before the magistrates, and Goodie
Ingersoll confirmed the devil's mark upon her back. Uproar moved
through the room like a living thing. Magistrate Corwin moved to her
side as the accused woman shrieked at those now shouting condem-
nations at her.

Elizabeth rose from between William and Rachel and pointed her
finger at the woman. "That woman's specter visited me last evening
and did tell me all sorts of evil things. She demanded that I sign
the devil's book!" The room fell silent, all eyes on Elizabeth. "When
I refused, she did torment me for hours, pinching and poking and
twisting my arm behind my back."

A loud thump announced that another woman had swooned.

William stood, Rachel rising with him. "I am taking our niece home."
Because he'd heard nothing about this supposed attack last night or
this morning while they were all under the same roof, and he didn't
wish to question Elizabeth in front of everyone.

"We should question her—" Hathorne began.

William pressed his palm in the man's direction. "She has told you
what happened. I will see to her care now."

Perhaps it was respect for his standing as a doctor, but for whatever reason, the crowd parted and allowed him to leave. He grasped Elizabeth's arm and pulled her behind him.

"Uncle, I can stay and answer their questions."

"Hush." Rachel's sharp reprimand reached William through the noise of the room. "Your uncle knows what is best for you."

"But I wish to—" Elizabeth's words clipped off with a muffled squeak.

William would bet his best pair of silver shoe buckles that he'd find a pinch mark on her should he look, and it wouldn't be from any specter.

Rachel did not suffer impertinence. She never had from their children, and she wasn't about to start with Elizabeth. William tightened his grip on the girl's arm and hauled her out the door of the tavern. He ignored her scowl when he released her and motioned for her and Rachel to precede him to the house.

Following them, he rubbed the middle of his chest where the ache had intensified. He needed a cup of strong tea, a quiet hour in a chair, and time to ponder what they were to do next. Being a doctor would not protect them from repercussions of Elizabeth's outburst. And from the glances the girl was throwing back toward the tavern, she knew it too.

What a horrible mess he'd landed them in. What he wouldn't give to roll back the clock several months. But such thoughts wouldn't safeguard his family now. What if Elizabeth pointed her finger at others in the days ahead?

His step faltered, and he had to grab the handrail at the steps to their house.

What if she pointed her finger at Rachel?

Chapter 21

C ALEB AND THE CHILDREN waited for Hannah and Verity to join them at the breakfast table, but Hannah appeared without the girl and took her seat. At his wife's nod, Caleb started the silent prayer. When they were finished, platters of pancakes, sausage, and fried potatoes were passed around, along with a crock of maple syrup.

"Is Verity no better?" Joseph asked.

Hannah shook her head. "Her fever has not broken. Poor Button will not leave her side. I do not approve of an animal on the bed, but I have not the heart to make him get down. She takes comfort from him."

Caleb set down his fork. "Should I fetch the doctor?"

Hannah paled. "Nay! 'Tis but a childhood cold."

Such a harsh response to his question surprised and somewhat alarmed him. His wife rarely reacted so forcefully. But come to think of it, had done so on other occasions concerning the orphan child. She may not think she was trying to replace their lost daughter with this one, but her responses, her actions, said otherwise.

Caleb let the matter drop, and they finished their meal with the children doing most of the talking, especially Jonathan who, at long last, had started to talk and seemed to love the sound of his own voice. Caleb didn't understand most of what he said, but Benji was always keen to interpret. The result was a table ringed with chatter and laughter. If only it could always be that way.

"We best get moving and change our clothing, or we shall be late for meeting." Caleb rose.

"Would thee like me to stay home with Verity?" Hannah Jr. faced her mother. "I would be happy to."

Emotions whisked across Hannah's face too fleeting for Caleb to decipher, but he got the impression that she'd like to refuse their daughter's offer. "'Tis of thee kind to offer. Please do." Hannah busied herself clearing the table as if she might change her mind without something to do.

Once they were arrayed in their Sunday best, Caleb Jr. brought up the wagon and team. They'd switched out the runners for wheels again, perhaps sooner than they should have as snowflakes dappled the backs of the horses, the wet, heavy flakes of late winter. Everyone piled into the wagon, including Joseph. Robert and the other children explained to Joseph about their service all the way to the meeting house. The ride was longer than usual, as they skirted the village rather than drive down the main street. The ground was still frozen, so they were able to avoid the road without getting stuck in mud. Best not to draw any more attention to themselves than they must.

The service went along as it usually did, with several men and two women rising to contribute what the Lord had given them to share. It appeared to be wrapping up when Elias rose.

Silence filled the meeting house.

Elias Barwick didn't speak much anymore during meetings, preferring to let the younger men lead. His voice wasn't as strong as it used to be, and his eyes were cloudy, but he stood straight as he said, "A great evil has visited the village. As I am sure all know, we have been avoiding it for a fortnight." He shot a glance at Caleb. "Most of us have."

Caleb ignored the other glances aimed his way. He'd not tried to keep his actions a secret, and everyone in the building knew of the barn fire and what he'd lost, what he must replace if he was to plant in a few weeks. While several of his neighbors had offered the use of their equipment, they had nothing extra to share. Loaning to him after they'd finished in their fields meant Caleb's crops would be in late and the harvest would also be delayed. If a delayed harvest met with an early winter, all could be lost.

He wasn't willing to take that chance.

"One of the Puritans came by my farm last evening to purchase a rooster, having lost his last one to a fox. I have spoken to this gentleman off and on over the years. He lives but a mile from my place and has always been fair and honest in his dealings with me." Light from the windows shone on Elias's bald head, giving him an almost haloed appearance. "He told me of their meeting yesterday that ended..." He let the sentence die off and surveyed the room. "Three women were examined and questioned on the charge of witchcraft. The slave woman of their reverend confessed before all."

Murmurings broke out. Goodwives hugged their young children closer, including Hannah across the aisle from him, who pulled Jonathan onto her lap.

Caleb put his arm around Benji, who leaned against him.

Elias raised his hands and quiet was restored. "In the end, Sarah Good was taken off to jail and charged with witchcraft." Another low round of murmuring started, but he continued. "'Tis my opinion, and mine only at this point, that we all need to stay out of the village." Again, Elias turned his face to Caleb.

This time, Caleb nodded.

"Are we in any danger?" one of the women asked without standing.

"If there is a witch, will she cast spells upon us?" one of the men asked, also not standing.

They were the types of questions that could draw unwanted attention. Several others voiced their concerns along the same vein.

Caleb rose, and the people quieted. "We all know what the Bible says, 'Little children, ye are of God, and have overcome them: for greater is He that is in you, than He that is in this world.' There is nothing evil can put in our paths that is greater than what our Lord can overcome. I know not how it is for the Puritans, but as for we Friends, we are under the Light of Christ."

In the hush that followed, Arthur Stokes rose. The steady farmer gestured to Caleb. "Caleb is right. We have nothing to fear from the evil that may have come over the village. But that does not mean the village will not visit evil upon us—the people, not spirits. 'Tis best we keep our distance." He sat again, and Caleb did the same.

More murmurings broke out, but a calmness had settled over them. Caleb could feel it, like a light breeze on a hot day, subtle and welcome.

When no one else rose to speak, the meeting was adjourned. The men gathered in groups, as did the women, to discuss what had been said. The children were kept indoors and not released to run outside and play as they usually were. Some raced up and down the center aisle, and no one chastised them. The youngsters needed to wear off the energy that had built up over a morning of sitting still in quiet contemplation.

David joined Caleb. "Are thee finished with the doctor's furniture?"

"Nay. Not yet."

"What will thee do?"

Caleb rubbed the back of his neck. "I wish I knew."

"Have thee been paid?"

Leave it to David to ask outright. "Indeed. The doctor insisted on paying for each delivery."

"Which now thee can do no longer."

"But I can still complete the order. Perhaps in time for the spring planting, 'twill be possible for me to finish the deliveries." Perhaps. Possibly. Too many uncertainties for Caleb to rest easy.

The congregation dispersed, wagons rolling out into the sloppy wet snow, the temperatures having risen while they'd met. Their horses labored to pull the loaded wagon, and it took longer than usual to reach home. Caleb's stomach growled, and the children laughed. As they approached the back door, Hannah Jr. burst outside.

"Make haste, Mother. Verity has taken a bad turn."

The church was packed, more full than William had seen it since their arrival. Every infrequent attender must have come to listen and gawk at the spectacle. And spectacle it was.

Reverend Parris announced that his lesson was from the book of Deuteronomy. He raised his voice and all but shouted the scripture verses. "'Let none be found among you that maketh his son or his daughter to go through the fire, or that useth witchcraft, or a regarder of times, or a marker of the flying of fowls, or a sorcerer, or a charmer, or that counseleth with spirits, or a soothsayer, or that asketh counsel of the dead.'"

When he paused to draw breath, the congregation erupted into chaos. Some people stood in their boxes and shouted in agreement. Women clutched their children and cried. Even more disturbing, some pointed fingers at those in nearby boxes. Toward the reverend's family box were aimed pitying glances, but quickly, as if looking at them too long might somehow taint the looker. All ignored the reverend despite his attempts to regain control of the situation.

There was nothing to be gained by staying. "Come, let us return home." William stood and assisted Rachel to her feet.

"I am staying." Elizabeth remained seated and tilted her chin up at them.

"Elizabeth—" Rachel was silenced when the girl raised her hand.

Anger—an emotion quite foreign to William—stirred within him to see his wife so treated by this slip of a girl, even if she was their niece. "Now see here, you will come with us."

"I am not your daughter." There was a forceful punch to her words. "And I am seventeen, not a child."

"You are part of our family. You live under our roof. You are in our care." Rachel's voice was calm and reasonable.

It was best William let her speak for them both. He rubbed the ache in his chest, then stopped when Rachel eyed his motion.

"I am also a part of this village. You saw to that." There was a smugness about her now. "I must stay and I must testify to what I experienced if it helps even one other person from having to withstand it." She pressed the back of her wrist to her forehead.

The chaos began to subside, but Reverend Parris had left the pulpit. The two magistrates from Salem Town climbed the steep steps. One of them clapped his hands, finally drawing attention.

"Come, Rachel." William took her elbow. "If the girl will stay, she will stay. But you and I have no need to be here."

Rachel glanced at Elizabeth, but the girl turned her face away.

With a sigh, Rachel allowed him to lead her out the door, the words of the magistrate following after them, telling the crowd that they would continue with the questioning.

On the Lord's day.

In the church.

Without even a prayer for guidance.

Though he was a man of science, he believed in God. No good could come of what was happening behind them, and William would have no part it in.

Hannah Jr.'s shout still hung in the air as Caleb drew back on the reins, but the horses hadn't come to a complete stop before Hannah scrambled off the wagon's high bench seat. She cried out when her feet hit the ground, and Caleb leaned over to see her better.

"Are thee hurt?"

She waved his question away as she hopped and limped to the door.

"Mind the little boys," Tamson said to one of her brothers, or maybe to all of them, as she jumped from the tailgate. She followed her mother into the house.

"Caleb Jr., come take the reins."

His son climbed over the bench seat's back, and Caleb waited just long enough to hand over the reins before climbing down. He didn't have to give the boys any instructions. They knew what needed to be done. But—"Put the horses in their stalls, in case we need to hitch them again in a hurry."

Solemn nods answered him, and Jonathan began to cry. Joseph shushed him and pulled him close for the rest of the ride to the barn.

Caleb sprinted up the steps, through the kitchen, and up to the upstairs hallway.

Tamson was charging out of the room she shared with Verity. "Mother said to bring cold water and cloths." Her dark gray eyes were wide, her mouth setting into a grim line.

He patted her shoulder and moved out of her way before stopping in the doorway.

Hannah sat on the edge of the bed while Hannah Jr. stood on the other side.

Between them, Verity was almost swallowed by the blankets heaped around her. Button's red-and-white head rested on her shoulder. The girl's face was flushed bright red, her breath shallow, and she appeared to be sleeping.

"How is she?" he whispered.

Hannah turned a haunted look to him. "I should not have left her."

"Nay, my dear." He came into the room and knelt beside her. "Thee have no blame in this. 'Tis a sickness, and nothing thee did made it any worse."

"But I could have been here when she needed me."

"Hush, now." He shot a glance at Hannah Jr. "Our daughter did everything thee would have done. Did thee not train her thyself?"

"Oh." Hannah dropped her face into her hands for a moment, then raised her face to Hannah Jr. "Of course thee did. I am sorry. I did not mean to imply—"

"I know, Mother." Hannah Jr. took her hand. "Think nothing of it. Thee are distressed."

"As are thee, I should have thought before I spoke."

"Who should have thought before she spoke?" Tamson arrived out of breath with a basin and cloths, her voice loud after their whisperings.

"Shhh." Her sister put a finger to her lips. "'Twas Mother this time and not thee."

"Perhaps now we know who thee inherited that from." Caleb winked at his younger daughter.

Verity coughed, a pitiful sound, as if she lacked the strength to expel more than a puff of breath.

"Verity, can thee hear me?" Hannah bent closer and smoothed the damp hair off the girl's brow.

"Uh huh." The reply was brought by another cough, and her eyes remained closed.

"We should prop her up on more pillows to ease her breathing," Hannah said. "Hannah Jr., bring me the two extras from the chest in our room. Tamson, set that basin on the side table. Caleb, would thee please see to setting out dinner. Thee and the boys can eat, and I shall see that the girls come down as I can spare them."

Gone was the helplessness and despair he'd walked in on, and in its place was his Hannah. As strong and capable a woman as he'd ever known.

In the kitchen, he sliced the bread, cheese, and a leftover roast Hannah had set aside. They ate a cold meal on the Lord's day so no one had to work more than was necessary. Unless, of course, someone took ill. He took heart from the fact that Verity had eaten well and filled out since coming to live with them. She wasn't the frail child of weeks ago. Even so, during the silent prayer, he asked the Lord for swift healing. He also prayed for safety for the rest of them.

They already had witch rumors in the village and barn fire losses to deal with, they didn't need a house full of sickness.

Chapter 22

G OODIE PARRIS BARELY LIFTED her eyelids when William entered the room and sat on the chair at the side of the bed. He'd been called to the house in haste shortly after daybreak.

"What happened this morning?" He took her hand from the top of the blankets. It was cold, the skin dry and bluish.

"I know not." She gave a feeble cough. "Samuel said he could not awaken me. He was in quite a state when I came around."

"But 'tis *your* state I am interested in. How do you feel?" By her appearance, not at all well.

"I am terribly tired, 'tis difficult to keep my eyes open."

"Allow me." He leaned forward and lifted her eyelids, one at a time. Her eyes were dull, which alarmed him. She was thirty-two years old, but looked twenty years older. The skin of her face was as dry as her hand. She needed more liquids, and soon. "What have you had to drink this morning?"

She shook her head, so he rose. "I shall return in a moment."

He stepped from the room, frustration mounting, and closed the door behind him.

Reverend Parris stopped his pacing in the hallway and turned to him. "What is it?"

William forced himself to keep his voice down. "She has had nothing to drink. Did I not leave detailed instructions about her intake of liquids?"

The reverend took a step back. "Of course. Of course you did. Without Tituba here we—"

"The lack of a slave simply means that *you* must fill the need." William spaced his words to make the point. Imagine, neglecting an ailing woman for want of slave labor. Not only was slavery morally wrong—and the leader of a church should be able to see that—it made people lazy, unwilling to do for themselves. "Brew a pot of tea and sweeten it with honey, or whatever you have. Very sweet, mind you. Add cream if you have it, at least enough to cool the tea so it may be swallowed at once. And make haste."

William turned and faced the door, then took a deep breath to calm himself. He plastered on his professional smile before entering again. "Your husband will fetch tea. I need you to drink it, every drop. And then you must have a piece of toast, two would be better. If you do not drink and eat, you will not get better."

"'Tis so hard to chew and swallow sometimes."

William took his seat and once again picked up her hand. "I know 'tis difficult, but you have your children to think of." When all else failed, he could usually count on maternal instinct to help him. "They need you to get better. Little Susannah especially is much too young to do without her mother."

"Am I that sick, doctor?" Her voice gained a little strength with that question. "Will I die?"

"We all must die at some point. If you will drink a cup of something each hour and eat, even small amounts, throughout the day, I think you will improve much. The body needs drink and food or it will cease to function."

"Indeed. I know this is true." She raised her other hand to her brow. "'Tis just so taxing."

"Life is difficult, is it not?"

"Sometimes more than others..." Her voice drifted off with the last word.

William patted the back of the hand he held. "I need you to stay awake, Goodie Parris. Your children need you to drink and eat."

Reverend Parris appeared in the doorway, a tray wobbling in his hands as if he'd never managed one before.

William rose and motioned him to take the chair. "You will probably need to support her head while she drinks. I shall give directions to the girls to prepare toast for her. She must drink a cup of something each hour and eat small amounts afterward. Food and drink will see her improvement."

"Thank you, doctor." The reverend sat without spilling the tea. "We shall do as you say."

"Indeed. You must." He stressed the last word and trusted that the man would understand.

Downstairs, Betty and Abigail were preparing breakfast. Trying to, at least. Again, reliance on a slave had stunted their abilities. Nevertheless, they must learn. "Girls, you will have to nurse Goodie Parris back to health."

"We know not how," Abigail said.

"Then heed what I am telling you." He used his strictest voice and had their undivided attention. He prescribed exactly what the good woman upstairs needed to eat and when and how it was to be prepared. Then he raised his finger as if in warning and said, "If you fail in this, she will fail as well, and you two will be raising the younger children."

At that moment, a sleepy-eyed Susannah came into the room, dragging a tatty blanket behind her.

The two older girls looked at each other, then at William, and nodded.

"I shall leave you to your tasks. I shall stop in again on the morrow in the forenoon, and I expect to see great improvement if you follow my instructions to the letter." With that, he headed home for his own breakfast.

"Doctor!" The call came across the street where the bulky form of the brewer, Buffington, motioned to him.

Whatever had happened to his dream of retirement? William met him in the middle of the street. "Have you need of me?"

"Nothing of the sort." The big man waved off William's question. "I wished to know if you need more firewood. Thomas Jr. and Benjamin—the twins—have time this week. They could fill your wood box."

"That would be most appreciated."

"Think nothing of it. 'Tis a relief to have a doctor in our midst again." He lowered his voice, an action which seemed foreign to him, and leaned closer. "Especially with everything happening to this village. Although, if you missed hearing, further examinations and questionings have been moved to Salem Town, the village not having its own jail."

"So our niece informed us last evening." He didn't want to think on that conversation, because it had seemed to solidify Rachel's opinion that Elizabeth was acting out to gain attention. His goodwife had tried to suggest that to the girl, and it had ended badly, with Elizabeth stomping off to her room and slamming the door. Had she been even a handful of years younger—and William too—he'd have taken the girl over his knee for her disrespect. As it was, Rachel had withheld her supper until an apology was forthcoming. It hadn't been. He'd left too early to see Goodie Parris to know if an apology had been given before breakfast.

"I do not mind telling you, 'tis glad I am to have it out of our village." The brewer straightened, and the booming quality returned to his voice. "I must be off. The lads and I are starting a new batch of spruce beer today. 'Tis good for what ails you." He gave a hearty laugh and strode toward the brewery.

The man wasn't wrong about the spruce beer. William had seen it work improvements on many ailing patients. Perhaps he should see that some made its way to the Parris house. But first, breakfast. He hurried home.

When he opened the door, no appetizing aromas greeted him. Rachel sat at the table, her head bowed over her clasped hands.

"What has happened?" William shrugged out of his coat as he moved to her side.

"She is gone." Rachel pushed a scrap of paper toward him.

It was a note from Elizabeth. She'd left the house before dawn to meet up with the Putnams and go to the proceedings in Salem Town.

William sighed and turned the paper over. "Do you wish me to go after her and fetch her back?"

"Nay. She has made her decision."

"This could ruin her reputation."

"As she well knows." Rachel lifted tired eyes to him. "But she cares not, and she is a determined young woman."

He took her hand and squeezed it. "Did we spoil her, do you suppose?"

"'Twould seem so from her actions and words, but we also taught her right from wrong. As with our own children, once they are grown, they must choose for themselves whether or not to heed our teachings."

"No good will come of her being there." He glanced out the window at the bright sunshine that mocked the darkness he felt inside over this turn of events. Then he faced Rachel again. "Someone is bound to find her out as a fraud, and then it will not go well for her."

"What I fear is worse."

"What do you mean?"

"I fear they will believe her, and in her state of mind, who knows who else she might accuse?"

A sense of dread rippled through William, erasing any desire for breakfast as it twisted his stomach. He dropped into the chair next to Rachel.

They'd had sharp words when Elizabeth had returned from the proceeding the evening before. What if—God forbid—she actually pointed a finger at Rachel, the woman who had taken her in and raised her when her parents had died in that accident?

What would he do, if he lost Rachel?

Caleb had shaved a bit more before the dovetail joint of the last drawer fit to his liking, but it was worth the effort. He smiled as he slid it in and out of the dressing table, hoping it would please Verity. She'd been no better that morning, but no worse either. He ran his hand over the top again, finding a little catch on his fingertip, and had picked up the wood plane to smooth it when the door to the shop burst open.

"Goodie Buffum says to come quick." Joseph panted to catch his breath. "Tamson has the fever."

It was spreading.

Caleb set the plane aside and whipped off his work apron, slinging it over the stool on his way to the door.

Joseph charged ahead of him as if he needed to show the way, but it did the boy credit that he was so concerned for more than just Verity.

Coughing reached him before he entered the girls' room. Both of them were now side-by-side in the bed, Button sandwiched between them. The young dog was devoted to the girls. There was no doubt of that.

Hannah bent over Tamson, adjusting a damp cloth on her forehead. She glanced up as Caleb entered. "It came over her suddenly while she was helping Hannah Jr. in the kitchen."

"The same symptoms?"

"Aye, but the fever is worse, I think, than Verity's."

They weren't supposed to go to the village. They'd all agreed only the day before in the meeting house. But this was his *daughter*. "Do thee wish me to go for the doctor?"

"I do, but..." She glanced at the girls and back again. "But should thee?"

"If thee think he is needed, then I should." If they were ostracized over this, so be it.

Hannah nodded, tears coming to her eyes. She followed him out of the room and down the stairs before stopping him with a hand on his arm. "What if...what if the doctor removes Verity from us?"

Spinning to face her, Caleb couldn't restrain the surge of anger that rose in him. "Our daughter is ill. She needs the doctor. Would thee have me risk her for the sake of the other?"

Taking a step back, Hannah pressed both hands to her chest, shoulders curving inward. "Nay. Never." She shook her head. "I did not mean that."

"We will handle whatever happens." Caleb grasped her upper arms and gave what he hoped was a reassuring squeeze. "Getting them well is the first priority."

"Thee are right. I am sorry." She lifted a shaking hand to her brow.

Heart aching, Caleb pulled her close. She leaned against him for a moment, all stiffness gone, as if the rift between them had—at least for a time—closed. He drank in the scent of her hair and the warmth of her arms when they reached around him.

"I know thee are fearful that we might lose Verity, but thee cannot let it distort how thee see everything."

Her muffled breath, heavy with a suppressed sob, heated his chest. "I will do better."

Dropping his chin to the top of her head, he savored the moment of closeness between them before stepping away. "I shall return as soon as possible."

With a teary nod, Hannah retreated up the stairs.

Caleb was out the back door and shouting for the boys to harness the team. Before he reached the barn, Joseph and Robert were in the paddock fetching Dolly and Dandy.

Caleb Jr. waited for him in the doorway. "How is Tamson?"

"Very ill. I must fetch the doctor."

"Would thee rather I go? Thee could remain behind with Ma." The worry in his expression showed that he'd noticed the change in his mother—and perhaps her fearfulness.

As tempted as he was to go back in the house and build on the closeness he and Hannah had just shared, Caleb shook his head. "Best if I go." He pulled one harness off its peg while his son shouldered the other.

"Because of the witches?" Caleb Jr. asked.

Joseph and Robert held the horses while Caleb and Caleb Jr. buckled on the harnesses. "We know not if there are actual witches, so choose thy words with care. 'Tis best to remain as neutral as possible until this situation resolves."

"And stay out of the village—except for thee," Caleb Jr. said.

Caleb paused with his forearms on Dandy's back. "I would not go either if not for the fever. If Tamson has caught it, any of us could be next."

"Benji and Jonathan?" Robert looked stricken, as well he should. It was usually the youngest who succumbed to such fevers. Caleb and Hannah had been blessed that all their children had survived so far, except the daughter lost when they'd had to flee before. The one born too early to survive at all.

Caleb straightened and threaded the lines through the harnesses. "Caleb Jr. and Robert, thee have spent the least amount of time with Verity and Tamson. I would like thee to take turns watching the little boys. Keep them in their room, the kitchen, or outside as much as possible." Caleb climbed into the wagon. "One of you run over to David's and tell them of the sickness. Pray none there come down with it."

"Aye, Pa." Caleb Jr. handed him the reins. "We will take care of things here. But thee have a care for thyself."

With a smack of the reins, the team lurched forward. They found good footing, so Caleb let them go faster than might have been prudent, especially with Dolly heavy in foal. But if it came down between losing a foal or losing one of his children, for Verity was also his child now, there was no question. He turned them out of the lane and onto the road, giving the reins another flick.

The first half of the trip to town was filled with what ifs, but by the second half, Caleb had calmed himself enough to pray and ask the Lord to intervene, and by the time he stopped the wagon in front of the doctor's house, he had found a semblance of calm.

Calm he was going to need for both himself and his goodwife in the hours ahead of them.

Chapter 23

"SOMEONE IN A WAGON has stopped in front of the house, William." Rachel lifted the curtain she'd sewn for the new house to the side. "'Tis the carpenter, but his wagon appears empty."

William rose from his chair at the table where he'd been bent over one of his medical books. The research on hysteria was doing him little good, so he welcomed the disruption—until he opened the door. It was Caleb Buffum climbing off his wagon, but his face was drawn and his movements hurried.

"Something is wrong." He pulled his coat off the peg and grabbed his satchel, then turned to his wife. "I hate to leave you when things are so unsettled here."

"I know." She handed him his hat. "But you are needed." She gestured toward the carpenter now standing on their porch. "Go and do what you can. I shall be all right here."

He gave her a nod and closed the door behind him. "Who is ill?"

"How did thee know—"

"Your face gave you away, man. I have seen the look enough times to know."

"I suppose thee must have." Buffum offered a steady hand on his elbow as William climbed aboard the tall wagon.

As soon as William could, he needed to purchase his own buggy, something lower to the ground, with a docile and trustworthy horse to pull it. An animal that would find its own way home should William nod off after a late-night visit to a patient. There was little chance the village would entice another doctor to move there until the witch hysteria passed. Who knew when that would be? While he wished to be retired, he couldn't ignore a call for help if there was on one else to meet the need.

Buffum sprang up onto the other side of the wagon and turned the team around in the empty street, then set the animals charging down the road.

William put a hand on top of his hat to keep it in place. "'Tis that bad?"

"I know not. 'Tis a fever that started with Verity, our— Then Tamson came down with it this morning, perhaps even worse."

It seemed wrong to feel relief that the problem was a fever and not fits or hysteria. William mentally went over all the things that could cause a fever in late winter, none of them good. He probed for more details. "How old are the girls?"

"Verity is eight and Tamson, twelve."

"Are they your youngest two?"

"We have Benji and Jonathan, who are five and three."

That wasn't promising. "What are the symptoms other than fever?"

"Cough, mostly. Sore throat. Tiredness."

"Any spots?"

The man whipped his face around to William. "Spots? Not that I know of."

"I am sure if there were, your goodwife would have told you."

"Indeed." He faced forward again, slapping the reins on the backs of the team already going faster than William deemed safe. At least there was no traffic to maneuver around.

Buffum asked, "Why is the village street empty? 'Tis usually in a hubbub this time of day."

"Then you have not heard that the witch trials have been moved to Salem Town?"

"Aye, we had heard. But surely the people of the village are not all there." He faced William again. "Are they?"

"'Tis almost like a circus." The truth of that weighed down on William as he said the words aloud. "People sitting to watch the spectacle as if 'twere an entertainment." There was little enough to keep a person busy in early March, with the ground still frozen and last year's work done. It was usually a time of rest, other than the normal chores of daily living. A time when people enjoyed a relief from the heavier labors of the spring, summer, and autumn months. But also, a time when entertainments were few and far between.

Then a thought struck, and William twisted on the seat, careful to keep his hold on its sturdy wood as they bumped over a rut in the road. "Have none of your Quakers been given any cause to worry over this outbreak the village is dealing with? Still no fits with any of your young women?"

Buffum flinched, an interesting response that William would need to mull over later. "Nay. There have been no fits, no cause for alarm."

"Fascinating." William sat back and faced front again. "Fascinating." What could it mean? For one thing, this whatever it was—demonic possession or witch specters or group hysteria—had not spread beyond the village limits. Or was it something else? Had it not spread to the Quakers because they simply didn't believe in it? He'd always heard they were simple folks, backward, not adhering to the true Church of England.

Heretics.

But his interactions with Caleb Buffum, and before him, David O'Sullivan, had not supported those assumptions, although they had not discussed things of the church. Neither was this the time as the wagon careened onto a farm lane. He couldn't be sure, but William suspected the wheels on his side may have left the ground for a moment. If he survived this trip into the countryside, he would purchase his own buggy and horse at the very first opportunity.

Buffum brought the wagon to a halt, the horses stamping and blowing, beside the door of a tidy farmhouse with barns in the background, one of which sported the scorched marks of a recent fire.

Two young men raced to take control of the horses as Buffum leaped from the wagon and came around to assist William to the ground.

A tall woman in a gray dress and white cap such as the Quakers favored opened the door.

"Hannah, this is William Griggs, the doctor." Buffum turned to William. "My goodwife, Hannah Buffum."

"Goodie Buffum." William removed his hat as he passed through a back room into a warm kitchen smelling of chicken broth, savory with herbs.

"Please, call me Hannah. The girls are upstairs." She led the way.

Given names, that was another difference. Quakers preferred to be addressed in the familiar, even by strangers. It was odd, but certainly nothing heretical.

William followed her to a small bedroom. The two girls were side-by-side except for a half-grown pup between them. He smoothed a hand over the red-and-white head when it lifted, the dog offering no sound or ill-will toward him. He'd always had a soft spot for the canine species. If Elizabeth hadn't been allergic, he'd have one even now.

Goodie Buffum went to one side of the bed but pointed to the girl on the other. "Verity's fever began two days ago, but I do not believe it ever got as high as Tamson's." She smoothed sweaty dark hair off the forehead of the girl next to her. "Tamson had a bit of a cough last evening, and her fever hit midmorning."

"I understand you have two younger boys." William bent over Verity, giving the girl his best encouraging smile, of which she returned a weak reflection.

"Benji and Jonathan." Goodie Buffum glanced toward the door. "We have kept them out of this room, and one of the older boys is watching over them now."

"That is for the best. Keep them as separated as you can."

He asked the younger girl several questions and got the expected answers, then checked her mouth and arms, chest and back, which were blessedly free of spots. He moved to the older girl. Her fever raged, but again, she was free of spots. She turned her head to cough, and William pulled a white handkerchief from his pocket and held it in front of her mouth, wiping it when she was finished. It was free of blood. Still, the fever was dangerously high. It needed to come down, and quickly.

"We must wrap the girl in a single blanket," William said, "and carry her outside."

The goodwife stiffened. "But, 'tis so cold."

"Exactly. 'Tis the cold that shall bring down her fever." He gave her a reassuring smile, hoping she'd trust him. "The blanket?"

She pulled one from the trunk at the end of the bed. Together, they got the sick girl onto it and wrapped in it.

"Allow me." Buffum scooped up the girl and carried her down the stairs.

William puffed as he hurried to keep up with the man's long strides. He followed him out the door and pointed to a patch of clean snow off the porch. "Lay her down there."

Buffum raised a brow, but did as he'd been bid.

"Ten minutes." William hunched deeper into his coat and pulled it tighter around him. "Leave her there for ten minutes and let the snow and cold relieve her of the heat."

"Will thee not bleed her?" Buffum asked.

"Nay." He had some rather strong opinions on bleeding patients, opinions that didn't always endear him to his compatriots in the healing sciences. He wasn't willing to say it was never appropriate, but he'd yet to see a fever victim show any benefit attributed to it.

"What else can we do?" Goodie Buffum asked.

"You have done well if that is chicken broth I smelled in the kitchen. Get as much of that into her as you can. At least a cup each hour. 'Tis fine if it is cooled. This one"—he pressed the backs of his fingers to her cheek which already seemed a bit cooler—"might take it more willingly that way."

"What is it, doctor?" the woman asked.

"'Tis winter fever, and it often spreads. Should anyone else come down with it, give them lots of broth—chicken is best, but any broth will help—cool cloths on their foreheads to help with the fever, and if it climbs higher, move them outside into the cold for ten-minute intervals. Have you any feverfew?"

"I have dosed them both with a tea from it." There was hope in the woman's eyes. "Will the broth, tea, and cold treatments bring them through?"

"If the Lord wills." William didn't want to squash her hope, but the realities were, winter fever could dissipate, or it could consume a body. There was no cure, only time, good nutrition, plenty of liquids, and God's blessings on the patient.

After ten minutes, Buffum carried the girl back upstairs, and Goodie Buffum tucked her back into bed.

William examined her again. Her color was better, and the fever had abated somewhat. She opened her eyes, and their gray depths were clear enough.

He straightened and faced both parents. "Should the fever climb again, repeat the process. You can do this twice an hour as needed. Do not let her grow any hotter than she was when I arrived."

"That could be dangerous?" Goodie Buffum twisted her apron in her hands.

"Indeed, it could. She will require constant monitoring." William lifted his satchel from the floor.

"We will continue to pray," Buffum assured him. "Before I return thee to the village, if thee have the time, would thee have some refreshment? Tea and whatever Hannah Jr. is baking."

William sniffed the hint of cinnamon in the air and patted his stomach. "I believe I can make the time." He followed Buffum to the kitchen.

A tall girl transferred golden-brown scones from the hearth to the table, steam rising from them. Without a word, she set out two plates and two cups and then unhooked a kettle from over the fire. She poured steaming water into a teapot before replacing its lid.

"It smells delicious," Buffum said to his daughter—the family resemblance to Goodie Buffum was unmistakable—and gestured for William to have a seat on a chair at the table. The whole table was surrounded by chairs, not benches as was much more common. But then, a carpenter could make his own.

"How are you coming on the rest of our furniture?" William asked as he accepted the chair.

Buffum sat and propped his elbows on the table, fingers steepled together. "I have finished the dressing table and its matching stool. I can take them back with us today. However,"—he raised troubled eyes to William—"I know not when I can make another delivery."

The girl put a crock of cream between them and a sugar cone with its nippers.

"Is there a problem?" William forced himself not to hold his breath, but the last thing he needed was one more problem.

"Aye. The problem in the village." Buffum dropped his hands into his lap and leaned back in his chair. "'Twas decided after our meeting yesterday that we Friends should remain outside the village until this...this unpleasantness ends. The decision was passed down from our eldest and most respected member."

Unpleasantness. That was one word for it. William's word choices were far more scientific or spiritual. Hysteria, possession, witchcraft.

"We have a gentlemen's agreement." William didn't want to pressure the man, but he owed it to Rachel to try. After all, it was his fault that they were in this village and not in their former Boston home.

"I have given it some thought." Buffum paused while the young woman poured cups of tea and handed them over. "I thought to ask Thomas Buffington if one of his sons might pick up and deliver thy finished pieces."

The girl froze for an instant, but no more than that.

William would have missed it altogether had he not been watching her retreat to the hearth. "He seems to be an agreeable man. And that would solve the issue of you driving into town."

Buffum shifted as if uncomfortable. "I have already defied the Friends' decision by collecting thee today and will again when I return thee."

"Will this bring trouble upon you?" Surely not. The man wouldn't be censured for seeking medical advice for his children. Would he?

"Nay. I think not. The circumstances will be understandable."

"I quite agree." William couldn't wait any longer. He took a pinch of the scone and let it melt on his tongue. It was heavenly. Rachel would love it and would ask for the recipe, if he knew his goodwife. "As far as I know, at least here in the village, it appears to be a female perversity and not found among men."

Buffum cast a glance at his daughter. "That brings little reassurance."

After a second bite of the scone, William said, "I agree. But it might settle some of the fears of your church elders."

"Nothing was said about citizens of the village coming to our farms." Buffum shrugged. "So if Thomas's sons were to come with a wagon and pick up thy furniture, I see no reason that would not work for each of us."

"Nor I, to be sure." William slapped a hand on the table. "I am happy we have a solution to that. My goodwife left much behind in Boston.

She is a stalwart woman, but even the most sensible of women enjoys her things about her."

"Indeed. Now, what do I owe thee for this visit to see the girls?"

William eyed the plate of scones, and then looked up at the young woman. "Would it short your family to send those home with me?"

Her smile was wide and genuine. "Not a bit. 'Tis no hardship to make another batch for them."

"And would you perhaps write down the recipe for my Rachel? I know she will want to try these." He lifted the one he'd already tasted and took another bite. "Mmmm."

"Pack a basket for the doctor," Mr. Buffum instructed his daughter. "Include some of thy cheese and a brick of butter." He turned his attention to William. "I am a carpenter, but we also have a dairy that our daughter manages. Thee will not find better cheese in this colony, even if 'tis bragging to say so."

William bit into the scone again. If the cheese was half as good, Rachel would be pleased. He'd have to make a note of how they'd arrived so he could find the farm again once he had a buggy. But he also wanted to speak with Buffum alone about the Quakers—Friends, he called them—on the return trip and see if he could figure out why they were immune to what was happening in the village.

Chapter 24

T HE SUN HAD BROKEN through, and its early spring warmth flowed on the breeze as Caleb turned the team onto the road toward town. He kept Dolly and Dandy to a slow trot, having worked them so hard already that morning. Goodie Griggs's dressing table and stool were tucked into the back of the wagon.

The doctor had checked on the girls one last time before they left the house and now sat beside him, Hannah Jr.'s basket held on his lap. "May I ask you some questions, Caleb. You might find them a little invasive, but I assure you that my only goal is to better understand what is happening around us."

Caleb stiffened but tried not to show it. The last thing he needed was to irritate not only a customer, but also someone whose word would carry much weight among the Puritans. "I will answer as best I can. I know very little about what is happening."

"You see, that is what intrigues me." The doctor turned toward him on the bench. "While the village is in an uproar, you and your—Friends as you call yourselves—appear to be untouched by it. As a physician, I cannot help but wonder why."

"I am sure I do not know." Nor did Caleb want to have the discussion. It could only lead to bringing the town's attention on the Friends, the exact thing they all wished would not happen. How was he to squash the conversation without irritating the doctor and perhaps doing exactly what he was trying to avoid?

"Please understand, whatever you say to me will go no further, as in, I would not name or quote you to anyone in the village. I believe I understand the delicacy of your situation."

Behind the round gold spectacles, the doctor's clear blue eyes regarded Caleb with compassion. Perhaps it was a look he'd perfected over the years as a doctor, but it appeared genuine. And he didn't press the matter, simply waited for Caleb to respond—or not.

"Our situation is, as always, precarious while living among the Puritans."

"And yet, you do not live among them, as I understand it. Your homes are all outside of the village proper."

"As they must be." The doctor's brows pulled together in a silent question, so Caleb continued. "Thee may not know, being new here, but 'tis in the village charter that only Puritan families may own property within the village limits."

"Indeed, I did not know of this." The doctor sighed. "Neither am I surprised. 'Tis not an uncommon line in any charter, I fear. However"—he raised a finger—"the new Massachusetts charter includes the right of all religious persons to live here, so things are starting to change."

"Except for Catholics and Jews." Caleb should have kept his mouth shut, but the words came out before he gave them thought.

"So you have heard. I believe that, in time, they will also be included." The doctor cleared his throat. "That is neither here nor there to the issue at hand. I would like to discover why your young ladies and girls remain untouched by what is happening to the Puritan young ladies and girls in the village."

"Perhaps the simplest reason is that our children and young adults are not encouraged to mingle with those of the village, and those of the village have shown no desire for it either."

The doctor rubbed the white whiskers that stubbled his cheeks. "If you are correct, then we have to assume the attacks on the girls are contagious, and I cannot think that they are."

"Why not, since it started in a single household?" Not that Caleb understood a lot about illnesses, but everyone knew that a contagious disease could spread through a house. It was why he'd been praying so hard for his family with the fever under his roof.

"Because it has spread beyond the house." The doctor seemed to back off, almost to shrink into himself as he turned to the front again.

Caleb should let the matter drop. After all, he didn't really want to pursue it, and yet, whatever he learned he could share with the Friends for their own protection. It was a slippery slope, but he plunged forward.

"How can something of this nature spread, if 'tisn't contagious?"

Silence followed that question for a while, the horses' hooves plopping in the slush and the jingle of the harness the only sounds.

Then the doctor cast him a glance, his blue eyes sad but sharp. "I wish I understood, but this event in the village, 'tis outside of medical. 'Tis a spiritual thing, of that I am certain. 'Tis something evil."

A cold chill crept down Caleb's spine. Would he ever grow accustomed to people speaking such words out loud? "And it has spread beyond the two girls in the Parris household?"

"Indeed. Even to my own."

Caleb had heard of it from Thomas days ago, but to have the doctor speak out so freely about one of his own household was unsettling.

"I see I have shocked you." The doctor ran his fingers down his face. "It shocked me as well. However, my goodwife believes that Elizabeth has not been visited by any sort of spirit. She believes the girl is acting the part."

"Why would she?" Not that it was any of Caleb's business, but once again the words were out before he considered them. He must do better—he usually did. The tension between him and Hannah, the stress over the girls' illness, and wondering if they'd have to run—his worries were wearing him down. Impairing his judgment.

"'Tis a long story, but the girl never wanted to come to Salem Village. She is a somewhat troubled young woman, orphaned at a delicate age, shuffled to live with a great-aunt and -uncle older than her own grandparents. 'Twasn't easy for her. My Rachel feels that she is reveling in all this new attention."

Caleb held his tongue and thought before he asked, "Could it be the same with the first girls?"

"Nay." The doctor's response was without hesitation. "I witnessed their distress during the fits, and I saw the marks upon their bodies.

Their heartbeats were incredibly fast, they contorted into positions one could not manage on one's own, and the one girl repeatedly tried to throw herself into the fire. 'Tis my professional opinion that neither girl was acting of her own volition."

Possession. Caleb managed to keep the word to himself, but it lodged in his throat.

"Have you heard that the slave woman, Tituba, has confessed to being a witch?" the doctor asked.

The meeting in the woods, the ritual she and the other woman tried to do with the old hound, the chanting heard by Hannah. It was all true. Someone had acted stupidly—for he could think of no other word to describe it—to court the presence of evil among them. To invite it into their midst. And now they were all paying the price.

"I had. And that Sarah Good was arrested."

The doctor snorted. "'Tis easy to point fingers at the outcasts of society. I doubt the woman is guilty of anything more than annoying her neighbors and turning her back on the church. The first is no reason to accuse her, and the second is a matter to be dealt with by the church elders and ultimately by God, certainly not by a public trial."

Caleb agreed and was thankful that Thomas had brought Joseph to them. Even if this was a female perversity, as the doctor had said, if more people like his niece started claiming afflictions and pointing fingers, it may not stay that way. All the more reason to keep close to home. Should he retract his offer to let Thomas's sons come and pick up the furniture? If he did, how would he plant when the ground was ready? How would he feed his cattle, sheep, and horses? Without tools, there'd been no hay cut. Without the animals and crops, there'd be nothing to feed his family come winter.

He had little choice.

Rachel had exclaimed over her dressing table, and it'd done William's heart good to be able to bring her that little bit of joy. Now, however, he pondered all the Quaker man had said earlier that day. He also regretted that he'd shared what he had concerning Elizabeth. But there was something about the carpenter that bespoke of a solid nature and a trustworthy being. It had lowered William's guard. William knew how to keep his own counsel. As a physician, that was expected. Time would tell if he'd judged the Quaker correctly, or if his loose tongue would cause problems.

The clicking of Rachel's bone knitting needles went silent. "Is something wrong?"

Other than their niece pretending to be possessed, and William spilling his guts to a Quaker man? He shook his head. "Heavy thoughts, that is all."

"Care to share them?" Rachel always asked and never assumed.

"Buffum says there are no afflicted girls or young women among the Quakers." He tilted his head and looked at her. "I cannot help but wonder why."

She settled her hands with her knitting in her lap. "You believe 'tis a spiritual battle, do you not?"

"Indeed, as we have discussed."

"Do you worry that the Quakers are more spiritually correct than we Puritans?"

He hadn't even considered that, and he resisted the urge to respond with a quick nay. After all, what did he know about them? Not nearly enough. And yet... "I do not think so. The slave woman who has confessed—she was in charge of the reverend's children and niece because of his wife's long-lingering illness. One thing I know about the Quakers is that they do not allow slavery within their midst." It was something he'd heard and probably remembered because he approved of it.

"Then you think this woman instigated the..." Rachel paused for a moment. "The evil, perhaps demonic possession, of those poor girls."

Did he? Or more to the point, did he want to admit it out loud? "'Tis a heavy charge to level at anyone."

"Indeed. One that should not be voiced outside of our walls."

"I know not what to make of the slave's confession. I fear she was pressured into making it. I wish I had access to more books here. I wish I could read and study about the islands from which the woman came." He pushed his glasses up and pinched the bridge of his nose. "I have a fuzzy memory of reading about their culture a long time ago. A practice called voodon or something like that. It included the conjuring of spirits."

Rachel rubbed her arms. "I like not the sound of that."

"Nor I, but it might help to understand it better."

"Perhaps understanding would only encourage such things to further invade our home." Rachel's words were clear and sharp.

And wise. "You are right." William let out a long breath. "Even to research such things could mean opening ourselves to unwanted consequences."

"'Tis best to let the pastors deal with spiritual matters and content yourself with matters of the body." Rachel resumed her knitting.

The rhythmic clicking of her needles lulled William into a semi-doze, but the lingering question of why the Quakers weren't afflicted didn't completely go away. And the notion that everything happening could come back to the evils of slavery took firm root.

In his shop that evening, Caleb worked on Verity's dressing table. He should start on the chairs for the doctor and his goodwife. The boys had the legs all sanded for them, but his heart wasn't in it. Instead, working on Verity's project calmed him. He'd popped up to see the girls before coming to the barn. Tamson's fever had remained steady without another trip to the snowbank. Hannah remained at their bedside.

The family had pulled together, as a family should. Two of the older boys, Caleb Jr. and Joseph, had taken the team to be cared for and would do the farm chores. Hannah Jr. prepared the evening meal. Robert entertained the two little boys, much to Benji and Jonathan's delight. Caleb would be sorry to see him and Joseph return to the brewery.

Assuming they didn't flee the area.

Even as she watched over the girls, Hannah was sewing sturdy canvas bags to pack their belongings into should they have to run. After Caleb's alarming discussion with the doctor, that might happen.

The doctor's questions had circled in Caleb's head for the entire ride back. If this was, indeed, a spiritual attack—at least in the beginning, according to the doctor's account—why had it not spread to the Friends? At first, he'd wanted to think it was because the Friends were correct in their belief that anyone could access the Light of Christ, any man, woman, or child. But to lean on that was to lean on self-pride, and he'd forced himself to move away from the thought. The next answer came back to the women in the forest, the chanting, and the witch cake, if that was what it was. All dabbling in the dark side of the spiritual world.

There wasn't much Caleb knew about the dark spirits, other than what the Bible taught about Lucifer falling from heaven, the angel called Son of the Morning because of his handsomeness. Lucifer had thought to exalt himself above the Lord, and as a penalty, had been brought low, even into the pit. From there he had contact with all those on earth to deceive and promote sinfulness. If not for Jesus, all would be under his dominion. But the Friends believed that the Light of Christ saved them from that fate.

Caleb believed that.

Almost as alarming was the doctor's admission that his niece was involved only for the attention she was receiving. That was also a sinful thing, the desire of self-attention. Pride. The sin that had toppled Lucifer. What if more young women succumbed to the desire for attention? How fast would that spread? Faster than the winter fever now invading in his home, most likely.

He set aside his tools and intertwined his fingers, elbows on the workbench. *Lord God above us all, protect my family from this evil in the village and from the sickness that has come into our home. Protect David's family as well. I pray none of them fall ill from having been here among us. Amen.* He started to straighten, then clasped his hands together again. *And Lord, if it be Thy will, allow us to remain here on our farm and continue the life Thee have blessed us with. May we never take it for granted. Amen, again.*

He picked up his tools with a lighter heart.

Chapter 25

C OMING IN FROM THE barn with Caleb Jr. and Joseph after morning chores the next day, Caleb saw movement through the trees near the road. He shaded his eyes from the sun's early brightness.

"'Tis David." Caleb Jr. had better eyesight. "He appears to be alone."

"Aye." Caleb motioned the boys toward the house. "Go and have thy breakfast. Tell thy mother not to wait for me."

"Because David can talk the ears off a mule?" Caleb Jr.'s smirk was good-natured, and Joseph turned his face away to hide his chuckle.

"Be not disrespectful of thy elders," Caleb said in his best stern-father voice, scowling at his son. Not that he didn't agree. So did David, for that matter, but it was the principle of the thing.

The boys dashed to the house, doubtless for the meal and not from any fear Caleb's words had instilled.

David pulled his team to a halt, the horses blowing plumes of mist into the chilly air.

"Welcome, my friend." Caleb lifted a hand to stop David from descending. "We have illness here. 'Tis best thee keep thy distance."

"Robert told us yesterday. I wished to assure thee that all are healthy at our place still. 'Twould seem the sickness came after we left." He leaned forward on the seat. "How are the girls? Have any else sickened since?"

"Nay. 'Tis only the younger girls."

"My family prays for them."

"We thank thee for that."

David sat back and appeared to get comfortable, a sure sign it wouldn't be a short visit. "I was in Salem Town yesterday delivering a musket to a customer there."

"And thee have news?" Caleb did his best to hide a grin. His son hadn't been off the mark in his comment. While not a gossip in the malicious sense of the word, David loved to share the news he gathered. Perhaps he should have been a pamphleteer or a town crier.

"Sure and I do. Half the village was in the town. 'Twould seem three of the women accused have all been detained in the Salem Town jail."

Caleb's heart went out to them. He'd seen the jail, driven past it a number of times. The building was not the best kept, to be sure. From what he'd heard, it was not a nice place on the inside either. Those detained were put below ground in a cellar, where it was always damp and cold.

"There be talk"—David leaned forward—"that himself, Cotton Mather, has been contacted about the situation."

The name was well known in Massachusetts Colony, a Puritan reverend of great importance for his writings as well as his preaching. He was the son of Increase Mather, another important man among the Puritans, who seemed to be as much politician as preacher. Caleb only knew what he'd heard, having never read anything written by either man.

"Do thee think he will come to Salem Town himself then?"

"'Twould put on quite a show."

"One I will be happy not to see for myself."

David nodded. "Their presence would keep me at home with my goodwife, I assure thee."

"Thee would miss the opportunity to see such an august personage as Cotton Mather?" It seemed the sort of thing that would draw David like a flower drew a bee.

"Aye." His friend frowned. "For the man thinks ill of our kind."

Our kind. He meant the Friends. "Do thee believe his coming might be cause for alarm among us?"

"I pray not, but 'tis best to be prepared."

How many canvas sacks had Hannah stitched together? Enough yet? But they couldn't flee with the two girls so ill. And the Puritan preacher's appearance wasn't a sure thing. And the truth was, Caleb didn't want to leave. He didn't want to be pushed out of their home. As alarming as his talk with the doctor had been, it had made Caleb see that.

He rubbed the face of the horse standing next to him. How much of what the doctor had said should he share with David? Perhaps it was best to keep it to himself for now.

"Thee have that look that says thee know things thee are not going to share." David's voice held no censure. "Has it anything to do with thee talking to the doctor?"

"Robert told thee I fetched him, I see."

"In his defense, I offered to go for the man myself if 'twould help thee. He assured me that thee had already left."

"Indeed. I know it breached the agreement—"

"Nay." David waved a hand to cut him off. "When thy children fall ill, thee goes for the doctor. There be no fault in thee for that."

His assurance was welcome, if not completely true. There were some who would fault Caleb for not relying on prayer alone and trust the Lord to heal the girls. Some of the Friends were as anti-Puritan as the Puritans were anti-Friend.

"Well"—David gathered up his reins—"I am on my way to Salem Town again. While there yesterday, I met a man who desires a pair of dueling pistols." He nodded toward a box on the seat beside him. "I told him I would bring a pair for him to inspect today. If I sell these, my goodwife can purchase new shoes for all the children this fall."

"I did not know thee made dueling pistols." It seemed an odd thing for a pacifist Friend to create.

David shrugged. "I never thought I would sell them, but I was curious if I could create a pair worthy of the title." He winked. "I shall know soon."

Stepping away from the team, Caleb waited until his friend turned from the farm lane onto the road. Dueling pistols. He shook his head. David must be the only Friend who would make such a thing.

Caleb walked to the porch and stopped with his hand on the rail. Should he ask David to make a pistol for him? The money from the doctor's furniture would cover his bill at the blacksmith for the tools he needed with enough left over for such a weapon. A weapon that could protect his family and his home.

A weapon created only to shoot another human being.

When they'd run from Puritans the last time, he'd managed to keep them all safe—except for the unborn babe. Now with six children of his own and the two orphans in his care, a pistol would give him added...

What was he thinking? He could never use a weapon against one of God's children. Never. It shamed him that he'd considered the notion for even a moment. He bowed his head, one foot on the step, one hand clenching the porch rail. *Forgive me, Lord. How quickly I can slip into a sinful mindset. Please guard my thoughts and keep me from doing anything so wrong. So evil. Amen.*

Evil lurked close to every human heart. He must be more vigilant.

The day before had seemed to stretch into a week, but as William walked down through the village, he was refreshed by the gentle breeze. It blew from the southwest and carried the faint scent of spring. Spring always made him think of newness and hope.

Elizabeth had returned the prior evening full of life and vigor, so unlike the listless young woman who had accompanied them to Salem Village. She'd been nearly giddy with the details of the questioning done to Tituba, Goodie Osborne, and Goodie Good. Widow Scudder was still missing. If Elizabeth had noticed his and Rachel's lack of enthusiasm, she hadn't shown it. Or she hadn't cared. And as with the previous morning, Elizabeth was gone before he and Rachel had risen.

William had half a mind to request that she stay with the Putnams to spare Rachel from having to witness—even second hand—the proceedings in Salem Town. Elizabeth gave every impression of preferring their company to that of her great-aunt and uncle anyway. Or maybe he was just looking for an easy way out of the whole affair.

When he knocked at the Parris home, ten-year-old Tommy opened the door at William's knock.

"How fares your mother this morning?" William removed his hat and coat and set them over a chair. The usually crowded house was eerily quiet.

The young lad shrugged. "She is upstairs with Susannah."

"Who else is in the house?"

"None other. Father and the girls went with Indian John to Salem Town to see Tituba." The lad looked up at William. "Will she come home again? Tituba?"

"We shall have to wait and see." William hoped not. This family needed to learn to take care of itself. And they'd better learn quickly. "Be a good lad and warm some broth for your mother."

Tommy's mulish expression wasn't promising, but he moved toward the kitchen. Had anyone cared for Goodie Parris at all that morning?

William marched up the stairs to the now-familiar room and tapped on the open door's frame. "Goodie Parris?"

"What?" The woman turned her face toward him and blinked. "Oh, doctor." She struggled to sit up while the little girl curled beside her stirred awake. "I did not expect you so early."

"'Tisn't all that early." William tipped the cup near the bed. It was not only empty, it was bone dry. "When did you last drink anything?"

She pressed the back of her wrist to her forehead, her hand trembling. "Last evening, I think." Her face was pale, her eyes too dull, and her voice wispy.

Anger churned in William's middle. He took a couple of deep breaths. He shouldn't judge too quickly. Reverend Parris must accompany Betty and Abigail, as they surely had been summoned to testify in Salem Town and were far too young to go by themselves. And it was doubtful any would come into the house to help out, for fear of their families becoming afflicted. It was a proper mess.

After asking her the usual questions regarding her physical condition and then shooing Susannah below to use the privy, he took her hand. "Goodie Parris, you will not improve if you do not drink the broth and eat at least a piece of bread with it, or a piece of cheese. You are starving yourself."

She pressed her hand over the blankets covering her middle. "How can I eat when my daughter and my brother's daughter are caught up in this terrible situation." Tears welled in her eyes. "Samuel said 'tis a spiritual battle with our girls. I feel as if I should fast and pray for them."

It wasn't that he didn't believe in fasting and prayer, which was a standard part of the Puritan faith, with whole churches often picking a special day for exactly that when it was warranted. But for the woman on the bed before him, fasting could be a death sentence. William would never claim to know the mind of God, but he was fairly confident that fasting was never intended to jeopardize the life of the faster. Convincing a woman set on saving her children, however, would be a challenge. He'd seen this sort of maternal dedication more than once.

He sat back in the chair. "If you fast at this time, you shall not arise from this bed. Would it not be more to the girls' benefit to have you up and about, able to physically care for them now that Tituba is gone?"

"You think she will return?" There was a spark of something, maybe fear, in the woman's eyes.

"I think it very unlikely." While he might have hedged with Tommy, his mother needed to know the truth. "She was arrested and charged with witchcraft. After that, do you want her back in the house with your children?"

Goodie Parris"s hand fluttered on the bed coverings before settling at her collar. "When you put it that way, then nay. I would not. But Tituba took such good care of the children that 'tis hard to believe what has been said."

"Have you heard that she confessed?" His words brought a soft cry, her eyes sparking again. Good. She needed something to bring back her will to live.

"I had not. Why did Samuel not say as much?"

"I suspect he is trying to shield you from the unpleasantness of the situation. But I know you are strong enough"—he raised a finger—"if you will but eat and drink as I have prescribed, to care for your children as I am sure is your wish." He leaned against her maternal instincts.

"Aye. That is so." She sat a little straighter when Tommy appeared in the doorway with a steaming cup held between his hands. "Thank you, son. Just what the doctor ordered." The smile she summoned for the lad was genuine.

"Then I will leave you to drink that broth." He put a hand on Tommy's shoulder. "And Tommy will bring you a slice of bread, buttered if you have any."

William ushered the boy down the stairs, then faced him, keeping his voice low. "You have been left the man of the house while your father is gone. Your mother needs to drink every hour, a full cup. Give her tea with honey and cream if you run out of broth. Make sure she takes a piece of bread with each, or cheese if you have it. If she does not drink and eat, she will not be able to get out of that bed."

The boy's eyes grew larger. "You mean she might die?"

From what William knew of Goodie Parris's history, the boy probably couldn't remember his mother ever being robust and healthy. For him, his mother remaining in her bed had become normal.

"Do your best, Tommy, and pray for your mother. That is all any of us can do."

The walk home gave William time to think and rub the pain away from his chest. It did him no good to get angry, not at Elizabeth, nor Reverend Parris, nor anyone who had a hand in what was going on in the village. If only they would see what these witch accusations were doing to the people around them. They seemed blind to anything other than the sensationalism of the event. If they could see past that, they would see how it was damaging lives.

Like the Quakers were able to see, which was why they avoided the village altogether, thought they were doubtless losing commerce because of that decision. He had the urge to speak with the carpenter again, but to what end? He'd answered William's questions, albeit guardedly. Why had the Quakers remained unaffected by this? That was what he really wanted to know. But he suspected Buffum didn't have the answer. Perhaps no living person did.

The science-minded doctor in him didn't want to let it go.

Chapter 26

"**A**RE THEE READY?" CALEB held out his hand to Hannah.

"I am, but I wonder what thee are up to." She wound a shawl around her shoulders before slipping her hand in his. "Thee have been awfully secretive these past few days."

It had been three days since the doctor's visit, and both girls were well enough to leave their bed. They sat at the table, still tired from their ordeal, as the midday meal dishes were cleared away by Hannah Jr. and Joseph.

No one else had become ill. Hannah had worried over Jonathan's runny nose, but it had cleared up without a trace of fever or cough. Young boys and runny noses seemed to go together.

"Come and see." He led her outside into the sunshine. The ground was soft, the snow having mostly melted away for a time. Early March often brought a false spring that would disappear in another snowstorm before April ushered in the true spring.

Hannah tucked her hand in the crook of his arm, setting off an explosion of emotions in Caleb. The rift between them had narrowed, a step in the right direction. With the improved health of the girls, it seemed Hannah had found a level of security. If only the walk to the barn were longer, so he might enjoy the moment more.

Caleb pushed open the door to the shop and stepped back, allowing her to enter first. She rarely disturbed him when he was working, so she didn't come to the shop often. She didn't have time, being the busy mother of a large brood of offspring, with a house and garden to tend.

She moved to the workbench and walked around it, studying the dressing table.

"What do thee think?"

"'Tis beautiful." She twirled her finger in the carved scroll he'd added to the front, her brow crinkled. "But I thought thee had delivered Goodie Griggs's dressing table when thee returned the doctor to the village."

"That I did. 'Tisn't for Goodie Griggs." He rocked back on his heels and enjoyed the moment while she sorted it out, smiling when her eyes lit up.

"I have mine, as do both Hannah Jr. and Tamson, so I have to assume"—she came close and wrapped her arms around him—"thee made it for Verity."

He pulled her even tighter. "Are thee happy with it?"

"How could I not be?" She glanced at the house and back at him. "I still fear someone might come for her. I prayed so hard when thee left to fetch the doctor."

He traced his finger along the curve of her cheek. "I prayed as well."

"But the Lord has left her in our care. And now,"—she pointed to the dressing table—"she will have her own dressing table. A sign that she is to stay with us forever."

"Only the Lord knows what the future holds," he reminded her gently. "We live each day as He wills."

"Of course." But when she turned her face back to him, there was a mischievous twinkle in her eye. "But so far He has willed that Verity remain with us, be one of us. Every time she says *thee*, I feel it here." She pressed one hand to her chest. "It makes me so happy."

He would do anything to keep the girl so his wife would remain as happy as she was at that moment.

Anything short of purchasing a pistol from David.

The *scritch* of William's pen against paper kept an odd sort of rhythm with the *click* of Rachel's knitting needles. He should have done this from the start. If there was one person on earth he could consult regarding the witch accusations, one person who wouldn't think him daft for questioning the events surrounding them, it was his oldest colleague, Marcus Witherspoon. They'd studied together more years ago than William cared to remember and had always kept in touch. He'd written Marcus with their new address as soon as they'd arrived, but didn't expect a return letter yet. Had it been only two and a half weeks?

It felt more like a lifetime.

He poured his doubts, his questions, his troubling thoughts onto the paper, filling both sides before adding his name to the bottom. Then he sat back and rubbed the center of his chest.

"William, when will you tell me what that is all about?" Rachel gazed at him from her chair.

"I told you, I am writing to Marcus." He picked up the paper and blew across it gently to dry the ink.

She raised a brow. "Your chest?"

"'Tis nothing of concern." He folded the paper, carefully not looking her way. But it didn't work.

Rachel rose and came to stand beside him, her hand on his shoulder. "Have I not been a doctor's wife these many years? I am not ignorant, William."

"Of course you aren't."

"Then do not treat me as if I am."

He bowed his head for a moment before meeting her concerned eyes. "'Tis old age. Nothing I nor you can change, my dear."

"Your heart, am I correct?"

"Indeed. 'Tis as old as the rest of me." He stood and took her hands. "But I am not at death's door. These pains are but the beginning."

"The beginning of the end?" Her steel-gray eyes bore into his, searching for the truth.

He would give much to be able to tell her otherwise, but as she said, she was not an ignorant woman. Nor one to be reined in when she had the bit between her teeth. "Indeed."

"What would you say to a patient with the same symptoms? What advice would you give?"

"To rest more, worry less, avoid strong drink, and eat well." He gave her a wry grin. "But 'tis the same advice I give to all, is it not?"

"Indeed." Her nod was crisp even though the tiniest tremor slipped into her voice. "And you shall follow it, with my assistance, to the letter."

William didn't have the heart—poor choice of thought—to tell her that it would make little difference. Having reached the age of four and seventy, his remaining days were few. He'd already outlived both of his sisters, he being the elder by several years.

"Rest easy, my dear." He pulled her into an embrace. "You have not lost me yet."

Her words were muffled by his neckcloth, but still firm. "I will do all that I can to prolong the day."

Oddly enough, the pain dissipated with her words.

With the girls occupied upstairs by some diversion Hannah had provided, Caleb went out to the shop with Robert and Joseph. He opened the door and entered, the familiar scents of sawdust, bayberry, and beeswax greeting him. He gestured to the dressing table.

Robert walked around the table, studying it. "'Tis a fine piece of work."

"Thank thee, son." Caleb was touched by the sincerity in the boy's voice, and just a little melancholy that Robert hadn't taken to the craft of carpentry. "'Tis for Verity."

Joseph gaped at the piece. "For Verity? All to herself?"

And then it hit Caleb—Joseph had nothing of his own. Had he made a grave error to include the boy in this endeavor?

With a gap-tooth grin, the orphan turned to him and dispelled his doubts. "She will love it. Widow Scudder took away all Verity's nice things when she came to live at the shack." The boy sobered. "Those things meant a lot to her, especially her momma's shawl pin. Verity cried long into the night. Not loud, but enough that I could hear, because she slept on the shelf above mine. It near broke my heart when I took it to the pawnbroker in Salem Town."

Children sleeping on wooden shelves. Forced to sell their family belongings. Caleb had to bite his tongue lest he say something he shouldn't. After all, the children had been removed and were in decent homes now. And truth be told, the old widow had probably done the best she could. She'd escaped capture by those hunting her so far, for which he was glad. Nobody should have to face such injustice, to be charged because of one's status in society.

"Perhaps this will bring Verity some peace." Caleb pointed to Joseph. "Can thee carry the bench by thyself?"

The boy puffed out his chest and spread his arms wide to hoist the bench. "Sure can."

"Robert and I will carry the dressing table. Take the other side, son."

They crossed the yard to the house and made it up the steps and into the kitchen without any uproar, so the girls hadn't seen them. Hannah Jr. turned from a pot at the hearth, a long wooden spoon in her hand.

"What have thee, Father?"

"'Tis for Verity," Joseph said before Caleb could answer.

The spoon splashed into the pot, and Hannah Jr. hurried across the room. "'Tis beautiful." She ran her fingers over the top. "Verity will be so pleased."

"Would thee fetch her?" Before the words were fully formed, his daughter was on her way out of the kitchen. Everyone seemed excited about the gift. Not that it could replace what the girl had lost, but if it brought her some joy, it would be worth it. "Boys, let us stand in front of the dressing table until she arrives."

Hannah came first, the two little boys following her. She ushered them out of the way as the tread of feet on the stairs signaled the girls' approach.

"Thee must go first." Hannah Jr.'s voice broke the silence that had gathered around them.

"But why?" Verity's question was filled with uncertainty.

"Thee will see. Go on."

At Hannah Jr.'s gentle urging, Verity appeared in the doorway.

Joseph's ear-to-ear grin must have reassured her, because she stepped into the room and looked around at everyone gathered there. Tamson and Hannah Jr. squeezed in behind her.

"Verity." Caleb motioned the boys to move out of the way. "This is for thee."

Her mouth opened, but no sound emerged.

Tamson, however, squealed with delight. "Thy own dressing table!" She fairly hauled the smaller girl across the width of the kitchen.

Verity put out a timid hand, one finger tracing along the table's top. "'Tis mine?" She looked up at Caleb, blue-gray eyes round and uncertain. "Truly?"

He knelt beside her. "I made it just for thee and thee only."

Two fat tears gathered on her lower lids, and then she threw herself into Caleb's arms, sobbing. He held the girl, but looked to his wife, whose eyes were also glistening.

Tamson had her arms around Verity from the back, and as usual, was not at a loss for words. "Are thee not pleased, Verity? Do thee not like it?"

The head burrowed against his chest, sandwiched between him and Tamson, nodded, but the sobbing didn't abate.

"You must like it," Joseph said. "'Twas made just for you."

Verity sobbed louder, shaking in Caleb's arms.

Hannah approached and rescued him, taking the child into her arms. "She is just overcome." She lifted the girl and carried her to a chair, settling Verity on her lap and lifting her face. "Are thee not, Verity?"

A nod, a few sniffles, and then a wobbly smile.

"I know it cannot replace the shawl pin," said Joseph, "but 'tis a handsome piece of furniture for your very own."

Verity let out a soggy hiccup. "I shall treasure it always."

All those years before, when Caleb and Hannah had fled with little Hannah Jr., they'd left almost all of their belongings behind. They'd had to start over. But Verity, she'd left more than just things. She'd lost her entire family, shuffled to an elderly uncle who had also passed, once again leaving her alone.

His own children had been blessed with an intact family, if one didn't count the sister they never knew, but for how long?

That evening, when the barn chores were done and the kitchen cleaned, Caleb called everyone into the parlor. It was time to talk to the children. They needed to be prepared.

When they'd all settled, some on the furniture, some on the floor, and little Jonathan on Hannah Jr.'s lap, Caleb cleared his throat. "'Tis time to speak of the happenings in the village. Thee know the Friends have decided to keep our distance from the village and from the Puritans who live there."

"But Father," Tamson said, "thee went and brought the doctor when I was sick."

"Indeed. And I would do so again, should the need arise. 'Twould be a good thing if we had a doctor among the Friends here, but we do not."

"I shall be a doctor when I grow up," said Benji from where he sat on a rug with Rags beside him, bringing a few chuckles in response.

"I hope thee will, son," Caleb said. "But until thee can step into that position, we Friends must rely on the village doctor."

"Will thee be censured for bringing the doctor here?" Robert asked.

Caleb shook his head. "I think not. 'Twas done for the good of my family, not to disrespect the decree of the Friends."

"Let thy father have his say now." Hannah's admonition and pointed look that swept the room quieted it.

"There is a possibility that we might have to leave this place—at least for a while."

"Why, Father?" As usual, it was Tamson who couldn't remain quiet.

How much should he say? He glanced at Hannah, who nodded. If they didn't know enough, they might not take this as seriously as they should. Caleb told them as much history as he'd already shared with Hannah Jr. Everything except about the daughter they'd lost.

"So you see, we may have to leave in a great hurry. Thy mother has been stitching canvas sacks, enough that each of thee will have one. Thee are to pack it with at least three changes of clothing, a blanket, and anything thee might need that will fit." He lifted a finger and made eye contact around the room. "But do not make it too heavy. Thee shall all have to carry thy own sack, except for Benji and Jonathan. Caleb Jr. and Robert will carry theirs, along with their own. Thy mother and Hannah Jr. and I will carry extra sacks of food. If at all possible, we shall pack Dolly and Dandy as well."

"We cannot leave the horses behind," Caleb Jr. said. "What of the cows, the sheep?"

"Our priority is our family and the horses, if we can take them, but the livestock we will set free to fend for themselves." Except for the milking cows, but he didn't want to upset the children by going into that. He'd do what he had to, if and when the time came.

Caleb and Hannah answered the questions that followed, even reassuring Benji that Rags and Button would go with them.

"If we had another musket," Caleb Jr. said, "Robert and I could hunt together for more meat to dry."

Caleb studied him, and the boy—the young man—didn't flinch. He wasn't trying to take advantage of a bad situation to get what he wanted. And he made good sense. If the family had to flee, they would need more meat wherever they wound up. Caleb nodded. "Go tomorrow and see David. Tell him what thee need."

With a solemn nod, Caleb Jr. said, "I will."

"I have told thee all these things because we must be prepared should we have to leave. But know this, 'tis my utmost desire to remain right here." He jabbed a finger at the floor.

"If thee go, will I go with thee?" Verity's voice was small and trembled.

"Of course thee will." Tamson put her arm around the younger girl. "Thee are part of our family now. Thee even have thy own dressing table."

Verity's eyes remained locked on Caleb.

He nodded, just a dip of his chin, but she returned the gesture before allowing herself to be tugged away by Tamson. The rest of the children rose and left the parlor.

Hannah came to him, and he stood, taking her into his arms. She leaned against him without a word, her head pressed against his chest, the scent of her hair like a breath of spring. Was this the end of the rift between them? Nothing would please him more.

Or was it just a truce? A coming together out of need, bracing for what might happen next?

Chapter 27

T HE WALK TO THE brewer's shop, breathing in the fresh air, revived William's lagging spirits. They'd had three days of rain, cold and insistent, the kind that frequented the middle of March and turned the snow into slop and then the slop into ankle-deep mud. Then another few days of gray clouds. This morning's sunshine, following a night of driving wind, had dried things out nicely. It'd been eight days since he'd been taken to the Quaker's farm to tend the sick girls. The road was finally dry enough to fetch home more of Rachel's new furnishings.

A cheerful thought after his morning visit with Goodie Parris. If only the woman would listen to him. She was eating and drinking some, but not enough. She was hanging on to life but far from living it. It frustrated him that her caretaker was a ten-year-old boy. Yet William understood the complicated circumstances for that family—the very tragic circumstances.

He reached the brewer's shop and scraped the mud from his boots on the blade mounted near the door for that purpose. A bell jingled overhead when he entered. "Hello?"

The room was empty except for the great vats of bubbling brew and the stacks of barrels and kegs everywhere, until a younger man popped up from behind a long counter on one side. "Can I help... are you not the doctor?"

"I am."

He whipped off a linen apron and tossed it aside. "I am Benjamin Buffington." He came around the counter. "Father said I should expect you when the weather turned. I am to drive you to the Buffums' farm. 'Twill take me a few minutes to harness and hitch the team."

"Slow down, lad." William raised his hands, palms out. "I am in no rush."

"Aye, sir." He motioned to a bench near the hearth. "Would you have a seat? I must fetch my brother to cover the shop, then I will bring the wagon around to the front." The words came like water rushing over a fall. The lad was very keen on running the errand, that much was certain.

William perched on the bench. "Take your time. I am quite content to enjoy the wonderful aromas in here."

Benjamin nodded and rushed out the back door.

Oh, to have such youthful energy.

The lad then entered through the front door.

How had he circled the building so quickly? Youthful energy was one thing, but he must be quite the sprinter to have achieved that feat.

"Can I help you?" the lad asked.

William pointed to the back of the shop. "You just left to fetch your brother—" At the boy's wry grin, William remembered that the brewer had twin sons.

"I am Thomas Jr., and that was Benjamin, I am sure."

"Indeed. I should have remembered."

The lad made a dismissive gesture, no doubt used to fooling people. The two young men were identical twins to the extreme. William had attended the birth of several sets of twins during his career, but they often grew to differ from each other with age. Not this pair. They couldn't be more than twenty, but looked like matching bookends.

Buffington came in through the back of the shop and stopped on the other side of the counter. "Doctor." His greeting filled the building. "Good to see you. How is your goodwife doing?"

"Rachel is as well as can be expected."

Buffington shook his head. "A nasty business, all that is happening in Salem Town."

Everyone knew that he and Rachel were not shepherding Elizabeth back and forth to Salem Town, that she was in the care of the Putnams.

It had been just over a week since the proceedings had moved there. For seven days, each evening, he'd had to listen to Elizabeth enthuse over which girl was accusing whom. At least they had suspended questioning on Sunday.

It was more than a little suspicious that those accused seemed to have been first the outcasts of the village. The whole situation was out of hand. No amount of talking to Elizabeth had changed the young woman's mind. She had convinced herself all that was happening was true.

William had been asked, again, to be part of the group to examine the accused for a witch's mark. He'd refused and would continue to do so. Hysteria had taken over other young ladies on the heels of what might have been an actual possession of the Parris's two girls and was now the root of the problem.

Time to change the subject. "I cannot thank you enough for letting me hire your wagon and strong son to fetch my goodwife's new furnishings."

The brewer's brows drew down into an uncustomary frown. "That was nasty business as well, the scoundrel selling you the house and all, and then making off with what he did. Shameful."

"'Tis all water beneath the bridge. Rachel is very pleased with the furniture from Caleb Buffum."

"He is the best carpenter around, I will say that. And a good man."

William shifted on the bench, sorting his words before he asked, "You are not put off by his being a Quaker?"

The large man glanced around the room, though none other had entered. "Nay. 'Tis neither here nor there to me. He and his goodwife are caring people. They have taken in an orphan girl, and they currently have the orphan boy who is apprenticed to me. I feared he might get swept up in—" He cut off his words and waved a hand toward the front door. "Better safe than sorry."

"Indeed. Better if none of us were caught up in this hysteria." There, he'd used the word.

Leaning forward, the brewer planted an elbow on the counter and dropped his chin to his fist. "Then you do not believe this is witchcraft?"

William would have to tread lightly. The brewer seemed an honorable man, but hysteria could frighten otherwise rational individuals. And frightened people sometimes lost their good sense.

"What I witnessed at first made me believe there was something spiritual happening to the reverend's girls. But what I am hearing now makes me think it has moved on to something else altogether."

A meaty hand smacked the counter. "As I said to my goodwife just last evening. 'Tis a shame what this had become, one family accusing another—a family they do not get along with over some piece of land belonging to a relative. I know not the extent of the feud, but it had been going on for years."

"So I have been told."

"And another thing"—Buffington pointed a finger at William—"why have we heard not a word about this spreading beyond the village? None are being accused in Salem Town, and yet they moved the proceeding there days ago."

"Nor has it shown up in the Quaker community, and their farms surround the village."

"I had not thought of that." The big man dropped his hands to the counter and leaned forward again, as forward as his belly would allow. "Have you an opinion on the reason behind it?"

"Nay, I do not." Perhaps he could broach the subject again with Buffum that morning.

The energetic lad bounded through the front door. "We are set to leave when you are ready." He fairly bounced on his toes.

"Have a care with the wagon," Buffington said. "'Tis still muddy along the way."

"Worry not, Father, I shall be most careful."

His father raised a brow above the gold rim of his spectacles, but said no more.

After sliding off the high stool, William strode to the door. "Thank you, again."

"'Tis no inconvenience at all." The lad held the door open. "Happy to help."

After being assisted onto the wagon's seat, William waited while Benjamin untied the horses, took his seat, and shook the reins over the matched black team. The heavy animals leaned into their harnesses and got the wagon moving.

"'Tis good you asked for our help." Benjamin glanced at him. "Our wagon is the sturdiest in the village, strong enough to hold dozens of kegs of cider and ale. Father had it made with wider wheels to handle better in mud, and it also has a set of broad runners, so we can deliver in almost any weather."

"Your father is a good businessman. Will you follow in his footsteps?"

"Thomas Jr. will, I suppose. But as for me"—he lifted and dropped one shoulder—"I would rather work outside in the fields or the orchard." Then he grinned. "Someone has to grow the apples for cider and the barley for ale."

No one who would interest Elizabeth then.

They lapsed into a companionable silence until he turned the horses onto the Buffums' farm lane. Two dogs barked their greeting. The red-and-white one had been on the girls' bed when he'd been here before. And since he'd not been called back, that should mean that the girls had recovered from their winter fever.

At least someone had listened and responded to his advice.

With a final sweep of the planer, Caleb set the handle for the new scythe aside and dusted off his hands. The heavy wagon coming up the lane with its bells ringing could only be the brewer's, so he took a rag and wiped away the loose sawdust clinging to the pair of dry sinks and the six table chairs he and the boys had finished for the doctor. By the time Buffington's son had the team stopped, Caleb had everything in order. He opened the door.

"Welcome." He started forward to help the doctor down, but young Buffington beat him to it, handing the older man down as if he were fragile.

And maybe he was. He must be into his seventies. Caleb's father had lived to be seventy and nine. In keeping with tradition, he being the youngest of the family, Caleb had brought his parents to live their final years here at the farm with them. More memories to leave behind if they must pack up and go. Yet another reason to stay.

His feet solidly on the ground, the doctor straightened his coat and looked at Caleb. "I hope this is a good time to collect more of my order."

"I have more ready." Caleb stepped aside and allowed the doctor to enter.

"Benjamin!" Robert raced across the yard with Joseph only a stride behind. The shout drew everyone's attention, and even Hannah Jr. stepped out of the dairy to watch.

"Those boys will have a good catch-up while thee inspect things." Caleb closed the door to the shop.

"Buffington mentioned you had his orphan apprentice staying for a while. 'Tis very kind of you to take him in."

"'Tis nothing. He is a good lad and gets along with our children."

"He also mentioned you had taken in another orphan."

Caleb's heart dropped, and he had to clear his throat to answer. "We did. A little girl." The less the doctor knew, the better.

"One of those I attended to on my first visit? I trust both are doing well."

He obviously wasn't going to let it go. Hannah would be beside herself if she were there. "The younger girl. Both are over their illness."

Caleb strode to the freshly dusted pieces and turned to the doctor. "Here are the dry sinks. I took the liberty of adding a little carved scrollwork along the fronts. Thy wife seemed to appreciate it on the side table." He pointed to the markings, and it seemed to distract the doctor from his questions.

"Very nice. Rachel will be so pleased."

"I hope thy niece will be pleased with hers as well."

The doctor rubbed the back of his neck. "I would hope so too, but the girl is most unpredictable at the moment."

How did one respond to that? Caleb's face must have mirrored his confusion.

"You have probably not heard all the news of the village, or rather, the news from Salem Town." Dr. Griggs huffed out a breath. "Our Elizabeth is overly caught up in all the witch accusation nonsense."

"Nonsense?" Caleb wished the word back as soon as he'd said it. The last thing he needed was to talk to the doctor—any Puritan—about the witch accusations and arrests and whatever else was happening. He should keep his mouth shut.

The doctor pointed to the stools. "May I sit?"

"Of course. Are thee all right?"

"Physically, I am fine. Oh, getting on in years, but fit enough for all of that." Being rather short in stature, he had to climb onto the stool. "'Tis all this witchcraft talk. It wearies a man, especially when one of his household becomes involved."

To not sit would be rude, so Caleb took the other stool, perching on it like a bird ready to take flight. Which he might if the conversation went in a bad way. A way that might point fingers at him or any of the Friends.

"Since our last conversation"—Dr. Griggs leaned toward Caleb—"have you had any ideas as to why your people have been unafflicted? 'Tis still so strange."

A bolt of fear shot through Caleb. It sounded too much like what had happened in the past. The Puritans had come to the conclusion that they must drive out—or kill—those who, they had convinced themselves, brought the sickness to the colony by way of evil spirits.

"You have gone pale." The doctor grabbed Caleb's shoulder with a surprisingly strong hand. "Rest easy."

How could he, when history was about to repeat itself?

Chapter 28

"**P**ERHAPS YOU SHOULD LIE down."

The doctor's voice pulled Caleb out of the dark memories. The angry shouts of the mob, the bellow of muskets, and the acrid smoke from burning buildings. Hannah huddled atop Samson, Hannah Jr. clutched in her arms, eyes wide with fear. The slap of tree branches against his face as Caleb led them through the dark forest, doing everything he could to muffle the sounds of their passing. To get them to safety. The memories had come over him as if they were happening again

"Mr. Buffum? Caleb?"

"I am fine." He pulled in a long breath and met the doctor's eyes, concerned behind the round spectacles. "I am fine. It just brought back..." It was time to stop talking.

"Have you experienced some sort of spiritual battle before?"

"Nay." He rose too fast, making his head swim, but he moved to the window. Outside in the sunshine, the young people gathered around the Buffington twin—Hannah Jr., Robert, Caleb Jr., and Joseph. Tamson and Verity were hurrying across the yard to join them with little Benji and Jonathan in tow. All those he'd need to get to safety.

Lord, how shall I manage this time?

"Caleb, something has distressed you. If 'twas something I did or said..." The doctor let his words drift off.

"Nay." Something niggled at Caleb's spirit, but he couldn't quite grasp it. He closed his eyes, thumb and fingers pressed against his temples. It was almost as if...

"If you would tell me what has upset you," the doctor's voice cut in, "perhaps I could be of more assistance."

Trust him.

They weren't words Caleb heard. They were words he felt deep in his spirit. As difficult as it was, trusting a Puritan he barely knew, Caleb heeded them.

"Can thee stop the madness of men who dislike and distrust others based on how they worship the God of heaven?" Caleb turned as the words came out, not sure where they'd come from. "Based on how they live and raise their families?"

The doctor sat straighter and blinked, taking his time to respond. "You are speaking of something that happened before, are you not?"

"I am." Caleb returned to his stool and sat. "And I will do whatever I must—short of raising my hand against another human being—to keep my family out of what is happening in the village."

"You have nothing to fear from me." The doctor pressed a hand to his chest. "I assure you. I wish only to learn how your people have remained unaffected by what is happening so close to you. You see, I believe 'tis a spiritual battle that was started by something dark. I cannot prove it. I have read everything in my medical books as well as reports on witchcraft written by Cotton Mather, but it tells me not how some are affected and others are not. That is what I wish to learn."

"Do thee believe in witchcraft?"

Dr. Griggs removed his spectacles, rubbed them with his sleeve, then replaced them and faced Caleb again. "I do. 'Tis in the Bible, after all. I will tell you this, because honesty between you and me will help me understand. I will not repeat anything said here to another person. I would appreciate the same pledge from you."

So the doctor also feared retribution. In the pause that followed, Caleb said, "Thee have it."

That seemed to satisfy the doctor. "I believe there was witchcraft—or something evil—when I arrived in the village. What I saw in those two girls could not be explained otherwise." He shook his head. "But what I am hearing now, what is playing out in the village and Salem Town, I believe 'tis something else." He cleared his throat. "I believe the evil that lurks in the heart of man is now at work."

Caleb cocked his head, at a loss for words. What was the doctor trying to say?

"Let me be clearer, and again, this must stay between us for now. I believe, as does my goodwife, that Elizabeth is seized by her own hysteria—not possession—as I told you before. There are discrepancies in her accounts, and she appears to be... Well, she appears to be enjoying the whole affair. " He let out a weary sigh. "I fear a good deal of the blame rests upon me. The girl never wanted to move here. She is high-strung, and we spoiled her, as her elderly guardians. Rachel believes she is acting out for the attention she is receiving."

Leaning closer, Caleb asked, "And do thee believe the others are acting out in a similar way?"

"Not the two girls of the Parris household." A vigorous shake of his head sent the doctor's wispy hair into disarray. "Nay. Their fits were beyond the physical, I would rest my reputation as a physician on that." His direct blue eyes backed up his words.

Could the evil conjured by the chanting have moved on, leaving the humans behind to continue the madness on their own? In many ways...

That was more chilling than the evil itself.

The man across from William was obviously shaken by what he'd revealed, but William still lacked answers. He'd opened himself up to Caleb. Would the other man not reciprocate? The long pause between them would have been silent but for the laughter of children outside, a glaring contrast to the tension within the carpenter's shop.

Caleb shook his head and straightened on the stool. "I appreciate thy honesty and trust. I fear I have no answers for thee, however. There has been no sign of hysteria among the Friends—or evil possession."

"Have you no guess, no matter how far-flung, as to why?" William pressed.

The carpenter ran a hand around the back of his neck. "Maybe one."

At last. William leaned forward against his crossed legs. "Which is?"

"When the orphan girl came to live with us, she was terrified of so many things. Of course she had been through much sorrow, but it seemed deeper than that. In fact, my goodwife and I spoke of it, the difference in how she reacted to things compared to our own children."

"And what did you decide?" William forced himself to breathe as he awaited the answer.

Caleb shifted on his stool, obviously very uncomfortable with the conversation. "The girl was obsessed with fear of sinning."

William leaned back. "As we should all be, should we not?"

"I believe we should be aware of sin and avoid it, of course, as the Bible teaches. But for Verity"—he shot William a look that physician couldn't interpret—"'twas more than that. 'Twas as if she understood nothing of God's grace and mercy."

God's grace and mercy.

The Puritans believed in those too. Of course they did. But William struggled to recall when he'd heard a reverend preach upon either, much less the two together.

"I wondered," Caleb continued, "if the constant fear of doing wrong was too much for the girl to handle, especially at her tender age. Too big a load for her to carry. My goodwife and eldest daughter spent a lot of time with her explaining about God's grace and mercy and the Light of Christ, which is available to all who believe in Him."

"And did that cure the child of her fears?"

"Not entirely. But she has lived with them for a long time. I believe 'twill take more than the few months she has been here for her to accept that her early teaching was"—he cast a glance at William—"overly harsh."

William wanted to bristle at the criticism of his Puritan beliefs, yet at the same time, he couldn't argue that some of their teachings were harsh. But so was life. "How would such a variance in belief cause the two young village girls to be...possessed?"

"Thee might not appreciate my thoughts on this."

So he'd noticed William's reaction despite his attempt to conceal it. Perhaps a man so perceptive should be listened to, no matter if it hurt his Puritan sensibilities or not. "Please. I would like to hear them."

With visible reluctance, the carpenter said, "I think the girls were more open to the evil visited upon them because they had no hope of overcoming it. Perhaps they were even enticed by it because it seemed easier than the constant strain of avoiding it."

He hated to admit it, but the man had a valid point. "How have you taught your children differently?"

"We have taught them that sin is wrong, temptations are many, but we can overcome through Christ—not on our own." Caleb leaned closer to William. "The Bible says, 'I am able to do all things through the help of Christ, which strengtheneth me.' We Friends believe that. As we also believe in forgiveness for those who fall short—if they repent. We have taught our children that grace and mercy and God's love cover our shortcomings through the sacrifice of Christ."

The carpenter hadn't mentioned teaching children of the church nor of the church's doctrine. But then, they didn't call their meetings church. There was no hierarchy. To them, everyone had equal standing before God.

Therein lay the heresy William had always heard about.

Well, William had asked for it, and in truth, he couldn't fault the man's logic. Even adults deprived of hope could mentally break down. He'd seen it more than once, generally after the death of a spouse. Betty and Abigail were but girls. Had the stress of living up to the reverend's standards—the Puritan's standards—been too much for them? Had they given in to evil because it was easier than continuing to fight it?

Plausible, disturbingly so.

That didn't explain Elizabeth or the other girls—girls older than Betty and Abigail—who were now claiming to be afflicted. Those fell under the category William had already surmised as girls wanting attention or acting out for other personal reasons. Pointing fingers at others and claiming false witness. Succumbing to a sin they found more enticing, more exciting than their staid Puritan life.

Caleb forced himself to remain still as the doctor took in his explanation. What would happen next? Would they need to leave the farm now? This very day? Had his impulsive words sealed their destiny?

The older man had hunched over on his stool, hand to his forehead, elbow planted on his crossed leg. Then he lifted his eyes to Caleb's, seeming to have aged another five years since he'd climbed upon the stool. "I believe you may be correct."

Not knowing whether to feel relief or deepening concern, Caleb kept his mouth shut, answering with the slightest of nods.

"I do not, however," the doctor continued, "have any idea how to stop what has been started."

"Nor do I." Caleb kept the eye contact. "Will thee discuss this with thy church elders?"

"Nay. I said I would keep it between us, and I shall." One frail shoulder lifted and dropped. "I do not think any would heed me at this point. 'Tis like a child's snowball, rolled along, picking up more snow, growing larger and larger until the one rolling it can no longer move it."

A shiver wormed its way along Caleb's spine. "So what will thee do?"

"Do?" The older man blinked several times, eyes roaming the interior of the shop, but not as if he saw anything there. "I have no idea."

Something nudged Caleb to speak. "I fear I must move my family."

"What?" The blue eyes came back to Caleb, sharp behind the spectacles. "Why?"

"The last time we were driven out by Puritans, 'twas just my wife and one babe. This time, I have a large family to move. I cannot wait until the houses start to burn."

The doctor straightened on his stool. "Why should it come to that? You are not afflicted. You are not to blame for what is happening, what has happened, in the village."

"'Twill matter little to some. Those who call us Quakers need little excuse to bring grief to our doors."

"If you run, you will look guilty."

The words hit Caleb square in the chest. He hadn't thought of it that way. "But if we stay, some of us might die. Some could be hanged as witches, others burned out or burned alive."

The doctor flinched.

"I have seen it with my own eyes." Why Caleb felt the need to explain, he wasn't sure. "The ruins of a house burned to the ground, the family locked inside. I have held my goodwife as she mourned the loss of our child, born too early to survive, in a shallow cave barely out of the weather where we hid from those with torches and muskets."

"She lost a babe?"

"Hannah was expecting another child at winter's end." He wiped his free hand across his brow. "But the child was lost to us the night after we fled. I know not why, perhaps the fear, or the shock, or the exposure to such cold as we hid in the cave, afraid to make a fire lest we draw those chasing us to our location. I helped her deliver a little girl not much longer than my hand. The babe was perfect and tiny. Although she kicked her feet and her hands opened and closed, she never uttered a sound or opened her eyes. Or drew a full breath. Within moments, she had slipped away."

"I am..." The old man drew an unsteady hand down his face. "I am so very sorry that you had to endure that." Then he lifted his eyes to Caleb again. "I promise you this—I will do all within my power to see that it does not happen again. Not here in Salem Village. I will keep our conversation private, as I know you will too, but I shall speak to those I believe I can trust among the Puritans about the situation in general." His lips lifted in a wry smile. "We are not all monsters such as you have experienced before, I assure you."

Did it assure Caleb? Maybe a little. The doctor was making an effort, holding out an olive branch. To not accept it would be ungracious. "I know thee are not, but how can thee stop those who might wish us harm, or just wish us gone so that our lands and our homes would be left abandoned?"

"We are both believers in the God of heaven, are we not?"

There may have been a time when Caleb would have refuted that question, but he'd met too many of the village Puritans who were nothing like those who had attacked them in the past. Men who had treated them with kindness and respect, like Thomas Buffington, Nathaniel Ingersoll, John Biddle, and the doctor who sat across from him. "We are."

"Then perhaps what we need is a little more faith—the both of us." The doctor sighed. "And more prayer."

"I pray for my family's safety every day, and for the safety of all the Friends."

"I shall join you in that prayer, and I believe there are others who will as well."

"Thee are new to the village—" Caleb stopped short when the doctor raised a palm toward him.

"Indeed, but I am not new to life, young man. People change little from place to place. Human nature is what it is. I will pray for your family, and in return, ask that you will pray for mine. For my niece, but also for my goodwife. My greatest fear is that someone might point a finger at her."

Caleb opened his mouth, but snapped it shut again. He'd given no thought to the fears of those in the village, even though he'd seen it firsthand. Those scurrying along the street, heads down, not making eye contact. Thomas bringing Robert home and then sending Joseph too. Puritans reacting out of—fear. But Caleb had worried only for his own. He drew in a deep breath. "I will add thee and thy family in my prayers every day."

"'For where two or three are gathered together in my Name, there am I in the midst of them.'" The old man's voice was worn and soft, but the quote was heartfelt. "Know this, Caleb. Should any begin to accuse you and your Friends, I shall stand against them and declare the injustice of it. I believe Buffington will too." He slapped his hands to his knees and slid off the stool. "Now, show me what else you have started working on over here."

It stirred something deep within Caleb. Something that rose in his spirit, not in a combative way, but in strength all the same. Could the two of them, a Friend and a Puritan, praying to the same God in Caleb's humble carpenter shop, change the outcome of what evil had brought to the village?

Chapter 29

"**W**AIT UNTIL YOU SEE the stuffed chairs he is making next," William said as Rachel examined the fine pieces of furniture he'd brought home the evening before. "He showed me the sketches while I was there. The man is talented."

Rachel gave him a side glance, then faced him and crossed her arms. "You are chattering like a squirrel, my dear. You only do that when you have something to say and yet do not wish to say it."

He rubbed the center of his chest until her brows rose, then dropped his hand. "The conversation I had with Caleb was...'twas enlightening, but not in a comfortable way."

"Have a seat and I shall make tea while you tell me about it."

William sat, enjoying her movements as Rachel bustled about making the tea. "We spoke of the differences in raising children between the Puritans and Friends."

Rachel paused, a plate of something smelling of cinnamon in her hand. "What friends?"

"'Tis what the Quakers call themselves, the Friends."

"Oh." She slid the plate onto the table and then brought the teapot over before taking her chair. "I did not know that they referred to themselves differently."

"I suspect there is much we know not about them."

She poured cream into each cup, and then the rich, dark brew from the teapot.

William took his and enjoyed the first sip, though it was still hot enough to fire its way down his throat. He sighed and sat back. "In the end, we believe in, pray to, and worship the same God, no matter what we choose to call ourselves. I believe that is what truly matters."

"But I have heard they are heretics." Rachel took a dainty sip of her tea, then cocked her head at him. "That they even allow their women to speak in church."

William chuckled and pointed a finger at his wife. "If we Puritans ever allowed such a thing, you would relish the chance, and you cannot tell me differently."

Her reserved smile brought back memories of a younger Rachel, her unique blend of strength, willfulness, and beauty that had so captured his heart in the end.

He looked to the ceiling, and then back at her. "I believe we would do well to embrace them as our neighbors and friends. We could learn from them—and they from us. In fact, young Buffington was quite enjoying his time driving me around. The Buffum youngsters and he were a lively bunch, talking and laughing and, by the time I was ready to leave, embroiled in some sort of a game involving throwing sticks. Perhaps we should encourage such interaction between the young before they become jaded by too much doctrine."

"Oh, my." Rachel set down her cup. "Such words could land you in trouble with the church elders."

"That is just the point, my dear. The Friends are also faithful. I believe it would do us good to reach out to them. What can it hurt to—?"

Their front door burst open and Elizabeth rushed in, her face flushed, hair escaping from beneath her bonnet.

Rachel stood. "What is it? What has happened?" Fear colored her questions.

"I had to tell you before we leave for Salem Town. This morning when I arrived at the Putnams', Ann Jr. told me that Martha Corey's specter visited her in the night." Elizabeth's face radiated satisfaction and excitement. "She will accuse the woman at the hearings today. You should come, both of you, to see this."

William stood. "We shall not." Perhaps he had spoken with more force than necessary by the frown his niece gave him. "Have we not met Goodie Corey ourselves and found her to be a pleasant woman?"

"Indeed." Rachel sank back onto her chair. "A most agreeable woman."

Elizabeth huffed, staring between the two of them. "You cannot tell a witch by looking at her. Everyone knows this." She lifted her arms to her sides and let them drop with another huff. "I cannot imagine why you wish to remain ignorant to what is happening in the hearings."

"That is quite enough, young lady." Rachel's reprimand was short and sharp.

"Well," Elizabeth crossed her arms, "I for one will not miss a moment."

"Then perhaps 'twould be best for you to stay as a guest with the Putnams." Rachel picked up her cup as if she hadn't a care and took a sip. Her hand was almost rock-steady as she returned it to its saucer.

"Perhaps you are right." Elizabeth drew herself to her full height. "If I can arrange it, I shall return this evening for more of my things." With that, she whirled.

William grabbed her by the arm and turned her to face him. "You are our family. You are welcome to return when this nasty business has concluded." He raised a finger and held it near her nose. "But not—I repeat—not if your aunt is in any way drawn into it. Have I made myself clear?"

Elizabeth's eyes nearly bulged, and she cast a glance at Rachel. "Aunt Rachel, I would never—"

"Nor your friends in this matter," William cut her off.

"" Elizabeth's tone turned whiney, as if he had gotten through to her.

"I believe you can, to a great extent." He crossed his arms.

"Aunt Rachel, I hope you do not think that I..." Her hands fluttered to her throat.

"I do not, my dear." Rachel's voice was soothing. "Your uncle is only being protective of me, and he would of you if you would only let him."

That brought a smirk to the girl's face that William distrusted. "Have no fear for me. I am on the right side of this." Drawing her wrap round her, she left.

William let out a gust of breath in her wake, then faced Rachel. "Are you sure 'tis best to turn her out?"

"Nay." Rachel shook her head. "I am not. Neither am I content to let her disrespect us any longer."

"And if the Putnams will not have her to stay?"

"I know not." She raised her face to his. "Perhaps we could send her to live with the Quakers for a few weeks and see what they could do with her." But the twist of her lips was more defeat than humor.

William rubbed the ache in his chest. The girl truly had gone too far, and they hadn't been able to rein her in, even with repeated attempts. The Quakers' ideas might have worked when she was younger, or sending her away to a boarding school. But she was ten and seven, old enough to marry.

And William and Rachel were too old to control her anymore. The timid young girl who'd come to live with her elderly relatives was barely recognizable in the defiant woman who'd stormed out the door. Defiant and unpredictable, and if Rachel was correct—dishonest.

A worrisome combination.

William took a deep breath and relaxed in his chair. Hopefully, his threat to banish her would keep her and her friends from pointing a finger at Rachel.

"I almost forgot." Rachel pulled an envelope from her apron pocket and handed it to him. "The tavern keeper, Mr. Ingersoll, delivered this while you were out. It came by courier last evening."

The envelope was worn, carrying the marks of having been well traveled. The wax held no mark that he recognized, nor was the handwriting familiar. He broke the seal and read the sparce message.

Dr. William Griggs,
It grieves me to inform you that my father, Dr. Mar-
cus Witherspoon, passed on to glory this past April the
eighth, before receiving your letter informing him of your
relocation.
Sincerely,
Patricia Dunbar

Gone. There would be no help coming from that quarter for the answers to his questions revolving around the witch trials. He rubbed the ache in his chest. William's longtime friend and colleague had reached the end before him. Oddly enough, he didn't feel much sorrow over the loss of his friend. Instead, he fought down an irrational stab of jealousy. In heaven there would be no more sickness, no more sadness, no more worries.

That sounded better to William every day.

With a restless night's sleep behind him, Caleb sought out Hannah the next morning after breakfast. She'd walked to the garden to see what the winter had damaged. It was the middle of March, the warmth of true spring still weeks away, but like any good gardener, she wished to be prepared. She stood at the garden's edge, the wind teasing her shawl and the rim of her bonnet while she hugged her arms around her middle.

He stopped beside her, looking over the ground. "'Twill be an easy cleanup this year."

"Will we be here to plant it?" She didn't look at him.

"I believe we will."

Pivoting, she searched his face. "Why?"

"The doctor and I had a long talk in the shop yesterday."

"So thee were not just showing him new sketches?"

"Nay. He asked questions—"

"What did thee tell him?" Her words tumbled out in a rush.

"I felt the need to be honest with him." Her scowl of disapproval might have made him angry if he hadn't seen the fear behind it. "As he was with me. The man has his own fears about what has happened—what is still happening—in the village and Salem Town. Even with his own niece."

"All the more reason to keep our distance." She wrapped her arms even tighter around herself as if shutting him out.

"Once, I thought that too. But he said something that I cannot set aside. He said that if we run, we will appear guilty of something, when we are not."

"Better to appear guilty and live than to stay and—" Her words clipped off with a half-sob.

"Come." Caleb opened his arms. For a moment, it seemed she would refuse his embrace, but she stepped into it. He wrapped his arms around her and nudged the bonnet from her head with his chin. The herbal scent of her hair was such a part of her, and he breathed it in. "We lost a child the last time. That does not mean we will lose another."

"But we could." Her words were muffled against his coat.

"Aye. As we could lose one to sickness, or injury, or accident right here on the farm." He rubbed her back. "Life can be fleeting for any of us, if the Lord so wills it."

"I know." She raised her face to his. "But we should not take chances."

Perhaps it was time to talk it all through. "Thee mean, like taking the girls into the forest with me? And accepting the work from the doctor after the church's decree?" When she stiffened, he didn't release her but kept rubbing her back. "Thee might have been right about the former, but I still believe the Lord presented the opportunity that the doctor's order gave us to restock the barn with tools after the fire. In fact, I sent Caleb Jr. with the order to the blacksmith shop for Stephan to get started. We should be able to plant on time."

They stood in silence for a long time, and then Hannah relaxed into his embrace again. "Perhaps thee are right."

Caleb raised his face to the sky, a silent *thank Thee, Lord,* in his heart. As he lowered his chin to rest on Hannah's hair, he caught a glance of Hannah Jr. walking to the dairy, a basket swinging from her arm.

It wasn't the right time to speak with Hannah about the hidden note, but he hadn't forgotten about it. With everything else happening around them, an admirer of his daughter seemed an almost trivial thing. Unless, of course, it was someone unsuitable. But his eldest wasn't the type to get herself involved with an unsuitable young man. Of all their children, she was the one least likely to bring out the gray already encroaching into his hair.

"So what shall we do?" Hannah asked.

"We shall do as the Bible says." The same words that had plagued him through the night and robbed him of too much sleep. "We shall love our neighbors as ourselves."

When she backed up to peer at him, he let her go.

"Thee mean the Puritans?"

"Aye. The Bible does not tell us to love only our own kind."

"But they hate us." She pressed one hand over her mouth for a moment, fear and sorrow filling her eyes before she took it away. "They killed our daughter. They could take Verity away from us."

Caleb needed to tread carefully, because his wife's fears and sorrows were justified. More than justified—they were real. But there was more to the Puritans than that. He'd seen it in the doctor, in Thomas, and in several others among the village. He took Hannah's hands and held them, squeezing gently. "Do thee remember Otis Parsons?"

"How could I forget. He should have been named Odious."

Caleb chuckled. "He was a very disagreeable Friend."

"Disagreeable?" Hannah's eyes flashed. "He treated his wife and children no better than his cattle, and they were a poor lot."

"Do thee remember what we did after the bull broke Otis's leg?"

She glared at him, having caught on to where he was going with the story. "We Friends took care of his family and farm while he healed."

"Why did we do that?"

"I get thy point, but 'tisn't another Friend we are speaking of this time. 'Tis a village of Puritans."

"And who did Jesus say our neighbor was?"

She pulled her hands free and turned her back to him, but she didn't move away, so he wrapped his arms around her and drew her against him. "'Tisn't easy for me, either. But there are people hurting in the village over what is happening, just as we are. People just as afraid as we are."

"What would thee have us do?" Her voice was soft, not angry.

"I would have us do what the Bible says, to love our neighbors, especially those who are fearful and hurting, as we are."

She turned and pressed her cheek to his chest. "How?"

"God will provide the way, if we open our hearts to His will."

"I know 'tis as simple as that, and yet..." Her words trailed off.

"And yet so very difficult." He pulled her closer. "As obedience often is."

She reached up and cupped the side of his face with one hand. "I am so sorry for the way I have been acting. 'Twas wrong of me, but I have been so"—she let out a shuddering breath against his neck—"so very afraid. In my fear, I lashed out at thee."

"I understood." He needed to be as honest as she was in that moment. "But I let it make me angry at times. And stubborn. Thee were right about searching for the cave. 'Twas only to fulfill my own need to *do* something."

"But thee kept the girls safe, as thee said thee would." She leaned back and looked into his eyes. "As I knew thee would."

The rift between them closed with an almost audible clap.

"Shall I stop preparing to leave?" Hannah asked.

"Keep the necessities close at hand and the sacks thee have made, but let us not plan to use them unless and until danger comes to our door."

"Do thee have any idea how we are to love our Puritan neighbors?"

"I promised the doctor to keep him and his family in my prayers."

"Then I shall add them to mine as well." She cocked her head. "Should we tell the children?"

A good question. He looked back at the buildings, the cows in their pasture, the sheep in theirs, and chickens pecking in the yard. Caleb Jr., Robert, and Joseph were spreading manure on the west field, using the wooden forks they'd made themselves in his shop. Tamson and Verity crossed the yard with Benji and Jonathan, Rags and Button following along. Hannah Jr. was probably churning butter in the dairy. All safe and happy, but the world around them was not.

"The more we have praying for our neighbors, the better. I shall talk to them after supper tonight."

Hannah snuggled back into his arms, and everything felt right for the first time in a month.

Chapter 30

A WEEK HAD PASSED since Martha Corey—an upstanding church member—had been accused of witchcraft and toted off to the jail in Salem Town. William continued his visits to Goodie Parris, who improved only marginally while under her son's care. Other than that, he'd spent his time talking to the townspeople, getting to know them, working to earn their trust.

Following his talk with the carpenter, William was convinced that logic and prayer would pave the path back to sanity. Maybe not for those caught up in the hysteria, as Elizabeth clearly was, but for those who were on the edge due to fear and distrust. Rachel often accompanied him, spending her time getting to know the women. They had discussed just the previous evening how well the visits were going, convinced they were helping to bring a feeling of community and well-being to Salem Village.

Which is why the news this afternoon had taken the wind from his sails.

Rebecca Nurse, a woman they'd visited at first due to her failing health and again two days after to get to know her better, had been accused of witchcraft by the reverend's niece. Goodie Nurse was at least seventy years old, weak from her illness, barely able to lift her head from the pillow. The accusation that her specter was flying around Salem Village tormenting girls and even one married woman was preposterous. Pure fiction.

William smacked his palm on the table.

Rachel whirled from the hearth where she'd been basting a chicken. "Husband, you gave me a start."

"I beg your pardon, my dear."

Setting aside the bowl and spoon, Rachel joined him at the table. "'Tis this mess with Goodie Nurse, I assume."

"How can anyone accuse that poor woman of witchcraft?" William practically bellowed the word, the first time he hadn't spoken it in a whisper. "Has the whole village gone mad?"

Rachel laid her hand over his on the table. "Mad? I think not. Fearful, yes. Most of them are that. But some are also vengeful and petty."

"You speak of Goodie Putnam, do you not?"

"Indeed. 'Tis clear to me she is no more afflicted than our Elizabeth. And since we have learned of the feud between the Putnams and the Nurses, 'tis not hard to see her motivation."

"Francis Nurse must be frantic. The poor man. He and I are the same age." William turned his hand over and grasped Rachel's. "Too old for such an atrocity."

"Fear not for me, my dear." Rachel squeezed his hand in return. "I shall keep my specter under tight control even as I sleep." Her grin allowed for a glimpse of humor.

William rubbed his chest with his free hand. "I do fear, especially with Elizabeth involved. Who knows how this hysteria has twisted her mind?"

"Which is why she is better off with the Putnams!" Rachel's face settled back into its serious lines. "I do love that girl, but she is lost to us for a time. We are safer with her gone from under our roof." She squeezed his hand again. "Both of us."

Had Rachel worried for his safety as he'd worried for hers? Of course she had. The woman was always a step or two in front of him in figuring things out. "Think you that men will be accused before all is said and done?"

Sorrow deepened the lines in her cheeks. "I fear so, and I would have you bundled and on a ship at first light if I thought 'twould keep you safe."

The words he'd spoken to Caleb came back to him—hitting home this time. "Were we to run, 'twould only make us look guilty."

"I fear so."

For the first time, William had a face-to-face encounter with the same fear that must have plagued Caleb for his family. But what could he do? One man, newly arrived in the village, elderly with a poor heart, had no power to do anything.

Or did he?

The wagon's bed was filled with happy chatter as the matched pair of sorrels pulled it into Salem Town. Unlike the village, the town was alive with wagons, carts, and buggies cluttering the street. People walked in and out of shops and along the boardwalks. Their voices carried on the breeze. Beyond it all, ships bobbed in the harbor, sails furled and lashed to their masts. A barking dog darted in front of Dolly and Dandy.

"Easy." Caleb pulled back on the reins as the gelding tossed its head. But he could hardly blame the horse. The street was chaotic compared to their quiet life on the farm.

"I had no idea the town had grown so much since last we came." Hannah gripped his upper arm, her touch a gentle reminder that the rift was gone from between them.

"It has," Caleb said, "which makes it easy to stay away from the jail and all the happenings on that side of town." David had reassured him that the trip would be safe. The witch proceedings had not filtered into the town proper, the jail being on the very western edge.

The children chattered in the back of the wagon, pointing out whatever had caught their attention.

How long had it been since he'd brought the family to Salem Town? It must have been two years at least. What they didn't provide for themselves, they obtained in the village. Or they had, before the accusations.

"There. I thought I remembered where it was." Hannah pointed to a small, round sign hanging in front of a shop. Painted on it were a spool of thread and a ridiculously large needle, but it served its purpose.

Caleb maneuvered the team through the soup of traffic to the boardwalk in front of the shop. "I shall tie the horses to the first empty spot I can find. Shall we meet there in an hour?"

"Oh, Father. Can we not shop longer?" Tamson dropped to the ground and looked up at him, her dark eyes pleading. "There are so many things to see."

Hannah's chuckle as he steadied her while she climbed down was enough to convince him. "Two hours then, but no more." He'd be amazed if they returned in under two and a half.

Tamson squealed and spun in a circle.

Hannah Jr. climbed down and helped Verity, then the two little boys. "We shall be there." But there was a twinkle in his oldest daughter's eyes as well.

Caleb knew when he was outnumbered.

"I shall find a suitable fabric for the chairs before we do anything else," Hannah assured him.

He'd have preferred to have Goodie Griggs pick out the fabric herself, but under the circumstances, this was best. Hannah had impeccable taste in such things anyway. Whatever she settled on would look lovely. As *she* did, with the late morning light teasing the wisps of hair escaping her bonnet and highlighting the excited flush on her cheeks.

Caleb needed to bring her to town more often, if only to please her.

"Where are we going first, Pa?" Robert's question brought him back to the task at hand.

"After we park, we should see what the mercantile has to offer." Caleb Jr. climbed over the back of the seat and took his mother's place.

"And so we shall." Caleb chirped to the horses. The first place they found to tie up was a quarter of a mile down the street in front of a bank building. What would it be like to have so much money one needed a bank to keep it in? Caleb Buffum would never know. "Here we are."

Caleb Jr. dropped down and secured the team while Robert and Joseph jumped off the back, Joseph whispering something Caleb couldn't make out.

"Can we go exploring?" Robert asked.

He cocked his head at the boys. "Can thee stay out of trouble?"

"Of course," Robert said, while Joseph nodded, his face like a cherub.

How long had it taken the orphan boy to perfect that look to achieve what he wanted? But Caleb had to admire the effort. "Two hours. No longer. Not one minute. Do thee understand fully?"

"Aye," they both answered at once.

"Touch nothing in the shops. Remember the rule—'if thee break it, thee purchase it'—and since neither of thee have money, 'twould fall to me to pay." He gave them his most stern fatherly look. "That would please me not at all. Understood?"

Two heads bobbed, eyes wider than before.

"Try not to get run over by a wagon. Thy mother would be most upset with me." He handed Joseph a coin. "Thee might find maple sugar candy at the general store. That should cover a small bag to share with the girls. Off with thee."

As the boys scampered away, Caleb Jr. snickered. "Thee know they are going to find some mischief, do thee not?"

"Probably." He leveled a look at his eldest son. "I seem to remember having to pull thee from an irate goodwife's duck pond when thee were about their age."

That brought a patch of red to Caleb Jr.'s cheeks.

Caleb swung an arm around his boy's shoulders. "Come. Let us see what is new in farming equipment. Every year there seems to be some new invention." And this year, he had coin in his pocket thanks to the doctor's prompt payment for his furniture. Even with the money set aside to cover the blacksmith's bill, Caleb could afford to look seriously at something new.

Especially as the weight of uncertainty had eased from his shoulders since his discussion with the doctor. It'd been a full week with no repercussions from that talk. The doctor had been true to his word and kept their conversation private. For the first time in two months, Caleb had space to breathe fully, fear having been pushed aside by prayer and the knowledge that at least two Puritans in the village, Thomas and the doctor, would not sanction pointing fingers at the Friends.

Upon returning to the wagon, Caleb was shocked to find Hannah already there with the girls and the little boys. When she spied him, she rushed to his side in obvious distress.

"Verity is missing." Her words came out in a rush.

"Missing?"

"Aye." Hannah looked around. "Where are Robert and Joseph?" Her voice rose on each word as she gripped his sleeve.

"They went exploring, as boys do." He glanced at Hannah Jr., who had the little boys in the back of the wagon, and Tamson, whose face was streaked with tears. "Tell me what happened."

"I know not. I was completing our purchases with my back to the door. I never saw Verity leave, and neither did the girls. She was just...no longer there." Panic seeped into Hannah's voice.

It tried to pry its way into Caleb's thinking as well. He took a deep, steadying breath before turning to Caleb Jr. "Have thee any idea where the boys have gone." He waited for his son's hesitant nod. "Find them, bring them back in all haste. And keep an eye out for Verity."

"Caleb, nay." Hannah pulled at his sleeve.

"Go, son." Caleb waved him off then turned to his wife. "The lad will be fine. We shall need the boys to help us search."

Tamson wailed and rushed to him, throwing her arms around his waist. "'Tis all my fault. I was so busy looking at things, I did not know Verity was no longer beside me."

Caleb rubbed her back. "Perhaps she just wandered off when something caught her interest."

"Nay, Father." Damp eyes raised to his. "She would not. Verity was too afraid to go off on her own."

"Afraid of what?" he asked.

"Of everything other than the farm. She only really feels safe there with us."

The little girl had been quiet for the drive to Salem Town, but she'd often been quiet, so he'd thought nothing of it.

"Caleb?" Hannah's quiet word cut through his thoughts. "What if...if they took her back?"

She meant the Puritans, of course. "Nay. I am sure that is not what happened. Who in Salem Town would even know that she was a Puritan child in our care?" He kept is . "'Tis far more likely that she got distracted. She lived here before, perhaps she recognized someone, a friend from her past, and slipped away to greet them." How he hoped that was the case.

"Nay." Tamson shook her head against his middle. "She had no friends here. The other girls were mean to her because she had no mother or father, just an elderly uncle to look after her."

Benji began to cry, and Jonathan followed suit.

Caleb put his hands on his wife's shoulders and looked her in the eyes. "Thee stay here with the little boys in the back of the wagon. Feed them from the hamper thee brought. I shall take the girls up the street in that direction." He tilted his head to indicate which way. "When the boys arrive, send them along in the opposite direction. We will find her." They must find her.

Verity was part of their family.

Chapter 31

I T WAS LIKE LOSING their babe in the cave all those years ago. Caleb watched the wagon until it was out of sight, taking the rest of his family back to the farm. Hannah hadn't wanted to leave, and neither had Tamson. But Caleb needed to know they were safe back at the farm while he, Caleb Jr., and Joseph remained in Salem Town and continued to search. Robert had driven the team, not that Hannah couldn't drive, but the little ones needed her. Hannah Jr. would have stayed, but the cows needed milking and Robert would need her help.

Caleb put one arm around Caleb Jr.'s shoulders and the other around Joseph's. "Come on. We will continue our search until dark, then find a place to sleep if we must."

Someone had to have seen the young girl—dressed in Friends' attire—even in a place as bustling as Salem Town. He'd had a brief wrestle with the idea of contacting the sheriff, but the man was knee-deep in the witch trial proceedings, and Caleb didn't want to draw any more attention to his family than absolutely necessary.

Caleb stopped at a bakery they'd passed and bought four small loaves of bread, handing one to each of the boys before tucking two into his coat pockets. They did the same, none of them hungry at the moment, but they would be eventually. They stood on the corner of two streets, nearly deserted at this late hour, so different from when they'd arrived. They watched the shopkeepers locking up for the evening, except for the pawnshop behind them. Caleb turned and looked in the window at the display of goods there.

"Look at that." Joseph pointed at a shelf with an array of jewelry. "'Tis Verity's shawl pin. They still have it."

"What?" Caleb took a step closer to the glass.

"This is where the widow told me to sell it." There was a note of misery in the boy's voice, no doubt from being a part of ripping everything away from Verity when she'd arrived. Not that he'd had any choice in the matter.

But there was something Caleb could do. He opened the door and entered, the boys following. "Get the pin." He motioned for Joseph to pick it out from the selection while he went to the counter.

An elderly man approached from the side of the shop, steel gray hair in a neat queue, matching whiskers growing under his chin in the manner many sailors favored, one leg thumping along the board floor upon a wooden peg. "Can I help you?"

"We need to return this item"—Caleb took the pin from Joseph and showed it to the man—"to its rightful owner."

The old sailor squinted at Joseph. "Did I not pay you for it, fair and square?"

"Aye." Joseph shot a sheepish glance at Caleb.

"Indeed. We shall pay thee a fair price for it." Caleb dug into his pocket, glad he hadn't found anything new in the farming line to purchase.

"Did this young scamp steal it?" The man demanded. "We have a sheriff here—"

"Nay." Caleb raised a hand to stop him. "Nothing of the sort, I assure thee. What is the price?"

The old man grumbled for a moment, shooting a dark look at Joseph before he named his price.

Caleb handed over the money, pocketed the pin, and left the store, stopping on the street. Where to start looking again?

"Caleb?" Joseph looked up at him.

"Aye?"

"I think it best if I strike out on my own." He shrugged and looked at his feet. "I know the ways of a town's streets after dark. I been there before." He looked back up. "Could be the people out there after dark will be more willing to talk to me alone."

"It could be dangerous for thee, could it not?" Bad enough to lose one child in his care. He didn't want to think about losing another.

"I know my way around, and begging your pardon, if those people hear your 'thee,' they will shut up tighter than an oyster."

"He is right, Pa." Caleb Jr. nodded toward where a poorly-clothed group of three young men emerged from an alley down the way. "That lot will not speak with us, but they might to Joseph. 'Tis worth a try."

With more than a little reluctance, Caleb nodded. "We shall wait for thee on the bench on the other side of the blacksmith's shop. If thee are not there in half an hour, we shall come looking."

Joseph gave a curt nod and slunk down the side of the street, moving as a shadow in the waning light.

"He knows what he is about," Caleb Jr. said.

"'Twould appear so." Caleb pointed down the main street in the opposite direction Joseph had gone. "Search that way. I will take this cross street. Half an hour at the bench. Do not be late, lest I worry."

Heading down the side street, the shadows long and clouds moving over the setting sun, Caleb prayed once again for Verity's safety. Why had God brought her into their lives only to have her snatched away again? Only to have his wife's heart broken again? Not just Hannah's, either. Caleb also felt the weight of loss, more than he would have imagined. The little girl had wiggled her way deep into his heart.

They had to find her—to make their family whole again. He reached into his pocket and felt the shawl pin there. He didn't believe in a talisman or a good-luck charm, but having something of hers to hold gave him an odd sort of comfort.

Half an hour of searching, calling her name down each alley, brought him nothing. He approached the bench where Caleb Jr. already waited. A shake of his head said he'd had no luck either. Caleb lowered himself to the bench like a man twice his age and pulled his coat higher around his neck to fend off the mid-March chill.

"I know who took her." Joseph's voice jerked Caleb and Caleb Jr. from the bench and onto their feet.

Where had the boy come from?

"Who—?"

"—How?"

Caleb and his son spoke over the top of each other.

"'Twas the Widow Scudder." Joseph's eyes were wide in the gloom. "The boys saw an old woman take Verity down an alley, and when they described her, I knew it was the widow."

"Did they see where the widow took her?" Caleb asked.

Joseph shook his head. "They stayed out of sight, you understand."

The boys were likely criminals, a street pack that hid from the law by day. "But thee believe they told thee the truth?" Caleb asked.

"Aye. They did. Their descriptions of both Verity and Widow Scudder were too spot on to be a lie."

"Where would she have taken Verity?" Caleb Jr. asked.

"The widow has been missing for some time." Caleb rubbed the back of his neck where the hairs prickled. "Ever since she was accused of... well." He glanced up and down the nearly empty street and lowered his voice. "Ever since she was accused. If anyone of the Friends might know where she had hidden herself—"

Caleb Jr. grasped his arm. "'Twould be David."

"Aye." Caleb glanced from one boy to the other. "Could thee find thy way to Thomas Buffington's in the dark?"

The boy puffed out his chest. "I can."

"If any among the Puritans were to know of the old woman's whereabouts, 'twould be Thomas." Finding Verity was the first priority, but what if they found her only to have the Puritan elders take the girl away? It was a risk Caleb had to take. The old woman wasn't right in the head. That had become obvious after the orphans were removed from her care. What might she do to Verity in her demented state?

"Come on, we shall split up after we cross the river, thee to Salem Village"—he nodded at Joseph—"and Caleb Jr. and me to David's."

Please, Lord. Keep Verity safe until we find her.

Thank goodness the reverend lived just down the street. William rubbed his tired eyes. Goodie Parris had taken a turn in the early evening, and he'd been sitting with her until she'd drifted into a normal sleep. He crept down the stairs and let himself out of the reverend's house.

He glanced at the moon, barely visible behind a thin layer of clouds. It must be after ten o'clock. He was too old for this. He should be retired, asleep in his own bed. He was covering a jaw-popping yawn when someone darted across the street in front of him, a small someone.

"You there," he called out. "Is something amiss?"

The boy stopped but looked ready to take flight again.

"I am Dr. Griggs. Can I help you?" So much for his warm bed.

"I must speak with Mr. Buffington." There was a breathlessness to the voice, as if the boy had been running for a while.

He approached the youngster, who stood his ground. "What has happened?"

"A girl has been kidnapped."

"Kidnapped?" How had William ever believed Salem Village to be a sleepy little town, the perfect resting place for his declining years? "What girl? From which family?" He'd met most of the town's residents now, and several of the farm families, since his purchase of a horse and buggy.

"Ah... I best be finding Mr. Buffington now."

Before the boy could sprint away, William caught a handful of his coat. "Tell me who she is, and I will help." Something in his tired old voice must have reassured the boy, because if he'd wanted to, he could have pulled himself free.

"'Tis Verity Manton. She lives with the Buffums."

"The carpenter?" Shock removed the last vestiges of sleep from William. "I will accompany you to the brewer's."

The boy had to beat on the door to rouse anyone within, and it was one of the twins. "Benjamin, I need to speak to your father. 'Tis urgent."

How could he tell them apart? Especially through a small opening while the young man was dressed in only his nightshirt?

"What has happened?" the young man asked.

"Verity has been kidnapped."

"Come in, both of you. I shall fetch him." Benjamin stepped back.

"No need. I am not deaf." Buffington entered the room with his shirt untucked but wearing breeches. "Joseph?" He stopped halfway across the room. "Doctor Griggs?"

"Verity was kidnapped." The boy went on to tell the story about a trip to Salem Town, the girl disappearing, and a street gang admitting to having seen her in an old woman's grasp being forced down an alley. "Caleb asked me to come. He hoped you might have an idea of the widow's whereabouts."

"That I do." Thomas turned to look at the other twin, a younger girl who must be their sister, and Goodie Buffington, who had joined them during the telling. "Boys, finish dressing and hitch the team." After they scattered to do his bidding, he focused on his wife. "We shall return as soon as we can."

"Find her." His wife laid a hand on his arm. "She is a sweet little thing and must be terribly frightened."

"We shall do our best."

"I will come too," William said. "The more eyes the better, even if mine are old and weary. I shall just let my goodwife know that I shall be gone awhile."

He moved before anyone could agree or disagree, and hurried down the street.

He stepped inside the house, where a candle burned in its holder on the table. Rachel always left him a light when she retired. She'd learned a long time ago that waiting up for him was a waste of her time and energy. He climbed the stairs to their room and sat on the edge of the bed.

"My dear." He nudged her until she turned onto her back and blinked up at him. "I have returned from the reverend's but am off again. There has been an abduction of a child."

Rachel struggled to sit, but he stopped her with a hand to her shoulder. "There is nothing for you to do. I will return as soon as I can. I am going with the brewer and his sons to search. Buffington believes he knows where the girl has been taken."

"Be safe." Rachel gripped his arm and then released it. "Have a care for yourself."

"I shall. Worry not."

She snorted and raised a brow at him.

"Worry no more than you must." He leaned down and planted a kiss on her forehead. "Go back to sleep if you can."

He returned downstairs, grabbed his satchel, and headed into the night.

The house was dark, of course, but Caleb's knock was answered in short order by David himself, who stepped out onto the porch. Caleb explained the situation in as few words as he could. "Do thee have any idea where the widow might have been hiding?"

"I do." David glanced behind them. "Thee walked here?"

Caleb nodded, his feet attesting to the journey in the dark, several toes sore from stumbling into tree roots and rocks along the way.

"If thee would hitch my team while I dress, we can make better time. 'Tis a bit of distance." He didn't wait for an answer, just ducked back into the house.

Caleb and his son had the horses' harnesses and were hitching them to the wagon when David appeared with his oldest sons, Matthew and Mark.

"Wait a moment." David disappeared into his shop and came out with three muskets.

"Why are thee bringing those?" Surely his friend didn't think they'd shoot the old widow, did he?

David handed a musket to each of the young men, then climbed onto the wagon's bench and took up the reins. "Where she be, 'tisn't the safest of places. Lions live there. And human lions." He cut a glance at Caleb. "Those who avoid polite society."

Mountain lions and outlaws. Caleb scrambled onto the seat while the three young men jumped into the back. They were barely aboard before David had the horses moving.

"Where is this place?" Caleb asked.

"'Tis north of the village in the hills near Wenham Lake." He shot a glance at Caleb. "On the edge of Indian country." Then he leaned back and said, "That be the musket thee ordered, Caleb Jr. Let us pray thee needs it not tonight."

Verity kidnapped. Mountain lions in the dark. A demented old woman. Muskets in the hands of their sons.

While David drove the horses as fast as he dared in the darkness, Caleb prayed.

Chapter 32

W ILLIAM WAS HAVING SECOND thoughts about joining the rescue attempt when the brewer's large wagon hit another rock or root or whatever and almost spilled him into the darkness beyond. But the boy, Joseph, had painted a grim scene. William remembered his encounter with the widow a few weeks past. The sick girl he'd tended was out there somewhere with a woman not in her right mind.

Another bump jarred his teeth.

"I am sorry 'tis not as smooth a ride as your new buggy," the brewer said in a low voice. That alone bespoke the danger, if the man's words didn't boom loudly enough to fill the forest growing denser on each side of the path they traveled.

"Where are you taking us?" William asked.

"'Tis a wild place, a rocky hill near Wenham Lake. It has come to my attention that several people avoiding the witch trials have taken refuge there. But should anyone ask, I will deny knowing it to my dying breath, you understand?"

"I do."

The brewer could find himself in trouble with the local law and the church if he kept such information from them, but with the hysteria ramping up, William could find no fault in his logic. It showed that the big man had an equally large heart. Something William admired.

There were good people in Salem Village. Under different circumstances, he'd be happy to live there.

"Pa, I heard something up ahead," one of the twins said.

The brewer brought his team to an abrupt halt.

All William could hear was the blowing of the horses, but then, his ears weren't as sharp as they used to be.

"I hear it too," said Joseph.

Buffington twisted on the seat and looked back at the boys. "What do you hear?"

"Horses." They said at the same time. "Pulling a wagon," the twin added. "I can hear the jingle of harness as well as the hoofbeats."

Buffington faced front again and cocked his head. "I cannot hear it, but the boys' hearing is keener than mine."

"It could be Caleb Buffum," Joseph said. "As I told you back at the house, he went to David O'Sullivan's for help. David has a stout team and wagon."

"For sure the widow has no horse." Buffington rubbed his jaw. "But there are others who may."

The twin who'd been speaking stood. "They have stopped."

William looked up at him. "Or maybe moved out of hearing range."

The twin shook his head. "The sound just stopped. It didn't die out."

"Let us go forward on foot." Buffington turned to the boys again. "Thomas Jr., you stay here and guard the horses. Keep your musket handy. There are lions and bears in this area. You two sharp-eared lads, come with the doctor and me."

William was considering the option of remaining with the wagon. After all, he was in no condition to try to outrun a lion or a bear, but the other young Buffington was at his elbow, ready to assist him off the wagon. The young man also had a musket in one hand, which made William feel a little better about going forward.

"Sound does not carry well in dense woods," the young Buffington said, "so they will not be too far ahead of us."

If that was supposed to encourage William, it failed.

Joseph slipped ahead of them, scouting the way. He'd been out of sight for only ten minutes when he reappeared. "'Tis the O'Sullivan wagon, with one of his boys standing guard."

"Did he see you?" Buffington asked.

"Nay. I know how to move in the dark." There was pride in the boy's voice.

Buffington stopped. "We should make ourselves known so as not to draw a musket blast. I know not how handy the Quakers are with a weapon, being pacifists and all."

"They hunt, the same as anyone else." Joseph shrugged. "But I can go back and let him know we're coming. 'Tisn't far."

"Do that, lad," Buffington said, and the boy disappeared into the inky darkness.

William wished he'd worn his muffler as the damp crept in around his collar despite the walk. Or maybe the cold was felt more because of their mission. How would the old woman react when they found her? Demented people could be...unpredictable. He'd treated enough to know that while some were simply confused and lived fairly normal lives, others could turn mean and even—in extreme cases—dangerous.

They had walked maybe five minutes when the wagon came into sight. As Joseph had said, a young man remained with it, armed with a musket.

"Where are your father and Caleb Buffum?" Buffington asked, his voice still subdued.

The lad pointed to the front of the wagon, where a tree lay across the rutted trail. "They went on when we could go no farther. There is a cave up ahead. Pa and I have been there before. 'Tis known of hereabouts. Pa thought the widow might take refuge there."

If she had, then she'd have shelter for the girl. That was something.

"We shall follow." Buffington took a step, then turned back to the lad in the wagon. "How many are with him?"

"Pa and Caleb, with Caleb Jr. and Mark."

The night was split by an eerie cry, and William's skin broke out in gooseflesh in response.

A lion.

The brewer twisted around. "Benjamin, run back and have Thomas Jr. bring the wagon this far. Stay with him and guard the horses."

William planted his feet. "Are we to go forward without a musket between us?"

Buffington reached into his coat pocket and withdrew a pistol. "Fear not, doctor. I am a very good shot with this." He left it in his hand and motioned Joseph and William to walk ahead of him.

Feeling somewhat reassured, William set off following Joseph and praying they would find the girl soon.

There was dark, and then there was what surrounded them. Caleb paused for a moment and scanned their surroundings. The forest closed in overhead, pine trees that towered to the sky, their needles blocking most of the light escaping the heavy clouds. The ground angled up in a steep climb toward a rocky outcropping, David and Mark barely visible in the gloom.

Caleb stopped when Caleb Jr. grabbed his arm.

"Pa, someone is coming behind us."

Caleb twisted and strained to hear. Too early for any night insects or frogs. It didn't take long to make out the crunch of dry needles beneath footfalls. Was the widow behind them? But it sounded like several people.

"Caleb Buffum?" A loud, if hoarse whisper reached him. Only one man had that voice.

"Thomas?"

The first to come out of the darkness was Joseph, followed by the doctor, and then the brewer brandishing a pistol.

Joseph hurried to Caleb's side. "Mr. Buffington thought they might be near here, but we did not expect to find you."

"David had the same notion." Caleb pointed to where David and Mark came toward them.

"We have grown in number, I see." David's eyes flashed in the low light as he took in the situation. "And in weaponry." He pointed to the pistol.

"Which fires as true as the day you made it," Thomas said. "We heard a lion scream from where we left the wagon, so I brought it out."

"A lion?" David whipped his head in the direction they'd left his wagon and team under the watchful eyes of Matthew.

"'Tis all right." Thomas reassured him in that hoarse whisper. "We had my boys bring our wagon near yours. Both have the muskets you made them. They will protect the horses."

Three to protect the horses and wagons were better than Matthew alone. Caleb pointed behind him at the rocky outcropping. "Thee also assumed the widow would be up there?"

"Indeed. 'Tis fairly well known, and a good place to hide if one wished to remain... out of sight."

"There is a cave not too far ahead," David said. "My guess is she will be there."

"'Tis a long walk from here to Salem Town." Caleb calculated that the widow had no more than a five-hour head start on them while they'd searched the town. Considering that she was elderly and walking the entire way, perhaps she was even behind them.

Joseph held up one hand and raised his face, sniffing.

Caleb drew in a deep breath, and then another. Was that—?

"Woodsmoke," Caleb Jr. said.

"This way." Joseph set off in a trot before anyone could stop him, David on his heels.

Caleb followed and, judging by the shuffling noises behind him, everyone else did too. Distance was difficult to judge in the darkness and traveling uphill, but they couldn't have gone more than thirty rods when Joseph dropped to the ground, motioning the others to do the same.

As quietly as he could, Caleb crept to the top of the rise where Joseph had flattened himself against the ground, David working to the boy's other side.

In the distance, a lion screamed.

A shiver ran over Caleb's back at the sound. He couldn't have pinpointed the direction, sound being a fickle thing in the dense forest, but at least it wasn't close.

A muffled cry came from in front of them. He wriggled himself into position until he could see over the edge.

Verity.

She sat with her back against a wall of stone, knees drawn up to her chest, arms wrapped around them.

"'Tis just a cat. Nothing to concern us." The old woman poked at a smoking fire in front of a long, low cave opening. She cackled. "Cats will not approach a fire."

"I want to go home." Verity's voice shook.

"Home?" The widow turned to loom over the girl, holding the stick in her hand. "This is your home, girl. Tomorrow, you will go begging rags, like you do every day." She went back to the fire, poking it. "Maybe you will find a piece of treasure in the dump. Something we can sell to patch the roof on the cabin." She pointed the stick at the cave's entrance. "It be leaking worse all the time. And the entrance could use a rug, if you find one."

Caleb started to rise, to rush to Verity's side and bring her out of that place, but the doctor seized his arm in a surprisingly firm grip.

"Wait a moment," the old man whispered. "We cannot predict how she will react to someone charging in. She could strike out at the girl."

"Why would she?" Caleb whispered back.

"Because she is not in her right mind."

"What if we fire a musket into the air?" David asked. "'Twould distract her, maybe long enough to grab the girl."

The doctor shook his head. "Or frighten her into pulling the girl inside the cave. How would we get her out then?"

Frustration clawed at Caleb. Verity was so close, and yet the situation was more precarious.

"Perhaps we can wait until the old woman falls asleep." Thomas had reached them. "She must be exhausted after that long walk."

The widow froze and peered toward them.

Oh, no. Despite his best attempts, the brewer's voice had carried.

"Who is there?" she called out, shaking her stick in the air. "Who are you? What do you want?"

Before anyone could say a word, Joseph was on his feet and moving toward the widow.

William bit back the words that wanted to recall the boy. It was too late for that.

"'Tis me, Widow Scudder. Joseph." He walked toward her with his arms swinging at his sides, as if he hadn't a care in the world. As if things were normal.

Good boy. That was the proper approach. William held his breath and strained to hear, wishing he had the ears of his youth.

"Where you been, boy?" The widow lowered the stick, at least, but anger rippled in her voice. "You been gone since breakfast."

She really was in a bad way if she thought the boy'd been gone only that long.

"Joseph?" The missing girl's voice quivered, but she didn't move. She was probably too frightened.

"I got chased by that old bull in the pasture by the creek. You remember, he liked to got me a few weeks ago."

Smart lad. Of course, he was one of the orphans taken from the widow not long ago. Doubtless he'd learned how to navigate the woman's eccentric ways.

The old woman nodded. "I told you to be careful."

Joseph stopped a good two rods away from the fire, on the opposite side as Verity. "But I found something." Joseph dug his hand into his pocket and made a great show of retrieving whatever it was. "Found it half buried in the dirt, I did." He held it between his thumb and finger—a coin.

The widow threw down her stick and hobbled towards him, snatching the coin with a gleeful cackle. "I knew you were good for something, boy." She turned the coin over and over in her hands.

Smart lad, indeed. He'd make a good doctor when he matured. He was doing exactly the right things to deal with someone of the widow's delicate mental state.

"While she is distracted, I shall try and get to Verity." Buffum moved, and this time William let him go. The boy had the old woman fixated on the coin. It should be enough of a distraction to allow the man to grab the girl.

The fire's light glinted off Joseph's eyes as they flicked toward Buffum. "I looked around for more, but there were none."

"Half buried, you said." The widow glanced toward where William and the others remained hidden, then back to the coin. "You go back there tomorrow, boy. Take something to dig with. The others might be farther down in the dirt." She slipped the coin into the folds of her petticoat, probably into a hidden pocket. "And you mind that bull, you hear me?" She had started to turn toward the fire as Buffum reached that side of the opening.

"But what do I do if it charges me again?" Joseph practically hollered his question, drawing the old woman's attention back to himself.

It created just the opening Buffum needed. He ran forward, scooped up the girl, who cried out, catching the old woman's attention.

She spun, eyes wide and wild. "Who are you?" Fury filled her voice. "What are you doing with my girl?"

Caleb was turning to run when three men stepped into the light behind Joseph, muskets raised.

Chapter 33

F EAR GRIPPED CALEB AS tightly as Verity's arms encircled his neck.

The biggest of the three men stepped close to Joseph and grabbed the boy's coat by the collar. "You got any more of them coins, boy? You holding out on this poor widow woman?"

"Nay, sir. 'Tis the only one I found."

"More?" The widow took her eyes off of Caleb and Verity and turned to Joseph. "Have you held one back?" Her voice rose to a screech.

"I found only that one, Widow Scudder, just like I told you." Desperation crept into his tone.

Caleb had never felt more helpless, looking into the barrel of the musket aimed his way. He didn't move his feet, just shifted Verity to his side. "Get onto my back," he whispered, "like when I carried thee out of the woods before. Remember? And hold on no matter what."

She nodded against his shoulder and then did as he'd said, moving like a crab until she was tight against his back.

"Put down those muskets." Thomas's voice boomed off the rock face of the cave opening.

All three men swung their attention to the bulky form of Thomas, again brandishing his pistol, while the doctor shouldered a musket. Behind them came David, Mark, and Caleb Jr. Two guns against three. Four men and three boys against three armed men and the widow.

"Well, well, well." The big man pulled Joseph to stand in front of him, using him like a shield. "Be you the village brewer?"

"Indeed, I am, and that lad you are holding is my apprentice. Release him."

"He is mine," the old woman shrieked. "So is the girl." She turned and glared at Caleb, walking toward him. "What have you done with my girl?"

"She is safe, Widow Scudder." Caleb held a hand out to stop her.

"Let the boy go"—Thomas advanced toward the fire, pistol raised—"and nothing will be said of you being up here in hiding."

"Who you gonna tell?" the big man sneered, jerking Joseph back against the front of his coat.

"Those in the village looking for people to name as witches," the doctor said.

Caleb didn't take his eyes off the three outlaws, but a shock ran through him at the doctor's words. People refrained from speaking the word *witch* out loud. Unease rippled through the two men behind the one holding Joseph, evidenced by feet shifting and eyes darting between the men advancing and David and the boys behind.

"Witches?" For all the big man's bluster, there was a thread of something uncertain in his voice.

"Surely you have heard of the witch accusation in the village." Thomas stopped his advance but kept his pistol pointed at the big man. "'Tis why the widow has hidden herself up here. She has been accused of being a witch."

That caught the outlaws by surprise, judging by their swift glances at the widow, the big guy with his mouth open.

"Witch, witch." The old woman cackled again. "They think me a witch because I am too smart for them."

"Indeed, you are," said the doctor. "Too smart to keep these children up here with you. Keeping them will only bring the elders searching, you know. They will not come all this way just for you, but for the children, they will come."

"They are mine." She pointed to Joseph. "He is mine." Despite the words, indecision deepened the wrinkles of the widow's face. She looked from the doctor to the one holding Joseph, and then she charged the big man, shoving into him. "Let my boy go!" She was slight, but with his attention still on Thomas, he lost his footing. He shoved Joseph away from him, and landed on his backside.

His musket discharged with a deafening roar.

Instinct kicked in, and William pushed the musket he'd been given into O'Sullivan's hands. He rushed forward, hardly thinking about what he was doing as the smoke from the shot cleared away.

Revealing the widow crumpled to the ground.

"'Twas an accident." The big man's voice shook as he climbed to his feet. He turned toward his companions, but they were high-tailing it into the forest. Ashen, that man swung back around, holding the useless musket at his side. "'Twas an accident, you all saw it. I was sticking up for her. I meant her no harm."

William dropped to his knees beside the widow. Her eyes had rolled back in her head, and when he covered her mouth and nose with his hand, there was no breath. The blast had caught her mid-chest and up close. Blood spattered the entire width of her torso. She hadn't stood a chance.

William drew her arms over her front and gently lowered her eyelids.

The big man groaned. "'Twas an accident."

"Go." Buffington pointed the barrel of his pistol toward where the others had disappeared. "Drop that musket and go. Never return to this place. Never return to the village."

"I never harmed nobody." But he put the musket on the ground and backed away. "Never laid a finger on that old woman."

"As thee said, 'twas an accident." O'Sullivan, pacifist or not, advanced with his musket raised. "Now, go."

Needing no more urging, the big man lumbered off after his companions.

"Can we go home?" The little girl asked in a frail voice.

"Indeed, we can." Buffum swung her off his back and gasped. "Doctor!"

William pushed to his feet and hurried to where Buffum was easing the girl to the ground. Her face was streaked with blood. Blood also dripped from Buffum's hair.

"Easy now." William knelt by the girl and leaned close in the smokey fire's light. She'd caught some of the shot from the musket's blast. He sat her up and looked into her eyes, which were wide and gray and frightened, but unharmed. He used his fingers as gently as he could to count four breaks in her forehead and two in her hairline. At her wince he asked, "Does that hurt?"

"Only a little."

She was likely still in shock from everything that had happened to her that day. All in all, the girl had been lucky. The lumps of whatever the man had loaded in his musket—likely pieces of pebbles scavenged from the hills around them—had not penetrated very far. William could feel some just under the skin, but he couldn't remove them until he had better light. "You will be fine once we get you home again."

"I can go now?" Her voice trembled on the last word, and tears welled in her eyes.

Caleb, on his knees on her other side, swept her into his arms again. "Indeed, thee can. Thee must. 'Twould not be home without thee."

"Let me look at your face," William said to Buffum.

The carpenter shook his head. "I am fine." He rose, the girl still in his arms, and walked toward his son.

Buffington came to William's side. "You would think the girl were his own, and not an orphan at all."

"Indeed." William returned to the body of the widow. "I suppose we should transport her back to the village for burial in the churchyard."

"Nay, I think not." Buffington crossed his arms and looked down at her, but not in an unkind way. "With her being accused, the elders would not allow her burial there. 'Twould be best to bury her up here. She preferred to live away from people. I think she would prefer to be buried away from them as well." He gave a wry chuckle. "She had no use for church people anyway. She was an odd one, even before her mind turned."

"Has she no family at all?"

"None that I have ever heard of."

"Everyone has a story." William sighed. "'Tis too bad there are none left to tell hers."

"Boys." Buffington motioned for the younger lads to come. "Find a few pieces of stout wood and let us dig a grave for the poor woman."

It was the least they could do. Such a sorry ending. A terrible accident, but it may have saved her from a worse fate if those accusing her of witchcraft had laid their hands on her. Nobody had been hanged as a witch in Salem Town yet, but if things didn't change, it was only a matter of time.

William rubbed the ache in his chest. His own end wasn't too far in the future. Selfishly, he was glad Elizabeth had moved out of their house. Neither he nor Rachel needed any more of the witch hysteria in their lives. Once he returned to the village, he was done with it. He'd tell the elders of the town that they needed to find a new doctor, and soon. He'd seen enough to last him whatever years, or more probably months, he had left.

His mind was made up, and this time, he'd stand firm. Dr. William Griggs was finally going to retire.

The sun had just broken over the treetops as David turned the wagon into the farm lane. Caleb sat beside him, a sleeping Verity in his arms. Caleb Jr., Joseph, and David's two sons slept in the back. Behind them came Thomas with the doctor beside him, the twins likely asleep behind them.

Verity roused, and rubbed her eyes with the back of her hand and winced when she brushed her injured forehead. "Are we home?"

"We are." Caleb had never been happier to see their farm. How had he ever thought they would walk away from this? It was *home*. It was where his family belonged. His whole family, including the girl in his arms.

The back door of the house banged open, and Hannah rushed out, her hair in a long braid streaming behind her, Rags and Button barking at her heels.

Hannah Jr. and Tamson charged down the steps next. Tamson's shout of, "Verity! Verity!" pierced the morning air.

Last to emerge were Robert and the two little boys, Benji with a piece of bread in his hand. They had probably been at the table eating breakfast.

"Caleb?" Hannah reached the wagon and stared at him, wide-eyed.

"'Tisn't as bad as it looks." David pointed to the wagon behind them. "And we fetched the doctor along to fix them up right quick."

Caleb sat Verity up on his lap. "I will let her down at the house. She is too tired to walk even that far."

Hannah reached up, grabbed Verity's hand, and walked beside them as the wagon rumbled forward.

"What happened?" Tamson asked.

"'Tisn't the time to tell the story." Caleb gave his daughter a smile to take any sting from his words.

"Girls, run back to the house and get a fresh pot of tea started," Hannah said. "Slice whatever thee can find to feed these men. And bring out cloths and a basin for washing. Thy father and—" Hannah looked up and aimed a watery smile at Verity. "Thy father and thy sister need tending to."

Hannah Jr. took Tamson's hand, and they raced off.

Then Hannah cocked her head at Caleb. "Thee will be telling me what happened, husband, as soon as thee are cleaned up."

He allowed the smile to spread and turn into a chuckle. "Indeed, I shall."

Hannah turned to the second wagon. "Come inside, everyone. Thee must be starving."

Someone's stomach rumbled from the wagon bed. "I know I am," Caleb Jr. said. Robert and Joseph agreed with him.

"Thomas has his two boys in the next wagon." Caleb dropped his voice. "I hope thee have enough to feed a small army."

"They helped thee bring our girl home. For that, we would kill the fatted calf."

Caleb couldn't agree more.

Chapter 34

I T DIDN'T TAKE LONG before the doctor had tended the injured, re-moving small pieces of debris and washing the wounds clean. All the while, David commented on the foolishness of loading a musket with common pebbles that blasted apart and shot in every direction.

Hannah Jr. and Tamson scurried around the large kitchen, bringing out more cheese, pouring fresh milk and tea, and slicing what was probably the last of their bread to feed all the young men at the table. Hannah, however, sat in her rocking chair, Verity cuddled on her lap and already fast asleep.

Thomas bumped the doctor's arm and pointed to her. "'Tis a picture worth painting, is it not? Makes me glad we could be there to help."

"Indeed." The doctor took off his glasses, cleaned them on his sleeve, and then resettled them on his nose. "Things turned out for the best, I would say."

"And yet, we let that man go," David said.

"Aye, but if we had taken him to the magistrate, in the end, we would have had to admit 'twas an accident," Thomas said.

"He held us at gunpoint," David continued his argument, "and that should not be allowed."

"Thee are right, my friend." Caleb lifted his cup of tea with a ban-daged hand and saluted David with it. "In a perfect world, it would not be. But here, and now, I care that my family is safe and together. At *home*." The bandage would remind him that keeping his family safe was his responsibility. He hadn't even realized he'd shielded Verity's face with his hands until they'd reached the farm and Hannah had spied the blood on them.

A man took care of his family.

And his home.

Caleb wasn't the frightened young father he'd been almost twenty years before, when disaster had reached their settlement of Friends. The years had seasoned him, given him wisdom, and deepened his faith. *Thank Thee, Lord, for seeing us home again. All of us.*

Any thought of running left him as he sat in their kitchen and took in all the blessings around him.

"Caleb." Thomas turned to him. "If I remember correctly, when we first left the young lass in your care, things were not settled as they should have been."

Hannah's head snapped, her blue eyes sharp with alarm when they met Caleb's.

"Indeed," the doctor said. "Although that was before I arrived, I was informed of the same." He nodded for Thomas to continue.

"As an elder of the village—the only one present since the others have taken themselves off to Salem Town to follow the witch trials—'tis under my authority to render a judgment at this time." Thomas cleared his throat. "'Tis my decision to proclaim that young Verity—" He let the name draw out and looked at Hannah.

"Manton." Hannah's voice was steady, but still uncertain. "Verity Manton."

"Of course, that young Verity Manton is to remain in the permanent custody of one Caleb Buffum and his goodwife, Hannah Buffum, as a member of their family, until Verity reaches her majority age of twenty-and-one, or when Caleb Buffum approves of her marriage to a worthy young man, whichever comes first." He banged a meaty hand on the table, startling Verity awake. "I have so ruled."

"And I have so witnessed," said the doctor, a smile creasing his weary face.

"On the morrow, I shall record it in the official village records." Thomas turned to the doctor. "Will you sign it as the witness?"

"I shall."

Hannah blinked back tears while Tamson's squeal filled the kitchen and started the dogs barking.

Tamson rushed to Verity's side and grabbed both of the little girl's hands. "Thee are staying with us, forever. 'Tis final now, and no one can change it. Thee are for always a part of our family."

Verity remained on Hannah's lap even as her arms went around Tamson's neck. She turned her face to Caleb, eyes shining.

"Oh." Caleb dug into his pocket for the shawl pin he'd forgotten. "I have something for thee, Verity." He reached across the distance between his chair and Hannah's. "Joseph found it in Salem Town yesterday." Had it only been the day before? It seemed half a lifetime. Verity opened her hand, and he dropped the pin on it.

She gasped. "Momma's pin." She pulled it to her chest. eyes shining with wonder.

"For thee to remember her by." Caleb's voice grew rough as he battled raw emotions after so much trauma. "Thee are part of our family now, but thee should remember thy first family too."

Hannah nodded, tears flowing down her cheeks even as she gave him a tremulous smile.

"There is more." Perhaps impacted by the emotional scene, Thomas cleared his throat again. "Dr. Griggs and I are in agreement that you Quake—Friends are in no way responsible for or involved in this witchcraft... What was the word you used, Doctor?"

"Hysteria."

"Indeed. The exact word. This witchcraft hysteria. The two of us, and I know several others in the village, will stand firm on this. Fear not that you will come under any repercussions from what is happening in the village or Salem Town."

Caleb's heart filled to bursting, right there in his kitchen, with his family and friends—even Puritan friends—around him.

"I am so blessed." Caleb stretched out on their bed and pulled the covers to his chin against the dampness and chill of March that crept into the room. Blessed, but exhausted, even though he'd taken a short nap after everyone had left.

Hannah finished her braid and turned on her dressing table's bench to face him. "I am almost afraid to believe it. Almost afraid that such happiness 'twill be snatched away."

"Nay. I think not. Not this time."

She rose and climbed into bed next to him, letting a whoosh of cold air under the covers.

"Thee did that on purpose."

Hannah ignored his grouch and put her cold feet against his lower legs. Such simple acts, so normal, so...right. "Why do thee think this time is different?" She pressed her back to his chest, her hair tickling his nose.

Caleb slipped his arm around her waist. "Because this time we have friends on the other side."

"Friends among the Puritans. 'Tis a lot to contemplate."

"Aye, and yet, I was there when they faced the outlaws—for our Verity's sake."

"Our Verity." Hannah snuggled closer. "Oh, how I love the sound of that."

"As do I." He enjoyed their closeness. *Thank Thee, Lord, that the rift between us has healed. May it never appear again.* Caleb would do everything within his power to see that it didn't. "With friendship comes responsibility, thee know."

"How do thee mean?"

"They came to help us when we were in great need. Should they have a need in the future, we are bound to assist them." What that would look like, he couldn't imagine.

"Aye, 'tis what friends do for each other."

"With the unsettledness in the village—and in Salem Town now—our newly formed friendship may be tested in the weeks and months to come."

Hannah rolled over and faced him, her nose inches away from his. "Then that is what we shall do. We owe them for their help in bringing Verity back to us and for Thomas's decree that she is now ours." The fear that had hovered over his wife was gone. Her eyes were clear, and serene, and indescribably beautiful.

The last thing he wanted was to bring up anything that might cause her fear to return, but they must settle one last issue. "To do that, we must remain here. If we run and go into hiding somewhere, we can be of no use to our Puritan friends."

Her eyes were clear and calm, the blue of peaceful waters. "Then stay we shall." Her arms slipped around his neck as she pressed her lips to his.

Whatever was to come before them, they would meet it together. He and Hannah and the Lord, who watched over them.

Author's Historical Notes

Among the Quakers of Massachusetts at the time of this story, two-thirds of first-born sons and daughters were given the forenames of their parents. Although it looks awkward to us today, both males and females were called "junior" to separate them from their parents. Another interesting custom was that when a child died, its name was usually given to the next-born baby of the same sex. This makes researching a family tree all the more interesting.

The 1600s were known at the Little Ice Age, and because of this, Boston Harbor froze over on several occasions. Today's warmer temperatures, plus the harbor having been dredged much deeper to allow larger ships access, the water no longer freezes over.

Captain Peter Henderson was the captain of the ketch *Margaret* out of the port of Salem. He and his crew were lost to pirates near Funshal, Madeira, in 1697. His trip from Boston to Salem in this story is, however, purely fictional.

The use of "collie" in Colonial America did not reference any certain breed of dog, as the word does today, but denoted the type of dog that would work on a farm.

The massacre in York, Maine, on January 25, 1692, flamed fears throughout Massachusetts Colony. At this point, Maine was part of the Massachusetts Charter—not its own colony. The French had sided with the Abenaki tribe, which killed over 50 colonists, took as many hostages, killed all the livestock, and burned the settlement. This action would compel King William III to take action, and the appointment of Sir William Phips as royal governor of Massachusetts was seen as a positive step.

Churches in Colonial America rarely had a fireplace due to the risk of a fire. Not only because of potential carelessness on a Sunday or lingering coals after services, but also from vagrants who might slip in and occupy the building during the week.

Mary Sibley, understanding that Tituba was from the southern islands and had knowledge of the black magic practiced there, approached the slave woman and asked her to bake a "witch cake." This was an old-time superstition of unknown origins. It was believed that the witch cake, a mixture of the afflicted person's urine with cornmeal baked into a hard biscuit and then fed to a dog, would enable the dog to identify the person who was bewitching the afflicted. Mary Sibley would admit to and repent of her actions and was later reinstated to membership in the Puritan church. She was never accused of or tried as a witch.

Today, some folks speak of "walking on tender hooks" when they mean being cautious not to start something bad. But the actual expression is "tenterhooks," which the people of Salem Village would have understood. Tenterhooks were sharp, S-shaped hooks used to secure woven cloth to a "tenter," or frame, during the process of "fulling" or finishing the cloth into a useable form for clothing.

Elizabeth Hubbard became one of the lead accusers during the witch trials. She testified against twenty-nine people, seventeen of whom were arrested. Thirteen of those were hanged, and two died in jail. Her backstory here is purely fictional, except that she was the great-niece of Dr. William and Rachel Griggs.

Reverend Cotton Mather is a real historical figure, a firebrand in Colonial America. He wrote the book *Memorable Providences, Relating to Witchcrafts and Possessions* describing what happened in Boston in 1688 with the Goodwin family. Depending on one's point of view, Cotton Mather was either a devout Christian or a crazy zealot. One could make either case, but I suspect the truth lies somewhere between the two. He knew the scriptures and firmly believed in Christ, but he sometimes didn't apply his knowledge and beliefs in the best way. The Salem Witch Trials were a prime example of that. Instead of a steady hand and calm head, he fanned the flames of fear and escalated the situation.

Rev. John Hale and Rev. Nicholas Noyes are real characters who were called to consult with Rev. Parris and question Betty Parris and Abigail Williams.

The first formal questioning and accusations took place at the tavern owned by Nathaniel Ingersoll. Salem Village had no proper law enforcement of its own, so magistrates John Hathorne and Jonathan Corwin were brought from Salem Town to oversee the proceedings. With more accusations, the proceedings were soon moved to Salem Town, where the jail was located. The events portrayed in this novel are a compilation of actual events, but the timeline may have been shifted for the sake of the story or because the actual timeline was not known or was represented in conflicting reports of the time.

The term "female perversity" is one I found while researching first-hand accounts of the witch trials. It was used prior to Giles Cory and other men being accused of witchcraft.

Winter Fever was the name given to pneumonia or bronchitis during the Colonial era.

The first pawnshop in Colonial America was started in 1690 in Massachusetts. It may have been in a different town, but for the story's purpose, I've located it in Salem Town here.

If you have read about the Salem Witch Trials, you will see I have woven together several of the theories regarding the cause of the girls' affliction: the overly-strict upbringing of the girls, true demon possession, and group hysteria. Another theory that has gained popularity in more modern years blames a possible type of fungus in the wheat crop that year, which can produce hallucinations. However, that theory doesn't explain why whole families—who would have eaten together at the same table—were not afflicted. And since the fungus was apparently discovered after the date of this series, I chose to leave it out. As to what really happened? Nobody knows for sure. I think weaving together the three major theories makes for a plausible story.

SALEM VILLAGE

BOOK TWO

The
Midwife

PEGG THOMAS

The Midwife

April 1, 1692

"'T IS A FALSE ALARM, but thy aunt was right to fetch me." Hester Fuller patted the back of Jane Biddle's hand. "There may be a few of them before the day is to come. I should think the babe will remain where it is for at least another fortnight."

The brown-haired woman on the bed gave her a weary smile. "I told my aunt 'twas too soon, but she worries so."

As well she should, but Hester wasn't about it admit it and upset the mother-to-be. This was Jane's fourth child, and as such, should have been less complicated. But she'd become pregnant of the heels of her last child, a little girl who had turned a year old last week, and not given herself proper time to rest in between. Hester firmly believed that two or three years between births was best for both the mother and the babe.

The aunt, Sarah Cloyce, sat on a chair on the other side of Jane's bed. "I am sorry for bringing you out for no cause."

"'Tis no bother." It never failed to amaze Hester that a woman could give birth—nine times in Sarah's case—and fail to remember the extend of the experience. Once the babe was in their arms, all thought of the process seemed to slip away. Perhaps it was God's blessing. "Do not hesitate to call me back if thee are unsure. A fourth child can make a surprisingly fast appearance."

Sarah sighed. "I remember my fourth, such a winsome child."

"I should be on my way." Hester lifted her basket and strode to the door before Sarah fully launch into her memories of all nine of her birthings. "And remember, do not hesitate to fetch me back. 'Tis only a short walk down the street." She slipped out the door and down the stairs.

"Midwife?" Jane's husband stopped his pacing in the parlor as Hester entered.

"'Twas a false alarm."

The air seemed to melt out of the tall man. Thin to the point of skinny, he bent forward, hand to his forehead, the faint light of morning filtering through the window behind him, dimming the light of the single lit candle on the side table. "Does it never get easier?"

Hester refrained from chuckling. Husbands came in two varieties, it seemed, those who suffered along with their wives, albeit from a distance, or those who regarded childbirth a woman's responsibly, and therefore of little concern to themselves. Hester much preferred John Biddle's reaction. It was her high averages for assisting with live births—something she took pains not to be proud of—that made her popular with her Puritan neighbors, but any birth had its inherent dangers. It did the man credit that he cared so much for the woman upstairs and their unborn babe.

"Each babe will come into the world in his or her own way, some easier than others." Even though she'd never given birth herself, she'd assisted well over a hundred women between helping her physician father, and then becoming a midwife after the death of her intended. That had caused a bit of a stir, even among the Friends, to have an unmarried woman as midwife. But there had been few options at the time, and her training had been exemplary. It hadn't taken long before she was accepted by both Friends and Puritans alike.

She wished John Biddle a good day, then stepped out into the fresh air of an early April morning. Smoke drifted from the chimneys in town, hanging low with the promise of rain to come. *Sweet April showers, do spring May flowers.* The old poem, as appropriate that morning as when Thomas Tusser had penned it some hundred years past, was one of her favorites.

If only the village were as peaceful as it seemed. If only a good spring rain could wash away the taint that hung over it.

Hester was the only Friend living within the village limits, which had a statute that restricted property ownership to members of the Puritan church. She rented a humble cottage from the innkeeper, Nathaniel Ingersoll, and the village elders permitted it because their women wanted a midwife they could count on nearby. Even though they had a new, rather elderly, physician in town, the women were generally more comfortable with a woman assisting in childbirth.

Which had suited Hester just fine before the accusations of witchcraft had begun.

Everyone knew that the first execution of a witch in the American colonies had been Margaret Jones, a midwife, back in forty-eight. A shiver crept up Hester's back. Margaret Jones had been a Puritan among Puritans. How much more vulnerable was Hester as a Friend living among Puritans? Several of the families among their Friends had offered her a place in their homes, but she'd resisted. Partly it was because she enjoyed her independence, and partly because she feared that the Puritan women—or their husbands—wouldn't fetch her from a Friend's farm when their time came. As accepting as they were of her, that might be too much for them. They were a stiff-necked lot, even if, taken one at a time, most were agreeable to be around.

She reached her cottage and entered through the back door, wiping her feet on a colorful rug one of the Puritan ladies had gifted to her after the birth of her child. None of the Friends would have created something so vibrant, preferring the somber, plain hues of soft grays, blues, browns, and greens. But it made Hester smile when it greeted her upon her return, and so she'd kept it.

Pushing aside the makings of another basket, Hester put her midwife's basket on the table. She stretched and yawned. No sense in going back to bed, as morning was already breaking. She'd mix herself a bit of porridge and then hunt in the forest for more basket-making materials. Spring was a good time to gather red-twig dogwood shoots, river willow withies, and woodbine vines. Selling her baskets in the village and in Salem Town, along with her midwife fees, allowed her to stay in the cottage. They created the independence she enjoyed.

Perhaps a little too much.

The alternative was to live as a spinster aunt with one of her brothers, which she did not favor, or marry a widower with a passel of children in need of a mother, which she favored even less. Not that she didn't love children, she did, but to be married to a man other then Timothy Newman? That she couldn't do. There'd only been one Timothy, and God can called him home far too soon. Far too young.

Perhaps it was knowing that she'd never have children of her own that made Hester so passionate about the babes and mothers she assisted. Timothy's death had changed everything for her, and perhaps for those children she'd successfully ushered into the world. It was good to think that God was working out his plan, and not that Timothy's death had been just a senseless farming accident.

It was still early enough in the year to let the cream rise in the dairy, so Hannah Buffum, Jr. poured the fresh milk into wooden troughs on her workbench. In another week or two, she'd need to haul the buckets to the spring house to keep the milk cool from the fresh water that flowed through it. With the cows out on pasture and grazing the early greens, the milk was thick and rich with cream. It was the best time of year to make her hard cheeses that needed to cure for several months.

Hannah Jr. enjoyed the process of cheese making. It gave her a purpose beyond helping her mother with the house and the children. The eldest of originally six children, eight counting the two orphans currently living with them, she split her time between the dairy and the house. She was also training her sister Tamson to work in the dairy, along with Verity, the orphan who had been given into their family by the Puritan elder, Thomas Buffington, just the past week. Hannah Jr. couldn't help but smile at the thought of having another sister.

The door separating the dairy from the main part of the barn banged open. Joseph, the orphan boy living with them until the situation in the village changed, poked his head inside, his straw-colored hair disheveled and his gap-toothed grin wide. "Old Buttercup is calving right now. Come and see." He disappeared as suddenly as he'd arrived.

The boy had been going on and on about witnessing a cow give birth for the first time. Hannah Jr. and her siblings were used to the rhythm of farm life—birth and death, planting and harvest. They took everything in its season. But to Joseph, a boy orphaned very young and shuffled from one house to another, it was all new. And very exciting.

Since the cream would rise without her watching it, so Hannah Jr. slipped off her dairy apron and hung it on its peg before following the lad through the barn, past the area that still smelled faintly of smoke from the fire last winter, and on to the cows' pen. Buttercup, their poorly named cantankerous cow, let out a raucous bellow as they approached. She was alone in the pen, the others having gone outside to graze after milking.

Robert and Caleb Jr. were already watching. Nobody would approach Buttercup unless they had to. While some of their cows were docile and allowed themselves to be handled even in labor, old Buttercup was against any human interference in the birthing process. Strenuously against it. Once, she'd even tossed Father over the top rail of the cow pen.

Another long and loud bellow brought Father out of his carpentry shop. He rested his forearms on the top board of the large open pen. He wore just his waistcoat in such fine weather, curls of wood from his current project clinging to his shirt sleeves. He was working hard to finish the large order for the new doctor in the village.

Hannah Jr. stifled the flutter in her middle at the thought of that order. Not the order, exactly, but who might come to collected it for the doctor—Benjamin Buffington. She shouldn't be thinking of him at all, but she couldn't help it. He was the only young man who had caught her eye. Three years her junior, he was two years from majority age, but that wasn't the real issue.

Benjamin was a Puritan.

The Society of Friends didn't intermarry with Puritans, and the Puritans would reject the possibility even more forcibly. The last thing Hannah Jr. needed was to replay some tragic version of *Romeo and Juliet*. She shouldn't even know about that play of William Shakespeare's, but her friend, Mary O'Sullivan, had somehow gotten a copy of it and had shared it with Hannah Jr. Guilt still pinched her over reading such a worldly story, and that'd been several years past.

Buttercup gave a mighty push, and the tips of the calf's front hooves poked out, and then disappeared again.

"I do not favor the look of that," Father said.

Tamson and Verity arrived with the little boys, Benji and Jonathan. "Why, Father?" Hannah Jr.'s twelve-year-old sister climbed onto the side of the pen until her head was level with Father's.

It was Caleb Jr. who answered. "Because there was no nose showing with the hooves."

"Is that bad?" Joseph's brow wrinkled as he looked to Father.

Father put his hand on the boy's shoulder. "It can be. We shall have to wait and see."

"Will she die?" asked Verity. She'd never witnessed a cow giving birth either.

"Death is as much a part of life as birth is." Hannah Jr. drew the girl to her side. "'Tis one of the things we learn early on the farm."

"I know about death." Verity's arms came around Hannah Jr.'s waist. "But I wanted to see a birth."

The words hit Hannah Jr. hard. This child, only eight years old, had suffered so much loss. Was it too much to ask that she be able to witness a happy occasion in the barn?

Buttercup sank to her knees, then with a groan, rolled over onto her side, her tail cocked as she heaved against another contraction, and the hooves appeared again, even farther this time—but still no nose.

Father rolled his sleeve up well past his elbow and took a stout piece of tree limb with a curve to it from its storage place near the pen. Caleb Jr. fetched a length of rope. Robert ran for a bucket of water. Hannah Jr. and Tamson kept the young boys out of the way. They'd done all this before, more than once.

Not always successfully.

"What is happening?" Joseph asked.

"They must assist Buttercup. 'Tis most likely that the calf's head is turned back."

"What will they do?" There was a tremor in Verity's voice.

Hannah Jr. squatted to her level. "They must turn the calf's head around so that it can come out of Buttercup."

Jonathan started to whimper, so Hannah Jr. scooped him into her arms. At just three years old, he hadn't seen this happen before either. Most birthings happened in the barn without any assistance.

Father and Caleb Jr. entered the pen first, the limb held between them. They waited for Buttercup to give another mighty push, then rushed forward, pressing the limb against her neck behind her head, pinning her to the barn floor. Robert left the bucket of water near her tail, then took Father's place holding one end of the limb.

Buttercup bellowed and kicked, but the boys and Father knew how to stay out of harm's way. Father wetted his arm, waited until after the next push, then grabbed the hooves with the rope in his hand. When the hooves disappeared again, Father's hand, arm, and the rope went with them.

Verity turned her face into Hannah Jr.'s petticoats, but Joseph let out a loud, "Ugh."

Robert spoke in a soothing tone to Buttercup while almost sitting on his end of the limb near her back.

Caleb Jr. kept both hands on his end, being careful not to cut off the cow's breathing by keeping the limb's curve up as he knelt near her throat. He was doing a good job of it judging by the increased volume of her bellowing.

The straw around Father's feet was mussed as he strained to reach the calf's head, groaning in his throat against the cow's next contraction. "I have the rope in its mouth." The words came through gritted teeth.

Verity peeked from Hannah Jr.'s petticoats, her hands still clinging to them.

Joseph had climbed to the top rail of the pen, and sat there open-mouthed.

Father groaned again as Buttercup bore down, but as soon as she ended the push, he dug his toes in and pushed back almost to his shoulder, other hand keeping the rope taut. "'Tis turned." Father's arm appeared—covered in slime and blood enough to make Verity blanch—and he got to his feet. "Let her up, boys, and get out of here."

Caleb Jr. and Robert dropped the limb and ran for the gate, Father not a full step behind.

Buttercup lurched to her feet with the closest thing to a roar that a cow could manage and turned to face them, the calf's front legs and nose swinging out behind her. Father got the gate shut a breath before the cow smacked into it.

Caleb Jr. grabbed Joseph from his perch before he could tumble into the pen with the irate bovine.

After another smack against the gate, Buttercup returned to the far side of the pen and bellowed, her nose in the air. Behind her, the wet calf slid onto the straw with a frightful thud. Hannah held her breath until it raised its head and shook it, wet ears slapping against its hide.

"Look at that!" Joseph pointed.

Buttercup ignored her babe and charged the bucket in the middle of the pen, driving her head into it. The sharp crack of study oak seeming to satisfy her, she returned to the calf, muttering to it as she licked it dry. The calf shook its head again, mouth opening and closing as it spit out the loop of rope that had guided its nose around.

"Ungrateful old beast." Father dried off his arm on a piece of sacking. "If she did not produce such fine milking heifers..." He let his threat remain unspoken.

"Will the calf be all right?" Verity asked.

Robert answered, "It should be right as raindrops now." Even as he spoke, the calf struggled to rise.

"She did it again." Father rested his forearms on the top rail. "Another heifer."

"May I name her?" Verity asked.

Father smiled at her. "And what would thee name her?"

Verity clasped her hands beneath her chin. "Buttercup Jr."

The boys groaned, but Father nodded his approval, so Buttercup Jr. it was, and the rule was, a named calf stayed on the farm.

Which meant another good milk producer for their herd. Hannah Jr. picked Verity up and gave her a squeeze, enjoying the girl's squeal of delight. The live calf meant so much to her, who had lost so many. Hannah Jr. had never suffered as Verity had, she'd never gone without her needs met by her parents, had never lost anyone she was close to. What right had she to pine over some young man who was beyond her reach?

It was time to put thoughts of Benjamin Buffington aside, and concentrate on being the best dairymaid she could be. The best daughter and big sister too. She who had known only blessings, needed to concentrate on being a blessing to others. That was a noble life for anyone, and honoring to God. The empty feeling in her middle would surely lessen with time.

Reviews are Golden

Reviews are the lifeblood of authors. Leaving a review on **Amazon**, **Goodreads**, and/or **BookBub** means that more readers will find our books! Reviews can be long or short - your honest opinion of the book. Shout-outs on any social media platforms also help!

About Pegg Thomas

Pegg Thomas lives in Michigan's Upper Peninsula with Michael, her husband of *mumble* years. She creates American stories with real history and fictional characters inspired by her ancestors who immigrated here in the early 1600s.

Pegg won the 2019 FHL Readers' Choice Award for novellas, was a double-finalist for the 2019 ACFW Carol Award for novellas, and a finalist for the 2019 ACFW Editor of the Year. She was a finalist in the 2021 FHL Readers' Choice Award for novellas. Pegg won the 2022 Selah Award for historical romance and placed 2nd with her second entry. She was a finalist for the 2023 FHL Selah Award, placed 2nd in the 2024 Selah Award, and won the 2024 Will Rogers Silver AND Bronze Medallion Awards. Pegg spent 3 ½ years as the managing editor of Smitten Historical Romance.

PeggThomas.com
Facebook
Goodreads
BookBub
Amazon
Newsletter signup